A CALL TO ARMS

ALLAN MALLINSON

BANTAM BOOKS

LONDON • NEW YORK • TORONTO • SYDNEY • AUCKLAND

A CALL TO ARMS
A BANTAM BOOK : 0 553 81562 8

Originally published in Great Britain by Bantam Press,
a division of Transworld Publishers

PRINTING HISTORY
Bantam Press edition published 2002
Bantam edition published 2003

1 3 5 7 9 10 8 6 4 2

Set in 11½/13pt Times New Roman
by Falcon Oast Graphic Art Ltd.

Bantam Books are published by Transworld Publishers,
61–63 Uxbridge Road, London W5 5SA,
a division of The Random House Group Ltd,
in Australia by Random House Australia (Pty) Ltd,
20 Alfred Street, Milsons Point, Sydney, NSW 2061, Australia,
in New Zealand by Random House New Zealand Ltd,
18 Poland Road, Glenfield, Auckland 10, New Zealand
and in South Africa by Random House (Pty) Ltd,
Endulini, 5a Jubilee Road, Parktown 2193, South Africa.

Printed and bound in Great Britain by
Clays Ltd, St Ives plc.

Acc[l...]

A CALL [...]

'Mallinson's books are far more than the ~~rattling g~~
might expect – though anyone who does will not be disappointed
. . . his tales are not only believable but delightfully informative
. . . a thoroughly satisfying and entertaining read'
Lyn Macdonald, *The Times*

'Once more Mallinson displays his extraordinary knowledge of
military history and practice. Throw in the fact that his usage of
English is as pure and precise as Jane Austen's and his imagination
as vivid as Kipling's and we have another cracking adventure in
what is proving to be an altogether outstanding series'
Birmingham Post

Hervey continues to grow in stature as an engaging and credible
character, while Mallinson himself continues to delight in the
minutiae and arcaneness of military life' *Observer*

'Thrilling . . . in addition to his exceptional knowledge of history,
Allan Mallinson shows his deep awareness of human feelings and
failings. This is an exceptional book' *Country Life*

'Mallinson is a good historian. He gives his people a well-
researched hinterland. He knows what it is like to command and to
serve. He is as good on the details – and it is detail we historical
novel buffs like – of the workings of a cavalry regiment in 1820 as
ever Patrick O'Brian was on the workings of an 1820 warship'
Spectator

'Oozing action, *A Call to Arms* is a military tale of epic propor-
tions that will leave fans counting the days to the next adventure'
Ireland on Sunday

'With each book, Hervey himself is becoming a more complex and
interesting character . . . Mallinson writes of his inner questionings
with subtlety and sympathy. This series grows in stature with each
book' *Evening Standard*

'Mallinson has lost none of his vigour for writing intense prose . . .
masterfully dovetails historical events to create an excellent
balance' *Good Book Guide*

A REGIMENTAL AFFAIR

'Mallinson deals with the historical and military minutiae with his customary panache . . . It is his consummate ability to incorporate the social details and niceties of the times that marks his novels out from the common herd of big boys' books of big boys doing jolly brave things . . . *A Regimental Affair* confirms his undoubted talents and marks him as the heir to Patrick O'Brian and C.S. Forester' *Observer*

'An assured and capable work that proves Hervey is worthy of a long series of novels' *The Times*

'Enthrallingly informative historical panoramas, as well as beautifully told tales of adventure . . . in Hervey, Mallinson has a character worthy of comparison with Forester's young Hornblower . . . And, as always, there is a splendid backdrop of action' *Punch*

'A riveting tale of heroism, derring-do and enormous resource in the face of overwhelming adversity. Season the whole with a generous sprinkling of riding expertise and military history – the author is an acknowledged master of both – and the book is another prime example of the unputdownable historical novel. In the lexicon of fictional military and naval heroes, Matthew Hervey has now joined Bernard Cornwell's Sharpe and Patrick O'Brian's Jack Aubrey as a creation of superlative skills and character' *Birmingham Post*

'Mallinson writes well and effortlessly across fields of conflict which cover a vast panorama from chasing smugglers in Brighton to Luddite violence in the English Midlands and ending finally and disastrously with a border conflict in the snows of Canada' *The Historical Novels Review*

'Many fascinating strands woven into this beautifully written saga endorse the author's mastery of narrative and of deep historical and military erudition. Sympathy, style and control mark the polished horseman; these talents are surely applicable to this talented writer' *Country Life*

THE NIZAM'S DAUGHTERS

'A marvellous read, paced like a well-balanced symphony . . . This is more than a ripping yarn . . . I look forward enormously to hearing more of Hervey's exploits; he is as fascinating on horseback as Jack Aubrey is on the quarterdeck' *The Times*

'Mallinson writes with style, verve and the lucidity one would expect from a talented officer of l'arme blanche . . . His breadth of knowledge is deeply impressive . . . Kick on, Captain Hervey, we cannot wait for more' *Country Life*

'An exciting, fast-moving story, full of bloody hacking with sabre and tulwar' *Evening Standard*

'An epic adventure . . . a book with a texture as rich as cut velvet, and a storyline as detailed as a Bruges tapestry. Patrick O'Brian may no longer be with us. But Mallinson has obviously taken up the historical baton' *Birmingham Post*

A CLOSE RUN THING

'An astonishingly impressive début . . . convincingly drawn, perfectly paced and expertly written . . . A joy to read' Antony Beevor

'Sparkling . . . The scope of *A Close Run Thing* is quite breathtaking . . . A sustained piece of bravura writing' *Observer*

'Cracking tale of love and heroism in the Napoleonic Wars . . . This is the first in a series of Matthew Hervey adventures. The next can't come soon enough for me' *Daily Mail*

'O'Brian's equal in accurate knowledge of the equipment, methods, weapons and conditions of serve of the fighting men of whom he writes . . . An imaginative feat of high order' *Country Life*

'Now at last a highly literate, deeply read cavalry officer of high rank shows one the nature of horse-born warfare in those times . . . *A Close Run Thing* is very much to be welcomed' Patrick O'Brian

'Marks the emergence of a new talent in historical fiction' *Irish News*

'Fast-moving, exciting, and above all, accurate. The author combines the experience of a serving cavalry officer with the knowledge of a military historian, blending the two into a colourful historical tale' *Army Quarterly & Defence Journal*

Also by Allan Mallinson

A Close Run Thing
*The Nizam's Daughters**
A Regimental Affair
The Sabre's Edge

*Published outside the UK under the title *Honorable Company*

A CALL TO ARMS

Drawn & Engraved by Charles Thomson, Ed.

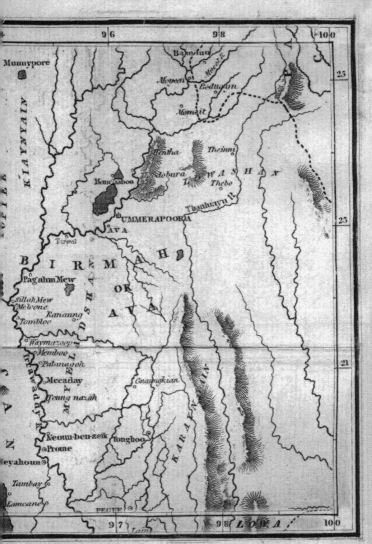

FOREWORD

In 1819 some 64,000 officers and men – all regulars – were stationed in Britain for domestic security, which meant, since the possibility of invasion had receded beyond imagination, for law and order. But after 1819 the threat of major disorder – of revolution, even – receded too, and by 1825 the number of troops in Britain had fallen to 44,000. Financial retrenchment generally was the order of the day. The army estimates in 1815 had been £43 million; in 1829 they were less than a quarter of that, and by the end of the decade they had fallen even further, for by then the army was less than half the size of its high point at the time of Waterloo. And yet, as today, the army found itself called on to do more, not less, as imperial commitments began to mount.

I have been surprised by remarks by otherwise kind reviewers on the question of what Captain Matthew Hervey and the 6th Light Dragoons would find to do after Waterloo, the inference being that the world was at peace. The answer, then as today, is that the British army is never at peace. Not one year has gone by since that great battle without a British soldier dying by hostile hand. No other army in the world, save perhaps that of India, can claim such a testimony. The army of today has been shaped over a long age, and some of the most important shapers have been small wars in distant places. They gave British officers and NCOs the habit – the *unrivalled* habit – of decision-making and responsibility at junior level; in other words, of *command*.

But the lessons were sometimes learned hard. The memory of victory over the French was like a dead hand at the Horse Guards as far as reform and innovation were concerned. In the colonial engagements of the three decades after Waterloo, superior British discipline and firepower – the same musket volleys as at Waterloo – were enough to see off the enemy. In the one arena that might have tested the army's readiness for large-scale war – India – jealousies and assumptions of innate superiority led to a general despising of Indian experience, for which the army was to pay dearly in the Crimea, and, indeed, in India itself at times.

So where did Hervey and his brother officers of the post-Waterloo army blood their swords, or at least draw them? In *A Regimental Affair* we saw the Sixth at police work in the Midlands to counter Luddite and nascent Chartist violence, and then in British North America in the wake of the War of 1812, where fear of territorial aggrandizement by the United States tied down 5,000 troops for years to come and saw a costly programme of fortifications and canals. And although Anglo-American relations developed harmoniously for the most part, there were periodic disputes and indeed the occasional rebellion in Canada itself. The settlements in Africa, at the Cape and the Gold Coast, drew the army into action in the 1820s and 30s; there were flare-ups throughout the Caribbean; expanding trade led to conflict with China; the troubles between settlers and Maoris in New Zealand were to occupy 18,000 troops at one point. Small wars in distant places. The sun never set on the British army.

And throughout, there was India, where an increasing number of King's (and later Queen's) regiments was needed to supplement the largely native army of the Honourable East India Company. And if it is true that, for the most part, all these distant imperial commitments were those of, in the Duke of Wellington's words, 'the best of all instruments, British infantry' (in the 1820s and 30s up to seventy-five per cent of the British infantry were stationed abroad or were in transit), nowhere was the mounted arm more valuable than in the presidencies of Bombay, Madras and Bengal, where speed of response could pay dividends out of all proportion. I commend the essay on soldiery in this period by Professor Peter Burroughs, co-editor of the *Journal of Imperial and Commonwealth History*, in the *Oxford Illustrated History of the British Army*. It gives a sobering picture of the conditions of service for the men whom, later, Kipling would call 'beggars in red'.

I am as usual indebted to several people in this, the fourth of my cavalry tales, and I am very fortunate that they remain the same people as before. I record here my continuing and sincere appreciation of their enthusiasm, patience and wisdom. I would make particular mention, this time, of Anthony Turner, who has worked on each of the manuscripts in the series. I am especially grateful for his keen and questioning eye.

And so, after the simple certainties of the Napoleonic Wars, and the year or two that it took for the Congress of Vienna to establish the new world order, we begin to observe how officers young and old had to settle to the new reality, just as they had to do in the decade that followed the end of the Cold War. Prospects for promotion were blighted, they knew; the army was not the place it was. Yet somehow these men carried the day in battles around the globe. But then, as in the aftermath of the Cold War, it was not so much the army that pulled them through as that 'accidental act of genius', *the regiment*: in 1817, Captain Matthew Hervey had left the army not by submitting his resignation to the Horse Guards, but by writing to the colonel of the 6th Light Dragoons, and then by sending his regimental commission to the Sixth's agents to be sold on. That was the regimental system.

CURSE GOD, AND DIE

He swalloweth the ground with fierceness and rage: neither believeth he that it is the sound of the trumpet.

He saith among the trumpets, Ha ha; and he smelleth the battle afar off, the thunder of the captains, and the shouting.

The Book of Job

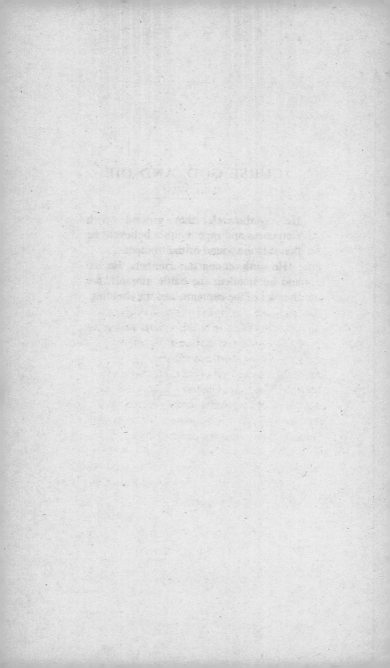

PART ONE

ENGLAND

An old, mad, blind, despised and dying king;
Princes, the dregs of their dull race, who flow
Through public scorn, – mud from a muddy spring;
Rulers who neither see, nor feel, nor know,
But leech-like to their fainting country cling,
Till they drop, blind in blood, without a blow;
A people starved and stabbed in the untilled field;
An army, which liberticide and prey
Makes as a two-edged sword to all who wield;
Religion, Christless, Godless – a book sealed;
A Senate, – Time's worst statute unrepealed;
Are graves, from which a glorious Phantom may
Burst to illumine our tempestuous day.

Percy Bysshe Shelley
'Sonnet: England in 1819'

CHAPTER ONE

CONDUCT UNBECOMING

The cavalry barracks, Hounslow, October 1818

'The regiment will form hollow square! First and Third Squadrons, at the halt, left and right *form*!'

A hundred and eighty dragoons in double rank began the manoeuvre that would transform the parade from extended line into a military amphitheatre. The time-beaters of the regimental band, and all the brass and woodwind, could not muffle the crunch of gravel and the ringing of spurs. 'Bonnie Nell', the Sixth marched to this morning. Herr Hamper's choice of music was always enigmatic: a year ago they had paraded for Private Hopwood's flogging to the strains of 'Seventeen Come Sunday'. Indeed, there were many on parade this fine autumn morning who were minded of that day, the last time the regiment had formed hollow square.

'Standfast Number Two Squadron. Remainder, inwa-a-ards, *dress*!' The regimental serjeant-major's voice echoed about the barracks as if he were shouting from a dozen places at once.

Heads and eyes in the flank squadrons shot right or left, boots shuffled forwards and rear, until the ranks were straight and aligned with the left and right markers of Second Squadron.

The RSM turned right about, advanced ten paces and

halted in front of the major, saluting sharply with his right hand. 'Sir, there are two hundred and eighty-five men on parade, sir!'

The major made no reply. The RSM turned to his right, saluted, and marched towards the right marker and thence for the rear of the centre squadron.

'Fall in the officers!' The major's words of command were more than an invitation, but feeble compared with those of the Stentor-RSM. When the officers had taken post, the major turned about in a little circling movement, unlike the RSM's emphatic pivot, and advanced ten paces to where the general officer commanding the London District stood with the Sixth's adjutant at his side. 'My lord, there are twenty-two officers and two hundred and eighty-five other ranks on parade.'

'Thank you, Eustace,' said the general quietly. He walked towards the open side of the hollow square, the major falling in beside him, and halted a few paces before it. 'By command of the Horse Guards, it is my duty to have read before the whole regiment, on parade, the following despatch from the commander-in-chief.'

Not a word was spoken, but there was a distinct buzz in the ranks. The adjutant took a pace forward, opened the red portfolio he was carrying under his scabbard arm and began to read. 'His Royal Highness the Prince Regent has been pleased to confirm the findings of the court martial convened on September the fifth, eighteen hundred and eighteen, to try the evidence against Lieutenant-Colonel the Earl of Towcester of the unnecessary hazarding of his command in the Americas and for conduct unbecoming an officer, contrary to the Articles of War. The court finds that Lieutenant-Colonel the Earl of Towcester is guilty of the grossest negligence in exercising his command in the face of hostile irregulars, and of conduct on numerous occasions beforehand revolting to every proper and honourable feeling of a gentleman.'

The buzz returned. The RSM threw his head to left and right, and though not a man could have seen him, the noise stopped abruptly.

'His Royal Highness directs that Lieutenant-Colonel the Earl of Towcester be dismissed from the service—'

The buzz returned louder than ever. The RSM maintained his eyes front, and the general waited patiently.

'Be dismissed from the service . . . with *disgrace*.'

The buzz continued, until the RSM silenced it again.

'The commander-in-chief directs that these findings be read out at the head of every regiment in the King's service.'

This last brought so great a shock that the buzz did not recur for some moments, but louder still was the noise when it did come.

'*As you were!*' The RSM brought three hundred heads back to attention in an instant.

The general would now have his say, after waiting for the silence to have its effect. 'This is an unhappy day for a regiment. It is an unhappy day for our country when an officer fails to do his duty. It falls now to every man of the Sixth Light Dragoons to do his duty to the utmost, as indeed you have done it in the past, conscious that the rest of the service looks at you. Let it see not the unhappy example of an officer unfit for his position, but the regiment of Corunna, Salamanca, Albura and Orthès. And of *Waterloo*!' He paused to a silent count of three. 'God save the King!'

'God save the King!' came the reply, but none too full-throated.

Major Joynson suddenly saw *his* duty. 'Light Dragoons, God save the King!' he roared, startling the RSM as much as anyone.

'God save the King!' bellowed the Sixth.

The general saluted and turned away. 'Carry on, Major Joynson,' he barked.

'Sir! Adjutant, carry on!'

'Sir! Regiment, to your duties, di-i-ismiss!'

At once the parade ground was a cacophony of words of command from the captains and serjeant-majors as each troop took itself off to stables, skill-at-arms or fatigues – whatever was the order of the day. A Troop more than the others could be forgiven if its collective thoughts were on what was past rather than on what lay ahead. Serjeant Collins perhaps spoke for them all as he fell in beside the troop serjeant-major. 'There's two men I should've liked to hear that.'

'Ay. And it's an empty place as well without Armstrong,' replied the serjeant-major.

'Fred, it's going to take more than Mr Lincoln to get things as they were.'

'Ay. An RSM can only do so much. I suppose Joynson'll become colonel.'

Collins hesitated. 'I suppose he will.'

CHAPTER TWO

PARADISE OF EXILES

The Caffè Greco, Rome, six months later

'Who is the severe fellow there?'

The enquirer, a boyish-looking man of about twenty-five, stood at the *bancone* of the meeting place of Rome's *literati* and *artisti*, drinking strong arabica.

'I do not know,' replied his companion. 'Save that he is English. Or that he reads English, at least, for I saw him with an English newspaper yesterday.'

The younger man brushed a dark curl from his forehead and took another sip of his coffee. 'But now he is reading Goethe, so by that reckoning he might equally be German.'

His companion gave a prolonged shrug.

'I have observed him here several times this week,' continued the younger man, draining his cup. 'He has a decidedly melancholic air. He takes not the slightest interest in anyone around him. He seems wholly absorbed in himself. And that, my dear friend, is singular in this city, even for an Englishman.'

'Then he would be dull company and not worth your regrets,' declared his companion. '*Giuseppe,*' he said to the *cameriere* on the other side of the *bancone*, nodding to the object of their curiosity. '*Il penseroso là – chi è?*' The Italian was without the accent of the country.

23

The *cameriere* shrugged his shoulders. '*Un'ufficiale inglese, dicono. Ma con me parla solo francese.*'

The younger man nodded. 'Does he have any companions, Giuseppe? *Ha amici?*'

The *cameriere* said something by reply, but fair though his Italian was, his questioner did not catch the sense.

'He says that a young woman joined him yesterday,' explained the other. 'Handsome but not dressed with fashion.'

'English too, then, certainly,' said the younger man, raising his eyebrows.

'But had she been German, she would likely as not have been neither fashionable *nor* handsome,' replied the older one, smiling.

'Oh, Rome is a harsh court in such matters! But in any event, an English officer reading Goethe has a sensibility I can respect.'

'*Dicono che ha combattuto nella battaglia di Waterloo,*' added the *cameriere*, helpfully.

The boyish-looking man's ears pricked. 'Now *that* is worth my regrets,' he declared, glancing again at the seated reader. 'He surely has a tale to tell. But I would not disturb his engagement with Goethe for all that. We shall see him at an assembly soon, no doubt. I am surprised, indeed, that we have not done so already.'

'Perhaps both he and his lady companion are of an unsocial disposition.'

'Perhaps.' The younger man placed a few *scudi* on the counter. '*Grazie tante, Giuseppe,*' he said, with an air of a man who had learned something of advantage.

'*Grazie a lei, Signor Shelley,*' replied the *cameriere*, as the two men turned to leave.

Matthew Hervey, for more than a year plain 'mister', and for more than a week an habitué of the Caffè Greco, still owned to mixed feelings at being in the city of the popes. One at

24

least of his father's profession – the rector of the neighbour-ing parish – had called the city 'the whore of Babylon' when Hervey and his sister had announced their intention to visit. And although there was nothing like so vehement a despis-ing of Rome in his father's parish, Hervey possessed the Englishman's instincts. He did not care for the picture of black spectres pursuing temporal ambitions, especially usurping ones. His history he knew very well indeed. And yet there was no doubting that he liked the easy ways of this city. He had seen no especial excess of luxury or vice. Even in the pages of Goethe he saw little that might seriously offend an unprejudiced conscience. What he did see in Rome was gaiety in large measure, and he was most glad of it. And his sister, too, always a sure weathercock of propriety, seemed as glad as he. That he was still, himself, restrained from joining with that gaiety did not diminish his appreciation of it.

One of the things that contrived to diminish any tendency to gaiety on his part this morning was the knowledge that he must go to the post office. The Rome post office, which stood half-way along the Via del Corso from where he now sat, was to his mind a true representation of bedlam. His two previous visits, to send letters to England and to collect others *restantes*, had been tedious in the extreme, and he now braced himself for another unedifying morning spent in what passed for a queue in this city. He paid for his coffee, tipped the *cameriere* too generously (why should *someone* not be pleased with his day?) and said *arrivederla* to the Greco's over-starched proprietor.

The sky was without a cloud, and the sun was already hot. He found it uncomfortable to walk any faster than a stroll, and he resolved to press his tailor to finish the two linen coats he had ordered a few days before. If he and Elizabeth were to stay here through July, he would need at least two more, and it was as well to know the cutter's capabilities as soon as possible. And Elizabeth, too, would need new clothes. He wondered if he would be able to persuade her of it. As he made his way along the Corso, he saw one exquisite female after another going in and out of the *palazzi*. He knew he simply had to persuade her.

When he reached the post office he was at first afraid that it might be closed (innumerable saints' days could catch out even the *romani*), for there was no press at its doors, only a mandolin-player with whom an official was noisily remonstrating. Hervey edged past them carefully (it was all too easy to be hailed as witness by one or other parties in a Roman dispute) to enter the cool, marbled hall. There, he was cheered further to see only a dozen or so people waiting, and he took up his place where he judged the queue to end, deciding there was little need to open his volume of Goethe to help the time pass.

Indeed, not many minutes passed before his attention was arrested by a tall, powerfully built man in a military cloak who suddenly turned to the man beside him at the counter and said very loudly, in English, 'What! Are you that damned atheist Shelley?'

The man to whom the charge was directed turned to face his challenger, and in that instant was struck by him with such force that he fell to the floor, stunned.

Hervey sprang forward at once, seizing the assailant's cane with his right hand. He jabbed his left fist into the man's face so hard that both nose and upper lip split bloodily. But still the attacker struggled violently to wrest the cane free, until Hervey drove his knee into the man's groin and followed through with his right fist to nose and lip again. The man reeled, brought both hands up to his face and dropped the cane. Hervey snatched it up and grabbed him by the collar, threatening to bring the cane down on his head if he resisted more. The man yielded, and Hervey pushed him to his knees.

Others in the post office had remained bystanders, but someone had sent for help, and two *gendarmi* now arrived.

26

A Swiss gentleman helped the victim of the assault to his feet, and Hervey, cursing himself for being so out of breath, was pleased to surrender custody of the assailant to the agents of the law. Wiping the blood from his hand, and concealing the stinging pain in his knuckles, he turned to the innocent party. 'Are you well, sir?' he asked, with more composure than the native bystanders could believe.

'I thank you, sir. I am quite well enough.' The man brushed the curl from off his forehead, dusted down the arms of his coat, and bowed briskly. 'Shelley, sir. At your service.'

Hervey returned the bow. 'Hervey, sir. May I enquire as to what induced that assault?'

'You did not hear?'

'I am afraid I did not.'

'I stood accused of the infamous crime of atheism.' Shelley's face was white, there was blood about his lips and tears in his eyes. 'I have been knocked down before, but never with so little forewarning. I wish I'd my pistols.'

'They would have done you no good before the blow, and might have caused you trouble afterwards,' replied Hervey, stooping to pick up Shelley's hat.

'I thank you again, sir. It is the very devil of a business when an Englishman is assaulted by another in a foreign place.'

The *gendarmi* were trying to tell them something, without success until the official from the altercation with the mandolin-player intervened. 'Signori, the *gendarmi* wish you to accompany them to the office of the *questura*. There are papers which must be signed.'

Shelley dabbed at his lips with a handkerchief and then at his eyes. 'I am sorry, sir,' he said to Hervey. 'I am not given to such emotion, but the blow stung horribly.'

Hervey smiled. 'Think nothing of it, sir. It was a brutal assault. I shall be glad to give what evidence I can.'

* * *

27

It took an hour and more for the *questura* to complete the investigation. When it was done, the two men left together. Shelley seemed recovered. 'You will permit me to give you a glass of wine, sir?'

'I should like that, yes,' said Hervey. At least he did not have to go back to the post office, for the official had obligingly brought his letters to the *questura*. They set off back along the Corso.

'You went at that wretch like a tiger, Hervey.'

Hervey raised his eyebrows. 'It is the only way if one is forced to fight, I assure you. There is little profit in dancing about.'

'You evidently have considerable experience in the matter, and yet you have not the look of a pug.'

Hervey nodded, obliged. 'You are very kind, sir.'

'You are a very soldierly man, for all your sensibility.'

Hervey was startled by the intimacy of his companion's knowledge. He did not reply.

Shelley frowned. 'Come, sir. I am reliably informed that you are one of the Duke of Wellington's men, yet I saw you lately in the Caffè Greco with a volume of Goethe.'

Hervey nodded very slightly again, as if taking the measure of what he had heard. 'You should not be so reliant on your informants. I am no longer in the King's service.'

'As you wish,' sighed Shelley indulgently.

'And you, sir? You have served of late?'

'I have not.' Shelley said it with what might have passed for disdain of the notion. 'But ought I then to think meanly of myself for never having been a soldier?'

'I cannot say what you should think. Your time has in all likelihood been spent honourably.'

'The wretch who assailed me would not share that view.'

'Perhaps he does not know you so well?'

'He does not know me at all, Hervey. And I know even littler of him.'

Hervey was wholly mystified. 'But he objected to you

most strongly – by your account as well as the evidence of my own eyes!'

'He had evidently formed an opinion of me at a remove.'

Only very slowly did it begin to dawn on Hervey who his new companion might be. The man himself had given no clues, save for the implication that he had a reputation beyond his range of acquaintances. Hervey knew that reputation only a little, and largely through his late wife. He had not himself read any of the work. 'Forgive me, sir. Are you the *poet* Shelley?'

Shelley smiled for the first time. His face was transformed. 'You have the soldier's directness, Hervey. What is there to forgive? I am indeed that atheist poet Shelley.'

Hervey felt the warmth of both smile and words. 'And *you* have the candour of your reputation, sir.'

'Ah, my reputation! Are we not all prisoners to what we would have the world think of us?'

'It was my understanding, sir, that your reputation was for not caring *what* the world thought!'

Shelley smiled again, though not so full. 'And your opinion of me will have been formed by the organs of Crown and Church, and you will not have read a word of what I have written.'

'I confess I have not. But neither has my opinion been so formed as to tend to anything.' Hervey might have explained that his sister had read his poetry, and Henrietta, but such confidences were not possible in ten times this intimacy.

They talked of the city for the rest of the way to the Caffè Greco. They passed any number of places in which they might have taken wine, but the Greco was familiar to Shelley, and the familiar was comforting. Giuseppe looked surprised by Shelley's reappearance, and in the company of the man who only an hour or two before had been a professed stranger. The *inglesi* were a strange people – always polite, but cool, even cold in their manner. Except Signor Shelley: he was a *gentiluomo* like the others, certainly, but Signor Shelley was also . . . *simpatico*.

Shelley called for a bottle of his favoured *rosso* from the Castelli Romani. 'Come,' he said conspiratorially to Hervey. 'Let us sit in the seclusion of one of these arches. I would know a little more of what brings you to Rome. You may learn of *my* reasons from any number of people, I dare say.'

They took up seats beneath a particularly vivid depiction of the rape of the Sabine women. Hervey sipped the thin red wine, which they drank chilled, and eyed his companion carefully. There was nothing he feared, but he was not inclined to vouchsafe anything either, no matter how inconsequential, to someone who might use it frivolously. 'I am here on indefinite vacation.'

'Good! A promising beginning. And do you find Goethe informative regarding the eternal city? Where *is* your book, by the way?'

Hervey looked surprised, and frowned. 'I recall that I have left it at the *questura*.'

'Never mind. We can go there tomorrow to retrieve it. But first tell me of it.'

Hervey was again surprised at Shelley's presumption of intimacy, though that was not to say he found it unwelcome. 'I find it a very faithful guide.'

'Then you have a keen understanding of German. I would that there were a passable translation.'

Hervey was now conscious that his conversation lacked the spontaneity of his companion's, and, unusually, it troubled him. 'And you, sir. What do you do here?' he tried, though sensing at once its inadequacy.

Shelley put down his glass and swept a hand about the room. 'I delve for the glory that was Rome, and seek in it inspiration!'

The words seemed entirely unaffected on Shelley's lips. Hervey searched for something by way of return. 'And are you here in company?' was all that the muse could summon.

'A wife and child. And you?'

'My sister.'

Shelley nodded. 'You were at Waterloo, were you not? That is my understanding.'

'I cannot think how you might know, sir, for I have not spoken of it since leaving England.'

'I should very much like to hear account of it. I have not met with any who was there.'

Hervey gave a sort of sigh to indicate the difficulty of obliging him. 'It was a very long day, and the field was enormous.'

But Shelley was not put off. He thought for a moment or two and then asked, 'Would you join us this evening? We shall be a small party, but an attentive one.'

It was the first invitation Hervey had received since arriving in the city ten days before, but he was still not greatly inclined to accept. 'I think I must decline, sir. As I told you, I am accompanied by my sister and she—'

'Then it would be doubly delightful, and not only for me, but for my other companions of her sex.'

Hervey was severely discomfited. He had no desire of excessive female company.

'Shall we say nine o'clock? Our lodgings are at the Palazzo Verospi on the Corso, number 300 – near the post office, I'm afraid.'

The mention of the post office engendered just the degree of sympathy necessary for Hervey to conclude that his declining would be an unkindness. 'I am much obliged. I can answer for my sister since we have no fixed engagements. We shall come at nine.'

'Good! So let us take a little more of this wine then – for our stomachs' sake, as St Paul would have us believe.'

Hervey frowned, even though he surmised the show of scepticism was for his benefit. But he took another glass, and there they stayed a full hour speaking of Rome and her glories.

* * *

31

Later, in his lodgings in Via del Babuino, *il ghetto inglese*, Hervey reflected on the morning's turn of events. He had befriended – was it not too strong a word? – an atheist, revolutionary and libertine. Elizabeth had lost no time in reminding him of the history of Mr Shelley and his elopements (half-remembered from Henrietta's teasing accounts), and the rest he had pieced together for himself, recalling the usual tattlers during the years that his attention had been distracted by those who would destroy the kingdom by the sword rather than by the pen. Shelley had by all accounts brought to bed two if not three or even four women – girls, indeed – so that there was issue out of wedlock, unacknowledged perhaps. And this the poet would defend as a right way of living – would propagate it, even! Who knew, therefore, what were Shelley's arrangements at present, and what dissipation he – Hervey – and Elizabeth might soon be a prey to? He could only ponder on what a journey he had made these past months, from honourable rank in His Majesty's light dragoons (some would say a primmish captain) to supper companion of a dangerous and amoral poetaster. Was he prepared to pay *any* price to put Elizabeth and himself an evening's distance from painful memories? He shrugged. He wished he had at least read some of Shelley's poetry. It would surely tell him more of the man than mere gossip could. But his own tastes in that direction had advanced only slowly, so that hitherto he had remained devoted above all to the Milton of his schoolroom. Through Henrietta he had read Coleridge, and with her Keats, but Shelley had not so far engaged him.

Elizabeth had not objected to suppering with the Shelleys, however. Elizabeth's pleasure was her journal, and it had often been her lament that its pages were full of things that no one could have the least interest in but herself. Not that she harboured literary ambitions; rather was she occasionally in despair of being, at no longer five and twenty, without anything more to record than domestic trifles. If only she could write of her time at the workhouse, or in the hovels of Warminster Common, her memoir might stand as something of real consequence. But good works were one thing. To itemize the meanness and dissipation of rural life in a lady's journal was quite another. Italy had seen her able to write infinitely more interesting pages already, but of the country-side and art; of people, her entries were as yet restricted. Save in the case of her brother, whose progress she noted with anxious attention – and of Henrietta, whom she missed so much more than any but her journal knew, sometimes through tear marks rather than ink.

At nine o'clock they took a carriage to Shelley's lodgings, for although it was not far, Elizabeth had been at pains to dress and Hervey had no wish to take the edge off her success by chancing to their feet. When they arrived at number 300 Via del Corso they found their host agitated. 'I am very glad to meet you, Miss Hervey,' Shelley replied, after Hervey's introduction. 'But my wife is unwell, I'm afraid, and makes her regrets. We shall go instead to Signora Dionigi's. She holds a *conversazione* this evening. It will be very diverting.'

Now Hervey was troubled. 'But we do not know Signora Dionigi.'

'That will not matter in the least. The signora likes nothing more than to meet new people.'

Elizabeth, whose face was suffused by a colour far from her usual, assured their host that they would be delighted to go to the signora's. 'For in truth, Mr Shelley, we have not been much in company these past months.'

Hervey did not care for the idea of this *conversazione*, which sounded like nothing so much as the flummery of some ageing widow's salon. Even the black humour which could descend on him of an evening might be preferable. But he could not deny his sister her diversion, even if he himself had no inclination for festive company.

* * *

Signora Marianna Dionigi was no dilettante, however. Ageing she might be, but she was also a painter of some distinction, an antiquary of impressive learning, and therefore unlikely to be seduced by worthless flattery. She was tall, upright. Her face, to Hervey's mind, was a little too farded, but her features were very fine. Her dress was distinctly Italian rather than French. Above all she had kind eyes. She took Elizabeth's arm and introduced her to the room, first in French, then in English. Elizabeth's shot silk was perhaps a little out of place among the dresses of the foreign ladies, but it did not matter greatly, for Hervey observed that she was as handsome in essentials as any in the room, and with expert assistance might outshine at least half of them.

For a quarter of an hour before supper began, Shelley tried in vain to engage Hervey in conversation, to draw from him some response to a question of fact, or some opinion on this or that. Perhaps, he thought, it was that Hervey watched too keenly for his sister, or that the liveliness of the company made it difficult for him to be at ease. At any rate, Shelley saw enough not to persist, and, with the utmost politeness, left him to himself as they made for the dining room. There, Hervey was relieved to find a table from which the guests helped themselves, so that he was able to slip unnoticed into the library. He had no appetite, and he could pass an hour or so pleasurably there now Elizabeth was at her ease and engaged in conversation.

But he was not long allowed his solitude, for Signora Dionigi was an attentive hostess, and she sought him out after a while. 'May I bring you some wine, Mr Hervey?' she asked, in French.

Hervey had in his hand a book of engravings of Roman antiquities. 'Oh, I beg your pardon, signora. I did not wish to appear—'

The signora smiled the more. 'Mr Hervey, we do not follow a *formula* at these gatherings. I had rather you took your pleasure in a book if it were not to be had elsewhere.'

'You are very kind, signora. I am not averse to company as a rule, but . . .'

'It is your business alone, Mr Hervey. We Romans are not nearly so constrained by obligation.'

Now Hervey smiled, gratified by her discernment. 'Thank you, signora. And yes, I should like a little wine, if I may.'

The signora despatched her attendant. 'Have you known Mr Shelley long?' she asked, now in English.

'We met only this morning, signora.'

'But you admire his poetry.'

He hesitated. 'I am very much afraid that I have never read any of it.'

'Would you like to?'

He had expected a tone of surprise, of disapproval even. The signora was indeed the most considerate of hostesses, as well as attentive. 'I would of course, madam.' So obliging had been her reply that he could not have said otherwise.

She took a small volume from the drawer of a writing desk. 'Here, Mr Hervey. You will see what a great poet is our friend Mr Shelley. Do not hurry: he will repay proper study. Join us only if you feel inclined. That should be the way with *conversazione*.'

Hervey bowed in appreciation. He truly felt disinclined to the gaiety of the room next door, and the signora had sensed it. And he did wish to read a little of Shelley's poetry, for he had a mind that it might tell him something of the man. Their time together that morning, although short, had endeared the poet to him to an uncommon degree.

Half an hour passed, perhaps more, during which Hervey was interrupted only by a manservant bringing him champagne. And from the first moments with *Alastor* – 'the demon spirit of solitude' – he recognized that the poetry stood comparison to any he had read. Equal, certainly, to Coleridge and Keats in the pleasure the words themselves gave, and equal in some respects even to Milton in heroic invention. He did not know how much it truly told him of the man, however. It seemed, in fact, to speak most aptly to his own condition – and so well, that he found himself reading lines aloud, twice over:

'. . . wildly he wandered on,
'Day after day a weary waste of hours,
'Bearing within his life the brooding care
'That ever fed on its decaying flame.'

And he marvelled at the poet's economy in describing what he himself could barely admit.

'And now his limbs were lean; his scattered hair
'Sered by the autumn of strange suffering
'Sung dirges in the wind; his listless hand
'Hung like dead bone within its withered skin;'

He shivered, almost, as he spoke this last.

'Life, and the lustre that consumed it, shone—'

But it was Shelley himself who spoke the culminating lines:

'As in a furnace burning secretly,
'From his dark eyes alone.'

Hervey looked up.

'You approve of my philosophy, Captain Hervey?' asked the poet, smiling with some pride.

'I am no longer captain, as I explained this morning. And I should have to read much more before I were able to make any worthy remark.' Even as he spoke, Hervey heard the stuffed shirt and inwardly he groaned.

But Shelley seemed only diverted by his reserve, and by what he considered to be further evidence of sensibility.

'Come with me tomorrow,' he said, on an impulse. 'To my favourite place in all of Rome.'

Hervey was intrigued. 'Where?'

'The place I hide from the world, and work.'

Shelley's eagerness could compel. Indeed, Hervey did not imagine he had met a more compelling man. 'I must make sure my sister will be content in my absence, but for myself I should say that I would deem it an honour.'

That compelling way also took Hervey into the music room, where he saw that Elizabeth was very agreeably engaged and smiling. And, he told himself, if Elizabeth could be so diverted, then perhaps his previous withdrawal was needless as well as selfish.

Next morning, Hervey left his lodgings in Via Babuino a little before a quarter to nine to walk by way of the Piazza di Spagna and Via Frattina to the Via del Corso. All along Frattina the sun was full in his eyes, and his progress was slow. As a rule he found Frattina an easier street to negotiate at this hour than Condotti or Borgognona, with their shops and stalls and hawkers; but even by this route he could advance but slowly this morning, so that he had to step out along the Corso to make his appointment on time. Only when he collided at full tilt with a ribbon-seller did it occur to him that he was not bound by any military obligation to be so exactly punctual. He caught but little of what the woman said, except that some of the ribbons, having fallen to the ground, were ruined. He stumbled in French and his few words of Italian to make amends, watched by a growing number of passers-by, and soon found himself with a good number of the fallen ribbons in exchange for more *scudi* than he supposed was strictly necessary. The immediate outcome was that he reached the Palazzo Verospi at ten minutes past nine, his hands and pockets full of brightly coloured streamers.

Shelley greeted him with an eager smile and an extravagant

handshake. 'I was afeard you would come very precisely on your hour as a military man and find me ill-prepared, for I could not lay hands on my notebook. But now I have it and we may leave at once. What do you intend with those ribbons?'

Hervey explained their provenance. 'I thought I might take them for my sister. She was complaining of a want of colour in her wardrobe.'

'How Italians do love ribbons!' declared Shelley, taking a broad yellow and white one and draping it across his chest to resemble some papal order. 'More so even than the French. I heard tell that Napoleon was a little too Italian in his love of them.'

'Bonaparte?' The imperial name was still unutterable to Hervey. 'Perhaps; I could not safely say.'

'I should not imagine *you* to be so easily seduced.'

Hervey frowned.

'You were very dull last night. Not a word of Waterloo did you utter within my hearing. Shall you be dull again today?'

Hervey could not find it in him to bridle against the remark. 'It is not my intention.'

'Good. Then let us be away.'

'Perhaps I may leave some of these for your wife?' said Hervey, taking another handful of ribbons from a pocket.

Shelley seemed dismissive. 'You may, but it will be some days before she is in humour to be gay.'

Hervey laid them on a table, without remark. He had not been so self-absorbed at the signora's not to have heard the speculation there. The Shelleys had had a turbulent time in Naples, it seemed, and the precise status of their travelling companion was evidently of some moment. 'Where do we go?'

'To the Baths of Caracalla. I'll warrant you never saw such a place in your life.'

The wager just permitted for Hervey to have seen them already, but in truth he had not yet explored them, seeing them only distantly and very indistinctly from the Palatine. It had been his intention to engage a guide and go there with Elizabeth in a day or so. He would not spoil Shelley's enthusiasm in the sharing of a secret, however, and he therefore made no reply.

Indeed, Hervey said little throughout their approach march, but it was not dullness that made him silent, only that the poet was a most zealous guide, and there was little to say beyond an appreciative word here or an interrogatory one there. They tramped the Forum, skirted the Colosseum, briefly traced the line of the ruined walls of Romulus, explored the Circus Maximus for a while, where Shelley was keen to hear Hervey's opinion of the turning circles and speeds of the chariots that had once raced there, and then followed the stream called Acqua Crabra for half a mile until they reached the object of their excursion. They came on it curiously abruptly, though the baths were as massive as any structure in the city.

'*Now*, Hervey, what think you? Tell me your thoughts ere I tell you mine!'

Hervey's immediate thoughts were of India. The jungled ruins of the great *Terme* of the Emperor Marcus Aurelius Antoninus – known as Caracalla, for he favoured that Gaulish mantle above the Roman toga – looked for all the world like the palace at Chintalpore overrun by the forest. He could therefore picture what must have been in this place, rather than seeing merely crumbling brick and tangled bines. 'Nature is remorseless, I should say.'

It was a prosaic response perhaps, but Shelley was heartened by it and expressed his approval freely. 'Nature is the ultimate barbarian, Hervey. The Goths cut the aqueducts which gave the baths their spirit, and others stripped the place of its marble, but it is Nature that overwhelms it in the end – crushes and devours it like an enormous serpent. Never was any desolation more sublime and lovely, though.'

Hervey nodded slowly.

'It thrills me more than I can say. Indeed, it is a scene which overpowers expression.'

But Hervey was not so transported that he did not see the paradox. 'If it overpowers expression, why does a poet seek inspiration here? Is there not other seclusion where you might summon the muse?'

Shelley smiled. 'Captain Hervey, you would have me believe your heart is of stone, or lead – no, not lead, for that is the soldier's precious metal! Come; there's a winding staircase here like a mountain path. We can reach the summit of these towers. And so wonderfully overgrown with myrtle is it that you will have no thoughts but of the wilderness.' He rushed ahead.

Hervey followed as if it were indeed a mountain path, having a care to place a hand at all times on something which might save him were the stones beneath his feet to expire after their sixteen long centuries of trampling. Shelley climbed carelessly, however, like a boy who knows the boughs of a great oak well and wishes to display that knowledge to another; except that Hervey was certain there was no such intention in his guide, for a man less affected in his fervour he could scarcely imagine.

All about them was Nature reclaiming – a thick entanglement of myrtle and bay and white-flowering laurustinus, of wild fig and countless nameless plants which the four winds had sown. High above circled buzzards, as if patrolling the Via Appia, sentinels to the two friends' solitude. And below them flapped hooded crows, which brought to Hervey's mind a happy boyhood at Horningsham, its jackdaws and their prankish flight. There were indeed special places, and this he would readily concede was one.

Shelley sat in an arch, a hundred feet and more above the ground, and took a black leather notebook from his pocket.

'Shall you write?' asked Hervey, wondering whether he should explore elsewhere in the ruins to give the poet his peace. 'I mean, shall you compose something as we sit?'

'No, not at once,' replied Shelley, removing the seal from an ink bottle. 'I shall sketch a little first. I like to compose the place when later I contemplate the lines.'

Hervey settled on the other side of the arch and took out his own leather-bound volume, much smaller.

Now Shelley was curious. 'What is that?'

'My prayer book.'

'And what will you find there?'

'I had it with me throughout the war.'

'So you find consolation?'

'I generally try to read the offices of a morning and evening.'

'Do you, indeed? Are you bent on ordination?'

Hervey simply smiled. 'It has been a habit for so long . . .'

Shelley made careful pen strokes, looking up occasionally at the arch. 'Tell me something of yourself, Hervey. Who are your people?'

Hervey placed the marker at the open page, though he did not close the book. 'My father is Archdeacon of Sarum.'

'Archdeacon of *Sarum*,' said Shelley, not looking up this time. 'That is a preferment which speaks volumes.'

'Ordinarily, perhaps, but in my father's case it does not. He is only very recently translated thus from an exceedingly poor country living. I beg you do not think us fattened by tithes and extensive glebe.'

Shelley chuckled, still intent only upon the arch and his sketchbook. 'I am glad he was not so poor that you could not come to Rome.'

'That expense was my own,' said Hervey, mildly insistent.

'The spoils of war?'

'Only in a manner of speaking.'

'*Everything* is but the manner of its speaking, Hervey.'

'I was lately in India and was rewarded for service to one of its princes.'

'India? A vast plundering-house for the Honourable Company!'

Hervey would not be drawn.

'And we know there is a sister of spirit and education,' said Shelley, sketching still. 'Who else?'

'I had an older brother in holy orders. He died five years ago.'

'I am sorry for it. How did he die?'

Perhaps it was Shelley's concentration on the pen strokes that made him so direct, Hervey supposed, but it startled him nevertheless. 'He died of a winter ague in Oxford.'

'Fellow of which college?'

Hervey hesitated. 'He was curate of a parish thereabouts. A poor one, I understand.'

Shelley stopped his sketching momentarily to look across at his companion. 'I am sorry.'

'He was a truly good man.'

But Shelley would not allow the mood to be sombre beyond the moment. 'And no female has secured this sensible military man and his fortune?'

Coming so soon after mention of John Hervey, it was as if a spent ball had struck him square in the breast, knocking out the wind. It did not matter that he knew it must come at some time. 'I was bereaved of my wife but a year ago.'

Shelley looked up again, his expression horrified. 'You too? My dear fellow, my dear dear fellow . . .' He placed his hand on Hervey's forearm, squeezing hard to impart his sympathy.

Hervey knew of Shelley's circumstances, for Elizabeth had told him. Harriet, Shelley's estranged wife, had taken her own life scarcely two years before. The circumstances could not have been more different from his own, and yet he was not inclined to imagine another's heartache was less than his. But although he might concede that, he was not yet inclined to entrust this man with his grief. He made no response.

'Now I see the cause of last night's melancholy, and the distance generally in your air. I pray you would tell me more of it.'

Shelley had laid aside his book, and he now looked him in the eye with a directness which spoke of candour. Hervey saw in that instant that if he did not now trust his grief to this man, he might never do so to any. He closed his prayer book, took a deep figurative breath, and began his story. He told of the earliest days, of Henrietta in the schoolroom, of his first going on campaign, of his returns and his fumbling courtship, of their becoming wed, and their short-lived bliss, and of the fruit of that passionate union. He told how he had struggled for half a year with his conscience respecting a craven and vindictive commanding officer and the obligation of loyalty to a superior. And then he related the circumstances and manner of Henrietta's dying: a cold, lonely affair – terrifying, knowing, above all *needless*. In the course of not one half of one hour, Hervey supposed he had spoken of more with this man than with any living soul.

When he was finished, Shelley, who had sat throughout with arms clasped about his knees like a rapt schoolboy hearing some dorrying tale, gazed silently into Hervey's eyes and saw what was left unsaid – yet which he knew must not remain so. 'And your love's cold grave is of your bringing, you believe.'

'It is. I could own to no other's accountability.'

'Not even your craven commanding officer? His guilt seems amply proven.'

'And that is the opinion of everyone. At his court martial he was censured for it, though there was no culpability in law. His destruction has given me no relief, though.'

Shelley looked out across the Roman plain. Countless thousands must have died by the hand of others there, and might do so again: why was a single life worth repining over? 'I would read you some fragments of verse I am composing when you have the inclination to hear them.'

Hervey would not have wished for the consolation of Scripture at that moment. He returned the kindness with a thankful smile.

Shelley reached into his pocket for a second notebook. 'You have read Goethe, so you will know the legend of Prometheus?'

'That is to make of my erudition what it is not,' warned Hervey, frowning. 'But yes, I know the legend.'

'You were reading last night of defying power which seems omnipotent.'

Hervey nodded. 'And convincing it sounded.'

'I write of Promethean resistance to the Furies, the ministers of pain and fear, disappointment, mistrust and hate. I write of the terrible alternative of giving way to Jupiter's tyranny.'

Hervey saw a lofty analogy, yet was not dismayed, for Shelley's was a wholly honest candour. 'When you are ready to read it, I would listen.'

Shelley grasped his arm again. 'My dear friend, the eagle tore at Prometheus' vitals by day, and by night those vitals were restored, so that the evisceration could begin anew in the morning.'

Shelley's warning, perhaps for its intensity, startled him. 'Do you tell me the pain must endure, then? Is that how your verse shall end?'

'No,' said Shelley, shaking his head decidedly. 'Jupiter shall be dethroned and Prometheus unbound, though I own I am undecided yet by what means. But until that day, Prometheus shall defy the Furies, or else it can never come. Here, let me read a little, rough-hewn as it still is.'

Shelley read him fragments, turning many pages at a time to find what he thought was most apt or diverting.

Hervey sat spellbound.

'And this is how I conclude; perhaps you might recognize, now, of what it is I speak:

'To suffer woes which Hope thinks infinite;
'To forgive wrongs darker than death or night;
'To defy Power, which seems omnipotent;

'To love, and bear; to hope till Hope creates
'From its own wreck the thing it contemplates;
'Neither to change, nor falter, nor repent;
'This, like thy glory, Titan, is to be
'Good, great and joyous, beautiful and free;
'This is alone Life, Joy, Empire, and Victory.'

Hervey did not know by what providence he had come to
trust this man, so different in every doctrine and practice
was Shelley to himself, but for the first time since
Henrietta's passing he wanted to speak his heart freely. And
it seemed that here he might find the means to do so.

CHAPTER THREE
HEARTS OF OAK

Two weeks later

Elizabeth Hervey kept her journal indefatigably, certain that
no one in her lifetime should read it but mindful that God
knew her heart and, consequently, the truth of her entries.
She took pleasure in her writing, and pride, too, for it
allowed her the exercise of free thought as well as literary
enterprise. However, the discovery that Shelley's wife was
an author, with work already published, had at first shaken
her confidence. She felt somehow intimidated that not ten
minutes' walk from the Hervey lodgings sat a woman
younger than her with far greater accomplishments. But
Mary Shelley was a sick woman – of that, Elizabeth was
certain. They had formed an attachment at once, rather as
her brother had with Mary's husband, but women's matters
perforce drew women into greater intimacy, and more
quickly, than men. Elizabeth knew about sickness. She had
seen a lifetime's fill of it in the Warminster workhouse and,
against her father's will, in the hovels of the fencing crib that
was Warminster Common. And she knew that Mary's sickness was as much of the spirit as of the body. Mary had lost
children (Elizabeth was not sure whether one or two), her
infant son was far from well, and her husband had treated
her with such indifference on occasions that Elizabeth

wondered what love there might truly be between them. And then yesterday, while Shelley and Hervey rambled once more about the *Terme* and their womenfolk took tea together, Mary had told Elizabeth she was pregnant, that she had been so since February and had not yet told her husband.

This morning, after a breakfast of oranges and very sweet chocolate, Elizabeth sat at the open window of her sitting room, with its pleasant aspect on the garden slopes of the Pincio, and made her longest journal entry in a month. After recording her fears for Mary's condition, she gave her opinion that her husband was, nevertheless,

a very engaging man whose manners belie all that I had previously read or supposed, and whose regard for Matthew in his bereavement is evident and genuine, for they share something in this respect, I believe, though Matthew's is infinitely more noble. Matthew for his part takes strength in their fellowship, and it is notable how freely he discourses on all manner of things that are novel and radical, for Mr Shelley is as eloquent in his speech in radical affairs as he is on the page, and he is very practised in the latter as we have known these several past years. It is a strange twist of fate that the two should meet and become intimates, and it could not have happened in England, where our relative positions would first have precluded it and then disallowed it. Perhaps it is one of the benefits of foreign travel, as is often said there are many, that one is propelled into intercourse with those whose society would otherwise be denied. Yet Matthew is far still from wholly sloughing off the melancholy, and I do so fear that our coming here will ultimately be to no purpose other than as a temporary amelioration.

Hervey knocked at the door. Elizabeth rose and went to it. 'Ah, brother! Have you changed your mind? Are you not meeting Mr Shelley, then?'

'Yes, but later. I came to see how you were. We hardly had an opportunity to speak yesterday.'

'I am very well. You know it. Mary Shelley is engaging company.'

'So you do not mind my spending so little time with you at present?'

'I had not *accounted* it, Matthew. We are here on in-definite vacation, as you have said. Allow me to address these letters I wrote last evening, and then I shall be all attention.'

Hervey sat and contemplated his sister as she attended to her familial duties. Her defiant good spirits had been his support for so many years, unsung, unrecognized even, that he marvelled at her constancy. And not only that. Henrietta had been her companion long before she had been his. Elizabeth's only companion. Her society since then had been the aged, the sick, the poor and the infirm. He, her brother, had shown scant regard for *her* bereavement. She held her-self ready to assume whatever duties he asked of her in respect of his infant daughter, or indeed of himself. A brother had no right to expect such devotion, the more so when it went uncherished. 'Shall we go to the opera tonight?'

Elizabeth turned. 'Why, Matthew! You have not once suggested we go to the opera since we came here. I should like nothing more. Are the Shelleys to go too?'

'I was not intending that we ask them.'

When Elizabeth showed surprise, her eyebrows arched so much that the eyes themselves seemed to grow larger. They had always been kind, but Hervey could also see they were eyes that might attract. And now that she had given up her ringlets, she ought to make men's heads at least pause, if not quite turn – as indeed he had observed at Signora Dionigi's *conversazione*. What suitors she had had in Wiltshire, truly, he was not sure, for in spite of his mother's lamenting that Elizabeth had willed herself into her unmarried state, there was no objective evidence that there had been any actual proposals. One way or another, he had better have a care of his sister.

'Matthew?'

'Oh, I . . . I beg your pardon. I was quite preoccupied.'

'I asked what is the opera this evening.'

'That I don't remember, save that the composer is Italian.'

Elizabeth frowned. 'I had not imagined otherwise. But you are very good to me to commit yourself to an entertainment about which you know nothing.'

Hervey nodded. Perhaps he had made a beginning.

'And now you shall spend the day climbing the ruins of the baths again?'

'No, not today. I'm meeting Shelley in an hour, but then I intend visiting the English College. I don't suppose he will agree to come with me.'

'I have resolved to move from the Corso,' Shelley announced.

Hervey sipped more of his cooling white wine, diluted and made *frizzante* by water from a sulphur spring near the city walls. 'For what reason? I think your arrangements there are admirable.'

'They are. But I confess to being out of sorts with the place ever since that business in the post office.'

Hervey sighed, and not without sympathy, although it had been the assault that had effected their introduction. 'I still turn over in my mind what could so animate a man to strike another without warning. Was it really dislike of your philosophy? Does such a thing move rational men to common assault?'

It was Shelley's turn to sigh. 'The magistrate was not inclined to examine his mental state, so we cannot be sure. In England, you know, we were subject to such social hatred as was impossible to bear.'

Hervey shook his head. 'You know that I dispute every bit

49

of that part of your philosophy, yet I could never harry a man for it. Tolerance is *the* English virtue, is it not?'

Shelley smiled. 'You and I are so very far separated, indeed, that I marvel we do sit here peaceably.'

'I hope it would be so in England, too.'

Shelley's expression changed to one of grim determination. 'I shall never go back to England!'

Hervey looked shocked. 'You must never say that! You cannot have so poor an opinion of your country.'

'For as long as there's a crowned head, I shall never set foot there!'

'But—'

'Nor a church established!'

'There is no institution on earth that can claim to be without fault, Shelley!'

'The Church of England is not so much without fault as without God! And certainly her religion is without Christ!'

Hervey frowned. 'Now you are being . . . *controversial*.'

'Am I? Am I indeed? You forget I was first at Eton and then at Oxford!'

Hervey prolonged his frown. 'There is a *little* more to the world than those places, Shelley!'

'I speak of institutions, and I count the Church in England no less corrupt than that here in Rome.'

Hervey would not respond. There seemed little point in addressing so vehement an opinion at the present.

'You are a queer fellow, Hervey. You would call me a godless revolutionary, and yet you choose to hazard your soul in my company.'

'I would call you more, but only to your face! But if you own to godlessness then the other sins are merely consequential.'

'Christ alive! I half believe you mean it. What makes you so sure of your religion? You've had cause enough for a whole charterhouse to doubt it.'

Shelley touched deep at that moment, and not solely

on account of Henrietta. Hervey said nothing.

Then Shelley's demeanour changed altogether. He gave a shrug. 'I myself contemplated ordination lately.'

Hervey fixed him with a disapproving look. 'And what decided you against so outlandish a notion?'

Shelley laughed and clasped his hand on Hervey's. 'You are, I think the saying is, "steady under fire".'

Hervey poured more wine, feigning not to take notice. 'I have a mind to visit the English College this afternoon. Shall you come?'

'You surprise me, Hervey,' replied Shelley, with a distinctly mock expression of it. 'Why should so unbending a son of the established church want to see the English College?'

'Why should I *not* want to see it? It has a claim to great antiquity. It is connected with King Alfred.'

'Since Rome is nothing but antiquity, how can that be any particular recommendation?'

Hervey was determined not to be drawn. 'Milton visited there, so I do not see that I may not.' And – though there was no point in saying it – John Keble had insisted he did.

Shelley looked sceptical. 'He visited, did he? Sacred Milton?'

'I am sure of it.'

'Then it is settled. I owe Milton too much to disregard his example.'

Hervey nodded, though in truth Shelley's contrariness could exasperate.

'Do you know his lines on the massacre in Piedmont?'

'Indeed I do,' said Hervey, pouring more sulphur water into his glass.

'I have often wondered in what manner Milton wished God to "avenge His slaughtered saints".'

Hervey was disinclined to discuss eschatology, however. 'You know, I can admire your Cromwell for the stand he took in the affair.'

51

Shelley looked wary, expecting a trick.

'Did you not know? He wrote to the Emperor and others on behalf of the Protestants, urging all sorts of visitations on the Duke of Savoy if he did not stop persecuting them. And it worked, it seemed.'

'It is curious to imagine there are *any* Protestants in Italy. The country is so unsuited to fervour in such matters.' Shelley took a sip of his wine, guardedly.

'Well I may tell you that there are, and very proud too, and called Valdensians, though I can't recall why. There is an Englishman who now ministers to them, who lost a leg at Waterloo. A general. I saw him carried from the field. Elizabeth and I thought we might call upon him on our way home.'

Shelley smiled. 'You have a very charming way of avoiding the material issue, but not an entirely effective one. I asked how you supposed that Milton wished vengeance to be accomplished?'

Hervey did not hesitate. 'Perhaps the wrath of God as well as the peace passes all understanding.'

Shelley raised his eyebrows and inclined his head, resigned to the knowledge that he could provoke his friend to no more.

However, Hervey was unsure whether the expression meant that Shelley acknowledged the reasoning, or that it was just the sort of rhetoric he had expected. 'In any case, you surely cannot lay blame at the door of the English College?'

'No, but it must have given rise to some very contrary sentiments.'

'We all live with those!'

Shelley now looked at him intently. 'Truly, you are a man of very decided certainties – even as regards contrary sentiments. I never had any thoughts of the army, as Coleridge and Southey had, but I think that were I ever to have served I should have wished to do so with an

52

officer like you. Certainty can move mountains.'

'Ha! I assure you, my dear Shelley, certainty in very senior officers is more often the cause of getting *lost* in mountains.'

'Now here indeed is someone who at last speaks his own mind rather than the institution's!'

'Shelley, at times you speak absurdities.'

'Very well, then. Let us speak *not* of absurdities. Where do we go this evening? I confess I shall be in need of gaiety after all the martyrdom at the English College.'

'I am taking Elizabeth to the opera.'

'And you did not ask me to accompany you? I call that dashed uncivil! Have you tired of me?'

Hervey frowned. 'I have neglected Elizabeth of late.'

Shelley was about to protest further when the Greco's proprietor approached their table, accompanied by a postal messenger. '*Signor 'Ervey? Una lettera, molto urgente*,' said the messenger, and there were twenty *scudi* to pay.

Hervey gave over the money, and a further three for his trouble in searching him out.

When they had gone, Hervey began to examine the envelope.

'It intrigues me why men tarry so long in contemplating an envelope when a moment's address with a paper knife would reveal what they puzzle over,' said Shelley.

But Hervey scarcely noticed. 'I do believe it to be from a most gallant acquaintance of mine. It is sent from Naples only three days ago.' He opened it and read the contents quickly. 'It is indeed from him. And it appears he is made commodore. He says he will be in Naples for a month and more, and would see me in Rome as soon as I am able to receive him.'

'And who is this gallant commodore? You have not told me of him.'

'I would need many an evening to do him justice. I sailed

53

to India and home in his frigate. He is uncommonly good company.'

'An officer of the wooden walls, another high Tory!'

'In that you suppose wrongly. There's a radical heart beating in Commodore Peto's breast – as well as one of oak. And you would not deride the latter, I'm sure?'

'No, no; I should not deride a brave heart wherever it beat. How did he know you were here?'

Hervey put the letter in his pocket and stood up. 'I knew his station was the Mediterranean, and so sent word to the embassy in Naples asking that the letter be forwarded when there was intelligence of his ship. I shall go to the post office at once and send him word to come at his pleasure. You will like him.'

'A radical, you say?'

'I did not quite say that. He has a radical bent. I would hardly think him a subscriber to the *Black Hand*, or whatever it is you revolutionaries read.'

'*Dwarf*, Hervey, *Black Dwarf*.'

'Just so. Shall you come with me to the college then?'

'No; on second thoughts I'm a little weary. My eyes are aching again. I have not slept well these past nights. And I want to engage someone at once to find other lodgings. You do not forget Signora Dionigi's party tomorrow evening?'

'No, indeed.' Hervey brushed the dust from his hat and placed it on his head a shade more carelessly than usual.

Shelley looked at him quizzically. 'I perceive a sudden spring to your step – at last.'

Hervey failed to hear more than an easy remark. 'Very well, then. Do we meet at the same time tomorrow?'

Shelley nodded, and with a wry grin. He had no words. And as he watched Hervey walk from the Caffè Greco, he wondered at the comradeship which black powder so evidently made.

There had been a night of rain and the Tiber had risen, so

that the sewers were stagnant again and enterprising hawkers were doing a brisk trade in nosegays. Hervey made do without, though now the stench was so bad that he clutched a handkerchief to his face, and consoled himself with the thought that there would be incense enough to cover this rankness at the college. He quickened his pace, too, almost to double time, so that it was not long before he was pulling the bell handle at the ironclad doors of the English College, the Venerable College of St Thomas *de urbe*.

The *portiere* opened them, but he spoke no English, much to Hervey's surprise – disappointment even – for John Keble had said the place was truly a piece of England in the heart of the old city, though he had not himself been to Rome. At length there came a tall man in a black cassock, and by the *portiere*'s manner, and a few of his words, Hervey supposed this must be the rector, which indeed the man confirmed as he held out a hand in welcome.

Father Robert Gradwell was striking in both appearance and bearing. Eyes that felt as if they pierced to the soul, albeit with gentleness, at once engaged the visitor; and when Hervey had detached himself from their hold he saw a face that might have been the Duke of Wellington's own, for the features were spare, hawklike, fervent. Indeed, so arresting was the comparison that Hervey made a very faltering introduction for himself, and took a little time to explain that he would deem it a great privilege if he might see inside the seminary. He half expected to be asked for what purpose, but Father Gradwell did not enquire; he simply welcomed him, warmly and without condition.

Although it seemed otherwise, Hervey knew that the rector could not have had long experience of showing the college to chance visitors such as he. The house had only lately reopened following Bonaparte's long occupation of what had variously been described as the Roman republic or the vassal kingdom of France's. But mercifully, the evidence was not as great as it might have been, although horses had been stabled where the *venerabili* prayed, and the tombs had been opened for their imagined treasure. Least spoiled of all was the little garden, a very singular feature according to the rector, for where in other *palazzi* there would be a *cortile*, with pots and running water perhaps, here was a place where in but a few moments an Englishman might think himself at home. Hervey, certainly, was able to cast his mind to Horningsham and to conjure an image of his parents, his father especially, for in no man could there be a closer unity of chancel and garden than in the Reverend, indeed now the Venerable, Thomas Hervey.

When the garden had pleased enough, the rector showed him some of the college's treasures – memorials rather than fine plate – and then conducted him to what he called the chapel of the Martyrs. 'I expect you shall wish to be in peace here. It is our custom to offer hospitality to any visitor. Please come to the refectory when you are quite ready.'

Hervey murmured his thanks, and the rector took his leave. He stood at the chapel door for some time before he felt ready to enter, for here was a place where the remembrance of English blood was as real as in the chapels-turned-dressing-posts he had seen too often in the 'never-ending war'. At length he went inside, got to his knees and closed his eyes. A quarter of an hour he remained thus, his prayers a ramble of pleas for the living and the dead – and for himself above all, for he could not in his heart believe that Henrietta needed his oration, nor yet that the living had more need of divine help than he. In his mind's eye he held the picture of Henrietta before him. It was a picture that no other had seen. Even in this most sacred place he had no scruple in conjuring the picture of passion which had transformed her face.

And then when he could no longer bear it, he opened his eyes and fixed them instead on Alberti's commanding allegory of persecution, so vivid a reredos, so prized a survivor of Bonaparte's occupation, Father Gradwell had said. So vivid, indeed, as to overpower. Hervey transferred his gaze to the crucifix on the high altar, wanting all the strength it could give. But he was not practised enough, and tears began to flow, gently at first, and then almost with convulsions, so that he had to take out a handkerchief and clutch it to his eyes. He sat back and picked up one of the cards from the pew. On it were the names of the *venerabili*, for whom a *Te Deum* was sung periodically. Such ordinary names they were, so very English, unlikely-sounding martyrs: Ralph Sherwin, John Wall, Thomas Cottam, Edward James – too long a list to contemplate without wondering what guilt for their deaths remained.

Perhaps he should not have come. He had wanted to see if a place of so much willing sacrifice might have some secret message, some hidden power to ease the pain which every day visited him no matter how determinedly he sought diversions. But there was no message, nor any power to dull the pain. Those who might know of these things – John Keble, Daniel Coates, his father even – had said that only time could ease, that a search for an opiate was at best futile and at worst destructive, and that what would see him through time was God, and his own strength of character.

The trouble was that God did not come to his aid, and that his own strength looked increasingly ill-matched with the trial. Hervey closed his eyes once more, and sought the simplicity of St Mark. 'Lord, I believe,' he murmured. 'Help thou mine unbelief.'

CHAPTER FOUR

THE FELLOWSHIP OF BLACK POWDER

A week later

When Commodore Peto arrived, Elizabeth recorded in her journal a distinct and immediate rise in her brother's spirits. Shelley noted it too, and was at first discouraged that his own company had evidently been deficient. But Shelley could not – even if he had been so minded – hold any part of that against the commodore, whose direct manner and decidedly radical sentiments he found altogether engaging. Their company in the first days was delightful to each.

The evening Peto arrived had been a private affair between the two old friends, however. Not even Elizabeth joined them for supper, for she knew her brother would only speak were she elsewhere.

'Tell me, then,' Peto had demanded when they took their table at his lodgings, the Albergo d'Inghilterra. 'What was done with Towcester? For you were silent on the matter in your letters.'

Perhaps most men would first have expressed sadness at the loss of a wife, even at the semi-orphaning of an infant, for the two had not met since the day of Hervey's wedding; but Peto knew he did not have to speak of it. Long days, weeks, months together in those close quarters of the frigate

Nisus had made for an understanding between the two men, and mere sentiment would have been repugnant to them both.

'I sent you the report in the *London Gazette*,' Hervey replied.

'A very dry account. I want to know how things went.'

The *cameriere* had come to the table again, and asked them in English what they wished to order.

Peto did not hesitate. Indeed, he had not even consulted the blackboard which the *cameriere* had previously brought. '*Trippa!*'

Hervey looked surprised. Peto's taste he knew to be choice, almost fastidious.

'Three months at sea gives a man a powerful taste for the byre!' was the commodore's explanation.

Other occupants of the dining room were now looking towards their table, though only Hervey noticed. He thought he had better share Peto's taste.

The *cameriere* began speaking excitedly, and in Italian. Hervey caught the word *Trastevere*, but little else. Eventually, one of the *albergo*'s men in authority came. He spoke with the *cameriere*, and then explained, in English and with great politeness, that it was not the practice of the Albergo d'Inghilterra to prepare dishes from the 'fifth quarter', as the Romans called it, but that if they were to cross the river to the Trastevere they could indulge their pleasure at liberty.

Peto looked at Hervey, as if his longer time in Rome might effect a change of practice. Hervey sought to accommodate both sides. 'What do you recommend in its place, signor?'

The man in authority was certain. '*Vitello*, signori. You will not taste finer in this city!'

Peto looked at him blankly.

'Capital,' said Hervey, keen to close the dispute. 'The fatted calf. Is that not appropriate, Peto?'

Peto might have wondered who was the prodigal, but his hunger got the better of his curiosity. 'Ay. It will do nicely.'

Hervey thought to distance matters further from the affront to the commodore's culinary discernment. 'And to begin with, I believe we should try the little marrow flowers which they do here in a light batter. They are very fine.'

'Good, good, but not *too* insubstantial, I hope. I'm fair famished.'

The problem was that Peto's voice was cast permanently to overcome the roar of the waves, the shrill of the wind, the groaning of canvas and the creaking of timber. He lowered it in company such as this, naturally, but from so high a volume that he never quite judged the decrescendo aptly. More heads turned towards their table, but Peto was still wholly oblivious to them – by design or not Hervey was unable to say. All he could do was pipe his own voice down still lower in an effort to have Peto follow him. 'Wine?'

'Barolo!'

The whole room turned.

Peto at last noticed. He nodded in turn to each table with an indulgent smile. 'They love a blue coat,' he said, turning back to Hervey, his voice now lowered to below the level of the wind and waves and canvas, as if he were at table in his own steerage, indeed – and at anchor. 'Now, the court martial: I want to know all of it.'

'Where should I begin?' replied Hervey, raising an eyebrow. 'It was a sorry business.'

'Where was it held? Who were the members?'

'At the Royal Hospital. It seems that the commander-in-chief wished to have it within London District, but not too close to the Horse Guards.'

'I would suppose it afforded the pensioners good sport.'

Hervey raised both eyebrows. 'They packed one of the galleries. Some of them had been in Holland when his lordship had first taken French leave. They tut-tutted throughout, and jeered terribly when it was revealed.'

'Good! In circumstances such as this an officer should be left in no doubt as to what his inferiors think of him. What did the president do? Who was it?'

'The Earl of Rotheram, the senior major-general. It was extraordinary: he merely asked them, very politely, if they would not make comment until after the proceedings were finished.'

'Wise move making one earl the president of another's court martial. Who were the others?'

'General Sir Horace Shawcross, a very choleric man indeed, from Lancashire I think, with one arm. He glowered at Towcester so ill throughout the trial that I could almost feel sorry for him.'

'The others?'

'Three colonels, none of whom I'd set eyes on, as I suppose was right.'

'And so how was he charged?'

Hervey took a large gulp of the Barolo, as if to fortify himself. 'I remember the words as if they were only just spoken: "Lieutenant-Colonel the Earl of Towcester is charged with the unnecessary hazarding of his command in the Americas, and for conduct unbecoming an officer, contrary to the Articles of War." '

Peto looked puzzled. 'The conduct unbecoming being that in Holland?'

'No. The Holland business was not revealed until the end.'

Hervey said it rather flatly, prompting Peto to another quizzical look.

'It seems the Judge Advocate General took the view that sending Henrietta away from the fort was ungallant beyond sufferance.'

'There wouldn't be many that could gainsay that. I wonder that he did not bring a charge of cowardice.'

Hervey tried hard to stick with the facts of the case. 'It

seems he did not believe such a charge had sufficient evidence. And Towcester's counsel were very active beforehand, threatening proceedings on vexatious grounds.'

Peto knew as much about military law as the next man. 'What? He would try suing the Crown?'

'He would try suing *me*.'

'Infamous devil! Why did you not call him out?'

Hervey huffed. 'How might one settle so with a dishonourable man? He would have found a way to prevail.'

'Shot at you in the back, I don't doubt! And how did he plead? Not guilty, for sure.'

'Just so. The case against him was then put in summary to the court by one of the Judge Advocate General's staff, and then the witnesses were called.'

'Who gave evidence? You, of course. You were, I presume, the principal witness?'

'Yes. And great play did Towcester's counsel make of supposed disloyalty and therefore unreliability. But in the material facts there were corroborating witnesses.'

'Your serjeant, principally?'

Hervey sighed. 'Regrettably not. He was still in-sufficiently well to give evidence, though he came to London for the purpose. The poor devil lost his senses a day or so beforehand. I even thought he had died, he fell so still in the hospital. No, the corroboration came from my lieutenant, Seton Canning, and Private Johnson, both of whom said far more than was strictly required to answer the questions. Towcester's counsel protested frequently, but so much did they reveal of his character that any predisposition to sympathy on the part of the court must have been wholly worn away.'

'Very satisfying,' said Peto, taking up the last of his marrow flowers and pulling apart another piece of bread. 'What else?'

'I believe the most damning evidence came from the

strangest place of all. There were two Indian guides who were with us the time when Towcester lost his head in the forest, when he thought we might be attacked. They made depositions to the officer in charge of the Indian department, and these were admitted in evidence. Towcester's counsel protested vigorously that the testimony of savages against a peer of the realm could not be borne. Curiously, this appeared to vex both Lord Rotheram and Sir Horace Shawcross equally.'

'No doubt, too, they felt affront that an Englishman could display such recreancy in that company.'

'No doubt,' agreed Hervey, shaking his head with the pity of it.

'How long were the proceedings?'

'Three days. At the end of the second morning the members retired, but the court reassembled in little more than a half-hour and pronounced his lordship guilty. Lord Rotheram then adjourned the proceedings until the following morning so that Lord Towcester's counsel could prepare a plea in mitigation of punishment. This was heard on the third morning, along with evidence as to character – which was given by the prosecution, of course. All the business in Holland came out, and it was then that the gallery roared its disapproval. Lord John Howard – you remember him, the ADC? – told me later that the Duke of York himself had ordered that the facts be revealed in open court.'

Peto nodded approvingly. 'The old fool's not in want of sense at *all* times.'

'And with the gallery still jeering, the members then retired to consider sentence.'

The *cameriere* brought two large plates of veal to the table, to Peto's obvious delight and to Hervey's relief. The commodore sprinkled black pepper over his in prodigious quantities and set about it lustily. 'How long were they out?' he managed between the first and second mouthful.

'It seemed no more than a dozen minutes, a quarter of an hour at most.'

'Always a sign they'd made their mind up even before the plea.'

'And then the president announced the sentence. "To be dismissed from His Majesty's service with disgrace."'

Peto remained silent for the moment, weighing the words. 'That must have given you satisfaction. More so than calling him out.'

Hervey looked pensive again. 'I confess I was astonished how in so very few words was the Earl of Towcester's destruction so utterly completed.'

'Indeed,' said Peto, laying down knife and fork, so profound was the notion. 'I cannot think that a capital sentence could have dealt him a greater blow at that instant.'

'The president then had to say the findings and sentence were subject to confirmation, of course, which drew the sting somewhat, but no one other than his lordship could have had any thought but that both would be confirmed.'

'Who was the reviewing officer?'

'In the normal course of things it should have been the general officer commanding the London District, but the commander-in-chief had reserved the appointment for himself, apparently.'

'And how long did it take?'

Hervey now smiled a little, evidence at last of his satisfaction in the proceedings. 'That is the extraordinary thing. It was said seven days. But the next evening there came confirmation of both findings and sentence from the Horse Guards, *and* with it the order that the judgment be read out before every regiment, on parade – *every regiment*!'

'It would have gone very hard with the Duke of York that a peer proved to be a coward. For all his faults, I imagine the old scoundrel holds to *noblesse oblige*.'

'I imagine so. And I wished for a moment that I was still under orders, for I should have relished being on the parade at which the Sixth had the findings read to them.'

Peto beckoned for their glasses to be refilled, and looked at Hervey a shade sceptically. 'Are you so sure of that? A ship's company becomes very low when the captain is dishonoured – not often that that is, thank God. Even when he is thoroughly despised there is some feeling that every man bears some part of it, and is shamed. It will be the same in a regiment, will it not?'

Hervey nodded. He knew full well it was so. He had thought about it often. Indeed, guilt had gnawed at him that when his troop's spirits must be at their lowest he was not with them – had deserted them, some might say. And he had been an instrument in the sorry business, had he not? If he had confronted Lord Towcester, even in Canada, late, then the terrible end might not have been. He had scarcely needed more evidence of Towcester's incompetence and cowardice, surely?

'You have not thought of rejoining?'

Hervey sighed. 'Frequently; I cannot help it. But in truth I am entirely repelled by a system in which such a thing might happen.'

Peto looked pained. He lowered his voice as if the table were a confessional: 'Hervey, my good fellow, we spoke long of these things during the Indian voyages. I do not believe it is necessary for an honourable man to quit a corrupt institution, so long as he himself is able to serve honourably in it.'

'That may be so.'

'I think it more than "may be". You recall those hours spent in talking of the right conduct of war? You said that Aquinas had ruled that a soldier might still take part in unlawful war as long as he comported *himself* lawfully. I see your present difficulties in that same light.'

Again, the argument was not new to him. Indeed, Hervey had been the first to rehearse it. His appetite now seemed suddenly to leave him, and he pushed his plate to one side.

'It is more than that. My daughter is without a mother. Would it be right for her to be without a father, too?'

Peto did not answer. These were waters in which he had no sailing experience and no right instinct, but he did have one more challenge for his friend, and he squared up to it direct. 'Hervey, are you in any degree fearful of having lost some aptness for command?'

Hervey was stung more deeply than by anything in months. No one had ever suggested this or anything like it. Only Laughton Peto could have imagined such a thing; not even Daniel Coates could read him thus.

Peto did not press his question. Instead he said simply, 'Such a thing would go ill with me, and would remain until next I had the chance to show otherwise. Isn't that the way with men under orders? Those at least who take their profession seriously?'

It was the first time that Hervey had seen Peto let slip the mask of command. And that a man as proud as he should have done so was high testimony indeed to their mutual regard and friendship. Hervey simply breathed deep, and resolved on a different path to their discourse. 'Let's leave it for the morning. Tell me how was your journey. We ourselves are intending to visit Naples.'

'Ha!' exclaimed Peto, his voice rising above the waves again. 'You'd do as well to take a ship. We were stopped interminably. Everywhere the talk was of Carbonari.'

'You were stopped by Carbonari?'

'No! By that ass Ferdinand's troops – "King of the Two Sicilies" indeed! I can think nothing of a man who requires foreign troops lest his own people try to depose him.'

Hervey looked askance. There were precedents closer to home. 'Had we not better have a care in France's regard, therefore?'

'Perhaps so. But at least theirs is a French king, and our troops are in barracks there. Ferdinand would not have a throne if it weren't for Habsburg troops tramping the roads.'

'I doubt that Bonaparte would have been worsted without the Austrians,' tried Hervey.

'*I* don't doubt it. But we didn't fight one tyrant only to replace him with another.'

'Well, I for one shall be pleased if it means we reach Naples without molestation by bandits, even if they do wear pretty ribbons,' said Hervey most emphatically.

The *cameriere* had returned, and Peto was taking more of the veal, with appreciative noises. 'By the way, how is your sister?'

Hervey smiled, pleased with the further evidence of Peto's approval of the veal, and at the thought of happy reports to be made of Elizabeth. 'She is very well. The country suits her, even if her heart is still at home. You shall see for yourself tomorrow.'

'I look forward to it. And have you any other acquaintances in Rome? I heard English spoken all along the street.'

'Indeed we have. The poet Shelley no less.'

Peto was all attention, but his eyes were narrowed. 'An intriguing man, indeed; perhaps in both senses of the word. I have read some of his essays. His sentiment's sound for much of it, but he goes altogether too far.'

Hervey smiled again. 'I should not be able to share even your limited generosity. But he's a great admirer of the Carbonari, and the most engaging of company off the page!'

And Elizabeth's journal recorded that Peto found it just so in the days that followed. And an altogether more agreeable occupation it was for her to write than before. 'They speak of martial things all the time. And even Mr Shelley seems much taken by it,' she noted at the end of the first week. 'I confess, too, there is much to admire about Commodore Peto. He is such a commanding man. He speaks plainly yet is not without sensibility.'

* * *

The pines on the Janiculum gave the little reconnaissance party shade and therefore, they supposed, some cover from observation as they scanned the great fortress of Castel Sant'Angelo below.

'Well, Commodore, could you reach it from here?'

'Just, I think. Two thousand yards, I'd say. One of my long twenty-fours, full charge and with the quoin out. What damage it would do those walls, though, I couldn't vouch for. The shot would be plunging. It'd make a pretty mess of the roofs, but little else, I fancy.'

'How close would you have to come to breach the parapet wall?'

Peto peered again through his telescope. 'I can't judge their thickness. It's not as if they were ship's timbers. I shouldn't trust to more than five hundred yards, playing on the same point with a whole gun deck. But how would you overcome the outer ramparts, and the moat?'

Hervey nodded, acknowledging the problem was no little one. 'I've been considering that a while, since first seeing them indeed. I don't believe they could be overcome in any direct assault. Every angle is covered too well.'

'Then how?'

'The weaker flank is the river. I think a storming party could get under those embanked walls and then scale them while sharpshooters kept the tops clear. I could see Henry Locke going at it, couldn't you?'

Peto agreed. Lieutenant Locke and his marines had never been concerned with tactics, only with audacious frontal assault, though he had paid dear for it – first with his fine looks and then with his life. 'Do we suppose the bridge is no longer standing?'

'I think we must, though even if it were I think it would be given the most severe raking by the defenders. The other weak point is what they call the Passetto, running through the Borgo.'

'A tunnel?'

'No. It looks rather like an aqueduct. It runs from the Pope's palace right into the north-west bastion.'

'For sorties?'

'The opposite: a bolt route.'

'Then it would surely be blown as soon as they were safe in the bastion?'

Elizabeth Hervey, standing behind them a little way, smiled. 'You see, Mr Shelley, my brother is restored to his former spirits. I do not know if he truly loves fighting, but he is wholly absorbed by the study of it. He cannot traverse a piece of country, no matter how pretty, without observing on its aptness to defend or attack. There is a farmer in our parts in Wiltshire who used to be a general's trumpeter many years ago, and he and Matthew will ride all day on the downs spying out the land.'

Shelley had observed the deeper change too, having had heed of it at the first meeting with Peto. 'I own to very great pleasure in your brother's company, Miss Hervey, but his true heart is always elsewhere. And I do not mean that it grieves the while for his lost love. Does that seem cruel?'

Elizabeth sighed. 'I do not think that any of us can say what is his heart or his mind, nor Matthew himself even, for there is such a confusion of sentiment. But painful though it is to say it, I am of the opinion that Matthew could only be free of his slough of despond if he were to put on uniform again.'

'Yes. I do agree. If a man quits the circumstances of his pain he only ever leaves the pain distant. Your brother, I judge, is hero enough to fight the demons on their own ground.'

Before their first meeting, every evangelical instinct in Elizabeth had tended to being appalled by Shelley. Yet now she considered him a true friend. Indeed, at their first meeting his very appearance and air had captivated her. She wondered how it might have been had they all met in Wiltshire, and then concluded that since such a thing was unthinkable, it was also pointless to imagine. 'He has received two letters, you know, asking that he would return to his regiment. But he will not entertain it. They are for India; that is half of the problem, I'm sure.'

'Then why cannot he go to another regiment that is not for the Indies? There are plenty about the shires alarming honest folk.'

'But that would not be the same at all, Mr Shelley,' replied Elizabeth, ignoring his barb. 'His attachment is to his regiment, not to *any* uniform. He would feel it a betrayal in any circumstances, let alone these.'

'Then I very much fear, Miss Hervey, that your brother will cease to be a pilgrim, in any sense. And I am very sorry for him.'

At Signora Dionigi's that evening they dined formally, *à la russe*, on account, said Shelley beforehand, of the presence of an English duchess. They were twenty at table, and Hervey was pleased to be seated at the furthest end from the lady (they did not sit promiscuously), for she seemed to eye him with a look that might have been disapproval. She had arrived late, after the signora had given up hope of her attending and they had taken their places, and there had been no introductions. Hervey could not imagine what offence he might have given her, and had first supposed that she mistook him for Shelley, except that the latter had then begun to speak of her in terms that indicated they were congenially acquainted.

'Do you not know the family?' asked Shelley when Hervey had confided his discomfort.

'Not really. I know the present duke, whom I suppose this lady must be stepmother to, but I only knew him after he had succeeded to the title.' In truth he would rather speak of other things, for the Devonshire acquaintance, distant though it was, brought only painful thoughts.

'She married the late duke only a little time before he

died. She is a very generous patroness of letters. You should be kind to her.' Shelley smiled, as if suggesting something faintly disreputable.

Conversation then became difficult because of a noisy troupe of mandolin-players, gaudily dressed and exuberant, in curious contrast to the formality hitherto. They put Hervey in mind of the feast at Chintalpore, when the *hijdas* had brought the dignity of the palace banquet to a raucous end.

'*Napolitani*,' boomed Peto from across the table. 'We had 'em aboard my ship a week or so past. Not these, but dressed the same. Hands mocked them something terrible to begin with, then they played so well they wouldn't let 'em leave.'

A sudden fermata left the commodore's words exposed, and heads turned his way. Hervey smiled, for Peto seemed not to notice. 'I recall your being fond enough of music to engage an orchestra for the *Nisus*.'

Shelley looked interested. 'Music calms the seaman's savage breast, does it, Commodore?'

Peto saw no irony in the proposition. Nor in truth did Shelley intend any. 'You should come and see for yourself, sir. A squadron of frigates in Naples Bay is a sight to stir any heart, let alone a poet's.'

Shelley looked tempted, but there was an objection. 'I have affairs overdue in the north, I'm afraid, else I should very much like to see them. We passed some months in Naples last year, and the bay was empty the while.'

'I should *certainly* like to see them,' said Hervey, the mandolins' crescendo forcing him to raise his voice a little. 'How long shall you be there?'

Peto consciously lowered his voice. 'A month, probably. We are waiting on some American frigates, and then together we shall make a sortie against the Barbary pirates.'

Hervey was all attention. When last they had spoken, Peto had despaired of ever getting command of a seventy-four, let alone of a squadron of frigates with their guns run out. 'Do they offend us?'

'It seems they do very much, especially the Americans. The Barbary states have made grave depredations on their merchantmen these past few years. Did you know we bombarded Algiers together while you and I were in India?'

Hervey did not. 'Shall you do so again?'

'We shall stand ready to, but our actions will be directed on the ships themselves. I hope to cut out a good many.'

And that would bring a further small fortune for Commodore Peto, mused Hervey. 'I half wish I were coming with you!'

Peto frowned. '*Half* wishing's no good to me, Hervey!'

Hervey was cut, and could make no reply for the moment. It was made all the worse by the mandolins' unexpected finale. But he was saved by the signora, who stood and invited the duchess to take coffee on the balcony of her drawing room.

The little procession of ladies left the men to their cigars, although Hervey himself declined his, disheartened still by Peto's reproof: was Peto – unconsciously at least – impatient of him now that his life was no longer mortgaged in the King's service? Hervey was, as Shelley would have put it, very dull in the ensuing conversation.

When they rejoined their hostess, it was for her to present each of them to her principal guest. She was a handsome woman, the Duchess of Devonshire: not yet sixty, Hervey supposed, and time had not been at all unkind to her.

'And this is Captain Hervey, Duchess,' said the signora, in English, 'although I regret that he prefers to be called plain "mister". I tell him that here in Italy it will not do, that every man has rank or title, or both. But he will not oblige me.'

The signora's happy prating did not induce the duchess to smile. She continued as at dinner to eye Hervey in an altogether unnerving manner. 'Hervey?' She pronounced the 'e' as if it were an 'a'. 'Are you family?'

Dull though his spirits may have been, Hervey was quick enough to make the connection, and he rallied. 'So distantly, ma'am, that you had never known of mine.'

The duchess looked at him quizzically. 'I did hear tell of a Hervey who married a Lindsay – Thynne's ward. Indeed, I once met her, at my sister's in Bath. That would not be you?'

A sick feeling came on him. Only his mind seemed to remain whole. 'Henrietta Lindsay was my late wife, ma'am. She died but a year ago.'

The duchess's expression changed to one of dismay. 'My dear, dear boy: how perfectly dreadful. Had I but known . . . '

'Mr Hervey, had I known too . . .' added the signora.

But Hervey stayed both their protestations. 'I have not been inclined to speak of it. There is no reason for your distress.'

The duchess took his arm and led him a little to one side. 'Was there issue, my dear?'

Hervey told her. 'She is called Georgiana.'

The duchess smiled. 'A good Devonshire name.'

'Just so,' he nodded, managing a little of a smile, but not seeing Shelley's more knowing one. 'Indeed, a godmother is Lady Camilla Cavendish.'

The duchess nodded. 'We were not close, I'm afraid. The duke died but three years after we were married. Not as cruel a severing as yours, Mr Hervey, and at our time of life these things are to be expected. But . . .'

Hervey put his hand to hers. There was no saying that the pain of such things was any the less with the years.

The duchess seemed to know his thoughts. 'Yes, my dear, but I would not have had it any other way, even had I known what was to be its outcome.'

It was a simple truth, and Hervey saw that it applied to him in equal measure. His own surprise silenced him for the moment.

'So I give thanks daily to the Almighty for those few

73

years, my dear,' continued the duchess, now placing her hand on his. 'For they might never have been.'

When it came for them to leave, Shelley told Hervey he would not be able to join them the following morning, for there were lodgings by the Spanish Steps that he wished to look at. The two friends exchanged a few words on the suitability of the location, before bowing and bidding each other goodnight. When Hervey had retrieved his hat, he found he had fallen behind his sister in their farewells, and so he hurried past one or two dawdlers on the staircase to see Elizabeth at the door with Peto. The commodore had evidently said something amusing, for Elizabeth threw her head back and smiled broadly – laughed a little indeed. Hervey checked, an instinct saying he should not intrude. It was the first time he had seen Elizabeth smile quite like that, and the first he had seen Peto looking anything other than a man of the quarterdeck. Truly, it took him by surprise. And how foolish he would think himself, later that evening, when he turned the thought over in his mind. For of what property did he imagine Elizabeth and Peto to be beneath what they were obliged to show to the world? Peto was not married to the sea, for all the poetic attraction in that saying, and indeed for all Peto's own protestations of it. And neither was Elizabeth his sister alone.

Despite these notions, however, and the thoughts which the duchess had planted in his mind, Hervey slept uncommonly well that night. He rose at seven-thirty next morning and went with Elizabeth to morning prayer at the Reverend Mr Hue's new meeting rooms in Piazza Colonna Traiana. It was the second anniversary of his marriage, a union that had brought him unimaginable happiness and fulfilment, and he intended to give unequivocal thanks to the Almighty. It was a holy day too, the feast of Saints Philip and James, and there was an infectious exuberance about the people in the Corso even at this early hour.

Hervey and his sister were the only congregation as Mr Hue began to read the Sentences. 'Rend your heart, and not your garments, and turn unto the Lord your God: for he is gracious and merciful . . .'

The rush-seat chairs held their backs erect, and the high ceiling was a sounding board for the minister, whose voice made full use of it. It was so far from the hushed ease of his father's chancel, and yet the words of Cranmer spoke to them both, in the Pope's very capital, as if they had been in Horningsham itself. Hervey was content, as if he were somehow awaiting the arrival of his bride. Indeed, he turned half-expectantly when he heard the scrape of feet as two more brethren joined them at the General Confession. At the Venite two sightseers joined them, curious. They all remained standing as the minister, in stark white surplice, began the Old Testament reading. 'The spirit of the Lord God is upon me; because the Lord hath anointed me to preach good tidings unto the meek; he hath sent me to bind up the brokenhearted . . . to comfort all that mourn . . . to give unto them beauty for ashes, the oil of joy for mourning.'

How apt did Hervey find Isaiah – always wise, always certain.

'I will greatly rejoice in the Lord, my soul shall be joyful in my God; for he hath clothed me with the garments of salvation, he hath covered me with the robe of righteousness, as a bridegroom decketh himself with ornaments, and as a bride adorneth herself with her jewels.'

How little had Henrietta needed to adorn herself with jewels! He could see her before him now as plainly as he had that day in the chapel at Longleat. He could almost reach out to touch her, as he had that day, when he had found a warmth in her hand that spoke more than any words might. For the rest of the office he heard little, neither readings, nor prayers, nor psalms, nor the comings of the faithful nor the goings of the sightseers. Only the familiar words of St Chrysostom recalled him, beseeching Almighty God to fulfil 'the desires and petitions of thy servants, as may be most expedient for them'. *Desires and petitions* – how he prayed for their fulfilment.

Afterwards, as they walked back to their lodgings, Elizabeth took careful note of her brother's mien without, she hoped, giving him the impression of study. She concluded – she hoped not over-hastily – that it spoke of something different in his heart. So it seemed, too, for he announced with uncommon brio that they would take their breakfast at the Caffè Greco.

And at that place, amid the greater than usual bustle of a Roman festival, Elizabeth observed that her brother was indeed a blither spirit. He took notice of what was about him, and in an approving way, whereas at times before, when he had not been sunk in introspection, he had seemed positively to despise the exuberance of the Greco's less contemplative patrons.

'Shall you go to your secret garden with Mr Shelley today?' asked Elizabeth brightly. 'Or does Commodore Peto command your attendance?'

Hervey returned her smile, but wider. 'Mr Shelley is looking at new lodgings this morning, near the Spanish Steps. He asked me to accompany him but I told him he would better take a sapper than a dragoon. He will make up his own mind whatever it is that I say.' He cut into a *crostata*, and none too neatly: sugar and crumbs spread about the table, so that Elizabeth began sweeping them together with a napkin, and a sisterly frown. 'Commodore Peto wants to go and see the graves of some sailors. Apparently there was an affair on the Tiber a few years ago, when the Navy saved the Pope's treasure from Bonaparte's men, or something very like it.'

'I should like to see them too,' said Elizabeth decidedly. 'May I come with you? Is it far?'

'Testaccio, the other side of the Aventine. I thought we would walk since he wants also to see the Circus Maximus, though I told him it was nothing but a cow meadow.'

'Then I shall dress for a country walk. It will be pleasant to spend a day out of the city. Do you not find the constant noise wearying?'

Hervey looked as though it was the first time he had considered the noise.

'I quite confess to missing silence. I had a mind, indeed, to seek out a convent for a few days.'

Hervey brushed more sugar and crumbs from his coat as he finished the *crostata*. 'That might be apt, for I had a mind to go to Naples for a few days. I should very much like to see Peto's command. Would that disappoint you? You could join us there later. The duchess said she would see Naples, and would welcome your company.'

Elizabeth was, in truth, disappointed, but she readily understood that her brother's return to full spirits needed the attention of a man under orders, and that she would break that peculiar fellowship if she travelled with them. Indeed, her withdrawal to a convent for a few days had been designed principally with that fellowship in mind. She nodded in agreement at her brother's proposal. 'I do not want to leave this country without seeing Pompeii and Vesuvius, though. But there is plenty of time, is there not? Did we not also speak of taking a ship from there to Sicily en route for home when the time came?'

'We did, and we shall. Goethe says it is not possible to understand Italy without seeing Sicily. And I think we must discover why.'

Elizabeth smiled. 'Then I shall get me to a nunnery. The duchess is bound to know which one is suitable.'

'Ah,' sighed her brother. 'The duchess has very decided opinions, does she not?'

She did indeed, thought Elizabeth. And her decidedness, though admirable, had made of her an exile, though it was of her own choosing and she was surrounded by attentive company if not actual friends. And she was a widow, not an old maid, taking obvious comfort in her former state. But

Elizabeth still shivered at the eternal image of the ageing, friendless and, as she thought, childless singleton, for it was a spectre that began visiting females such as she, respectable women 'out' in society beyond the usual time and still without a lace cap.

When they returned to their lodgings that evening, around six, Elizabeth was tired and said she would take her supper in. Hervey said he would be glad to keep her company, for Peto had told him there were three days overdue in his 'log', and he did not allow himself four. 'And I suppose I must reply very soon to this,' he sighed, taking a letter from the writing table. 'A second from Lord Sussex in as many months. He writes that the regiment is certain for India next year. He asks me once again to take a troop.'

Elizabeth, her bonnet already off and her hand on the door to her rooms, hesitated only for an instant. 'I believe you should.'

Hervey looked at her intently.

She narrowed her eyes just a little. 'I believe you *must*.'

Hervey stood silent for the moment, seemingly astonished. 'How can I possibly!'

'How can you be *here*?'

'That is hardly the same. There is a short end to Italy. India would be years. How can I abandon my own daughter?'

'If you insist on the word "abandon", brother, then I despair for you – and not much less for Georgiana. I have thought about it a very great deal these past weeks, and I am of the opinion that Georgiana's best future will not be served by any cloying proximity of yours. I am sorry to speak so brutally, Matthew, but that is my opinion.'

Hervey had been for so many years in awe of his sister's opinion that he at once checked the instinct to lash out against so hurtful a proposition.

Elizabeth did not want to lose the initiative. 'There are

three options, as I see them. And none requires that you are in attendance. Georgiana may remain at the vicarage, and we can find a governess when the time comes. Or else she can go to Longleat, or even to Chatsworth it seems, for the duchess suggested as much, did she not?'

'I don't recall that she—'

'And the choice depends on what prospects you wish for Georgiana.'

Another option occurred to him, but he dismissed it at once as being the product of an entirely selfish impulse: if Elizabeth would accompany him to India with his daughter, then most of the objects would be accomplished. It was impossible, of course. Elizabeth could not leave their ageing parents, nor could any right-minded man submit his infant daughter to the trials of such a climate as India's. 'The only prospect I can rightfully own to is her health and happiness,' he conceded.

'We should all say "amen" to that, Matthew, but you must make a choice as to how best that is secured.'

Still Elizabeth remained with her hand to the door, as if she would not let him go without a decision. Hervey had not felt himself so tried in a long time. He knew he ought to have expected that Elizabeth would not let him off lightly. He had never flinched from decisions as a young cornet, nor lieutenant, nor even when first a captain. But his indecision in the affair of Lord Towcester had cost him very dearly. Had he grown indulgent?

'I believe the air at Naples will do me good,' he said suddenly, folding the letter and putting it in his pocket. 'I think I shall take a walk and then call on Shelley. Shall I ask for collops for you?'

Elizabeth sighed. 'Very well, brother. Perhaps a whiff of sulphur in Naples will be efficacious.'

Hervey looked at her, unsure as to whether she intended any ambiguity. 'And the collops?'

'No, Matthew.' She smiled. 'I think that would be a little

dull. I might as well be in Horningsham. I should like some macaroni and some red wine, and I shall sit with Miss Austen at hand. *She* is never dull.'

Hervey smiled back. He hoped profoundly he would never outlive his sister, for he could not imagine how he might subsist without her good sense. He kissed her forehead. 'One day I shall read Miss Austen, since she has held both you and Henrietta in such thrall. But not just yet.'

'I hope you won't be so soon gone that you mayn't see my new lodgings. They're very pretty rooms.'

'Near the Spanish Steps, you say?'

'Ay. Not a stone's throw from the Caffè Greco. I should be content to lodge there far longer than I have taken them.'

It was curious, thought Hervey, how Shelley rarely spoke but in the singular. Gossip in many a *conversazione* held there to be an uncommon alliance between Shelley, his wife and her stepsister. But Elizabeth had warned her brother that all was not happy with Mary, with whom she had become quite intimate. It was certainly not a matter that he and the poet might discuss. 'You are intent on travelling north for the summer, I hear?'

Shelley raised his eyebrows a little. 'It is not settled.'

'Where might you go?'

'Pisa, perhaps. Or Leghorn.'

'But you would leave Rome altogether if you did?'

'I should not keep the rooms, no.'

'We might travel home by way of Leghorn.'

'I wish that you would.'

They sipped Marsala for a while in silence.

'The duchess is an engaging woman,' said Hervey at length, almost by way of something to break the silence.

Shelley smiled. 'Oh, engaging indeed. You did not know she was a Hervey?'

'There was no reason to. I should be unable even to draw a design of our connection with her line.'

'You thought her handsome, no doubt, too?'

'Handsome indeed!' replied Hervey readily.

'Perhaps a *little* old for my taste.' Shelley smiled again.

Hervey frowned in mock disapproval.

'My dear friend!' Shelley's smile had turned indulgent. 'I am only too glad to see that your impulses remain that of a man. The duchess has always exercised a powerful attraction.'

'Well, very evidently it was so with the last duke, but—'

'Hervey, she was his mistress for years, and of Lord knows how many other dukes. She has so many children salted about Europe that—'

'Shelley, I really do not think that—'

'And there was always talk of her association with Georgiana, the late duchess.'

'Infamous! Shelley, you would do well not to repeat such things.'

But Shelley merely smiled the more. 'Ah, but see what a woman such as she wrought of your demeanour this evening and last.'

Hervey relented, his smile broadening almost into laughter. 'There is nothing about him that a good woman would not put right, and more so, even, a bad one!'

'*Vero! Vero!* You see, Hervey, what a few months away from that hypocritical land of ours does for the spirits.'

Hervey nodded, but his smile was now one of some caution. 'In the short run. But how may we know if it endures?'

'Hervey, you exasperate me with that dogged faith of yours, for that's what lies at the root of your melancholy. You know, when we walked around St Peter's together, there was but one inscription that did not excite revulsion in me.'

'Indeed?' said Hervey, trying to sound surprised that Shelley had found even one.

'Indeed. It was the *memento mori* above the entrance to the sacristy. But not for the reason it was placed there.

Rather because it reminded that our prospects of pleasure are limited.'

Hervey looked at him intently. 'And the rest is silence?'

'Yes, Hervey. It is.'

Hervey sighed, seeming to weigh his words a good deal. 'Shelley, I might wish it were so.'

CHAPTER FIVE

QUO VADIS?

Three days later

Despite the temptations, they stopped only once along the Via Appia before it became wholly a country road. Ruined sepulchres on either side stood regular and imposing, like street-liners for a procession. Here and there a man looking not much better than a vagabond would importune them to stop and descend some dank, dark, subterranean steps to view a catacomb, but the duchess and others had warned Hervey and Peto very emphatically that *banditi* would fall on them with the utmost savagery if they did, and so Hervey had resolved to come another time, in greater company, to explore these holy vaults. Where they did stop, at Peto's wish as much as his own, was the tiny church of Domine Quo Vadis. Indeed, so compelling was it, the turning of history in the turning of a single man upon this spot, that to have passed without a prayer, at least, would have seemed to them both a blasphemy. And Commodore Laughton Peto, for all his hardening years aboard men-of-war, stood awed and speechless at the spot for several minutes, half expecting some command or apparition in the silence of the empty Roman plain.

Their carriage was a more compact affair than they would have had in England, resembling a small hard-roofed landau.

Although it was well sprung even by English standards, the carefully dressed stones that had once afforded the legions rapid marching between Rome and Capua were now worn, uneven and broken, so that at times the carriage's progress was bone-jangling and noisy to the point where talk gave way to near-shouting. But when they were a dozen leagues from the city, the road acquired a surface less cruel; thus conversation was resumed for an hour or so, before a halt for a *collazione* of *spigola* brought that very hour from the blue Tyrrhenian which had been in and out of sight for the last dozen miles. And the rough white wine of the *hostaria*'s own vineyard, much stronger than either Hervey or Peto had expected, soon induced slumber even as the carriage picked up into a good trot with the new horses. They dozed for a long while in the growing heat of the afternoon.

The carriage stopped suddenly. Both men awoke abruptly to shouting, angry and insistent. Hervey, now fully alert to danger, reached for the cavalry pistol on the seat by his side. In an instant its muzzle was roofwards, his thumb on the hammer ready to cock – he had primed it as they passed through the city walls – and with his left hand he pulled out his watch, as he did instinctively at any alarm. Four o'clock: they could be anywhere.

Peto, sitting opposite, facing forward, was likewise ready for action at the offside. 'What are they saying?'

'I can't tell. Not a word.' Hervey crouched by the open window to see where the shouting came from.

'Do we get down?'

'We're safer inside, I think. The driver may make a bolt for it any second.'

But the driver had no such thoughts. Hervey saw him and the guard climb down from the box and raise their hands. Before he could even think what to do next, the doors were wrenched open, and big, bearded men crowded both sides of the carriage. They wore brown cloaks, despite the heat of the afternoon, and tall pointed hats with ribbons round the peaks: red, blue, black – fire, smoke, charcoal. '*Carbonari?*' he asked defiantly.

'*Si, signori. Scendete, per favore.*'

They were courteous enough, thought Hervey. And, curiously, they did not appear to be armed. But he was not minded to threaten his pistol. He motioned to Peto to do nothing but alight.

'*Austrienni?*' said the biggest of the Carbonari, taller by several inches, and easily in excess of six feet.

It was a strange thing to enquire of a man's nationality before robbing him, thought Hervey. '*Inglesi.*'

The big man seemed impressed, but then sceptical. '*Avete dei documenti per provarlo?*'

Peto looked puzzled, but Hervey thought he caught the intention.

'*Siamo officiers inglesi.*'

The big man seemed puzzled by the admixture of French.

'*Caballeria,*' Hervey explained, pointing at himself, hoping the Spanish would be near enough. '*E marinare,*' he added, pointing at Peto.

The big man turned and gave what was obviously an order to another behind him. Hervey now saw the butt of a musket sticking out of the bottom of the man's cloak. He glanced at the others: it was the same with them. These were cool fellows, indeed, not at all anxious to be off with their booty.

Still the big man looked wary of the two travellers. '*Non avete documenti?*'

But Hervey could only shrug. Then a woman with fierce black eyes pushed her way to the front, her dress as gaudy as the men's was plain, with red, blue and black ribbons tied around her waist. '*Parlez-vous français, monsieur?*' she asked brusquely.

Hervey sighed to himself, no little relieved at being in a position to communicate at last. '*Oui, madame. Nous sommes officiers anglais.*' He went on to explain their exact qualifications, taking care not to give any impression that his commission was sold a year ago.

The woman relayed all this to the big man, who relaxed visibly, smiled almost. He asked her several things, some of which she seemed to answer of her own accord, others which she repeated to Hervey in French. The big man wanted to know why they were travelling this route: it was not the usual one to Naples. Hervey said he didn't know, that the driver was charged with taking them to that city, where his companion's ship lay at anchor.

Only as he said it did Hervey realize he was upping the ransom price which these brigands might have in mind, for that could be their only object if they were not simply to take all the travellers' possessions and make off. Yet something in the big man's manner made him less menacing than he ought to have been. Not once had they threatened violence, nor even revealed their arms.

'Who are you?' he asked, in as unruffled a way as possible.

'He asks who we are,' relayed the woman.

'*Siamo Carbonari*,' replied the big man, with so much pride that the others threw their heads up at the word.

'First Austrians, and now Carbonari,' groaned Peto. He thought to raise his voice for clarity. 'You are very good fellows, but we have no gold worth your taking. We are English officers.'

But the voice that from the quarterdeck could send hands aloft in a howling gale was greeted by indifference.

Hervey turned to him. 'They asked if we were Austrian. Do you think we're in Naples already?'

Peto shrugged. 'There was no customs post on the journey up, as I recall.'

Hervey asked their interpreter.

She appeared to know, but asked the big man nevertheless.

'*Si*,' he nodded. '*Sulla frontiera*.'

Perhaps this explained the men's composure, thought

Hervey. They were abroad on the margins of the Pope's domain and the kingdom of the Two Sicilies, where the writ of both monarchs ran weak, and where the fastness of the mountains to the north offered rapid refuge. But even so, the leisure with which they now proceeded was curious in his military eyes. 'Since we are not Austrian, and you are honourable men,' he tried, 'may we now continue on our way?'

The woman stared at Hervey a while before turning to the big man and explaining.

The man shook his head impassively. '*Venite con me,*' he said, beckoning and turning about, the press of men behind parting for him.

Hervey was vexed, but he was no more than a shade apprehensive, for somehow there seemed no menace in these Carbonari. He thought it strange that no attempt had been made to disarm the two of them. Perhaps they were covered by many more Carbonari concealed about this lonely stretch of road. It was certainly not a place to make a dash from. A couple of hunting dogs, lurcher types, fell in beside them, as well as several women, none of them older than they themselves.

The growing band climbed the rocky hillside, beneath pines and through scrubby bush. Hervey heard the carriage moving below, and looked back. '*Ne vous inquiétez pas, messieurs*. Do not worry at all,' said the fierce-eyed woman. 'We take it away to hide, that is all.'

Hervey was sure her French was not the native's, but it was most convincing.

Peto was becoming indignant. He knew a little French, and now was the time to deploy it. 'I am Commodore Laughton Peto of the Royal Navy and I demand to know your intention, sir!'

Hervey winced. A commodore, in common parlance an admiral – he would carry a heavy price if the Carbonari were minded to ransom.

The big man bowed in acknowledgement when the woman translated.

'The comandante says he is honoured to have so exalted an officer in his company, and wishes to offer you our hospitality,' she explained, throwing out a hand to indicate their encampment.

They had by now come up to the mouth of a cave, big enough to enter without stooping. A fire burned without smoke at the mouth, and a pot hung above it on a tripod. Beyond that there was little sign of camp comforts. 'Why do you detain us, sir?' asked Hervey.

The man appeared to understand much of the French, but he would not speak it, and he waited each time for the woman to explain before replying in Italian. 'Because if I had let you go on you would have run into Austrian patrols. And if you had gone back it would have been the same. I could not risk you telling them of us.' He took the pot from the tripod with a piece of leather. 'Would you like coffee, signori?'

There seemed no reason to decline.

'But we saw no troops of any sort on the road,' pressed Hervey.

'That is difficult to believe, signori. There are always pickets along that road, and in strength.'

'I assure you, sir,' replied Hervey, shaking his head. 'We saw not a man. Although I confess we were sleeping for the past hour or so. But they surely would have stopped us?'

The comandante began hurried consultation with the half-dozen other men who had followed them to the cave. His voice had turned more than a touch anxious. He turned back to Hervey. 'Do you swear, sir, by your soldier's honour that the road is free of troops?'

Hervey frowned. 'I repeat, sir, that we saw none at all in our progress. If they lay concealed in the trees, or ditch or I know not, then I cannot say.'

Clearly this intelligence had some effect on the plans of

the Carbonari, but in what way Hervey could neither understand nor deduce.

'What d'ye think agitates them so?' asked Peto, becoming
weary of the business.

'I can't tell. Either they're planning an ambuscade and
their birds have flown, or—'

'You will stay here, signori,' said the comandante
suddenly. 'And you will stay with them, Maurizia.'

The woman nodded, looking anxious for the comandante.

'*Venite!*' he commanded the others.

When they had gone, Hervey glanced at Peto.

The woman saw. 'Do not try to leave, messieurs. There are
men posted. They will shoot.'

Hervey and Peto exchanged looks which postponed the
notion of escape. Hervey sipped his coffee, bitter though it
was. 'Your French is excellent, mademoiselle. May I ask
how you acquired it?'

'Why do you wish to know?' she replied defiantly.

'I have no motive other than curiosity, mademoiselle.
Mine I was taught by a Frenchwoman who lived in England.
I did not set foot in France until I was three and twenty.'

She smiled a little. 'I have not even been to Rome,
monsieur.'

'Then you too had an able teacher.'

'King Joachim.'

Hervey did not catch her meaning. 'How so,
mademoiselle?'

'I was his mistress, monsieur.'

Hervey was stunned. Here was both honesty and history
in uncommon measure.

Peto had followed the exchange, and looked eagerly for
the particulars.

'Not his only mistress, of course. But I believe he
favoured me above the others for a time. Certainly among
those who were not of the quality.'

Her candour was wholly disarming. It was not difficult to

appreciate what Murat had seen, for her fierce eyes could surely blaze in an altogether different light. Hervey and Peto looked at each other in some confusion. 'What are you doing here, mademoiselle, with these Carbonari?' asked the former.

'The Carbonari fight for our liberty, monsieur. We want no other sovereign but our own, Italian. And perhaps not even a king. We make a beginning here, in Napoli, but in time there will be Carbonari in all of Italy.'

'And you yourself, mademoiselle?'

She looked at Hervey strangely. 'I am Carbonara, too, monsieur. And my place is here, with the comandante, my man!'

Hervey was silenced by her passion.

'From silk sheets to pine needles,' said Peto, just loud enough for him to hear, and in a tone more of puzzled admiration than reproach.

Hervey was inclined to admire her too, though who could tell her true motives in being here? Perhaps she herself could not. But the life must hold few comforts. 'Mademoiselle, what is the comandante's intention here today?'

Her look at once became distant again. 'Why do you wish to know?'

'Well,' he began, with a smile, 'we are detained by you, and might wish to know what shall be our end, and when.'

'You will come to no harm, messieurs.'

'But why was the comandante so sure we had seen Austrian troops on the road?'

The woman hesitated at first. 'There is a company in the town a mile or so along the road from here to Napoli. We intend capturing their weapons. They send patrols along the road to the frontier each day. They return about this time. You should have seen them.'

'Well, we did not. How many men does the comandante have, mademoiselle?'

She did not answer.

'Mademoiselle, I am a soldier. It is my interest to know, that is all.'

'Enough,' was all she would say.

Hervey thought for a moment. 'Has the comandante placed pickets about the camp?'

The woman looked uncomprehending.

'I mean, has he placed sentries all around the camp, at a distance, beyond the range of the camp's noise?'

Again she looked as if she did not grasp the intent.

'So that an enemy's approach might be detected in time to have the comandante's men take post.'

Hervey's question was answered in part by a distant welter of musketry. He sprang up and past the woman in an instant. From the mouth of the cave it was clear the firing came from the direction they had travelled, but from up the hill rather than the road below.

The camp was now all alarm, running, cursing and shouting the order of the moment – *a posto! avanti! presto! presto!* Peto looked about with a disdain bordering on contempt. Drill was what they needed at a time like this, and drill was very patently not what they had ever tried, let alone perfected.

Hervey moved instinctively to the protection of a tree trunk, taking his pistol from his belt and porting it high. He called and beckoned to Peto, who was still standing at the mouth of the cave as if on his quarterdeck, for a naval officer did not seek cover in an engagement.

Peto almost strolled to the tree.

'As soon as they're all atop that rise' (Hervey pointed with the pistol to where Carbonari were scrambling for all they were worth) 'we can steal back down the hill and try to find the carriage.'

'Very well,' said Peto, as if he were agreeing to nothing more exacting than a change of sail.

The firing was now intense, perhaps no more than a

hundred yards off. It was volleying for the most part, and regular enough for Hervey to estimate there was a full company, for no foreign troops could volley at that rate in a single rank.

Shots peppered the silence between volleys, the Carbonari answering defiantly.

'We must grant they have pluck,' said Hervey to Peto.

But Peto was dismayed to find that sticky pine sap had dripped onto the shoulder of his coat. 'I had this made only last month in Naples,' he complained.

Hervey turned to look, but a ragged volley from atop the hill took him by surprise. A ball hit the branches overhead, sending down pine needles and bits of bark. He looked back to see white coats coming over the crest. Carbonari, until that moment unseen, rushed forward past him, taking cover behind the rocks and returning the fire determinedly. He saw one whitecoat fall to what looked like a Baker rifle. Now was the time to slip away. He turned to search for his line, but shots over to the right made him look back.

The fierce-eyed woman fell as if dead not thirty yards from them.

As one Hervey and Peto sprinted to her. She lay moaning, blood spread the length of her back.

'We can't move her,' said Hervey.

'I think we must,' insisted Peto. 'To the cave, at least.'

They made to take her by her arms and legs, but lead whistled their way again, and bark flew from the tree next to them. 'Christ!' cursed Hervey, reaching for his pistol. He swung round to see a whitecoat rushing them with the bayonet twenty yards off, another close behind. Had he any choice? He levelled his pistol and fired in one movement. The first man fell stone dead.

Peto took aim at the second, fired, then cursed. Hervey dashed to the dead man, seized up his musket and rushed at the second with the bayonet. They met at the charge, but the whitecoat flinched at the last minute and Hervey's blade drove in beneath the ribcage, running the man back a full six feet before he fell.

Out came the bayonet – easily enough, thank God – and Hervey stood on guard as other whitecoats came over the ridge. Shouting behind him, Italian shouting, made him glance over his shoulder. He flung himself to the ground just as the gun fired. A hail of metal whistled over his head and scythed through half a dozen whitecoats who had left the cover of the trees. He got up and scrambled back to find that Peto had all but reached the cave with the woman.

Carbonari were now swarming up the slope from the road, three dozen of them, perhaps more. Four giants of men hauled the gun back into alignment – it looked as big as a carronade – as women little more than girls carried powder from the cave.

A line of Carbonari now faced the attack, taking standing cover in the trees. Down the slope in a headlong rush came what was left of their picket – half a dozen men – to rally behind the firing line. Last man down was the comandante, his cloak and hat still in place, ribbons flying loose, the lurchers loping along at his side. As he reached the line he saw the woman lying at the cave's mouth, and Peto kneeling over her trying to stem the bleeding. He called to Hervey. 'Save yourselves, signori. This is not your fight.'

Peto took no notice, even if he understood. Hervey was re-priming his pistol. He looked up and called back, 'Have a care of your flank,' indicating the direction of his skirmish.

The comandante looked right, saw the whitecoats lying dead, and beckoned the picket to that quarter. They were firing within the minute. The comandante looked round and nodded to Hervey grimly.

Soon there were whitecoats the length of the crest not seventy yards away. They presented, fired as one, but too high to have effect. A shower of needles and bark fell on the Carbonari line, then the whitecoats gave point with the bayonets and began doubling down the slope.

'*Aspete, aspete!*' called the comandante, glancing left and right to reinforce the command.

Hervey wondered where he had learned his nerve; it took a practised eye to await a bayonet charge.

'*Aspete, aspete*,' he continued, as the whitecoats quickened their pace. Then, at thirty yards, '*Fuoco!*'

The effect astonished Hervey as much as it shocked the Austrians. Hardly a ball failed to find its mark. The few whitecoats not hit seemed to falter, the touch of cloth now gone from left and right. Carbonari stepped boldly from behind the trees and began taking careful aim with pistols. It was over in a minute.

There was no despatching of the wounded, though, as the Spanish *guerrilleros* would have done. Hervey watched as Carbonari who had fought desperately now sought out those of both sides with life remaining, staunching blood, offering water. By rights they should have picked up their wounded and gone, for there was no knowing what other troops were even now marching towards the sound of the gunfire. Having once been caught off guard, it was, thought Hervey, imprudent to remain.

'She needs forceps,' called Peto from a few yards away. 'I can feel the ball but it's tight-lodged.'

The woman was conscious but perfectly still, making not a sound. Where he might find a surgeon's bag, Hervey had not the first idea. 'Do not trouble, signori,' said the comandante in broken French, pushing new cartridges into the bandolier beneath his cloak. 'The *muli* will come soon, and Maurizia she is strong.'

Hervey did not doubt it, though he thought that neither mules nor the woman's strength would be enough. Her colour had turned almost grey.

But the stretchers came soon, and with a string of mules; their *sconci* ran ahead with long lead ropes, letting the animals extend up the uneven slope. For Maurizia they lashed a stretcher between two mules, and Peto, Hervey and the comandante lifted her into it and lay her face down, head to one side. She managed something which passed for a smile at her deliverers, a smile which plainly said her thanks. Then she turned her eyes to her comandante; they spoke of defiance still. She coughed the words, '*In bocca al lupo, Domiziano. In bocca al lupo.*'

The comandante took the ribbons from beneath his cloak, red, blue and black, and pressed them into her hand. '*Crepi il lupo, Maurizia. Crepi,*' he said softly.

At his nod the *sconci* led the tandem off, up the slope and towards the mountain fastness. Not for Maurizia and the wounded Carbonari the hospital of the town below. That was for the whitecoats. They would take them to the road and leave them for their comrades; and better would be their chances than those of Maurizia and *her* comrades.

Hervey watched the comandante as the train of mules passed. The man's lips moved, but without a sound. Was he cursing, or praying? As the last mule passed him he made the sign of the cross then turned back to his unlikely comrades-in-arms. 'Signori, you have done more than I can thank you for. Only it is time for you to leave now, or you will be fighting more.' He spoke slowly and carefully, his French well chosen.

Hervey understood. He held out his hand.

The comandante took it, and Peto's, then beckoned to a Carbonaro and gave him instructions to take *nostri amici* to where the carriage had been concealed.

Hervey looked about as the last Carbonari began striking their meagre camp. He wiped his brow with his sleeve. It was strange to see the streaks of powder smoke after so long. His clothes were blood-spattered, his hands too. He pulled the pistol from his waistband to draw the charge. How strange it all felt. But it felt strange because it was so familiar, almost comfortable.

'Time for us to be hove off, Hervey,' said Peto, guessing his thoughts.

'Ay,' nodded Hervey. 'I've seen ghosts here.'

They spent the night in an uncomfortable *hostaria* not two hours' drive from Naples. The horses were tired, and the coachman had had enough of a fright not to want to risk more by continuing in the dark. And both Hervey and Peto felt the need of a bath. It was nearly eleven the following day, therefore, when they reached the place just beyond Capodimonte which first afforded a view of the bay. Peto was soon searching with his telescope for sight of his squadron's tops, and Hervey saw an already happy man become perfectly content when at last he saw his frigates' ensigns. He himself had already concluded that his only chance of peace lay, ironically, with his return to arms. He would not say at once to Peto why, but he would ask him if they might go first to the post office before rowing out to *Nisus*.

CHAPTER SIX
HAPPY RETURNS

London, two months later

Horse Guards Parade of a sunny July morning was a sight which both commanded attention and pleased the eye. After all the grand places they had visited in Rome, Hervey was unsure how the capital of the greatest military power in the world would compare with that which had once claimed the same title. It was only his fourth or fifth visit: he could hardly profess any certain knowledge. But his sister had been not once, and to her therefore he was an accomplished guide.

'So this is where sits the Duke of York?' she said, remembering the mixed fortunes it had spelled for her brother in the past five years.

'It is,' replied Hervey, taking out his hunter. 'And not many minutes before we shall see the changing of the horse guards.'

They had walked from their respective lodgings in Charles Street, he at the new premises of the United Service Club, Elizabeth at a comfortable hotel for ladies, and she had thrilled at the elegance and pulsation combined that was St James's. After crossing through the park to the parade, they now waited to see the daily spectacle of colour and military discipline. A company of foot guards (to Elizabeth's disappointment her brother confessed that he could not tell from which regiment) were drilling in the middle of the parade ground, their band, thirty-strong and more, using the echo from the buildings on three sides to swell their music so that it rose above every competing sound from the busy thoroughfares nearby. The march they played was Irish, thought Hervey, for he had heard it many a time in Irish bivouacs in the Peninsula, but he could not put a name to it. Five minutes before the hour by the Horse Guards' clock, the old guard – a cornet, a corporal of horse carrying the cased standard, a trumpeter and seven private men of His Majesty's Life Guards, three remaining sentinel at the Whitehall entrance – filed through the arch below and formed up in line, in close order, to await their reliefs. The horses were impatient for a good trot on the way home, having been confined to the little yard of the headquarters for a full twenty-four hours. They fidgeted and bobbed their heads until their riders managed one by one to collect them.

'Let's get a little closer,' said Hervey.

'Oh, may we?' enquired Elizabeth, rather surprised.

'As close as we like. Come,' he smiled. 'It will be the first time I have walked this ground entirely at my own volition. I think I may like the feeling.'

'Especially since it may be the last time for some years to come,' she replied, smiling doubtfully at him.

He smiled back. 'I suppose, yes. If there is no fault with the agents.'

The clock began striking the hour as the reliefs arrived at the walk from the Mall, the same number exactly from the Royal Horse Guards, the 'Oxford Blues'. Their trumpeter sounded the approach, the Life Guards brought swords to the carry, and the Blues formed up facing them. There followed a curious colloquy between the cornets, rein to rein, which Hervey strained to hear, but without success. He supposed it must be a report of the foregoing twenty-four hours, but after a while he came to think it was probably no more than idle chat, a conceit to hold in thrall the onlookers.

'Is it the same in the Sixth?' asked Elizabeth when the ceremony was over and the guards began dismissing to their respective duties.

'No,' he smiled. 'I'm afraid you would be very disappointed on that account. Our guards are mounted *dis*mounted.'

'What a contradictory locution,' she teased.

'Though we are as fine a sight on parade,' he added quickly. 'If perhaps not so imposing; these are bigger men on bigger horses for the most part.'

'Matthew, I am sure I should be equally mystified by what passes in the Sixth as here.' She took his arm again. 'Do we proceed?' she asked, turning away.

Hervey arrested the turn. 'Through the arch.'

'*Through* the arch. I should have thought—'

'No, you may walk right up to the door of the Duke of York's headquarters itself. Don't you think that is very *English*? Could you have imagined the same in Paris in late years – for all that talk of *égalité*?'

'I cannot imagine Paris at all,' sighed Elizabeth.

'You would be disappointed after Rome.'

'I am so pleased to have a brother who is a man of the world,' she said, putting a hand to his forearm. 'It makes me feel a little less provincial.'

Hervey was not sure of the precise measure of his sister's irony. 'I should never call you provincial. No more than I should call myself a man of the world. I think it more than travel alone which makes the latter. Shelley was more a man of the world, though he had but crossed the English Channel and I two oceans.'

Elizabeth's expression indicated that she agreed. 'I do wish I had had a little more time with Mary Shelley. I told you, did I not, that she asked me to winter with them in Italy?'

'No, you did not. That would be very agreeable, I think.'

He hoped he sounded convincing, but he had a care for her reputation, and the prospect of joining the Shelley house-hold was not something to be viewed lightly. And then there was the question of Georgiana, over which he had daily been growing more troubled. He was relying on Elizabeth's super-vision in great part.

Silently though her brother had borne those troubles, however, Elizabeth had sensed them. 'I cannot of course do so. There will be so much to detain me in the parish,' she said dismissively.

But 'detain', in its ambiguity, was not a comforting word for Hervey. Elizabeth might well insist that parochial calls and the poor-relief committee were the principal demands on her liberty, but he knew it would be otherwise. He was about to reply when the dismounted sentry in the arch came to attention, bringing his sword upright from its point of rest on the shoulder. Hervey raised his hat in acknowledgement.

Elizabeth blushed at the salute. 'Matthew, does that man *know* you?' she whispered.

Hervey smiled indulgently. 'No, Elizabeth. He cannot know me. Lord John Howard told me they are instructed to salute those whom they believe are officers, which they guess by some process best known to them only, I imagine. I rather think it a little game they play. Lord John says that their own officers are not averse to strolling through the arch out of uniform with a lady whom they seek to impress.'

Elizabeth sighed. 'And others would do the same had they the chance, no doubt. But you are not yet an officer: ought you to have returned the salute?'

He raised an eyebrow. 'I could not have disappointed the man.'

'Nor me?' She gave a wry smile.

He smiled too. 'Well, I assure you I did not walk this way with that object.'

'Soldiers! They are all the same.'

He thought it would be to no avail to dispute it with her.

* * *

At the premises of Messrs Greenwood, Cox and Hammersly, in Craig's Court behind Scotland Yard, they were received with unusual civility – unusual in that each time Hervey had entered the establishment before, he had found the insouciance of the clerks to be verging on the impudent. But on this occasion he was received by one of the partners, offered hospitality and made to feel a valued customer of the regimental agents rather than a mere book-keeping item.

'The papers have been prepared, sir,' said Mr Cox, a man of a type Hervey did not meet as a rule – a commercial man, fiftyish, of some substance certainly, but perforce deferential. The nearest he could imagine was the regiment's surgeon, paymaster or veterinarian – not an officer in the usual sense, but sharing an officer's milieu. They were never entirely at home, being just a degree above the class of artisan in the minds of many. It never worried Hervey; it always seemed to worry them.

'And by what date shall the commission be effective, Mr Cox?'

'Three days hence, Mr Hervey. It is all explained in a memorandum I have had prepared. At signature today you will forthwith be cornet in the 6th Dragoon Guards. Tomorrow that cornetcy will be sold on, and you will advance by purchase to a lieutenancy in the 82nd Foot – it was the most expedient, you will understand, sir.' (Hervey had to suppress a smile at the agent's need to apologize for having him gazetted to an infantry regiment, even for a day.) 'And the day following, the lieutenancy shall be sold and the captaincy in the Sixth purchased.'

'There is no risk of . . . misadventure?'

'Not at all, sir. We hold the respective bids in bond. It is an entirely regular affair.'

Hervey raised an eyebrow and smiled dubiously. 'It was always my understanding that it was most irregular.'

Mr Cox raised both hands just a little and bowed. 'In

ordinary, it is irregular, sir. As you will know, a year must be spent in each rank before the next may be purchased. But in a case such as yours there are many precedents. It is not something to which an objection would be raised: of that I can assure you, Mr Hervey.'

'I am gratified, Mr Cox. And when do you say I shall be gazetted?'

'The *London Gazette* will publish the commissioning and first promotion on Thursday and Friday of this week, and your captaincy on Monday.'

'It would be amusing to spend Friday with the Eighty-second,' said Hervey, smiling again. 'Where are they?'

'I am very much afraid that I do not know, sir. I *think* they may be in the West Indies.'

'Ah,' said Hervey, frowning. 'Disagreeable as well as impractical.'

'Quite. And so, Mr Hervey, if I might be so bold as to trouble you for the draft . . .'

Hervey had been that morning to the St James's offices of Gresham's bank, and there made the arrangements to draw on his account the sum of £4,125, being the price which, by ruses best not known, the regiment's colonel, the Earl of Sussex, had struck with the seller. It was, he knew, an expensive way to purchase an annuity of £270, but so few were the commissions compared with but five years ago, when the cavalry stood at more than twice the number of regiments, that the price was the seller's for the asking. They were supposedly regulated – the official price for a captaincy in the cavalry was nine hundred pounds below what he was now paying – but the Horse Guards turned a blind eye to the practice of overbidding. It suited, now that there was a general peace in Europe, to have the army returned to the proprietorship of those with considerable independent means, for on the whole they were less ambitious and less troublesome. Hervey handed an envelope to the agent.

'Thank you, sir,' said Cox, laying it to one side on his desk without, of course, opening it. 'That completes the formalities, as I imagine you will recall. Is there any other way that we might be of service?'

There was, and Hervey handed him a list of requirements touching his pay and credit arrangements in India, all of which the agent said would be arranged with very little trouble.

'I am obliged to you then, Mr Cox. And if you will now excuse me, my sister and I have certain other errands to be about. I am staying at the United Service Club until to-morrow only; I shall see tomorrow's *Gazette* there promptly, but I should deem it a service if you would have my page sent down by express to Wiltshire. I have no doubt that the arrangements are made, but I have come to value exactitude a little more than I formerly did.' He said it with a smile, but he meant it.

They left the agent's and took a chaise to Piccadilly, to the premises of Mr Gieve, the tailor who held the sealed patterns for the uniform of the 6th Light Dragoons. Hervey's pleasure in the anticipation of this was easily evident to Elizabeth, who had insisted on accompanying her brother on business he had scarcely imagined would interest her in the slightest – despite what was commonly held to be a female's inescapable captivation by regimentals.

They were greeted warmly by Mr Rippingale, the same genial cutter who had refurbished his military wardrobe at the end of the war, five years past, and attended him since when there were changes to be made. 'How very gratifying it is to see you again, sir,' he said, bowing. 'We received your letter only a few days ago, but we have made a beginning. Is this your good lady, sir? We read of your nuptials in *The Times* with considerable pleasure.'

Hervey faltered only momentarily. 'No, Mr Rippingale, the lady is my sister.' He turned to Elizabeth: 'My dear, this is Mr Rippingale, who can cut and stitch an overall-stripe straighter than any I have observed.'

Mr Rippingale beamed at the recognition. 'Good morning, madam. I am flattered by Captain Hervey's approval, though I must say my work is made easier by the captain's having an exceedingly good leg for a stripe.'

'I have observed so, Mr Rippingale,' replied Elizabeth, returning the smile.

'Well, then, Captain Hervey – I may call you that, may I not, sir?'

'I do not see why not, Mr Rippingale. From Monday I shall anyway be gazetted as such.'

'Yes, indeed, sir. And may I say how glad I am that you are returning to the colours, so to speak.' As he did so, he pulled aside the curtain of an open-front wardrobe, revealing a rack of uniforms part-made. 'Your measurements we have had for many years in our order book, sir.' He turned again to Elizabeth. 'They have not changed greatly with the passing of the years, madam.'

That it was genuine enough praise was without doubt, and Elizabeth saw in her brother's face the look of a man who might have received some approving remark from a superior officer. She had perhaps learned more about the soldier in him in a single morning than in all the years before: what simple precepts animated him at root – simple, yet not unexacting.

Hervey first tried the jacket: a good fit, as Mr Rippingale had predicted, as too was the pelisse. 'Not as dashing as the hussar's, Elizabeth, I'm afraid,' he said, frowning a touch as the pelisse was hung on his shoulder to check the fall.

'May I ask what it is for?'

'Well, I imagine it served originally as a surtout, but I've never had my sleeves through one. If it is cold we wear a cloak.'

'Then it serves no purpose?'

Mr Rippingale maintained a detached air during the exchange, although with the suggestion of a smile. Useless embellishments were not unwelcome in his trade.

'It serves the purpose of smartness, I suppose,' replied Hervey, a little put out by Elizabeth's utilitarian questioning.

She nodded. 'And the braided belt, too?'

'Oh,' he said, puzzled, as Mr Rippingale took the crossbelt from its brushed cotton wrapping. 'That is not the Sixth pattern.'

'Ah,' replied Mr Rippingale. 'There has been a change in the regulations. There is no longer a red stripe.'

'Indeed?' said Hervey approvingly.

Elizabeth looked curious. 'Why should that be, do you suppose, Matthew?'

Her brother smiled. 'The stripe was a bone of contention in the mess when first I joined. Some commanding officer come from another regiment had said he wanted his officers distinguished in some way, so that he might recognize them instantly. And so the stripe was added. Before that the uniform had no red whatsoever, and of that the officers were inordinately proud.'

'And so your new lieutenant-colonel has obliged the former tradition.'

'It would seem so. And I am disposed already to like him for it, although it must have stung in the pocket rather.'

'And I understand, sir, if I may,' added Mr Rippingale diffidently, 'that the red cloak has also been replaced by a blue one.'

'Excellent!' said Hervey, smiling wide. 'It was ever a nuisance for covert work. And all because someone had bought so much red cloth years back.'

'I think I prefer red,' said Elizabeth, examining a scarlet coatee hanging nearby. 'I thought the Life Guards looked much nicer than the others this morning.'

Hervey looked pained. 'You sound like one of Miss Austen's heroines.'

Elizabeth pulled a face. How her brother was enjoying this! It tokened well.

They were another half an hour at Mr Gieve's. With each

minute Hervey parted with yet more of his modest savings. True, there was a margin to his account before he would need to mortgage his pay, and he had not yet received the past year's rents of the Chintal jagirs; but he was still most conscious of the need for economy. And half of him believed that to be a very good thing in a soldier (for it would keep him lean, so to speak), while the other half craved the means to be an independent-minded officer. If only he had not so precipitately disposed of all his former uniform.

When they left, Hervey asked if they should look for dining rooms. As Elizabeth said she was not hungry, he took her instead to see Mr Bullock's 'Museum of Natural Curiosities' a little way along Piccadilly. He thought to show her the elephant which stood as the centrepiece in the Egyptian hall, so that he might better give her an account of his struggle to save the Rajah of Chintal's hunting elephant when that great beast had become stuck fast in the quicksands of the Sukri river. But Bullock's was more than usually crowded, the main exhibit being no less than Bonaparte's carriage – the very same that had carried the Great Disturber from the field of Waterloo when all was lost. Hervey paid over his two shillings for them both, dismayed that the price had exactly doubled since his last visit three years before, and made straight for the centre of attention. But oh! – the scene before them. Over the carriage and into it were clambering all manner of sightseers, each anxious to be able to crow some proximity to the tyrant, like a child taunting a caged beast at a menagerie. Hervey was as revolted by it as he would have been by the child's prodding stick. 'I own freely to never having had a moment's admiration for the man, but this disrespect is gross unseemly.'

Elizabeth was more philosophical. 'You must not take against them. We were all so afeard of the bogeyman of Europe, and for so long, that it is but relief.'

Hervey relented with a raising of his eyebrows. 'I hate to

see any soldier dishonoured by those who would never have the courage to face him in life.'

Elizabeth put a hand to his arm. 'You are not wrong, brother dear. But you must allow for differences of temperament, as indeed you seemed more willing to do of late.'

Hervey was minded to dispute his sister's thought in this. Instead he simply took her arm, and they walked about the exhibits for a while in welcome solitude, the carriage having drawn most of the sightseers.

'Matthew,' said Elizabeth suddenly, starting at the python coiled round a palm tree, yet trying not to be dismayed, 'I saw a poster proclaiming the Waterloo rooms in Pall Mall. Is that far from here? Would you like to see them?'

Hervey had seen the poster too. 'They're but five minutes' walk, though I have no very strong desire to see them. I'll warrant they're full of gruesome pieces scavenged from the field, taken from dead and dying alike, or else fanciful pictures and accounts. I confess I have no stomach for it. I should rather go and see this new bridge they call Waterloo. It is very handsome, I hear tell – a full half-mile of granite.'

Elizabeth was disappointed. 'It would be nice to have *some* notion of the battle; that is all. It is difficult to conceive of your part in it with so scant a knowledge as I possess.'

But her brother seemed not to hear. He had been studying a mounted knight in full armour for some minutes. Elizabeth wondered what it was that engrossed him so. When he emerged from his thoughts it was as if he had been turning over some profound question. 'Elizabeth, would you come with me to Hounslow? Tomorrow, on our way to Wiltshire, I mean. It would be a courtesy to call on the lieutenant-colonel rather than merely to write.'

Elizabeth thought she knew her brother's mind better now than she had ever done. She was certain of what the trouble was: there were ghosts to lay in that place, and although her brother would face them alone if need be, a sister might be a powerful support. But would it be any kindness? Would it not be better to plead some reason why she could not go with him, thus making him face the ghosts alone? There would certainly be others in time, for it seemed to her that he had condemned himself to a perpetual haunting.

But it was not in Elizabeth's nature to abandon her brother. On their journey from Rome he had spoken a good deal about the change in the Sixth of which the Earl of Sussex had written. And yesterday, when they had called on him at his set in Albany, the colonel had repeated his opinion that there was much work to be done. This had fired Hervey, it was true, but Elizabeth sensed also a certain anxiety. Its root she could not tell for sure, and this uncertainty, combined with simple sibling loyalty, determined her response. 'Shall your commanding officer not think it a trifle strange that you should bring me?' she asked, thinking the question fair no matter what the other considerations.

Hervey was quick to reassure her. 'If he reveals it then I shall know I have made a grave error in returning.'

It was so stark an opinion that it fair took Elizabeth aback. She had not supposed that the question was so contingent on the character of one man, and she said so.

Hervey now sensed her surprise, and was dismayed that she had not seemed to grasp the essentials of what had gone before these past two years. 'The commanding officer is *everything* to a regiment's soundness and fortune.' He meant to say it kindly: he was sure he had meant it kindly, but he knew it must have sounded otherwise. He felt a terrible rush of despair in Elizabeth's incomprehension. Henrietta would have understood.

Next day was St Swithun's, and to general relief it was not raining. Indeed, it was as fresh and bright a morning as any they could remember of late in Italy. Matthew Hervey had advanced overnight from cornet of the 6th Dragoon Guards – the Carabineers, as some knew them – to lieutenant of the

82nd Foot, the Prince of Wales's Volunteers. He had not worn any uniform of the Carabineers, nor would he of the Eighty-second. He did not think of himself as an officer of either regiment. This was a paper transaction only, the means by which he was proprietorially reinstated with a captaincy in his former regiment. It was a curious system by any measure. Indeed, he was not himself fully aware of its intricacies. He had tried, with varying degrees of success, to explain it to others as he did now to Elizabeth, but why there should be such a system he did not rightly know. Although it had served the country well these past twenty years, on the whole it had not been without its scandals and shortcomings. Had not the Duke of York himself fallen foul of it a little while ago – an unedifying affair of dubious trading in commissions? But of one thing Hervey was sure: it was a most expeditious way of restoring him to the Sixth. And as the travelling chariot he had engaged for the journey to Wiltshire drew up to the gates of the cavalry barracks at Hounslow, his only care was whether he might sufficiently conceal his pleasure at being . . . *home*.

He did not recognize the sentry, nor the corporal of the guard, but entrance was arranged easily enough. He did not announce himself by rank (a lieutenant of line infantry would only serve to confuse), instead handing his card to the corporal and declaring that he was come to see the lieutenant-colonel. The corporal did not even look at the card: that was an officer's business. Instead he gave it to an orderly with instructions to 'accompany the gentleman to regimental headquarters'.

'He did not recognize you, Matthew?' said Elizabeth, curious, as they drove towards the single-storey building on the far side of the square.

'It's been more than a year. And before that we worked by troops, in the main. It's possible we never saw each other before, if he joined after Waterloo. But it is unusual.'

He was recognized at once at the regimental headquarters,

however. Mr Lincoln, the serjeant-major, was just leaving for his second rounds with the usual attendant party of picket-serjeant, provost-NCOs and orderlies. In an instant he transferred his whip from his right hand to under his left arm and threw up a salute so sharp that it quite startled Elizabeth. 'Good morning, Captain Hervey, sir! We had word this morning you were to rejoin.'

Hervey raised his hat by return. 'Elizabeth, this is Mr Lincoln, the regimental sar'nt-major. Mr Lincoln, my sister.'

'An honour, ma'am,' replied the RSM, saluting her in turn, though not as violently. 'Captain Hervey has been very much missed these past twelve months.'

Hervey smiled just enough to reveal his gratification. 'Is the commanding officer at orderly room, Mr Lincoln?'

'He is, sir,' replied the RSM, turning to one of his orderlies. 'Wiles, go and tell the adjutant that Captain Hervey is calling on the lieutenant-colonel.'

Hervey nodded. 'Good, good. Then I'll let you be about the lines, Mr Lincoln, and look forward to being back there myself soon.' He resisted hard the temptation to ask him which would be his own lines, for that should properly come from the commanding officer.

The RSM took his leave with another salute of absolute precision, and struck off for the horse lines followed by his attendant NCOs, each trying to emulate the master in the business of saluting.

Hervey turned to Elizabeth and smiled in a way that conceded it was all rather . . . different. Elizabeth gave a smile and raised her eyebrows, perfectly grasping his meaning. But there was no sign of diffidence on her part, and Hervey was impressed by it. She had visited the regiment before, in Ireland, but she had not come so close to the heart of things as here this morning, on the very steps of the headquarters. Hervey was glad she had come, and so was Elizabeth.

The first thing he saw inside the building, well lit by its clerestories, were the two guidons, the lieutenant-colonel's and the major's, lodged against the far wall and flanked by a semi-arch of old-pattern sabres. It was a good display, proud and telling of the business the regiment was about. Then the adjutant stepped from his office, and Hervey was surprised to see it was Assheton-Smith; the adjutant was as a rule from the ranks, not a troop-officer. But before either of them could say a word there came a voice from the door of the further office. 'Hervey, my dear sir! I am so glad you have come! I am so very glad we meet at last!'

A man perhaps ten years older than him, about his height and build, with the fine, unmistakably patrician features of the brother who had once been his idol, advanced with a broad smile and outstretched hand. Hervey took off his hat, smiled as broadly and took the hand. 'I am very glad to be back, Colonel. May I present—'

'Miss Hervey, I presume? My brother spoke of you.' Sir Ivo Lankester bowed.

Elizabeth curtsied, returning his easy smile. She had met Hervey's erstwhile troop-leader in Ireland, and had liked him very much. His brother appeared to her to have all Sir Edward's good manners, and perhaps even more of his charm. She at once concluded that Matthew need have no concerns on his commanding officer's account, at least.

'Would you care to come into my office, Hervey? And Miss Hervey too, if that would not be too tedious. I shall send for coffee. Or perhaps you would prefer tea, Miss Hervey?'

Elizabeth was sure she would not find it in the least tedious to accept the invitation. 'I should be very glad of coffee, sir.'

'Capital,' Sir Ivo exclaimed, turning to the side and indicating the open door.

It was Elizabeth's first encounter with so intensely masculine a room, and she was evidently much taken with the buttoned leather chairs, the sabres and spurs, the drums, the oils of bloody battles and illustrious officers, for she quite failed to catch the commanding officer's enquiry.

'Elizabeth?' prompted her brother.

'Oh, yes, er . . .?'

Sir Ivo smiled. 'I merely asked, Miss Hervey, if your time in Rome had been agreeable. I myself was there for some months before Oxford. I own that I might never have returned home had war not resumed.'

'Oh, I liked it very much too, sir, very much,' she replied, now repossessed of her former senses. 'I liked its gaiety above all, I think, though they say it is nothing compared with Naples, but alas we were not able to travel there because of brigandage.' She glanced at her brother; the explanation would suffice.

'Who are the captains, Colonel?' asked Hervey briskly.

'Rose has A Troop, Barrow has B, Strickland C. And D is sold to a man from the Bays whom I have not yet met. Yours will be E Troop.'

'So there are to be five troops only?' Hervey's voice betrayed a certain disappointment.

'Five, yes. That is to be the Indian establishment. I confess it dismayed me to begin with, but so it shall be.'

Hervey glanced at Elizabeth, who seemed not greatly to care about the Indian establishment, engaged as she was by the intricate wirework on a shabraque laid over a chairback settee. 'And who shall be my lieutenant?'

The commanding officer hesitated for a moment, as if he could not recall. 'There is none at present.'

That need be no bad thing, thought Hervey: he could soon have a new lieutenant on the bit. 'Cornets, Colonel?'

Colonel Lankester looked discomfited. 'I regret there are no cornets either, Hervey.'

'Oh.' Hervey could not conceal his surprise at the squadron's being without any officers whatsoever.

'No, well . . . you see, Hervey, I'm afraid there is no troop in being. Third Squadron was disbanded nine months ago. I rather thought you might know this. I imagined that . . . well, no matter. We must raise a full troop inside five months before we embark for Hindoostan. That is why the colonel was so very particular in wanting you to return to duty.'

Hervey's heart sank fast. A troop of widows' men to command, and five months only to find recruits and remounts: he might as well be with the Eighty-second and yellow jack in Jamaica after all.

CHAPTER SEVEN
THE SERJEANT-MAJOR

They left the barracks an hour later, Elizabeth in good spirits, her brother tolerably so. He leaned out of the window when they were well clear of the gates and called to the postilion to ask if he knew the Windsor road. He did, and so Hervey bade him put the pair into a trot as soon as possible for the Spread Eagle at Datchet.

Well might Elizabeth look pleased, Hervey mused. She had received much flattering attention, and seen the regiment in hale condition. All *he* had been able to see was blank troop-rolls and empty stalls. True, he had been told that he could draw on Mr Lincoln's seniority list of corporals, and that Lincoln also had a promising list of chosen men. And Sir Ivo Lankester had been straight and fair with him. 'I will sign any reasonable promotion order,' had he not said?

At once Hervey had sought to probe what was reasonable to Sir Ivo's mind. 'I should wish for Serjeant Armstrong to be my serjeant-major, Colonel. I trust that would not go badly with the seniority rule?' he asked squarely.

Sir Ivo had shaken his head. 'Promoting Armstrong would *not* go badly with the seniority rule,' he had replied. 'That is, it would not go badly if Armstrong were with us still.'

Hervey was stunned. The colour drained from him in an

instant. 'I . . . I had no idea that . . . When did he die, Colonel? Where is his family?'

'No, no – not dead, not at *all* dead. I mean that he was discharged these six months and more.'

Hervey's relief was palpable, but the very idea of Armstrong unbooted was only a partial consolation. 'Why did he have his discharge, Colonel? He had made a fine recovery, had he not?'

The lieutenant-colonel furrowed his brow. 'I don't rightly know. I had not been in command many months – weeks, indeed – when he applied. Mr Lincoln says he had become listless. Perhaps if he had returned to a troop instead of light duties with the quartermasters . . .'

'And how goes he now? Do we have word of his family?'

'Again, Mr Lincoln would best advise you. I know that he keeps a posthouse near Eton.' Sir Ivo knew because he had himself arranged for it, though he did not say so.

Hervey knew that it was not a time to explore his own culpability in Armstrong's listlessness, nor in Armstrong's estrangement from the regiment, which he had made his family when his own had been destroyed by a firedamp explosion fifteen years before. But guilt pricked him hard nonetheless. No matter how pressing his duty here, and to his own family in Wiltshire, he must see for himself that Armstrong was sound in soul as well as body. He glanced at Elizabeth. 'With your leave, Colonel, I should like to take a look at Mr Lincoln's promotion lists and then make a start for Wiltshire. I should like, if I may, a fortnight in which to set affairs right at home, and then to report for duty.'

Sir Ivo smiled indulgently. 'Of course, Hervey, of course. Take as long as you need. There's no profit in having you begin before you can give it your heart.'

Hervey had known Sir Ivo but a half-hour, yet he thought he had known him an age, so thoroughly regimental was his view. He could have been Lord George Irvine, Joseph Edmonds or Sir *Edward* Lankester for that matter. How right

Lord Sussex had been, if not entirely fulsome with detail, when he had said that he was certain the Sixth were restored. Hervey rose and took up his hat, and held out a hand to Elizabeth. 'I shall spend a little while with the adjutant and Mr Lincoln, then, Colonel, and afterwards drive west.'

'I cannot prevail on you to stay to luncheon?'

Hervey had glanced at Elizabeth, as a courtesy, but he had then declined.

'Then while you are with Assheton-Smith and the RSM, allow me at least to show your sister the horse lines.'

Elizabeth had accepted without waiting for her brother's leave.

Hervey left his sister to take in the sights of the Berkshire countryside while he himself sat back to contemplate the reunion ahead. He had no very clear idea of what it was he would say to Armstrong, a man he counted more than just his erstwhile serjeant. There was so much he could say: what he owed him, what he had failed him in, what he might do for him yet – confused notions which swam before him as the chariot picked up speed on the Windsor turnpike.

And what a very agreeable mode of posting was the travelling chariot. Had he but had one in Italy, where the full vision forward would have afforded them many a longer preview of the glorious sights of that country! He knew full well it was an indulgence he was unlikely to be able to afford for many a year. Indeed, he had only been able to engage the chariot for the two days, which would mean their changing at Andover, or perhaps even Newbury, to something altogether more utilitarian. They sped past fields of ripening barley, empty now of the hoes which for months had tramped up and down the drills. In a few weeks or so they would be filled again, with scythes and rakes, by men and women who like as not had known nothing other than husbandry, and never would, and yet seemed content that it was so. It was from men such as these that Hervey must find his recruits, willing volunteers. He could go to the courts and arrange with the bench for felons to be given the choice of being sent down or taking the King's shilling, but all he had seen of that sort of recruit was trouble. No, not all of them, not every one, for was not Private Finch called 'Chokey' for the manner of his enlisting? And could anyone doubt there was a truer man in a fight than Finch? But the effort in finding one good man was too great. Hervey had never been enamoured of those 'paying with the drum', nor had any of the Sixth's officers or serjeants for that matter. And Armstrong had always added a practical as well as a principled objection: if a man were caught at petty crime, he would not have the wit to be a good light dragoon.

'Are you going to say what is on your mind, Matthew?'

Hervey sighed. 'I had so hoped that the troop would be well-found.' He would admit to no more.

Elizabeth said nothing. She could not be certain, but she supposed her brother's despondency was caused not so much by the absolute state of numbers, but because he would not have around him those who had previously been his succour. His mind had been set on boot and saddle for a full month now, and to find a troop of widows' men, as it was known, was disappointment indeed. That his serjeant and others of the like were gone was even greater discouragement to him. And yet Elizabeth was not so sure that this was necessarily for the bad, for she had observed in her brother over many years that he was not content with things as he found them: there was always the urge to adjust, to change, to *improve*. In fact, she was very much of the opinion that raising a troop – recruits and remounts alike – was just what her brother needed to engage every atom of mind and body these next five months. It was a high price for her, and their parents – that she knew well enough, for his time would not be theirs – but it was a price which any who truly loved him would pay willingly.

'And Serjeant Armstrong,' added Hervey suddenly, after a

full minute's silence. 'I cannot bear to think of him as . . . diminished.'

Elizabeth looked puzzled. 'By his taking a posthouse, you mean?'

'No, not that especially. By the loss of vigour, I suppose – mental *and* physical. When last I saw him he walked slowly, and had fearful headaches.'

'And what did Colonel Lankester say of him now?'

'Oh, he has not seen him in many months. It seems he went to Ireland in the summer with Caithlin to see her people and has not been near Hounslow since.'

'Well, you could scarce blame him for wanting to put a little distance between himself and the regiment.'

Hervey raised his eyebrows: didn't he, of all people, know about wanting that? 'Ay, that's fair enough. But Armstrong so likes the company of his peers . . . it's difficult to imagine him—'

'He has his *family*, Matthew.' It was perhaps a little cruel to remind him of that, but Elizabeth considered it important that her brother should approach this reunion with a proper understanding.

He turned to her, half smiling, and placed a hand over hers. 'You are very good to me.'

'I always was,' she insisted, smiling back. 'And see where it has got me. I shall end an old maid in your service!'

'I should not mind that,' Hervey teased. 'Indeed, I shall call you Dorcas, for you are full of good works.'

'I suppose I would rather be called Dorcas than Tabitha!' replied Elizabeth, frowning.

Hervey admired as well as loved his sister. It was not just her public charity and her devotion to him; it was the daily evidence of a good mind – a self-improved mind – yet a mind that was prepared to sacrifice what it might become for the sake of the rest of her family, whose needs had varied with the years, and whose number had so lately seen increase and decrease. He had left her with scarcely a thought when he was little more than a youth, and had now returned in the unspoken expectation that she would accomplish whatever he required of her. He had seen how Commodore Peto had been gladdened by her company, and she by his, and yet he had sped his sister away from Rome the instant he decided to answer the colonel's call. And he would leave Georgiana in her care just as he had Jessye with Private Johnson, exonerating himself by the notion that it was his own life that had greatest need of amendment. But he was still half afraid the worms might eat at him from within, for Dorcas had died a maid doing her good works, and he was not Peter to raise her up again.

The Spread Eagle was a smarter-looking establishment than Hervey had feared. As the chariot hove into the yard a pair of ostlers ran out from the stables and had the leader out of the traces almost before the postilion had dismounted; these were men practised with the mails, whose proud boast it was never to touch the same strap twice. But Hervey wanted no relief team this minute. He intended to dine here, he said, and then they would take four horses, not two, for the longer haul to Newbury – or, if fortune favoured them, Andover. And he wanted to settle the amount now, before seeing Armstrong.

'Three shillings per mile, sir,' said the horsemaster. 'With two postboys, that is.'

Hervey groaned to himself. Posting to Newbury, let alone Andover, would cost him the best part of five pounds. He had better reacquire the habit of thrift soon, else the expenses of the Sixth would oppress him sorely. 'Very well, in an hour, say?'

They left the yard to the ostlers and headed for the post-entrance. Inside, a cherub-faced bootboy showed them to a private sitting room, and Hervey asked for the postmaster. The boy bowed and tugged at his forelock enthusiastically, but with a clumsiness that suggested he was still a novice;

after a fumbling encounter with the door handle, he took his leave.

'The Armstrongs are evidently well set up here,' Hervey ventured.

Elizabeth nodded, glancing about the room. The wainscotting was newly polished – a fair enough test, she thought.

Hervey was pleased for them, pleased that they should have found so fitting a billet. On the other hand he was displeased for himself, for there was scant likelihood of Armstrong leaving such a place for the uncertainties of the regiment.

Within the minute the door opened again, to Caithlin Armstrong. Her copper-red hair was pulled back severely, yet still not enough to make her face anything but as warm and welcoming as when Hervey had first seen it those five years ago in Kilcrea, the time she had soothed his blistered hands with balsam.

'Captain Hervey, and Miss Hervey ma'am, what an honour this is!' She did not curtsy, but her pleasure was real enough. Caithlin Armstrong, even Caithlin O'Mahoney, had never revealed a trace of guile in all the difficulties she had faced since first encountering the Sixth.

Hervey bowed, a shade self-consciously. Not so long ago he would have kissed her, but things were different now. Elizabeth smiled full and easy. Although they had met but half a dozen times, she admired her independent spirit, her cheerfulness (for it was plain to all that Caithlin had wits far beyond the run of things, and that these were scarcely tried). And, what was more, Elizabeth would concede that for all the difference in their respective traditions, Caithlin's devout religion was heartening in the extreme. 'Good afternoon, Mrs Armstrong,' she replied for them both. 'I hope we do not call at an inconvenient hour.'

'Not in the slightest, ma'am,' replied Caithlin. 'My Jack will be returned from Windsor at any moment. He has gone to the horse fair.'

Hervey was encouraged the more. This sounded like Armstrong restored in spirits as well as health. 'And how are you . . .' – he hesitated – 'Caithlin?'

'Oh, I am very well, thank you, Captain Hervey.' Caithlin had reverted to the formal way as soon as she had become engaged to Armstrong. 'We have a son now, too.'

'A son? Indeed!' Hervey was very happy for her, for them both. His happiness was almost enough to ease the twisting in his gut.

Elizabeth asked if she might see the children, and Caithlin consented proudly.

They left Hervey to himself and ascended the stairs at the back of the posthouse to a simply furnished bedroom with pretty flowered curtains through which the afternoon sun came softly and warm. Son and daughter were sleeping as Elizabeth and Caithlin tiptoed to the bedside, but Elizabeth saw that they were fine babies. In her heart she knew her brother's purpose here was futile. Indeed, she wondered if it were at all honourable.

When they were back in the sitting room, tea was brought, and arrangements for a travelling dinner were made. Hervey and Caithlin exchanged reports of Italy with news of Cork, and then, when they were finished with tea, Caithlin asked if they had just come from Hounslow.

'Yes,' said Hervey, uncertain as to how she had concluded that.

'Would you be going back to the regiment, then, Captain Hervey?'

Her manner was as matter of fact as it was candid. Hervey tried not to sound hesitant. 'Yes, yes I am.'

Caithlin smiled. 'So you shall be but a short drive from here. My Jack will like that right enough. And you too, Miss Hervey?'

'No, not I, Mrs Armstrong. I must stay with my parents, I think.' Elizabeth spoke lightly, as if it were of little moment.

'The regiment is for India soon,' explained Hervey. He

thought how repellent it must sound to a wife and mother.

'Oh, India!' she sighed. 'When Jack hears he will beg you to take him as your groom.'

Hervey laughed politely.

'It is true, I assure you!' protested Caithlin. 'There isn't a day goes by without his lamenting for a parade. And when those Life Guards from Windsor go by it's like seeing an old horse prick up its ears at the hunt passing.'

If this were so – and Caithlin had never been a one for exaggeration or idle gossip – then Hervey was dismayed. True, he had come to Datchet with a half-formed notion of rescuing the Armstrongs from penniless drudgery, taking his erstwhile serjeant back to the regiment with him, restoring his rank and more. But here was neither penury nor menial labour: he had no right to tempt this woman's husband, even for a moment. Better that he made his excuses now and left with his respects and good wishes for Caithlin's worthy provider.

But Caithlin would have none of it. Perhaps she sensed Hervey's purpose. She certainly spoke with fervour. 'Captain Hervey, you see us very well-found materially. And we are ever so grateful to Colonel Lankester for that. But Jack's heart isn't in it. Oh, he does a fine job all right. He does it for me and the bairns, as he calls them, but for himself he is dispirited, and very deeply, I think. It has troubled me a very great deal these last months.'

Hervey could scarce comprehend that Armstrong too had found himself thus, for he had supposed that his own dispirits were occasioned wholly by his widowing. Armstrong, with a wife he adored and two children with a fine mother, could not pine so much for the Sixth, surely? 'But is he recovered in body at least, Caithlin? Colonel Lankester spoke of headaches and lassitude.'

'Oh, gracious Mary, he's as fit as when first he rode into Kilcrea. He throws himself into work just to tire himself out. I'm sure of it.'

'But the headaches ... the colonel said his discharge papers spoke of neuralgia. I think that was the word.'

'He has not had a headache in months, Captain Hervey. Well, not one whose cause was not manifestly apparent.' She frowned with a sort of mock disapproval.

'Caithlin, wait a moment. Are you truly telling me that Geordie Armstrong, landlord of a going place as this, would exchange it for the ranks of the Sixth?'

'I am. On condition.'

Hervey looked quizzical.

'On condition that I did not object. Six months ago I would have hidden all his clothes had he so much as mentioned it. But I see now he is not the man I married. And I can't be happy if he is not.'

Hervey recalled the selfsame words a year and a half before, when Henrietta had pleaded with him not to accept the sinecure of the yeomanry command.

The landlord of the Spread Eagle returned within the hour. Hervey heard his voice in the yard outside, unmistakable: 'Them are two bonny mares, me lad. The best hay only for them!' He rose in anticipation.

'Caithlin, me love, I—' Armstrong stood open-mouthed as he saw his captain.

'Hello, Geordie,' said Hervey, holding out his hand.

'Well, I'll be damned!' said Armstrong, oblivious to all else but the reunion. But then he saw Elizabeth, and reddened. 'Oh, I beg your pardon, Miss 'Ervey,' he stammered, glancing at Caithlin, who was already frowning. 'I didn't see—'

'Nor me either, Jack Armstrong!' said Caithlin.

'Oh, I'm sorry for you too, love. Captain Hervey here quite took me aback.'

Hervey was almost laughing. It was not every day he could see a serjeant – even one no longer serving – so completely abashed. 'It's very good to see you, Geordie. And so obviously at home!'

123

Armstrong grinned. 'Ay, sir. I'm at home all right. And right pleased I am an' all to see *you*. And you, too, Miss Hervey. You're looking proper well, ma'am.'

Elizabeth smiled. Armstrong had charmed her from the first moment he had visited them at Horningsham. 'Thank you, Serjeant Armstrong. Or "Mister", I should say.'

'Either way, ma'am, either way. Most folks as know me round here still call me by rank. "Mister's" too much like an officer for my ear! Have you had some tea, by the way?'

'Yes we have, thank you,' replied Elizabeth. 'And seen your beautiful children.'

Armstrong beamed with pride. 'Ay, they're two bonny bairns as ever there were.'

Caithlin now determined to take charge of matters. 'Miss Hervey, would you like to look at the garden? It is not very large, but quite pretty.'

'Yes, I would indeed,' said Elizabeth eagerly, knowing full well the purpose in the invitation.

When they were gone, Armstrong bid Hervey sit down. 'Something to drink, sir?'

'In a minute, maybe. But I want to ask you something first.'

'Can I ask *you* something first, sir?'

'Of course.'

'Have you just come from Hounslow?'

'Yes.' Hervey said it cautiously, not sure what Armstrong might be getting at.

'Then I know what you're going to ask.'

'*How* do you know?'

'Oh, there's always NCOs coming here for a wet. It's E Troop, isn't it! You're going back and taking over the Chestnuts!'

Hervey smiled and nodded. 'Except that it's D, now, that has the colour.'

'And you want me to come back an' all as your serjeant!'

Hervey let the smile go. 'No! Indeed I do not. You are quite wrong in that!'

Armstrong looked perfectly crestfallen. So much so that Hervey at once felt heartless for the joke. 'I do not want you as serjeant. I want you as serjeant-major!'

Armstrong now looked wholly taken aback, though less pained. 'Good God, sir. I never thought I'd hear such a thing. Never in a lifetime.'

Hervey was puzzled. Promotion was never easy, especially for an NCO of Armstrong's stamp, but he never imagined it would not have been forthcoming had Armstrong stayed with the colours. 'I don't think I want to have command of E Troop *unless* you're its serjeant-major. There isn't a man better suited. It's as simple as that.'

'Can we have a drink now, sir?'

'Yes, I should like that. A little port if you have it to hand.'

'I do.' He went to the door. 'Port and a flagon, pots-lad!' he called, then returned to his chair. 'I have two a day, only. That much is better at least than when we were serving.'

Hervey nodded. 'Perhaps I shouldn't say this, but Caithlin gave us to believe she would not be sorry to return to the regiment, else I should never press you to it now.'

Armstrong sighed. 'Caithlin's said it a dozen times if she's said it once, that I'd only be happy wearing blue again.'

'*You* don't sound so sure.'

Armstrong shifted in his seat. 'Look, sir, every man in the Sixth knows what went on in Canada – and before, for that matter.'

'Well? You've nothing to fear in that respect.'

'I'm not afeard of anything, least of all what the canteens are saying. I'm just not sure it'd be the same.'

Hervey was even more puzzled. 'Nothing's ever the same. But you and I are no worse soldiers for all that happened.'

Armstrong shook his head. 'I'm not so sure about that. That savage got the better of me, from behind – me not seeing him even. That should never have been. I'd have bawled out a recruit for not watching 'is back like that. And they all know it at Hounslow. It wouldn't be fair on you.' He did not say that in that lapse he had let his captain down. But Armstrong believed it. That no one else even thought it, let alone believed it, would never be consolation to him.

Hervey pictured the scene of Armstrong's undoing – his raging, perhaps for an instant losing that field sense which keeps the good soldier alive. And he saw Henrietta, perhaps more terrified still by the invincible Armstrong's destruction before her very eyes. He shook himself. 'Look, we had all this out a year ago. Theory's one thing, but it can't always *be*. I got that spontoon in my leg at Toulouse in the same way, but it didn't mean I was finished in the eyes of the troop. Everybody knows you went single-handed at a bunch of savages and fought like a tiger. *That's* what they think of Geordie Armstrong, not that one of them got the better of him.'

'Ay, maybe.'

'Look, you used to admonish me when I said I couldn't be done with the shame of Serjeant Strange's death. Well, it's the same now with you.'

The pot boy came in with a tray. Hervey took his glass in silence, Armstrong likewise. A long time they sat, without a word, sipping occasionally. This was not a matter to be rushed, and Hervey was not inclined to be the first to speak. He would wait, however long, to hear the evidence of what had truly become of Geordie Armstrong.

CHAPTER EIGHT
HOME TRUTHS

Salisbury Plain, a week later

Hervey eased himself into the ash dugout which Daniel Coates regarded as the chair of honour. The room had moved on to oak and then mahogany over the decades, but still that piece was Coates's pride, for he had fashioned it himself from windfall when first he had married. It was all, indeed, that now materially remained of those days. There was a way of sitting in it which was tolerably comfortable, and Hervey, having bent to take off his spurs, shuffled until he found it, and then took the glass of purl which Coates's manservant brought.

'Tell me what are the designs regarding your widow's troop,' Coates asked.

Hervey looked at him, quelling a smile. They had just ridden the downs together and the old soldier had pressed him every minute of it to details of the regiment and his imminent fortunes. Yet, even now, there was more that Coates would know. It was the same Daniel Coates of his boyhood, without a doubt. The hair was white and thinned, the cheeks sunken and the back a little bent, but in all else Coates seemed as he had always been.

'Matthew?'

'I'm sorry, Dan; what—?'

'How shall you raise the men? And where shall the horses come from?'

Hervey sighed. 'Well, the second question's a sight easier to answer than the first. There'll be no remounts until India. And as for recruits, I'm very much afraid it will be the usual fashion. The colonel's made a start sending out parties under the more active serjeants, and he's offered a special bounty to any man who'll enlist his own brother. He's very much of the opinion that brothers exercise a beneficent effect on each other.'

'I only ever saw one lot myself, and they was the biggest pair of rogues in the regiment. They were both in chokey at the same time at one point. But I think they 'listed as a pair, though; nobody was to know.'

Hervey had no cause to dispute it, but he supposed the colonel was a discerning man when it came to brothers. 'Well, he's confident of filling the ranks ere the summer's out. He told me he believed my concern would be drill and not recruiting.'

Coates looked puzzled. 'How are you to drill dragoons without troopers?'

Hervey raised his eyebrows. 'I suppose the riding master must have sufficient to introduce them to the saddle, but there'll be no jockeys this side of India, that's for sure. It doesn't much matter, says the colonel, for we're hardly going to the seat of war. Hindoostan has been quiet these past three years since the Pindarees were seen to.'

Coates did not look entirely convinced. 'It's always a business taking over another regiment's horses. You're better off with roughs nine times out of ten.'

'And I think roughs are what we'll get, for I gather the regiment there has been on a much reduced establishment.'

'Ay, well, your work'll be cut out, Matthew.' He took a match and relit his pipe, letting the smoke rise a while before breaking the comfortable silence. 'And how's that yearling of yours? Haven't seen him in months.'

'He's as fine as you could want. He'll make a charger all right.'

'And Jessye: have you had her under the saddle yet?'

'We hackneyed through Longleat park yesterday. And she would have had a good run if I'd let her.'

'I should put the stallion to her again, Matthew. Never has the demand for roadsters been greater. The mails are running up and down the turnpikes like quicksilver these days. She'd make you a pretty penny.'

Hervey nodded. 'Perhaps if I were staying . . .'

'That groom of yours going to India too, then?'

'He is indeed.' Private Johnson would have preferred to keep his cosy billet in Horningsham, of that Hervey was sure, but as Johnson himself had said when first Hervey had told him of his intentions, beggars could not be choosers. Johnson's only fear, which was his only secret too, was the workhouse. 'I thought of attaching him to my father, but . . .'

'*I* would take him, if you like.'

Hervey smiled. 'Now you're gainsaying your earlier counsel, Dan. I gave him the choice, and he made up his own mind, though it was probably Hobson's choice.'

Coates inclined his head, as much as to say there was more to Hervey's observation than perhaps he thought. 'Hobson's was not a *bad* choice, Matthew. It was to spare his horses, if you remember.'

'Yes, I do remember, now.'

Both of them knew also that Johnson had been as devoted to Henrietta as a groom might be. Coates, at least, knew that this bound him more fast to his master now than ever. 'Shall you stay for a bite of dinner?'

'I thank you, Dan, but no. We have Mr Keble calling on his way back to Oxford. You remember him?'

'I do. He made that pleasing sermon at your wedding. I shouldn't forget 'im.'

Hervey looked forward keenly to seeing John Keble again, but he knew that wounds would probably reopen thereby. 'It will be the first time since the wedding that we have met.'

Daniel Coates was not for treading lightly about the subject. 'And how are things at the big house, Matthew?'

'You mean with Lord Bath?'

'Ay. It can't help, that son of 'is running off with yon Harriet Robbins.'

The elopement of the Marquess of Bath's son and heir with the daughter of the turnpike-keeper was the talk of west Wiltshire, and it had indeed made for greater strain in Hervey's own intercourse at Longleat. He was certain that Lord and Lady Bath, despite their solicitude when first he had come home from Canada, must hold him to blame to some degree for Henrietta's death. 'She was a deuced pretty girl, Harriet, as I recall. And old Robbins was an honest man. There's every reason to suppose—'

'There's none at all, Matthew, as very well you know. I've a lot of time for Bath. He's as good a man as you might want in that house. But he's proud, too.'

Hervey could not gainsay it. He had always supposed that his own connection with Longleat had been viewed by the marquess more with resignation than approval, even though Henrietta had been his ward, not blood. 'You're right, Dan.'

'You go there every day, I trust?'

'To the nursery, yes, but I don't always see the family.'

Coates nodded. 'Keep with them, Matthew.'

Hervey knew that he must.

'And our prayers should be with his lordship, for never was there a steadier hand at such a troubled time. Oh yes, the troubles there have been these last months, Matthew! But he is still of a mind to have a proper police in this country, and speaks of it in parliament often. He brought all the magistrates together a week ago. These reformers are playing a merry dance about the country. A lot of what they say is only right and proper – his lordship himself agrees with much of it – but the manner of it is very ill. It leads only to trouble. That Hunt as I knew, when the family was across the plain at Upavon, he's nothing more now than a rabble-rouser. He conceals it just sufficient to keep from arrest, but his lieutenants do the dirty work. His name draws the crowds now. Did you read of that meeting in London three days ago?'

Hervey nodded. 'They won't recognize any laws passed from now on.'

'Ay. Thousands there were at that meeting by all accounts. Hunt was waving a tricolour, they say. Did you ever hear anything so damnable? Lord Bath has the yeomanry prompt at hand, for that sort of thing travels all too easily, and there's too much distress in the county.'

'Well, I for one should never want a part in aiding the magistrates again,' said Hervey, very decidedly. 'The yeomen are most welcome to it!'

The dining room of the vicarage in Horningsham was not large, but neither was the party that evening, consisting of, besides the family, the incumbent of Upton Scudamore, his wife and the Reverend Mr Keble. It was, however, an occasion for the best china and glass, as well as Mrs Hervey's family table linen. She had fretted that there had been no fish to be had in Warminster, save common trout, and that the beef, fresh-slaughtered off the high street the day before, was not as tender as ought to have been. But cook had done her usual best, and there could be no cause now for fearing that her guests would be affronted.

And the candles were of the best quality, too – not the everyday ones that could whistle and spit at inopportune moments. Not that their light was needed at this hour of a summer evening, but fashion required that they be lit, and if the conversation detained the party more than a couple of hours – which, with Mr Keble *and* the vicar of Upton Scudamore present, it might – there would certainly be the want of it. Perhaps at this hour, though, the candlelight might have been better employed in illuminating the family portraits, thought Hervey, for these, being of clergymen, were so colourless as to make them disappear. He himself had no need of a candle, of course, for he knew each feature and fold of them. Their presiding presence had been both a comfort and a caution all his life – like his parents indeed, his father especially, who had of late become as venerable-looking as the portraits.

Canon Hervey had joined the party last, having returned late from the bishop's palace. He was eager to tell them of it. 'I should have been very much later without that curricle. It fair flies,' he explained, with a distinct twinkle in his eye.

'Father bought the former archdeacon's equipage, Mr Keble,' explained Elizabeth.

'I wonder the former archdeacon didn't have a sulky,' declared Mrs Hervey. 'For who would wish to drive with such a disagreeable man as he!'

'It is a very elegant carriage, Archdeacon,' said John Keble. 'I own to having but a very modest gig in my new parish.'

Hervey was as ever pleased that John Keble found the opportunity to stay a night in Horningsham. Keble had become a friend, albeit for the most part in adversity. If he did not yet freely confide in Mr Keble, he had nevertheless a sense that if ever there came the time to do so, he would find an uncommon understanding of the human condition – far in excess of what might be imagined of a donnish young man in his first parish.

'I never knew that our roads and carriages were so much better than any on the continent until our visit to Rome,' said Elizabeth, hoping to draw her mother further from the subject of the former Archdeacon of Sarum. 'We scarcely ever seemed to go at even a moderate trot.'

'By all your brother has told me, Miss Hervey,' replied Keble, looking particularly earnest, 'the continent is inferior in many respects of human endeavour. And for that I believe we must be thankful for having seen nothing of an invading army these many years past.'

'Just so, Keble,' agreed Canon Hervey, laying down his glass. 'It is a terrible thing to have to bury one's silver every other year.'

There was an empty place at table. Mrs Hervey explained that the new incumbent of Upton Scudamore was to have joined them, but he had sent word only this last hour that he had a chill which had gone to his head and did not wish to share it with the family.

'You would have liked Harrison, Keble,' opined Canon Hervey. 'He is lately chaplain at Christ's College in Cambridge, and a strong member of the "intellectual party" there. I am very pleased to have him in the archdeaconry, I may tell you.'

Hervey smiled at his father. 'So now there is high ground, to be of mutual support, on *both* roads between Salisbury and Wells.'

The table enjoyed the joke. 'Just so, Matthew. Just so,' agreed his father.

'And you can signal to each other with incense smoke.'

'You see, Mr Keble?' said Elizabeth, feigning despair. 'My brother cannot speak but in military metaphors.'

Keble replied with equal gravity. 'Of course, Miss Hervey. Your brother is a soldier to his fingertips. How else must he be expected to speak?'

'Matthew,' she replied, with a note of challenge, 'is not signalling with smoke dangerous? Can it not be seen by an enemy, too?'

'Yes,' he conceded at once. 'But if the enemy already

know you are there, then nothing will be revealed so long as you employ a code.'

Mrs Hervey looked alarmed. 'No message can be concealed with incense. We have had *quite* enough trouble with the diocesan to last a lifetime. I beg you would not mention incense ever again. It is an abomination unto me!'

The late charges of 'Romish practice' against his father being evidently of present memory to his mother, Hervey felt obliged to deflect the conversation. 'How does your work on Archbishop Laud stand, father? Is it near ready for the publisher?'

Canon Hervey sighed. 'Not in its complete form, I fear, for there is still too much to be done with it. But I am preparing a monography on Laudian decorum for the *British Critic*.'

Hervey had deflected the conversation insufficiently, however, and Mrs Hervey needed further reassurance that her husband's scholarship would not lead to a recurrence of activity in the consistory court.

John Keble was able to allay her worst fears. 'I heard a sermon at Oriel only last month on like matters. There is little appetite, I think, for troubling over what is said or written if it is in the manner of scholarship.'

'Oh, I am very pleased to hear it, Mr Keble,' declared Mrs Hervey earnestly. 'And now, if you please, let us have no more talk of these things. Matthew, tell us some more of Italy. What of its art?'

'And its music, if you will,' added Keble, equally anxious to avoid further disputation on the Church of England and its tangled rubrics. 'Did you see the opera?'

Elizabeth giggled. 'Mr Keble, you must know that Matthew has no music in him save the drum and the bugle!'

'That is unfair *and* inaccurate. We do not have drums in the cavalry.'

'Not even kettledrums?' challenged Elizabeth.

'Oh, well, yes. But not drums as I supposed you meant them.'

'And I thought the bugle was what the infantry played?' added Mrs Hervey.

'No, the cavalry too, for mounted calls. It is pitched an octave higher than the trumpet, so the call carries further.'

'We did go to the opera, Mr Keble,' Elizabeth assured him. 'In Rome. And Matthew sniggered the while!'

Hervey looked uncomfortable. 'Well, it *was* a very singular business. And I was not the first to laugh.'

'How so?' asked his father.

Hervey looked at his sister and raised his eyebrows as if censuring her for what would be revealed. 'It was an opera by an Italian called Rossini: he is very famous there. And he himself directed it from the piano. He came into the orchestra wearing the strangest coat the colour of cream, and it caused great hilarity. Then after the overture – which was, I must say, very lively – a tenor came on stage with a guitar to serenade his love, and all the strings broke at the first chord. The audience hooted with laughter, and very many of them clericals.'

'I might have done the same,' said Canon Hervey.

'And I, too, Archdeacon,' added Mr Keble supportively.

Elizabeth frowned at them both.

Her brother, emboldened, warmed to his story. 'Soon afterwards the same happened to someone with a mandolin, and then there came someone else who fell straightway onto his nose and there was blood all over his robe. The hooting and catcalls were so bad that Signor Rossini fled the orchestra and the whole thing was abandoned. We had our money back and went to a firework display instead.'

'Which Matthew liked because it looked as though the castle there was under siege. I tell you, Papa, he has no appreciation of anything but the sound of the trumpet and the thunder of the captains!'

'And the shouting?' added John Keble.

'Oh, I should imagine *especially* the shouting, Mr Keble!'

After dinner Hervey and Keble walked together in the garden. There was a full moon, and it was warm. 'Not unlike an evening in India, I should suppose,' said Keble, looking up at the sky. 'And the stars will be the same in those latitudes, no doubt.'

'Yes, I believe you are right. Though I shall be further north this time, in Hindoostan.'

'And Georgiana: she will remain here, with your sister?'

Hervey did not reply at once. There were so many things he might say to qualify the simple 'yes'. 'I confess it will be harder than I ever supposed. She is no longer a mere babe in arms.'

'She will have a Christian upbringing. That is more than most, I fear.'

'I've settled all Henrietta's property in trust to her. I was intending to ask if you might consent to be a trustee.'

'I am honoured.'

'It would mean your going to the attorney's in Warminster tomorrow.'

'I see no objection in that.'

'You are very good. And to my father too. He prizes your counsel highly, you know.'

'Hervey, your father has nigh on forty years' cure of souls, and I scarcely a tenth of that. My counsel, as you put it, can in his respect only ever be from a standpoint of theory.'

'Well, without experience, theory is the only resort.'

'That seems a good military precept. Will you write to me from India? Does the regiment take a chaplain there? I fear I do not know who is to be this new bishop in Calcutta.'

'I shall indeed write. I don't know whether we take a chaplain, nor even whether it is a good or a bad thing; their quality is little admired. We have spoken of this before, you and I.'

John Keble stopped and turned full towards him. 'You

must be steadfast in your daily prayers, my good friend. Now of all times. I do not ask if you are.'

Hervey sighed to himself. It was just as well that Keble did not.

CHAPTER NINE
THE RECRUITING PARTY

Hounslow, a month later

'Well, Sar'nt-Major – we have a troop orderly room and an acquittance roll, and scarcely more than a quarter-guard's-worth of names to enter on it.'

Troop Serjeant-Major Armstrong huffed. 'Them bringers have been about as useful as a sewn-up arse! I've a mind to go down there meself.'

'Twenty-two in all. Not bad-looking men on the whole. And six that can read and write. At least the bringers've not been sweeping the gutters.'

'We might have to do that yet, sir,' said Armstrong. 'If we leave for India under strength it'll be a year before the depot troop can send us the rest. I reckon we'd be broken up inside that time.'

'I well know it, Sar'nt-Major. And I'm not sure I want every man that elects to stay from the regiment that's leaving. Half a dozen, maybe, but more would be a veritable combination.'

'They do say a married man in India's a better soldier. But I'd take some convincing.'

Hervey allowed himself a smile. 'I'd not trade you for a singleton, Sar'nt-Major.'

'And in truth, sir, I wouldn't ever want to be one – not

even to be shaved in bed of a morning like them char-wallahs do.'

'I thought char-wallahs brought them tea, don't they?'

'Probably that an' all.'

'A punkah-wallah cools them with a fan, as I remember . . .'

'Well, if we don't get active, sir, they'll be fanning empty beds. I'd like to send Collins into London today. He's a good eye.'

'That I grant you, but London's yielded up precious few to the regimental parties.'

'We won't get the best there, that's for sure. But I don't see as we've time to be traipsing round the county looking for likely men. And sure as hell we don't want to take any as is paying with the drum.'

'Well, at any rate, not any that have a large payment to make. The odd fellow who's fallen foul of the bench of a Saturday night oughtn't to be too much of a problem.'

Hervey knew that his serjeant-major was not wholly convinced of the corrective qualities of soldiering. Despite his rough and ready ways, his quick temper and his fondness for a drink, Armstrong held strongly to the notion that character would out as soon as the guns began to play. In the infantry this did not matter so much, for the bad characters were held in line by the NCOs close by them, and all the line had to do was wheel and form and deliver volley-fire on command. In the cavalry it was not so easy. A dragoon was much more upon his honour as regards his horse, doing outpost duty and going to it with the sword. A rough could be redeemed by military discipline, but a bad hat – never. And the trick was always to know which was the one and not the other.

Hervey observed closely as his serjeant-major took up the acquittance roll again and began examining the names. Armstrong's new uniform fitted handsomely, showing off the barrel chest and powerful arms that had made him so formidable a fighter in a mêlée. The regiment would not have been the same without him. And how good did that fourth chevron look – at last.

'Do you want to see those as came in yesterday, sir?'

Hervey did, so they walked to the pump in the yard outside E Troop's empty stables, where dragoons were throwing buckets of water over half a dozen brought men. It would have been the same in the depths of winter, and the dragoons went at it with a will, since they had no wish to share the lice and other vermin which recruits brought with them.

'Why ay,' exclaimed Armstrong suddenly. 'Corporal Mossop, fetch that red-'eaded man over here.'

Mossop half dragged the man in front of the serjeant-major; trying to march him over would have taken all day. 'Sir!'

'Turn 'im about, Corporal!'

Corporal Mossop knew the order would be pointless. He jerked him round to face rear.

Armstrong pulled the man's long red hair roughly to one side. 'I thought as much!' he snarled.

Hervey, too, saw the 'BC' brand on his shoulder.

'Why can't them bringers look properly? About turn!' he barked.

The man spun right-about like a top, ending up with his hands at attention by his side and his eyes set distant, exactly as if on parade.

'And what might your former service be, my bonny lad?'

The man's voice faltered. 'Six years, sir. Thirty-fourth Foot.'

'And why did the Thirty-fourth discharge you?'

'Rather not say, sir.'

'"Rather not say." I *bet* you wouldn't.' He turned to Hervey. 'Sir?'

Hervey knew his serjeant-major wanted him to say 'Throw him out of the gates', for that was what the army

140

intended when it branded a man 'bad character'. But he recoiled more from the notion of branding than from the letters themselves. 'Can we not see how he goes to his work while we try to find out why he was discharged?'

Armstrong suppressed a sigh. 'I wouldn't want him messing with the others to begin with, sir.'

'He can sleep in the guardroom, can he not?'

'He can, sir. Corporal Mossop, double this man away. I want an eye on him at all times.'

'Sir!'

'Not a good beginning,' said Hervey. 'How did you know to look for a brand? There were no lash marks.'

'Just an instinct, that's all, but I only thought there might be a "D".'

'Trying it on for the bounty?'

'Ay. There was a man 'anged not six months back for it. Deserted and then 'listed again eighteen times before he was discovered.'

'Well, five pounds and four shillings is an attractive bounty. But I wonder that someone on the take doesn't go to the infantry for the other guinea.'

'Maybe we've a soft name, sir.'

Hervey frowned. 'Yes, we've both of us seen men who thought they were enlisting to an easier life because they rode to battle rather than walked.'

Armstrong screwed up his face. 'But I'll 'ave that bastard if 'e does prove a bad character. And I'll 'ave that Mary-Anne – *Mossop* – for not being sharper. I'll stop his bringing-money, that's for certain.'

Hervey was beginning to wonder if one more recruit was worth the trouble. 'The others look clean-limbed. You can't fault Corporal Mossop for that.'

'Ay. They do right enough. Yon dragoon!' he shouted.

A smart-looking private man doubled over to them and saluted. 'Sir?'

'Who are you, lad?'

141

'Ashbolt, sir. C Troop.'

The keen eyes said it all. Hervey sighed to himself. He wished he had twenty like him.

'Well, when you've finished dusting them with that evil-smelling powder, line them up for inspection.'

'Yes, sir.' Ashbolt saluted and doubled away.

In as straight a line as the keen eyes could manage with them, the six recruits stood as upright as they could.

'Name!' barked Armstrong at the first, a well-made lad.

'Harkness, sir.'

'Work?'

'Cooper, sir. Then there was insufficient so I was laid off.' Broad shoulders told that he must have been useful when work there was.

'Read or write?'

'I can read a little, if you please.'

'No "if you please", lad: just plain "sir".'

'Yes, sir.'

'And that "sir" is addressed not to me but to the officer on parade.'

Harkness looked confused.

'You'll learn soon enough,' said Armstrong, moving to the next. 'Name?'

'French, sir.'

'I'd change that quickly if I were you, lad.'

'Please, sir?'

'Never mind. Work?'

'Counting-house clerk, sir.'

'Lost your character, did you?'

'*No*, sir.' The boy – for that was all he looked – sounded indignant. His black curls bobbed as he shook his head. 'I didn't like the city, sir.'

'Country, are you? Do you know horses?'

'I've driven a pair, sir.' His voice was not of the common stamp.

Armstrong eyed him suspiciously and moved to the third. 'Name?'

'Smith, sir.'

'Oh yes?'

'Yes, sir. I was a boiler with the Oakley. I have a testimony from Lord Tavistock, sir.'

'Why did you leave?'

'I wanted to 'list in the horse guards, sir. But they said I was too short, sir.'

'Read and write?'

'No, sir.'

Armstrong turned to the next. '*Your* name, lad.'

'Sisken, sir.' The words were barely audible.

Armstrong looked down at the spreading pool by the man's left foot. 'Good,' he said simply, and moved on.

'Name?'

'McCarthy, sor.'

Hervey looked closer. Armstrong continued: 'Employ?'

'Private man, Hundred and fourth Foot, sor.'

Armstrong's suspicions rose like storm cones.

'I had my honourable discharge, sor,' the man insisted, the gentle Cork lilt now plain.

'The Hundred and fourth were disbanded two years ago, Sar'nt-Major,' explained Hervey, stepping forward a pace. 'We have met before, have we not, McCarthy?'

'We have, sor.'

Armstrong looked at Hervey for enlightenment.

'In Le Havre – a little affair of rebellious Frenchmen. Private McCarthy has a cool head under fire.'

'Thank you, sor.'

Armstrong eyed him up and down, taking his own measure, and moved to the last man. 'Name!'

'Mole, sir.'

'Occupation.'

''Ireling, sir.'

Mole looked to Armstrong to be little more promising

143

than Sisken, a harelip giving his face a permanent expression of alarm and rendering his speech awkward. 'Read or write?'

'No, sir.'

Armstrong turned to Hervey and saluted. 'Carry on, sir, please?'

'A word with them first, Sar'nt-Major.' He looked left and right at the six recruits. Somehow by the miracle of military training and discipline they would become handy dragoons in his new troop. But at this stage he could be excused for doubting the existence of miracles. 'I want no men who will not put their heart into their work,' he began. 'For there is little time before we sail for India. I will grant any of you a free discharge – on repayment of the bounty only, no smart money – up to tomorrow midday. Thereafter I will expect you to bend your backs to it without complaint. That is all. Carry on, please, Sar'nt-Major.'

Corporal Mossop had by this time returned to the yard. 'Corporal Mossop, carry on!' barked Armstrong.

Mossop saluted as they turned away.

'I doubt they'd be able to raise one man's bounty between 'em,' Armstrong opined. 'They'll have pissed it against a wall by now. That Sisken, or whatever his name is, is pissing it still. You know what he'll do the first time he gets a *real* fright! Who's this Irishman, by the way, sir?'

'McCarthy? A Cork man, I think. You ought to recognize the accent better than I.'

'Ay, I'd place him as a Cork man right enough.'

'There was a riot of French prisoners in Le Havre when I was en route to India. They broke free from the guard – McCarthy's regiment. The officer was killed and the serjeant was a funk. There was only McCarthy with any presence of mind. I seem to recall he said he'd been a corporal. Yes, I remember, because there were stitch holes on his coat where the stripe had been.'

'That's all we need – a busted chosen-Paddy! I dare wager

a day's pay the charge was fighting aggravated by drink.'

Hervey smiled ruefully. 'Serjeant-major, have you become a Methodist?'

Armstrong frowned determinedly. 'I never said as I wanted a troop of Armstrongs.'

'Well, I for one would settle for *half* a troop as things stand.'

'And I don't like would-be gentlemen in the ranks either. If that French has driven a pair then why isn't he an officer?'

Hervey sighed. Some things were better not enquired into. 'We've barely two dozen men, for all the weeks the recruiting parties have been out. Why is it, d'you think? Have they been going to the wrong place? Isn't the bounty enough?'

'Well,' began Armstrong, sighing also. 'There are too many parties fishing in the same bit of water, for a start. Mossop said there were bringers from the Second Dragoons and three foot regiments in the same alehouse last night.'

'Has India anything to do with it?'

Armstrong shrugged. 'Who knows? What's it matter how far from home a man is if he's not there? Half these jack-heads won't have the first clue where India is.'

Hervey supposed it must be true. 'Look, we're wasting our time here. Collins will find another half a dozen, and choice men we hope, but we're going to have to do more ourselves. I've a mind to take a party down to Wiltshire. The recruiters are not nearly so active there.'

'Well, anything's better than sitting and waiting.'

'The thing is, there are always hirelings in Warminster each week at the market, and there's not much work to be had. The price of wool's dropped like a stone. If we took the band we could make quite a go.'

Armstrong looked impressed.

'I'd better go and speak with the major.'

Major Eustace Joynson was a much happier man these days.

He rarely had a sick headache, and when he did he could alleviate it with the new morphium from Leipzig, though it cost him a pretty penny. All the mess knew that the cause of the headaches was no more, for in the new commanding officer Joynson found an able and considerate man who knew how to use his second in command's strengths, all-be-they limited to painstaking administration. And some of the mess suspected, too, that the death of the major's wife had come as a merciful relief, for so addicted to laudanum had she become of recent years that she was to all intents and purposes an invalid. So now Major Joynson could happily immerse himself in the regiment's administrative detail, to the gain of both parties. And in the evenings he had the consolation and support of a daughter not yet one and twenty.

'The band is a very good idea, Hervey,' the major agreed, 'but I'm not clear how we might pay for it. They couldn't post down to Wiltshire, that's for sure. Are there any stages?' He knew well enough that the band had been to Wiltshire before, but then it had been at Lord Bath's expense to play at Hervey's wedding. Joynson was not going to be the first to mention that, however.

'I thought we might ride there, sir.'

'I'm not sure that all the bandsmen ride. And that would cost dearly, too. Why not take three or four trumpeters? They'd make a goodish noise.'

'They would, but I thought some pretty tunes would draw people in.'

'I don't deny it. And how many recruits would you expect to get?'

'I'd be disappointed with fewer than thirty.'

'Thirty!'

'I don't see why not, sir. My part of Wiltshire is much distressed. There are many men paid outdoor relief. My intention would be to get their names from the parishes and offer them the bounty.'

Major Joynson looked thoughtful. 'How will you get them all back here?'

'That, I'm not sure of yet. They might have to walk.'

'I'll see what is to be done with the band, Hervey.' He got up and opened a cupboard. 'Would you care for sherry?'

'Thank you, yes.'

Joynson handed him a glass of very pale Montilla and indicated a chair. 'You find the regiment to your liking, then, Hervey.'

'Yes. Very much. Times change, but I think the best of the old spirit is probably returned.' Hervey took a good sip of his wine.

Major Joynson took off his spectacles and rubbed his eyes. He hoped profoundly that the best of Hervey's old spirit, as well as the regiment's, had returned. From the day Hervey had joined, he had never shirked his duty, regardless of what others said. But although he had never been a 'yes-man', there had perhaps been a willing compliance with him that would serve admirably in field rank, but take him no further. Joynson thought now that he detected a sterner core, however.

He replaced his spectacles and looked directly at him. 'Hervey, I've said this to you before, but I'm more than a little conscious that had I acted more . . . resolutely, then things might not have happened as they did.'

Hervey nodded. 'And I think I replied that if I myself had so acted then things very *assuredly* would have been different.'

Silence followed for a while. 'You are content, then, to go alone to India?'

'Content' was not the word Hervey would have chosen. 'I am in two minds still about my daughter, but I cannot see that to inflict a sea journey of six months and more, and then the vagaries of that climate, would be right.'

'No, I am sure that must be so. Frances is to come with me, though.'

'That will be pleasant, sir.'

'I hope so. For Frances I mean. Do you believe India a proper place for her?'

Hervey hardly knew Frances Joynson. She seemed a sensible enough girl. 'I only know Madras, sir, not Hindoostan. But I saw Englishwomen there who were very content – and altogether freer, I should say, than here. One who is the sister of a Company official who was at Shrewsbury a little before me went about the country as she chose, and with only a maid.'

'Mm . . . I do not say I could imagine allowing Frances such licence, but perhaps I shall become used to it once I have been there a while.'

A week later the recruiting party left its lodgings at The Bell in Warminster high street and took post outside St Laurence's chantry, the intention being to draw onlookers from the livestock market further up the street, and taverners from the breweries and alehouses down the hill to their left. Although there were only four trumpeters (for despite Major Joynson's best efforts no money could be found to send the band to Wiltshire), they were an imposing sight. Serjeant Collins had had the five dragoons from C Troop up half the night bringing their uniforms to a high order, and the trumpet-major had not spared himself or his three trumpets either. They wore buff breeches and hessians instead of overalls (Collins would not have them taken for infantry), silvered buttons, epaulettes and sabres which glinted in the sunshine, and pipeclayed crossbelts and sword straps that looked as white as the finest flour. Shakos topped with plume, white over red, sealed the impression of especial smartness and regularity. Hervey could not have been prouder as he rounded the corner on Gilbert and returned the salute. And Gilbert could not have done them greater service in appearance than with the black sheepskin and shabraque, and hooves which Private

Johnson had brought to a high gloss with his fish oil.

Private Ashbolt stepped forward to hold Hervey's charger by the bridle as he dismounted. 'Thank you, Ashbolt. Good morning, Sar'nt Collins. I see we have attracted a fair crowd already.'

'Yes, sir. If we could put women in uniform we should have a troop by mid-morning.'

There was no denying it. The onlookers were for the most part women and girls. Not that the dragoons minded; there would be time stood-down this evening, they supposed. 'Shall we see what answers to the trumpets, then?'

'Very good, sir. Trumpet-major, would you oblige us?'

The four unhitched their trumpets. The trumpet-major had checked the pitch before leaving The Bell; it was a warm day and he was confident the instruments would not have flattened. They raised them as one and blew a short fanfare in unison, followed by another in four parts. A very pretty sound it was, thought Hervey – not a note cracked or overblown. The effect on the onlookers was favourable but momentary: they thrilled, but then shrieked and scattered as half a dozen oxen stampeded past them, followed by the teamsters cursing the trumpeters for their 'caterwauling'.

The indignity might have been fatal to Hervey's purpose had he not taken action at once. 'Again please, Trumpet-Major.'

Another fanfare, with the same precision, announced that the military meant business. The evening before, Hervey had had bills posted up and down the town announcing his purpose, and he would trumpet it now until he got results.

The poster had been most carefully composed. Hervey had seen a good many which seemed contrived positively to make men take to their heels, and some so ludicrous as to attract mockery. He recalled one of the Seventh's, which had been put up derisively in many a barrack-room, which announced that 'since the regiment is lately returned from Spain and the horses young, the men will not be

149

THE
SIXTH
Regt. of
Lt. Dragoons
Commanded by that gallant and noble hero
Lieut. General
THE EARL OF SUSSEX

YOUNG Fellows whose hearts beat high to tread the paths of Adventure, could not have a better opportunity than now offers. Come forward then and Enrol yourselves in a Regiment that stands unrivalled, and where the kind treatment the Men ever experienced is well known throughout the whole Army.

Each YOUNG ADVENTURER on being approved, will receive the largest Bounty allowed by Government, and may elect to serve in a new-raised Troop commanded by

Captain Hervey, of Warminster

A few smart Young Lads will be taken at Sixteen Years of Age, 5 Feet 2 Inches, but they must be active, and well limbed. Apply to Serjeant Collins, at

THE BELL INN

allowed to hunt more than one day a week next season'.

He had first consulted Serjeant-Major Armstrong. Armstrong had argued for command to be ascribed to the colonel rather than the executive officer, the lieutenant-colonel, for although titular, he argued, the rank of lieutenant-general and earl would reassure a recruit that he was joining a regiment which would not be too ill-treated by government. Then there had been much discussion about whether to make the usual reference to being a hero, but Serjeant Collins had argued that now the war with Bonaparte was ended there was already quite evidently no regard for 'heroes' in the country: 'adventure' might be a more useful appeal, although he thought the bounty was probably the strongest inducement if distress in the neighbourhood was as great as Hervey said. Armstrong had wanted reference made to the law that no man enlisted could be arrested for prior debts below £30. Hervey had been tempted, but judged that the immorality of it outweighed the attraction. The usual reference to smart uniforms was omitted, since they would be able to judge that for themselves – besides which Hervey was not sure it was so great an inducement in the young men of that corner of Wiltshire, although had he imagined the animation among the townswomen on the first appearance of regimentals he would doubtless have included it. And Private Johnson had later added the reference to Hervey himself and the new-raised troop. 'Y'see, sir,' he had argued, 'if I was a young'n wanting to advance, there'd seem more chance in summat new. And they'd like to think they was officered by someone as knew a bit about where they came from.'

'Unless they wanted to get away from that,' Hervey had countered.

But Johnson had persuaded him that for every man who stepped forward there would be another who could not quite bring himself to do so, and the thought that he might be among friends – at least, that there was an officer who was not quite so remote – might just make the difference. 'You might even get somebody from 'Orningsham as knows thi' family.'

'That would mean from Lord Bath's estate, and I don't think that would do.'

'It's a free world, Cap'n 'Ervey.'

'Of sorts.'

The longest discussion had been on the question of India. Hervey had been adamant that the fact of their posting be advertised. 'We cannot fail to declare such a thing!'

Again, Armstrong had countered that it would make no difference to the recruit himself but might set his family or sweetheart against it. 'We should tell a man once he comes to us, before he takes the shilling. Then it's his own doing. He might be looking for an excuse to leave the girl!'

Hervey pulled a face.

'Come on, sir. This is the army, not New Lanark!'

'And what if the news gets around? Won't it seem we can't be trusted?'

The arguments were finely balanced. Hervey was adamant that he would not trick any man into joining.

Armstrong was equally adamant that the bounty itself was a trick. 'We pay him five pounds and then make him spend ten on clothing. That's hardly fair, is it?'

At length, Hervey agreed to the compromise: recruits would be told about India before they took the shilling.

Hervey left Serjeant Collins to his duties and rode to Upton Scudamore to see Daniel Coates. He had no intention but to pass the day with him, an unexpected pleasure, but it did indeed prove fruitful to his recruiting. Coates had sat the day before on the Westbury bench and had had to deal with, as he described it, a particularly distressing case involving a shepherd he had once employed but who had left for a better position. 'It appears he had a wife in common law but she

152

had taken to another man on account of the nights he spent with his sheep. When he discovered them together he struck the man and did him no little damage. And although he wanted his wife to stay with him she left that night.'

'I'm surprised a case should have been made for the magistrates, Dan. It would hardly seem the other party received more than he deserved.'

'Ah,' replied Coates, suggesting Hervey was right. 'But it was not that simple, for the other man turned out to be a son of his employer.'

Hervey sighed. 'The social order in west Wiltshire was thus threatened!'

'That is what Sir George Styles seems to have imagined.'

Hervey's jaw dropped. 'You mean—'

'Ay. The very same.'

'As if his brother was not trouble enough; God rest his soul.' Hugo Styles had courted Henrietta, ineffectually, commanded the Warminster Troop of the yeomanry just as ineffectually, and died at Waterloo very probably in a state of terror. 'What did you do with him, Dan?'

'I couldn't bring myself to do anything. I adjourned the court, and first thing this morning I went to see Styles senior to ask that the evidence be withdrawn. The shepherd has no position now, he's lost his so-called wife, and their cottage: what more punishment might there be? But I can't very well set him free. It would scarcely be exemplary.'

'I suppose Styles refused?'

'Would hardly hear me out.'

Hervey sighed again. 'You're thinking of inviting him to pay with the drum?'

Coates returned the look grimly. 'Would you take him, Matthew?'

'Would you recommend that I should?'

Now Coates sighed. 'The Lord only knows whether he'd make a soldier, for I don't. But there's nothing for him hereabouts now. And I fear for him. He was a good shepherd. I don't think he'd let you down willingly.'

'Then if he'll come I'll take him.'

'He'd have to attest before I released him.'

'Well, you're the magistrate, Dan: he can attest before you. I can have a dragoon bring him back to Warminster straight afterwards.'

'Thank you, Matthew. Let us pray he sees sense, then.'

'I'll warn my serjeant this afternoon. What is his name?'

'William Stent. Your father buried his at Imber, as I recall.'

'Very likely. Well, it's not a bad connection. By the way, I didn't say as I have some officers at last. Seton Canning will be my lieutenant again, which I'm right pleased with, I may tell you. And the cornet will be Lord Huntingfield's younger son. I knew his brother in the Eighteenth in Spain. He ought to have the makings.'

'I'm glad of that for you, Matthew. You'll want good officers by the sound of things.' Coates now paused, seeming to contemplate something else. 'Matthew, I'm pleased you're come. I can't tell you how glad am I to see you back in regimentals. You were not your true self without them.' He reached into his pocket. 'We may not have a chance to make proper farewells. I want to give you this.'

Hervey was taken aback by the sudden reminder of his transience on the Plain. He took the leather case and opened it carefully.

'I sent to London for it. It has hands which luminesce. I scarcely believed it – but they do.'

Hervey examined the watch closely, but in vain. It showed no sign of luminescence. But he saw the maker's name, George Prior: the same as d'Arcey Jessope had given him five years earlier, and he was at once confident that, come the evening, the hands would somehow be visible. And in that name he saw, too, the extent of Coates's generosity as well as his thoughtfulness. 'Dan, this is so very good of you, I—'

'And *this*,' added Coates enthusiastically, reaching into the other pocket. 'See *this*, Matthew!'

Hervey looked at the instrument curiously. He had not seen a compass outside of a binnacle, and certainly not one as small.

'The strangest thing. I was sat at the Devizes bench a month ago, and a man entered it in lieu of payment of his fine. The clerk wouldn't have it at first, but I gave him sufficient to pay his fine and a good deal more. I reckoned I might have use of it on the downs of a night. But then I thought you would make more of it in the Indies.'

Hervey smiled gratefully. 'Dan, you are the most solicitous friend a man might have. Why do you not follow to India in a year or so? I ought by then to know the safe ways.'

Coates clapped his hands together and laughed. He had ever had a mind to see the east, but Hervey's caution on his behalf sounded like the wheel turning full circle. 'Matthew, a very handsome offer that is. But if I should come, I should not want to see only the *safer* ways. And, I might say, Captain Hervey, neither should you!'

Hervey laughed, and assented with a nod.

A few moments of contented silence passed, and then Coates spoke quite gravely. 'And everything is right with you otherwise, Matthew?'

' "Right", "otherwise", Dan?'

'Ay. Are all your affairs put in order?'

Hervey balked at the directness. But Daniel Coates had picked him up when first he had fallen from a pony. 'Dan . . .'

Coates sat down.

Hervey half sank into the ash dugout, and with a further sigh. 'Elizabeth will take Georgiana to Longleat just before I leave. They'll stay there until I'm gone.'

'I should think that's very wise of her, Matthew.'

Hervey remained silent for a while, trying to think how

best he might explain it. 'She is not two years, Dan, and yet she has everything about her that is her mother's.'

Coates nodded. The silence returned. 'She's *not* Henrietta, of course, Matthew.'

'No, that I understand. When I am able to reason, that is.'

'Oh, Matthew, never surrender that power to reason.'

Hervey smiled. 'No, I don't believe I shall – not willingly, at any rate.' And then he frowned. 'I should have liked a little more time, though.'

'Perhaps it's better you hadn't, Matthew. It would go harder with yon infant.'

And with himself, Hervey knew.

Late in the afternoon, at the time that Canon Hervey was saying the evening office, Hervey strolled with Elizabeth through the village. It was warm, perhaps as warm as an evening in India early in the summer. Swifts, swallows and martins were everywhere, jinking and diving, and a continuous stream of rooks headed west towards Longleat park. There were labourers about the fields still but not nearly so many, the work of haymaking done for a week or so; and cottage tables were claiming the menfolk at this hour. 'How do you persuade a man to leave this for the barrack-room and India?'

Elizabeth looked at him, puzzled. 'You don't!'

'Yet we have to fill the ranks somehow.'

'Well, there's little profit in trying to persuade a man with a wage and a sound roof. There'll be one or two who might like the thrill of it, I dare say. But in truth you had better look elsewhere.'

'You're right, of course. We had a fair bag today, but not as good as I'd hoped.'

Elizabeth raised her eyebrows. She could never fathom the town. 'Why don't you go to the Common?'

Hervey looked at her, pained. 'We're recruiting for the

cavalry and India, Elizabeth, not a penal battalion for the West Indies!'

Elizabeth smiled. 'You're not recruiting very much for anywhere, by your own admission, brother! Didn't your Duke of Wellington say that his men were the scum of the earth?'

Hervey did not answer at once. 'Elizabeth, you go to the workhouse, and I admire you much for it. But can you have a true notion of what the Common is?'

'Why do you suppose otherwise?'

Hervey looked at her quizzically. 'Father has forbidden your going there, has he not?'

'Father forbade me to *visit* there.'

He furrowed his brow again.

'He did not say I could not go about workhouse business.'

'Are you saying you go *into* those hovels?'

'I do. But I do not *visit* with them.'

Hervey said nothing, but his look betrayed his disapproval.

'Matthew, *someone* must attend there. Last Monday we took in an unwed girl and her child from a single room in Marsh Street. The child's father was her own father. Yesterday the constable arrested a young woman not one and twenty who was carrying on her trade while her common-law husband lay three days dead in the room upstairs. And this morning he turned out a young man who slept in the same bed as his unmarried mother. A singular week in numbers, perhaps, but not otherwise. Shall I say more?'

Hervey was speechless.

'There is life there which cannot be any worse in the London rookeries. In the main I grieve only for the children now. But some of the young men might have redemption. The Methodists are doing fine work, but they must break through so much with the younger men.'

'Elizabeth,' said Hervey, muted. 'I cannot do God's work with these men. All we may do is make soldiers of them.'

'I have seen enough to know what that would do.'

'Yes, but you can't make a good soldier out of a bad character.'

'And I am not suggesting you try to. Only that you look for young men whose character is not yet formed.'

'Elizabeth, you astonish me,' said Hervey, the admiration evident. 'But I'm afraid that nothing could induce me to go to Warminster Common in search of recruits!'

CHAPTER TEN

THE SCUM OF THE EARTH

In the course of the next three days, the recruiting party enlisted fourteen men, including William Stent, lately shepherd to Sir George Styles of Westbury. A dozen more had presented themselves to Serjeant Collins at The Bell, but these he had rejected on various grounds.

'Two were so punchy, sir, that between them they'd have stood no higher than a noseband,' reported Collins, carefully consulting his notebook. 'One was badly scalded about the face, there was another with leg sores that stank very ill, two had crooked spines, one was an idiot, one was taken off by his mother before I could do much more than take his name – more's the pity, for he was a smart lad.'

Hervey cocked an ear.

'One had eyes that were very blear,' continued Collins. 'One was too close to forty for me to pretend he was under thirty, and two were dead drunk and haven't returned.'

Hervey shook his head. 'Were any put off by the notion of India?'

'Not one, sir.'

'It is disappointing indeed to have only the fourteen when it might have been double.'

'But I will say the ones we attested look promising, sir.

That Stent has the makings of an NCO, without a doubt, but he's an unhappy man at the present. He told me he was missing his sheep – not his wife, mind, sir – his sheep.'

Hervey simply raised an eyebrow. 'And who was this lad whose mother took him away?'

'Rudd – a well-made lad, about your height, sir. And smart as a carrot new-scraped. I reckon he'd put on his best clothes.'

'And his mother just came and took him away, you say?'

'Ay, sir. She's a milliner. Premises in Silver Street, the lad said. Reckon she has better things in mind for him than going for a soldier.'

'You spoke to her?'

'No, she gave me no chance, but I made enquiries afterwards and went to her shop, but she threatened to bring the constable.'

'Did she indeed? Well, Serjeant Collins, we're going to have to make one last effort tomorrow. You're going to Westbury for the fair this afternoon?'

'Ay, sir. But I've been told there was a company of foot there for a month and more and took a fair number of men with them.'

'Yes, I'd heard that too, which is why I'm contemplating going onto the Common to see what we can find.'

Collins looked wary. 'Sir, there were men in here last night – and not preachy types – who said that the best thing that could happen to Warminster Common was for the plague to take a hold and then the flames.'

'Are you saying we should not go?'

'Sir, with respect, it's you who are from these parts.'

'My sister believes there are some likely men.'

Serjeant Collins accepted without question that his captain's sister could properly know such a thing. 'Has she names, sir? That would be a start.'

'Three, yes.'

'And how would you wish me to do it, sir – with the trumpets, as here?'

'We could try that, yes. But I shall come with you, Sar'nt Collins. I can't very well ask you to go to the biggest fencing crib this side of Bristol while I sit at home waiting.'

Hervey expected a protest, but Collins was of quite the opposite opinion. 'It's bound to have an effect. I'll warrant they never see a gentleman there other than the parson.'

Hervey stayed an hour with him, but no 'Fellows wanting to tread the path of Adventure' came to The Bell in that time, and at eleven he left to go to the milliner's in Silver Street. He was not content to leave so promising-sounding a recruit to the protective clutches of a 'respectable' mother.

Hervey wore plain clothes this morning, and was doubly glad of it since he supposed he would not therefore be immediately barred entry from Mrs Rudd's shop. She smiled at him, indeed, when he entered, and asked him to take a seat while she attended to another customer. He sat looking about him at the lace, the ribbons, and all manner of fancy goods that might brighten a townswoman's day. There were hats, too, in various stages of construction. Here was a skilled and artistic trade, and it was evident that Mrs Rudd was a true proficient. He wondered if Elizabeth had ever come here.

When Mrs Rudd's customer was gone, Hervey made himself known at once. This put the milliner in a difficult position – as he had gambled – since in her trade she could ill afford to be abusive and dismissive of a gentleman, even if she were inclined to be. 'Mrs Rudd – I may call you that, may I?'

She nodded guardedly.

'I understand that your son expressed an interest in joining my troop.' He had decided to make his approach as personal as he could.

'The boy is very young, sir, and does not know his own mind.'

161

Hervey saw how to deal with both objections. 'My serjeant was most impressed with him. Although he may be young, my serjeant – who is but seven and twenty himself – believes he has the makings. And if you are in any degree troubled that he might not be suited to the profession, then I give you my word that he may have his free discharge at any time during his training.'

'I am obliged, sir. But it has always been the intention that Stephen continued in this trade. He has made a very good start.'

Hervey judged it better not to try to counter a mother's hopes. 'They are beautiful hats, Mrs Rudd.'

'Thank you, sir.' She managed a sort of smile.

'And there seems no reason why Stephen should not continue in the trade after serving the King.' He judged her loyalties to be firmly Tory.

Mrs Rudd looked uncomfortable at the inference which might be drawn if she persisted. 'May I speak freely, sir? And I mean no offence. And we are all grateful and proud of what was done in the wars. But you see, sir, to have a son go for a soldier is not . . . that is, families in respectable trades such as ours . . .'

Hervey smiled as benevolently as he could. 'Of course, Mrs Rudd. I perfectly understand. But we are light dragoons. You saw what sort of man my serjeant was, and those about him.' It was perhaps fortunate at this exact moment that Armstrong had not been in charge of the party; there could be 'misunderstandings' with Serjeant-Major Armstrong.

'We attend divine service every Sunday at the Minster, sir.'

'I myself am a clergyman's son, Mrs Rudd. And a bible and prayer book are provided for every soldier by the Naval and Military Bible Society.' He sensed he was beginning to overwhelm her objections.

'And he would be properly treated?'

Hervey could answer with absolute assurance. 'The

officers have as close a feeling for their men as any in the service, Mrs Rudd.' He judged it now the moment to make a personal guarantee. 'You would be most welcome to communicate with my father, the Vicar of Horningsham, at any time.'

Next morning, Hervey rode early to The Bell, to find Serjeant Collins looking troubled. 'Have you seen the news, sir – about Manchester?'

Hervey had not. Collins handed him the *Daily Courant*:

Manchester, August 16th

SLAUGHTER OF INNOCENTS

This day in Manchester has been witness to scenes so infamous as to beggar description. At One o'clock p.m. a large but peaceable assembly of respectable men together with their families was at St Peter's field to hear the Radical speaker Henry Hunt address them on the propriety of adopting the most legal and effectual means of obtaining a reform of the Common House of Parliament. The Magistrates had sworn in four hundred Special Constables to serve on the day of the meeting, and also had at their disposal a military force composed of Cavalry, Infantry and Horse Artillery. Shortly after One o'clock Mr Hunt arrived to great acclamation and bands playing, and began addressing the crowd which by various estimates were in excess of Fifty Thousand Persons, but no sooner had he begun but the Magistrates ordered a Troop of The Manchester and Salford Yeomanry to arrest the speaker, and thereupon the Corps charged the crowd with great violence so that within a short time there were many dead and dying on the field and divers more cruelly maimed, and the exigency was made the worse by the appearance soon afterwards of Troops of Regular Cavalry, namely the Fifteenth Light Dragoons, who disported themselves with no less restraint than the Yeomanry.

'That is very ill news indeed, Serjeant Collins.'

'Ay, sir. Half the town will think we're heroes, and the other butchers.'

'I cannot believe the Fifteenth would have behaved so. What does *The Times* say?'

'I have not heard tell, sir.'

'We had better get along to the Common before this becomes street tattle. Did the milliner's son return yesterday, by any chance?'

Collins smiled. 'He did, sir. He is coming here this afternoon to attest before one of the notaries.'

It was some consolation, at least. Hervey had still not seen the lad, but Collins's recommendation was enough – that, and the respectability of the mother.

Thirty or so onlookers watched the recruiting party file out of The Bell's stable yard, hooves ringing on the cobblestones beneath the arch. The little crowd seemed to no degree different from the day before, and Hervey was relieved that they could go about their business without abuse in the high street, for they would surely meet with it on the Common.

It took but ten minutes at the walk. Hervey had never been to the Common before, but the stench on this hot summer's morning alerted him to the rank nature of the place from a quarter of a mile. As they neared the first dwelling, a dismal hovel with a broken roof and a wall which could never stand another winter's storm, he saw that the Rehoboth stream, whose plentiful sweet water had first been the draw of the squatters, was now but a trickling midden. Children stood all about barefoot in filth. Dogs, cats, pigs, poultry, a cow and even donkeys wandered freely, adding excrement to the mud and ash that was the main street, a foul faecal mulch which the dragoons would curse when it came to boning boots that night. In what manner this was superior to the meanest villages he had seen in India, Hervey would have been hard put to it to say.

Serjeant Collins looked about disdainfully. What adult males were abroad at this hour did not impress by their appearance. 'Over there looks about best, sir,' he said, indicating the chapel, the only substantial building to be seen.

Hervey agreed. They halted and dismounted. 'Calls, please, Trumpet-Major.'

Children appeared, some evidently delighted by the colourful sight amid the drabness of the settlement, others wary, recognizing perhaps the ingress of authority to their free and easy camp. A few women came, one or two owning to motherhood by taking charge of their offspring with a cautionary slap to the ear. Some of the children came closer, wanting to touch the horses. The dragoons received them willingly, but one by one they were hauled away. Before long the party was without an audience except for two young women who stood by the corner of the preaching house, and for a purpose which its sparse congregation of a Sunday would vehemently condemn.

'Do you want me to begin looking for these three men Miss Hervey has named, sir?' Collins's voice carried neither enthusiasm nor reluctance.

Hervey sighed. 'To tell the truth, Serjeant Collins, I little imagined squalor such as this. I can't see how any half-decent recruit might come out of here.'

'A good hosing and a week's drill and any of these could look likely, sir. It's all a question of whether they *want* to lift themselves out of this sink. You never know: there might be such as have been waiting the opportunity for years without even knowing it.'

Hervey nodded. 'Well, we'll take no recruits by waiting; that much seems certain. Sound off again, please, Trumpet-Major. And you and I had better begin visiting,' he said to Collins, grimly.

The dwellings had no numbers, and although the streets had customary names they were not displayed. But Elizabeth had provided directions for each of the three.

Good directions, too, for the first they found very quickly. Collins knocked at the door – closed, as were the windows, even on so warm a morning as this. It opened to reveal a single foul-smelling room with a dirt floor partly covered by furze cut from the edge of the Common, and on it a sleeping woman with, next to her, like piglets at a sow, half a dozen infants no older than three. Collins bent to the door's opener. 'Does Jobie Wainwright live here, love?'

The little girl stared, turned to seek assurance from her mother, who slept soundly the while, and then looked back at Serjeant Collins without a word.

'Is Jobie Wainwright your brother?'

Collins's tenderness was unpractised, but effective. The little girl nodded.

'Do you know where he is?'

The little girl wanted to help – her expression said it – but she shook her head.

'Will he come back soon, do you think?'

She nodded.

Collins stepped past her carefully to take a better look at the room. Hervey stepped forward gingerly and looked in too. The walls had no plaster, there was not a stick of furniture, and in the corner was a pile of ragged and filthy linsey, evidently the entire wardrobe of the brood – family seemed so inapt a name. 'This is a job and a half, sir,' said Collins as he came out. 'She's soused in gin by the look of it, and them babes is probably too sick to stir.'

'My sister said it was a wretched household. They're one step from the workhouse, I'd say. Did you see any food?'

'No.'

'Nor I.'

The little girl suddenly pointed and called out happily. 'Jobie!'

Hervey and Collins turned to see a boy of seventeen or eighteen approaching with a small sack under his arm. His step did not falter as he approached the cottage. 'Good mornin',' he said as he came to the door.

'Jobie! Jobie!'

Jobie's face was clean, unlike the little girl's – or, indeed, any they had seen since arriving at the Common. And shaven, too. He had bright blue eyes and hair the colour of horse chestnuts, and a ready smile for his half-sister. He gave her the sack and she ran inside with it. 'Only bread,' he explained to the visitors. 'I go for it evr'y mornin'.' He showed no apprehensiveness on account of seeing strangers in uniform.

'I am Serjeant Collins of His Majesty's Sixth Light Dragoons, and am authorized to enlist young men of the best character.'

Collins had not wanted to introduce confusion in the lad's mind by speaking of his officer, but Jobie Wainwright glanced at Hervey and then back at the serjeant. Even to an uninformed eye the difference in quality of uniform was apparent.

Hervey smiled. 'I am Captain Hervey of the same corps.'

'I reckoned as much, sir. I saw the posters in the town. And it's your sister as comes here.'

'Steady on, young 'un,' said Collins, checking his instinct to bark that he would speak to an officer only when given permission.

But Hervey saw an opportunity. 'It was my sister who told me you might care for a soldier's life.'

Jobie did not hesitate. 'That I would, sir, if only for a regular wage.'

Serjeant Collins now sensed further opportunity. 'Are there others who think the same, Jobie?'

'Two or three, Serjeant.'

'Well, if you bring them and they enlist, you are entitled to a bringer's bounty. Will you do that?'

'Ay, Serjeant, I'll bring them. But I wouldn't want the money for it. They must have that for themselves.'

'You shall have the money, Jobie, and you may give it away as you please. For that is the procedure. Come to the chapel within the hour. We cannot be here all day.'

'Ay, Serjeant, I shall do that.'

Hervey and Collins walked back to the chapel pleased with their easy success, and after so unpromising a beginning. 'As decent a lad as ever I saw,' declared Hervey. 'Clean, well-made, he reads, and he has an honest stamp. Or at least, he would not try to profit from his friends.'

'Ay, sir. A very satisfactory sort.'

'You sound unsure.'

'Oh no, sir. I'm sure right enough. That little lass's face told you he was a good'n. I was just thinking how contrary it all is. Here's the filthiest place you'll see outside a London rookery, and out of it comes a lad like that. Gives a lie to poverty being the breeding bed of sin, don't it, sir?'

'Don't let's begin on that, Sar'nt Collins. I had ample of it last night at home. You would not imagine so many opinions there might be in one family.'

'Well, sir, there'll be plenty more in the days to come, no doubt, after that business in Manchester.'

'Oh yes, indeed,' sighed Hervey. 'You may be sure of it.'

Three-quarters of an hour later, Jobie Wainwright and three others of his age came to the chapel and asked if they might know the bounty and pay if they enlisted.

'Five pounds and four shillings,' replied Serjeant Collins. 'And pay is one and twopence a day. For the infantry a shilling only. And there is one penny a day beer-money too.'

The potential recruits looked encouraged. Hervey, sitting in a corner, lowered his copy of *The Times*.

'And all our keep is found, Serjeant?' asked Jobie Wainwright on their behalf.

Here was the rub, thought Hervey. And here was when an unscrupulous bringer would dissemble or even lie. Better that he himself speak to it than leave Collins to have to apologize for the subsistence and off-reckonings which would take away so much of their pay. 'Three-quarters of a pound of beef and one pound of bread every day. That or its equivalent,' he said, reassuringly.

The four looked even more encouraged.

'And for this you pay no more than sixpence a day.'

They looked disappointed.

'And you must, of course, buy that part of your uniform and necessaries which would be a man's everyday working dress whatever. Serjeant Collins has a list of these. He will show it to you.'

Only Jobie Wainwright made to look at it. To the others it would have been no more helpful than a page of Greek.

	£	s.	d.
Flannel drawers		5	11 ¼
Flannel waistcoat		7	5 ¼
Shirts		7	5
Worsted stockings		2	6
Stable trousers		7	9
Forage cap		2	6
Stock and clasp		2	0
Shoes		8	0
Boots		18	0
Gloves		1	8
Hair comb			6
Razor		1	3
Shaving box and brush		1	3
Shoe brush			11
Cloth brush		1	2
Curry comb and brush		4	0
Mane comb and sponge			8 ½
Water sponge, per oz.		2	2 ¼
Horse picker			1 ½
Turnscrew and worm		1	0
Corn bag		1	6

169

Oil tin	1	0
Scissors	1	6
Black ball		10
Valise	12	6
Saddle blanket	18	11 ¼
Braces	2	6
Night cap	1	8
	5	16	9

'Sir, it comes to more than the bounty,' said Jobie anxiously.

'The usual way is that a recruit is given twenty-one shillings at once, and the remainder is kept back for these necessaries. The difference is advanced to the man, and from his basic pay instalments are made until the advance is paid back.' Hervey did not say that it was the troop captain who lent the man the cash, and on very disadvantageous terms to himself.

Jobie looked a little relieved.

Serjeant Collins judged the catch was ready to land. 'You will receive a free issue of overalls, a stable jacket and a dress coat annually, and an allowance of six shillings for boots and three for gloves.'

They seemed encouraged again.

'There are other clearings,' said Hervey, 'but you shall receive not less than three shillings each week. And in India you may live much higher than ever at home.'

'India, sir?' said Jobie, his voice suggesting neither favour nor otherwise.

'Yes. The regiment is for India soon. I have been there. It is the place for adventure.'

The four looked at each other. Jobie spoke for them. 'If we enlist, sir, can we stay together?'

'You will all serve in my troop,' Hervey reassured them.

Serjeant Collins sealed the affair. 'Bring the measuring

stick, Prax. Let's see if these likely-looking lads stand sixteen hands and a half.'

They all did, though Hervey could not suppose there was more than a leather's thickness to spare with any of them. Not to worry; regular meat and riding school would do its work.

'Here is a shilling each for you, then,' declared Collins gravely. 'The King's shilling, that is. His token of trust in you. Come to The Bell at nine o'clock prompt tomorrow morning, and the magistrate will swear you in once the doctor has certified you fit for service.'

'Jobie, Jobie!' called the little girl from the other side of the street. 'Mam says didn't you get her gin?'

Jobie looked uncomfortable. 'Can I go now, Serjeant?'

'Ay, lad. Be there at nine sharp, though.'

'Jobie, are you going for a soldier?' asked the little girl as he took her hand.

Collins turned to Hervey. 'Christ, sir. What do you do?'

'I know, Serjeant Collins; I know. Try not to think about it, I suppose.'

The following day, a special edition of the *Warminster Miscellany* carried a further report of the disturbances in Manchester. The Herveys' manservant brought it just before midday to the dining room at Horningsham, where Hervey and his father were sitting with the remains of a pot of coffee and a salted mutton ham.

'PETERLOO' CASUALTIES

We are informed by the Manchester Observer *that the affair of the 16th Instant, dubbed 'Peterloo', has accounted for the deaths of sixteen persons, including a special constable, and Four Hundred injured, with no fewer than One Hundred and Fifty suffering from sabre cuts. It is further understood from the Officer Commanding all of the Troops that day, one Colonel L'Estrange, that Sixty-seven of his own men received slight wounds, while twenty cavalry horses have been hurt either by striking or by being stabbed.*

His Royal Highness The Prince Regent has sent a letter of strong approval to the Magistrates for the firm way in which they dealt with the lawbreaking.

The archdeacon read the report again carefully. 'I should say that, notwithstanding the title, the paper is indifferent in its tone. While the stabbing of the horses cannot be compared with the sabre cuts to the people, the two being juxtaposed in the report serves to ameliorate the shock that is felt. For it suggests a predisposition on behalf of some in the crowd to do mischief. I suppose the Prince Regent had to commend the poor magistrates, but I cannot help but feel it would have been the better to hold silence until the facts were established.'

'I wish it made some distinction between the regulars and the yeomanry,' said Hervey.

'I am afraid that if you are at the receiving end of a sabre stroke it matters little whether it be regular or otherwise, though I agree it is dispiriting for those who are proficient in the business of soldiering.'

'It's the very devil of a business keeping a troop in hand in the face of a crowd. The horses sense their riders' unease, I'm sure of it. I still hold a picture of poor Wymondham being thrown to his death in the street in London. Is there any more, Father?'

The archdeacon nodded. 'There is. And it troubles me, I confess.'

SIX MEASURES TO BE ENACTED

We have it on the most reliable authority that Lord Sidmouth will announce in Parliament six measures to be enacted which shall permit of the most summary dealing with the Radical agitation which now disturbs the greater part of the Country. Assemblies of over fifty persons shall be prohibited.

Magistrates are to have powers to search private dwelling houses for arms. Drilling and military training by civilians, except the Yeomanry and the Militia shall be strictly prohibited. The Laws against Blasphemous and Seditious Libel shall be strengthened. There shall be a limitation on the right of an accused to adjournment of trial to prepare his defence, and there shall be an increase in Stamp Duty on newspapers and pamphlets to Four Pence.

The archdeacon took off his spectacles and shook his head. 'By any standard, taken as a whole these are repressive measures, though three are reasonable in themselves, I suppose.'

Hervey assented with a nod. 'Daniel Coates told me that Lord Bath intends proposing a measure to form veterans' battalions to act as police.'

'Well, that has merit, for they would be men used to discipline,' declared Canon Hervey, replacing his spectacles and taking up the newspaper again. 'Ah,' he said, after reading more. 'Lord Bath is to embody the Warminster Troop.'

'That won't be greeted well in some parts, but it's only prudent. The Hindon people are a combative bunch, by all accounts. I shall be happier leaving you knowing there are a few sabres about the place, even if they *are* yeomanry.'

Canon Hervey looked thoughtful. But he withheld any fears for the peace of the parish and his family's safety. 'We shall see you again before you embark, Matthew?'

'You may depend upon it, Father.' Then he frowned. 'And it will be very much harder than ever before.'

Canon Hervey nodded, and rose. 'And not only for you, Matthew. Will you come to evening prayer?'

Hervey stood, but his brow was still furrowed. 'I beg you would excuse me this once, Father. There are things I ought to be about.'

Hervey sat for a half-hour, alone, when his father was gone.

The house was silent but for the ticking of two clocks, and there was nothing but his thoughts to disturb him. *Five years*. The house would not change in that time. The garden, perhaps – a branch fallen here and there, plantings come to maturity. His parents? It were better not to imagine. Elizabeth? He became fearful. And Georgiana? He rose hesitantly, then hurried to the stables.

In a quarter of an hour he was at Longleat. He entered the house unannounced and went to the nursery. The door was open but, hearing the sounds within, he stood to one side to observe without being seen. Elizabeth sat with her face half-turned from the door, contented-looking, happy even. Georgiana shuffled towards her on a little wheeled horse, gripping its woollen mane, her nursemaid by her side ready to support with an outstretched hand. The child giggled when she reached Elizabeth, and threw her head back. Hervey swallowed hard. He had never imagined he might look on alone like this. Next time, when he returned from India, the horse would not have wheels. Georgiana might even be free of the leading rein. And he would have missed all of it. And he had not imagined, until now, what it was that he would miss.

CHAPTER ELEVEN
ROUGH-RIDERS

Hounslow, three weeks later

'Keep them 'eels *down*!' bellowed the rough-rider serjeant at the six recruits as they attempted to complete a circuit of the riding school without stirrups. 'A sack of flour'd look better in yon saddles!' The old commands, the old quips – Hervey smiled to himself as he left the school and walked to regimental headquarters. In another five months the riding master and his staff would make dragoons of these green-heads, as they had done many times before.

The trouble was, they didn't have five months. In seven weeks they were due to sail for Calcutta, and there would be little they could do aboard ship by way of training save for musketry and sword practice. He would land with a half-drilled troop, at best.

'But that should not trouble you,' said the commanding officer, indicating a chair and pouring two glasses of sherry. 'You have done admirably in filling the ranks. I had not thought it would be so difficult. The adjutant's efforts in that direction were commendable, but his bringers netted a very feeble catch in the end. And your enlisting so many from one town must be a strength, I think. There ought to be a quicker fellow feeling.'

'I believe there will be, Colonel. And three of them are

already showing well – one that is paying with the drum, too, though it was scarcely much of an offence.'

Sir Ivo Lankester nodded approvingly. 'You'll have time enough when we get to India. I'll not expect your troop at regimental drill for a full six months.'

'That will be sufficient, Colonel. They'll come on capitally as soon as they've passed out of riding school.'

'Good, good. How many have you lost, by the way?'

'One only, sir. He coughed up blood each time they did anything strenuous.'

Lankester sighed. 'He'll be dead sooner outside than in, but it can't be helped. Now, I'm afraid I'm going to ask you to do one more thing, and it's only right that *I* should ask and not Joynson, since it is my notion and it may vex you to be distracted by it.'

The commanding officer's courtesy was such that Hervey was already disarmed. What could possibly vex him?

'I have decided that we shall take three dozen or so troop-horses to India, as well as all the chargers. I want the non-commissioned officers to be properly mounted. I know it will be a month at least before they're used to the climate, but better in the long run we begin with a well-mannered horse out of condition than what the Indian garrison might leave us.'

'I saw some fine horses in India, Colonel, but I agree there is no certainty of our having them at once.'

'It seems to me that the whole business will come to nought, however, if the horses don't travel well. Lord knows how many you and I have seen that were served ill by foul transports.'

'Indeed, Colonel.'

'Barrow says you took your charger there and back.'

Hervey smiled. 'I did. We sailed both ways in a frigate, with an uncommonly obliging captain.'

'Then you will know better than any what is to be done to a ship to make her fit to transport horses over so great a distance. And I should very much deem it a favour if you would supervise the making ready of the Indiamen which are to take us. As I understand it, they'll be at Tilbury in a fortnight's time for refitting.'

Hervey saw now why the colonel had been so concerned to make the approach himself, for Tilbury took him away from his troop – such that it could be called at this stage – but also, and more important, from his family in Horningsham. Yet the military necessity Colonel Lankester had spelled out with perfect sense, and it was to Hervey's advantage, too, that his own charger be carried in best condition. 'Of course I shall be able to do it, Colonel . . .'

'I know you would have liked a lengthy furlough before embarkation – as the rest of us – but there is no reason why you should not take leave when the job is done, and make the passage by a later ship.'

Hervey was much encouraged by the commanding officer's solicitude. 'Thank you, Colonel. I am mighty grateful, but unless something untoward occurs, I should want to sail with the others. Besides ought else, Calcutta will be' – he smiled – 'a heady place, I think, and if I am not there with my troop from the outset all manner of things might happen.'

'Admirable, Hervey, admirable. I should not have thought of you any the less, however, had you opted for the other course. And if circumstances change between now and then you must adjust your plan without fear that any shall think ill of it.'

'Again, thank you, Colonel.'

'Well, then – let us to the mess. Joynson says he has found some very fine burgundy, and there's woodcock. The general will be joining us.'

Next morning, as he was busying himself for the journey to Tilbury, Hervey received an envelope bearing, on the reverse, an embossed ducal coronet. Inside was a double-thick demi-octavo card:

Field Marshal The Rt. Hon. The Duke of Wellington
requests the pleasure of the company of

Captain Matthew Hervey

at Dinner

at Apsley House on 23rd September 1819
at 7 o'clock p.m.

Hervey wrote at once to accept, sent for Private Johnson to arrange despatch of the letter, and then took the regimental phaeton to the Red Lion in order to post to Tilbury.

His journey, overnight, was a not altogether comfortable affair, but on arriving at the port he was soon restored by the arrangements he found. The Honourable East India Company, being an institution of longer lineage than the army, had at least as many regulations, but as it was a company of merchants, the purpose to which all the regulations were drawn up was commercial. The arrangements put in hand by the Company for the regiment's shipping to India – for it was the Court of Directors who paid the costs of a King's regiment in India – were, in the main, sound. Two good-sized ships had been engaged, one for the major part of the regiment, the other for the horses and their attendants. But the surplus capacity was to be filled by general merchandise, and therefore any additional space requested meant a corresponding diminution of that profitable extra – not a matter the agent would be inclined to let pass easily.

Hervey asked if he might first look over the transport assigned to the horses. This was arranged without too much difficulty, although the captain was not in port and all questions were therefore dealt with by the first officer, who was clearly in fear of his master's wrath. She seemed a well-found ship, and clean. Hervey asked if he might see the plans for the stallage.

'I think you will find they comply with the horse guards' usual requirements,' said the agent.

Hervey did not know the regulation size of a stall. Those he had seen in the Peninsula hardly seemed to have the stamp of any sort of order.

'Six feet by two feet six is the allowance. Here is the plan for the lower deck, which is where they are all to be had.'

Hervey sighed to himself. Jessye had had twelve feet square on the *Nisus*. He studied the plan carefully. 'I see there is a gangway between the backs of the stalls and the side of the ship.'

'Yes,' replied the agent, without needing to check the drawing. 'Two feet, as specified, in order to permit of cleaning out droppings and soiled bedding.'

Hervey considered how best to make his proposal. 'When I took my mare to India, she had a loose box which could be turned into a standing stall in case of foul weather. But we soon found that she chafed badly, fore and rear, as the ship rolled. So we let her have her full length back and trusted to her own balance – and she did not suffer in the slightest. I think it would be very much the better for them if we did away with the gangway and extended the stalls to the side. It would be cheaper to build that way too, I would think.'

The agent heard this last with interest, but then remembered the regulation. 'My understanding is that the gangway is absolutely necessary to do the work of cleaning, Captain Hervey.'

'Not *absolutely* necessary. With a few free stalls in each section it is perfectly possible to move the horse and then muck his stall. That would be a matter for the regiment. You would not need to trouble yourself over it.'

'Then so it shall be, Captain Hervey. Would these spare stalls need slings, too?'

'None of the stalls need slings. They cause far more damage than good. Four or five only, for sick or injured horses. With the extra length of stall they'll keep themselves up well enough, believe me.'

The agent was all delight at the further economy.

Hervey judged it the moment to drive the bargain a little harder in respect of the spare stalls. 'Four per every twelve animals, then. And built so that they can be turned into one loose box. That way a sick horse may be allowed space to lie down and stretch.'

The agent checked the plans and agreed that it was not unreasonable.

The negotiation of gangway space in which to exercise proved a little harder, but the agent and the second officer saw how it could be done. Some of the orlop's capacity had to be sacrificed (all of the hay would now be stored there rather than some on the horse deck), but the savings overall were still considerable. There were numerous details to be agreed, but both parties were well satisfied. Only the question of windsails and ventilating shafts was unresolved. Hervey judged it better to wait a little while: there were bound to be savings he could suggest to offset his demands in this direction.

And so, in the next few days, Hervey found himself as much afloat as ashore. It was not a disagreeable state, but six months at sea in an Indiaman would not be the same as being guest of a frigate's captain. He decided he must turn his thoughts to the day's routine on the horse deck, and who best should be there, for without doubt Sir Ivo Lankester would next ask his opinion of that. The more he thought, however, and the more he wrote, the more he wished the six months could be past now. He had been gazetted captain since July, and still he could not rightly say he was returned to the saddle. This he would not be able to claim until they reached India, and even then only when he could take the head of his troop and have them wheeling and forming behind him as one body. In truth, he sighed, he would not be in the saddle before next year's summer was out.

181

CHAPTER TWELVE

NUMBER ONE, LONDON

The anniversary of the battle of Assaye

Hervey rose before dawn and took the morning stage to London. He intended being in good time for the Duke of Wellington's dinner, with sufficient in hand that if the coach were to meet with any delay, he could engage a saddle-horse to complete the journey. However, the *Quicksilver* was true to her name. She covered the distance not very greatly slower than the post by virtue of being exempt from the prohibition on galloping to which the government mails were subject. What she lost in the leisurely team-changes, and indeed the quality of the roadsters, she partially made up for in celerity over the macadamized turnpike.

For more than six months now, the duke had been Master General of the Ordnance with a seat in the cabinet, and the signal honour of this invitation had given Hervey much pleasure in the anticipation; as much, indeed, as the consolation which the duke's letter of support had given him eighteenth months before. Doubtless the invitation was but a formal conclusion to his earlier employment, which had ended somewhat unceremoniously, the duke being preoccupied with affairs elsewhere than Paris. Yet even if this were the case it was a handsome gesture still. He would savour the occasion, speak only when spoken to, and drink only very moderately.

182

Having spent what remained of the afternoon with the regimental agents seeing to various advances and allowances, at ten minutes to seven he climbed into the elegant dress chariot which he had engaged for the evening and left the United Service Club for Apsley House. Charles Street to Hyde Park Corner was a walk of but ten minutes at most, but in that short distance the edge could be taken off his ball dress – d'Arcey Jessope, of late lamented memory, had once regaled him with the story of how, similarly accoutred, he had been passing White's club when the contents of a fish kettle were hurled into the street and over him. And so while Hervey told himself it was to be his last extravagance before India, it was at least to a practical purpose.

A large crowd had gathered to see the arrival of the guests, and there was a steady parade of carriages to the porticoed entrance to the yard at the front of the house. They deposited their elegant occupants, female and male, and then drew away through the toll gates at the top of Knightsbridge to wait in Hyde Park. At once Hervey knew that the expense of his equipage saved him at least from disappointing the crowd; there had been times enough of feeling the country cousin. Indeed, as he stepped down, and rather to his surprise, he noticed several men raise their hats. But then if regimentals did not receive a cheer outside Number 1, London, where in the land might they?

Inside the walled yard he was able to get a better impression of the house, bought only recently by the duke from his elder brother, the former governor-general in India. Hervey was disappointed. He had imagined something more imposing. Next door was an altogether grander affair, twice as large, stone-faced instead of brick, with classical columns and pediments. But the disappointment did not dull his anticipation; in the yard the band of the Grenadier Guards was playing a merry tune, and in front and behind him were officers and their ladies who were also taking evident pleasure in the invitation. He recognized no one, and so contented himself with observing what he could without making it obvious.

The queue advanced steadily until Hervey stepped into the entrance hall which, although painted rather drably, was brilliantly lit. He handed his hat and cloak to a footman, together with his card, and followed the other guests towards the spiral staircase which would take them to the principal floor. But at the foot of the stairs several of the guests had stopped to examine the towering statue of a nude Bonaparte, presented to the duke by the Prince Regent. Hervey stopped too.

'Is it a fair representation, do you think?' came a female voice behind him.

Hervey turned, for the question sounded as if it were directed at him.

A tall woman in her thirties, strikingly handsome and very elegantly dressed, glanced from the statue to him and then back again, her smile suggesting amusement in the obvious difficulty her question posed.

'Twice life size, I should estimate, madam,' replied Hervey. It was as good a response as any might make. He looked about for the woman's escort but could see none.

'I had not thought of Napoleon as so . . . athletic.'

Hervey was doubly cautious. 'I believe the artist exercised some licence.'

The woman looked at him, with the same smile still, and inclined her head. 'I believe I have rankled, sir?'

Hervey was not without practice in this sort of conversation. 'No, not at all, madam. I merely relay what I heard in Paris, where the statue was set up originally.'

'Oh,' she said, in a delighted sort of way. 'You have been in Paris.'

'Yes. I first saw the statue in the Louvre palace.'

'And who is it by?'

Hervey paused. 'I'm afraid I do not recall, madam.'

'Well, it is of no matter. Not a Michelangelo, that is

for sure. *He* would never have dissembled with a fig leaf!'

Hervey counted it fortunate that at that moment the guests began again to ascend the stairs, allowing him to follow without need of more words. At the top was a footman to whom he handed another card, which was in turn passed to the master of ceremonies.

'Captain Hervey, Your Grace,' came his announcement.

The duke, wearing the levee dress of the Royal Horse Guards, of which he was colonel, nodded approvingly and held out his hand. 'I am very glad you are come, Hervey. All is well with you?'

'Yes indeed, thank you, sir,' replied Hervey, taking the duke's hand for the first time.

'I am glad to see you returned to the colours. In all the circumstances it is the place to be.'

Hervey bowed appreciatively.

'Lady Katherine Greville,' announced the master of ceremonies, the signal for Hervey to move on and into the Piccadilly drawing room, but not before he saw the duke's face light up with pleasure at hearing the name.

Inside the drawing room, with its classical friezes and ceiling an altogether finer affair than the exterior of the house would lead to suppose, Hervey took a glass of champagne and looked for a face he might know. Here and there he recognized one from the Peninsula, general officers all, not least the unmistakable profile of Sir Stapleton Cotton – now Lord Combermere – his face even browner after two years as governor in Barbados than when he had commanded the cavalry in Spain. But there was not a face he might present himself to, and so he made instead for a painting of Lord Uxbridge – new done and by Sir Thomas Lawrence, he surmised. It would both engage him agreeably and cover his knowing no one. However, scarcely had he time to verify the portraitist when a field officer in rifle green approached him.

'Captain Hervey?'

He turned. As ever with the Rifles, the rank was difficult to make out at first sight, but the man was about the duke's age, and his face more weather-beaten. 'Sir?'

'I am Colonel Warde, the duke's secretary.'

Hervey bowed. 'Good evening, Colonel.'

'We have a little time before dinner is announced. I wonder . . . may we have a word, privately?'

Hervey looked surprised. 'But of course, Colonel.' He glanced about the room, now becoming quite full.

Colonel Warde drew him away to a corner, taking another glass of champagne as he did so. 'This affair of Peterloo – a damnable business. It has already caused the duke great embarrassment.'

'I imagine so, sir.' The duke had sent a letter to the magistrates commending their action, just as had Lord Liverpool, and there was much popular resentment at both.

'It was, of course, a noble and brave thing to do, Hervey. The duke was mindful of the clamour there would be against him, and yet he was of the opinion that if the Manchester magistrates were not publicly supported, then others would shrink from their duties.'

Hervey nodded.

'But by heaven he is disturbed by what he reads. General Byng – the same that was with us at Waterloo – has the northern district, but his despatches have only an immediate account by the military. The duke believes there must be more to things than in the official despatches, but is not inclined to support a public inquiry. He wonders if you would go there and judge the various reports.'

'*I?*'

'Yes. You have experience of these things, do you not? And the duke trusts you.'

'Well, sir, greatly flattered as I am by the duke's trust, I do not consider that I am qualified!'

'The duke is of the opinion that you *are*,' replied the colonel, a shade testily.

Hervey sighed to himself. He ought to have seen that coming. 'But in only a few weeks I sail with my regiment to India!'

'I am sure you can be spared, Hervey. Sir Ivo Lankester will not object when I have spoken to him.'

There was a moment – perhaps no more than a second or so, though it seemed an age – when Hervey's mind rested in the balance. Eighteen months ago he would have received a request from a senior officer as an order. From the Duke of Wellington it would have commanded his instant, un-questioning obedience. But not now. He had his judgement – *percipient* judgement, the duke had once called it – and he had seen the consequences of disregarding it. 'No, sir. I am afraid I must insist that I have my prior duty.'

'*Mm.*' Colonel Warde's eyes narrowed. 'The duke *said* you might be recalcitrant. Well then, you can at least give your opinion of various statements that have been made?'

'Sir, I really do not see that that would be of any merit, since I have no special insight. For me to express a worthy opinion I should have to do more than merely read what might any other officer.'

'You really are most obdurate, Captain Hervey!'

'With respect, I trust not, Colonel. I think it would be wrong for me to undertake an assignment that the duke believed would yield some particular result when I am not in a position to do so. And a wrong opinion by me would be greatly to the duke's discomfort in no time at all.'

Colonel Warde sighed, most displeased. 'I cannot think what the duke will make of this. He was most adamant we had your opinion.'

The master of ceremonies announced that dinner was served.

Colonel Warde sighed again – huffed, almost. 'Come then, we had better take our seats. The duke's sister-in-law acts as our hostess this evening, in case you are presented.'

Hervey looked uncertain. 'In the circumstances, sir,

would it not be more proper for me to make my apologies and leave?'

'Don't be an ass, Hervey!' snapped the colonel, beckoning him on behind. 'I'll show you your place. You have very agreeable company – better than you deserve, I dare say.'

Colonel Warde made his way to the centre of the room, to the woman who had questioned Hervey at the foot of the stairs. 'Lady Katherine, may I introduce Captain Hervey, who shall be your companion at dinner. Hervey, this is Lady Katherine Greville.'

Hervey bowed, and his dinner companion made a part-curtsy by return, but with the same knowing smile as at the statue.

Colonel Warde eyed Hervey sternly again. 'After dinner we must resume our conversation.'

'As you please, Colonel,' said Hervey, offering Lady Katherine his arm.

'I see I have intruded on affairs,' she said. 'I have a mind that dinners such as these are mere interruptions to the serious business with which men concern themselves.'

'Not at all, Lady Katherine,' protested Colonel Warde. 'They are most necessary to the cultivation of proper society, which in these times we must not take for granted.' He glanced meaningly at Hervey.

They passed through a mirrored lobby, in which Hervey noticed that his face had reddened somewhat.

'We are the first to dine here,' explained Colonel Warde, who seemed anxious to keep up his conversation. 'The duke has had the room made only this year.'

That much was at once apparent to Hervey, for it was a most masculine room, most military indeed. The walls were a buff colour, not unlike his own facings; the doors, dado and cornice were oak, the chairs red leather and the table, almost groaning with silver, was mahogany polished to a high gloss, so that countless candles reflected from silver and wood alike.

They arrived near the far end of the table. 'I shall leave you in the hands of Captain Hervey, then, Lady Katherine,' said Colonel Warde, bowing again.

'What a delightful prospect, Colonel,' she replied, inclining her head slightly.

Colonel Warde bowed more formally. 'Until later, Hervey.'

A footman held the chair for Lady Katherine as she sat, allowing just enough time for Hervey to introduce himself to the aide-de-camp seated on his left, a captain of foot guards. He turned again to his companion.

'Colonel Warde seems most anxious that you speak together, Captain Hervey,' said Lady Katherine. 'You are evidently of some consequence.'

Hervey smiled. 'Oh, I think not, Lady Katherine. I am a regimental officer.'

'Indeed?'

Lady Katherine's smile seemed fixed in a bemused, disbelieving fashion which Hervey was beginning to find slightly unnerving.

'As a regimental officer, you could tell me what all this silver signifies.'

Hervey was relieved but still inclined to be guarded. 'I confess I do not know it intimately, but the centrepiece was presented to the duke by the Portuguese a year or so ago. The ornament in the middle of it shows the four continents paying tribute to the united armies – of England, Portugal and Spain.'

'It is quite magnificent, if perhaps rather severe for my taste.'

'When I first saw it, in Paris, there was a chain of silk flowers linking those dancing figures about the base. It was then a little less formidable.'

Lady Katherine inclined her head as if to say she might have further questions on the matter. 'Colonel Warde tells me you are to go to India soon.'

'Yes, madam. My regiment is posted to Bengal in two months' time.'

'And does this please you?'

'Yes, yes it does please me. I was there three years ago, though in Madras, which is much further to the south, and for only a very few months.'

A footman leaned between them to serve a plate of soup.

'My husband spent some time there, though he never speaks of it.'

'I do not know your husband, Lady Katherine.'

'Over there – Sir Peregrine Greville.' She nodded to the other side of the table, further towards where the duke sat. 'To Lady Combermere's left, she in the blue.'

Hervey saw a general officer who looked twice Lady Katherine's age. 'Forgive me, madam, but what is your husband's appointment?'

'He is Governor of Alderney.'

'Ah.' Hervey was not a polished conversationalist – he knew all too well – but even so, this was an appointment that did not make for a ready reply.

'*And* of Sark,' added Lady Katherine, mischievously.

Hervey returned her smile involuntarily. Her eyes caught the candlelight and for an instant tempted him to some equally mischievous reply. He had had only the one glass of champagne, though, and he thanked God for it, too. 'That must be very agreeable, madam. The climate, especially.'

'Oh, I don't know about that, Captain Hervey. I visit there but very infrequently, and then only for a very short time.'

Hervey knew he was making a poor show of it, and the knowledge did not improve matters. 'Your husband is not resident there, then?'

'Indeed he is! This is one of his few returns. He says that since the war there is little to engage him from a military point of view, so he can indulge his passion, which is fishing. There is nothing he likes more than to spend the day in a little boat among lines and pots and I know not what.'

Sole, only half warm, had followed the soup, and then there was partridge. And all the while Lady Katherine pressed Hervey to reveal his exploits in the war, explaining that her husband had nothing to tell her of but the toings and froings of ships past his islands. And all the while Hervey tried equally to deflect the conversation to something less sanguinary. The effort was so great that he ate little, sipped his wine perhaps too often, and was altogether relieved when at last the arrival of the sweet confections allowed the officer on Lady Katherine's right to engage her attention, and him to seek relief with the ADC. However, the ADC was engrossed in conversation to his left, so Hervey instead occupied himself with a survey of the room.

They were thirty-four at table. Besides two or three junior officers such as him, there was an equal number of generals in their braid and ladies in their finery. Hervey mused that each in his or her own way had dressed to please or gain the attention of their host. There was no end of pleasing him, at the most exalted and the most personal levels alike. The fruits of victory at Waterloo were bountiful indeed. The gifts alone spoke volumes: the marble nude of Bonaparte from the Prince; the Portuguese service, a thousand pieces of silver and gilt; the Saxon service, finest Meissen; the Prussian service, Berlin green china, with its magnificent obelisk centrepiece depicting the duke's orders and titles, perforce incomplete, for the honours still came; the Deccan service; the Egyptian service; paintings, furniture, statuary, porcelain of every description; field marshal's batons of half a dozen nations and more. And many hundreds of thousands voted by parliament so that the duke might acquire a country seat, as Marlborough before him had acquired Blenheim. Hervey could scarcely believe that he himself had refused the duke what little he had to offer.

'Do you enjoy your evening, Captain Hervey?'

He turned to the ADC and smiled. 'Yes, I do, very much.'

'Let us hope His Grace does, for he has been in high dudgeon these past three days.'

Hervey knew it was not a rare occurrence for the duke to be discomposed, but he had had no intimation of ill humour on arrival. Quite the opposite in fact. 'Indeed? How so?'

'Do you know what day it is?'

'No.'

'I think you must. The duke's time in India?'

Now that he was given the hint, the answer came quickly enough. 'The battle of Assaye.'

'Just so. The duke had invited Sir John Vandeleur to be guest of honour, as colonel of the Nineteenth Light Dragoons, whose victory it was, in large part. But he declined in protest of the disbandments.'

Hervey was intrigued. He had heard that the Twenty-first were to disband – the Twentieth had gone already – but nothing more. In any case, the Nineteenth, the heroes of Assaye, had only lately become lancers – with the Sixteenth, the first in the King's service. 'I am very sorry for it, on all accounts.' There were evidently other men, then, who were not disposed to obliging the duke in every particular.

'Indeed. So we must hope that the ladies are sufficiently diverting this evening.'

Hervey glanced up and down the table. 'For the main part, I should say there is no doubt of it!'

The ADC smiled and nodded while tucking into a cheese-cake with surprising gusto after all that had gone before. 'Lady Katherine is engaging company,' he suggested between mouthfuls.

'Yes, yes,' said Hervey, a little unsure. 'We have had plenty of conversation.'

'She greatly enjoys company when she rides every day.'

Hervey heard the suspicion of a warning, but before he could press the ADC to more, Lady Katherine turned again to him. 'We ladies are being bidden to retire. Will you attend upon my husband and me afterwards, Captain

Hervey – when, that is, Colonel Warde has done with you?'

'With great pleasure, madam.' He rose as a footman drew back her chair.

She smiled warmly at him. 'Until later, then.'

Hervey turned back to the ADC, but that officer was already moving to attend on the duke, as, it seemed, was the officer who had been on Lady Katherine's right. So he himself closed further towards the middle of the table, to begin an interesting discourse with a peer, whose name he did not catch, about the prospects of reform. But soon the several conversations deferred to the duke's, in which he expressed himself glad to see so many of rank and distinction at his table, that he considered it a worthy 'inauguration' of his new dining room, and that he intended hereupon to hold a banquet each year in commemoration of the battle of Waterloo.

The unreforming peer on Hervey's right evidently wanted some association with Waterloo too, if only in conversation (for he did not have the look of one who had ever served). But he sadly misjudged his subject. 'Did you have a good view of the battle, Duke?'

The duke's benevolent smile turned at once to a look like an angered hawk. Hervey felt himself trying to lean as far away from his neighbour as he could.

'I generally like to see what I am about,' came the icy reply.

It fair chilled the company. Hervey did not relish an encounter with the duke in such a humour.

The day was saved by the only man at the table who could do so. 'And thank the great God that you do see what you are about, Duke, for I am in no doubt England would not have triumphed without you!'

The great man turned to his right. 'Thank you, Bathurst.' He said it gravely rather than with any surprise or gratitude. He had heard as much many times.

Earl Bathurst, Secretary for War and the Colonies for the

past seven years, had been raised in Apsley House, indeed had sold it to the duke's elder brother, but it was not the time to make any reference to it. 'And we thank you for your magnificent hospitality this evening.'

There were tentative 'hear, hears' from around the table.

The duke nodded. Then he rose suddenly. The gentlemen were to rejoin the ladies, and sooner than both had expected.

In the drawing room, Hervey refused any more wine and began to contemplate instead his opportunity to take leave. Colonel Warde had not sought him out, and he had just judged the moment right to approach the duke; but to his considerable surprise he saw Lord Combermere himself striding across the room towards him.

'Captain Hervey, I fear I did not recognize you at first. It is a long time since that day at Toulouse, and indeed Paris. Do you recall?'

Hervey smiled broadly at the recognition, and at Combermere's engaging humility. 'Indeed I do, sir. Of course I do!'

'You're back with the Sixth, I gather?'

'Yes, sir.' He presumed 'back' referred to the assignment in India.

'Lankester's a good man. The Towcester business – dreadful, quite dreadful.'

Hervey was astonished that Combermere should know of it, but he had not time to reply before a hand grasped the general's arm. 'What do you say to this officer, Combermere? He refuses an order.'

Combermere threw his head back. 'Hah! I should think he has very good cause, Duke!'

Hervey felt the same hawklike gaze on him as he had seen at table.

'That is just as I told my secretary. I shall say good night then, Hervey. I wish you fortune in the east.' He turned again to his former commander of cavalry. 'A word with you, Combermere, before Bathurst leaves.'

'Of course, Duke,' said Lord Combermere, and then, holding out his hand, 'Good fortune to you, Hervey!'

When they had turned, Hervey placed his coffee cup on a side table and made to leave, but he felt a tap on his shoulder.

'You did not keep your word, Captain Hervey.'

He turned to find Lady Katherine. 'Oh . . . I am sorry, madam. We were overlong in the dining room, I fear. I was about to leave.'

'You do not have to leave London this minute, do you?'

'No, madam, but it has been a long day, and—'

'Of course. I would not detain you, Captain Hervey. I know how hard is an officer's day in service. Why do not you accompany me in the park tomorrow? I ride most days there. You will find it most invigorating.'

'I . . . I did not bring a horse, Lady Katherine.'

'Then I can certainly provide you with one. Where are you staying?'

Hervey saw there was no way out of it save by the severest measures. But Lady Katherine's eyes twinkled very appealingly, and her face had a most tempting blush. 'The United Service Club, ma'am.'

'I shall have one of my grooms there at eleven, Captain Hervey. And you shall join me for luncheon afterwards. Oh, and you must call me *Kat*.'

Hervey did not sleep well that night. His pleasure in Lady Katherine's eyes, her entire form indeed, was intense, for they were charms which even prodigious effort could not have ignored. And then in the middle hours, when the wine had begun to lose its effect, he had been visited by remorse in succumbing to her attractions. Repose came only after four, but he was woken as arranged at seven, whereupon he rose and penned a letter to Lady Katherine explaining that duty would prevent his keeping their luncheon appointment (he considered that riding in the park need have no improper tendency), and craving that she would forgive him. He called a steward to have an express boy run with the letter to Holland Park, then he shaved and ate breakfast before walking to Mr Hatchard's bookshop in Piccadilly to buy the new edition of Clator's *Farriery*. He was greatly discomposed when he learned that it would cost him twelve shillings, and he returned to his club, to meet Lady Katherine's groom, in even poorer spirits than in which he had left.

When he took the post to Tilbury that evening he thanked God that his duty called him away, for such had been his pleasure in Lady Katherine Greville's company in the park that he was glad of not being put further to the test. She had, however, extracted a promise from him to write to her with a description of Calcutta, and that, he now saw, was indeed a perilous pledge.

PART TWO

INDIA

The European Power which is now established in India is, properly speaking, supported neither by physical force nor by moral influence. It is a piece of huge, complicated machinery, moved by springs which have been arbitrarily adapted to it. Under the supremacy of the Brahmins the people of India hated their government, while they cherished and respected their rulers; under the supremacy of Europeans they hate and despise their rulers from the bottom of their hearts, while they cherish and respect their government.

Abbé Dubois
A Description of the Character, Manners and Customs of the
People of India, and of their Institutions, Religious and Civil, 1810

CHAPTER THIRTEEN
THE BAY OF BENGAL

Calcutta, six months later

THE CALCUTTA JOURNAL

Yesterday there were received at Fort William Lieutenant-Colonel Sir Ivo Lankester and the officers of His Majesty's Sixth Light Dragoons, who are to augment the Company's Bengal establishment, and in their honour there was given a fête-champêtre by the Governor-General and Lady Hastings. The gardens were brilliantly illuminated with many thousands of coloured lamps; an eminent operator in fireworks had been brought from Lucknow to display his talents; the company appeared in fancy dresses, those that chose it wore masks. Ranges of tents were fixed in different parts of the garden, wherein tables were laid covered with all the dainties the best French cooks could produce, for the accommodation of three hundred persons, besides which every room in the Fort was stored with refreshments of every sort and kind; different bands of martial music were stationed in several parts of the gardens, and also in the house, with appropriate and distinct performers for the dancers. The road approaching the Fort was for the last mile lighted up with a double row of lamps on each side, making every object as clear as day. In short, nothing could exceed the splendour of the preparations. And this being the first such occasion after the conclusion of the Thirty Days of official mourning for His Late Majesty's passing, many were the opportunities taken to drink to the long life and health of His Majesty King George the Fourth.

For Hervey, however, nothing could have made the evening more agreeable than the inclusion of two particular names in the Governor-General's list of guests. He had been able to call on them the afternoon before, but only for a short time, so active were his duties with horses and men alike. A card had awaited him at the regimental agents in the city, delivered promptly with letters from home brought by the overland route through Alexandria. 'Mrs Eyre Somervile' was engraved on pearl-white card, struck through by the pen with 'Emma' written below, and in the same neat round hand 'wishes you would call on us at Number 3, Fort William on the earliest occasion.'

Almost the last letter Hervey had written from England had been to Eyre Somervile at Fort George, Madras, with the payment of a considerable premium so that it should go overland too. The card came as no surprise therefore, except in locating its sender in Calcutta, for the marriage of the Collector of Guntoor and Philip Lucie's sister had long been a presumption in Madras. But it did not diminish Hervey's delight at the early prospect of seeing them again. To both he owed, at the least, the preservation of his reputation; and very probably his life.

And now, the day after the *fête-champêtre*, he was dining with them both as their sole guest, his duties done until two days following, and thus with an easy repose before him.

'You are the toast of Council, Hervey,' said Somervile, refilling his glass and passing the decanter to his wife. 'Likely as not they'll vote you half a lakh next week. It is a prodigious achievement.'

'Five horses only!' agreed Emma Somervile. 'The native

200

cavalry lost that many last summer in one day when the Hooghly was in spate.'

Hervey smiled with satisfaction. 'We were fortunate in having a landing at the Cape. But the saving was in the arrangements aboard the transport. The captain was uncommonly obliging. There are half a dozen troopers with wounds and sprains, though. My own groom's mare is still on the sick list.'

'All the same, Hervey, to bring ashore so many fit horses is truly remarkable,' said Somervile emphatically.

Emma's ears had pricked at the mention of Hervey's groom. 'Is he the dragoon who was with you before? The one who spoke so strangely?'

'The same.'

'A good and faithful servant indeed,' she replied, smiling. 'I shall look forward to seeing him again. Do you recall him, Eyre?'

It had been three and a half years since last Hervey had shared a table with Eyre Somervile, and with Emma Lucie as she had then been; but the years had fallen away in as many hours this evening, and the fellowship born of those few but strenuous months in Madras and Chintal was now returned in full and easy measure. Time played its tricks in India, the Rajah of Chintal had once told him, and in the silence that Somervile took to light his cigar, while Emma Somervile cast a sharp eye over the khitmagars clearing away the last of the Company china (these Bengalis were not to be compared to her trusty Madras Telingas), Hervey imagined himself once more in that comfortable dining room at Fort George, the day he had swum ashore through the Coromandel breakers with Jessye. That was, indeed, where he would have wished to be, with all that then lay before him. And he was surprised when it next occurred to him that Henrietta's death was closer in time to that day than to this; so often he could barely remember what had filled the months since her passing, so that it now seemed only as yesterday. Six months at sea had served to dull a little more of the ache, but such was the ship's routine, its monotony often as not, that the passage might have been one month or twelve. On good days he could go for hours without even the remembrance of Henrietta. These were usually days when the weather was ill or the horses distressed, and the body was so active that the mind was somehow uncoupled. But there were other days when suddenly, his thoughts vacant, a black cloud of despair would settle over him, and only the knowledge that he must face his dragoons could shift it. And once – but only once – he had leaned long on the rail watching the Atlantic swell, wondering what release the cold depths brought to those who were cast, one way or another, into the ship's foamy wake.

Smoke billowed ceilingwards from where sat the erstwhile Collector of Guntoor, now fourth in Council of the Bengal Presidency. He had put on weight. A stone, Hervey thought, perhaps more. And he had less hair than before. But with these gains and losses had come an evident increase in contentment. There was none of the disputatiousness of that first dinner, where he had seemed at pains to challenge hosts and guest alike – Emma especially – on each and every matter. Hervey thought it the contentment of the man whose standing in the world was growing, and his fortune likewise. Above all it was the contentment of the married man: that, he could recognize assuredly.

Emma, for her part, had not changed to any appreciable extent. She had ever been content, or at least at ease with herself and her faith. Her hair was perhaps a shade lighter, but she did go about without a hat. The colour of her skin was little different from many a native girl from these parts.

'Hervey, I shall leave you a quarter of an hour,' said Somervile looking at his watch. 'I am lieutenant-governor of the Fort this evening and have to certify that the gate is closed and barred.'

Hervey was much diverted by the notion of Somervile's

doing picket duty, and liked the idea of some exercise following their ample beef dinner. 'I'll come with you if you like.'

'No, no. It's a turgid affair. The khansamah will bring more port. Sit fast.'

Since Emma looked set to take more port, Hervey gave way.

When her husband was gone, Emma suggested they walk in the garden. 'It is nothing by day, I'm afraid – a poor affair of pots – but by night it is very pleasing. The stench of the city is not so bad, for one thing.'

Everyone in the Sixth, from colonel to private, had been complaining about the Calcutta stench, and colourful had been the comparisons. Private Johnson had thought it 'worse than Fargate of a Saturday night', which Hervey learned was a place of singular olfactory torment. But the Somerviles' garden was a delight to the senses at this hour. There were thuribles about the place, from which a constant stream of incense smoke sweetened the air. The day's heat, becoming oppressive even now in mid-May, had given way to a gentle balminess, and in the sky were familiar stars again, which for a full three months in the middle of the voyage they had not seen.

'There is an owl, too,' said Emma, taking his arm. 'A Scops owl, Eyre says. Eyre is very knowledgeable about birds. But I have only seen it once by day. He has little tufts above his eyes. He looks very arch.'

Hervey was charmed. At this moment they might be in Wiltshire. 'Does it make any noise?'

'Oh yes. But not like the owls at home, for he seems to have but one note only, and very soft. And he just repeats it at intervals. It sounds as if he is speaking direct with one.'

'Then I hope we shall hear him. I suspect we have scared him away.'

'Oh no,' said Emma, shaking her head. 'He is very

assured. If he were here he'd be watching us yet. He prefers the middle branches of that cedar there.'

Hervey peered unsuccessfully into the semi-darkness, for the lantern lights about the place lit only the ground.

Emma pressed a hand to his arm. 'Matthew, this is the first occasion I have had to say anything to you but on paper concerning Henrietta.'

He had known it must come. He tried not to stiffen. 'You spoke very generously in your letter.'

'Of you both, I hope you will think.'

The owl called.

'There!' said Emma. 'Nothing shrill, as an English owl.'

Hervey silently thanked the bird for his intervention. ' "I am a brother to dragons, and a companion to owls." I remember in Madras how the night noises seemed so muted after the day's tumult.'

Emma smiled. 'Tumult indeed. And yet nothing to those days in Chintal.'

The owl called again . . . 'Oo . . . ooh' – the same note, just as soft.

They said nothing, listening instead for a third.

'Oo . . . ooh,' it came after a while, and just as before.

Hervey sighed, perhaps inaudibly. 'You know, I lay sleepless in my berth on the ship night after night, without her. I just lay there thinking about her not being there. And then I would think about my not sleeping for thinking about her. There seemed no way out of thinking. And it's the same still. No matter which way I try to go it's the same. At first it was like fear, as I felt before battle. And then just an awful ache, and I had no will to do anything. Nothing seemed worth it. I must force myself even now to believe that anything is worth it. And things do seem worth it for a while. And I begin to be as before. And then the futility of it all comes back on me.'

Emma had never heard him speak from the heart. Indeed, she could not recall hearing him talk of any interior matter

204

save religion – and that in the sense of theology rather than faith. But it did not discomfit her, and although she had no direct experience of the condition he described, she had a sense of the despair at his core. And she saw at once the danger in the belief that nothing mattered. Yet she was almost as heartened as she was troubled: it was now a full two years since Henrietta's death, and the practice in India was for such rapid re-marriage – months, sometimes only weeks afterwards – that she had begun to doubt whether a man could be truly constant in life. Hervey's constancy was so admirably apparent. 'Matthew, you have not spoken of God in this.'

It had not been Emma's intention, let alone expectation, but the mention of the Divinity had at once a most salutary effect. Hervey stiffened, braced himself up. It was as if his commanding officer were approaching with a 'Captain Hervey, you have duties to attend to'.

Emma pressed him to the point. 'You remain faithful, I trust, Matthew? I could not suppose it otherwise. And He must have been a light through these last years, as before?'

How could he explain? How could he *begin* to explain? How could he tell her that each time he had looked for that light it had been in vain? That at times it was like going to the house of an old friend to find the gates closed, the door locked, the shutters fast; and then the bell unanswered. How could he say that it was only Job who spoke to him, from the page, and at times contrarily?

But again, this she sensed. 'You had an admirable practice of reading a psalm each day, as I recall.'

Hervey smiled to himself, as if at some distant happy memory. 'The psalms appointed for the day, yes. And I do still, occasionally. To hear a familiar voice, I think.'

Silence descended once more. Then the owl called again.

'View-halloo!' came Somervile's voice from the house, imitating the bird. 'A dozen paces to your right, second branch up!'

There indeed it was. 'How in heaven's name did you spy him from there? I can see him only against the sky,' exclaimed Hervey.

'I couldn't. That is where he always sits.'

Hervey smiled. 'Then I wish you had met the duke's chief of intelligence. You would have had much to speak of in the question of humbug.'

'You cannot be sure that I have not.'

Hervey narrowed his eyes mockingly, but he was largely hoist on his own device, for secrecy in such matters was the very essence of intelligence work. 'No, you are right. I cannot be sure.'

'Calculation and just the right degree of humbug. That would be the essence of intelligence work, would it not?'

'I suppose so. And am I to calculate now?'

'There is nothing to calculate, Matthew,' insisted Emma, turning to her husband. 'Really, Eyre! I think there must be more to the skills required than being an ornithologer.'

At dinner Hervey had noticed how much of a teasing dominance Emma had achieved. It appeared to be in direct proportion to Somervile's own diminution in dispute, and left the impression of a thoroughly happy balance. Theirs was indeed an altogether admirable union.

Two days later, Hervey was standing at the rails of the sandy arena which served as the summer riding school in the cavalry lines. In a couple of hours' time, mid-morning, the place would be a great cloud of dust if so much as a single horse trotted its four corners. But the bhistis had been at work from soon after dawn, and would bring their watering cans in continuous relays to damp down the manège until the sun drove all to seek the shade. Hervey knew it would get hotter, too. This May heat was nothing compared with the heavy air that would settle on them before the monsoon broke, although, being close to the sea, their discomfort would be minor compared with the garrisons on the plain further west. It was difficult to imagine that the Calcutta garrison would have need of the big, whitewashed stone school which served all three regiments during the winter. Not that the regiment was labouring greatly in the heat, Hervey had been pleased to observe; the weeks coming up through the Indian Ocean had served to acclimate both men and horses well. He had five men sick this day, probably no more than would have been the case in Hounslow, although the surgeon's prognosis in the case of Private Carrow was not good. Poor Carrow had not seen India other than the inside of the isolation hospital. He had been laid low with a fever since the transports had entered the Hooghly, and had been taken off by stretcher in a delirium as soon as anchor had been dropped. It was the last thing that Hervey had wanted, for the smiting of Carrow as soon as they had come within breath of the land had put a terrible fear into the troop. Even 'Chokey' Finch, old Indiaman that he was, had been unable to shake off the dread that they would all be taken by the Hooghly's notorious miasma before laying a foot ashore.

But Finch had rallied after a few days, and with Chokey Finch in decent spirits once more, the others had soon followed suit. Hervey congratulated himself on persuading B Troop's captain to give him up to E, for an old sweat had good tricks to teach as well as questionable ones. Watching his troop at riding school, and with a heavy heart, Hervey wished he had a dozen more sweats. Before leaving Hounslow the new men had had a rude introduction to military equitation at the hands of the rough-riders, just enough to make them secure at the trot; but now they looked like raw recruits again.

'Three months at least before a field day I reckon,' opined Serjeant-Major Armstrong, taking off his watering cap and mopping his brow with his cuff. 'But some of them have the makings, for sure. "Boiler" Smith can sit secure, as you'd expect. And Rudd has a good seat, and Wainwright too. And neither of them had been on a horse before. It was worth going to Wiltshire just for those two. And Shepherd Stent's at home in the saddle, except that he won't do as he's told. Look at that leg!'

It was not where it should be, that much was certain. Yet Hervey observed that he had his mount in hand.

'Get them 'eels down, number three, and the leg where the girth is!' bellowed Rough-Rider Serjeant Smollet. 'This is His Majesty's Light Dragoons, not a flock of sheep drovers!'

'Six months was what the colonel said we could have. It certainly won't be a *handy* troop inside of that.'

'You just missed French. I'd be the first to say I judged him too hasty. That lad puts everything he has into it.'

Hervey agreed. No one had worked harder than French on the voyage out. It could not have been easy for a youth of evident education to be below decks. 'He seems very content in his lot. Yet I believe him to have ambition.'

'Oh, I hope so, sir. Mind you, it's your credit for things, getting him to teach the likes of Mole to write. Have you seen how they look at him? As if he's a corporal already.'

Hervey smiled a little with satisfaction. 'But I was wrong about Sisken.'

Armstrong sighed. 'Ay, well . . . I could've insisted more.'

They watched a while longer in silence.

'Half the trouble is those remounts,' said Hervey, after the second of the 'Warminster pals' had dismounted involuntarily. 'They're as green as the recruits.'

'Well, I doubt we'll see better this side of Christmas, no matter what the RM says. Them 'Indoo 'orse next door reckon they've scoured the country from here to Lucknow and still haven't enough.'

Without a doubt, thought Hervey, these were the poorest-looking troop-horses since the Peninsula – and very disobliging. 'I don't understand it. I saw more quality in the rajah's stables in Chintal than I've seen in years.'

'Word in the bazaars is that the agent's got the option on every screw in Bengal.'

Hervey sighed. 'It'll be a sorry affair if we have to go and find our own remounts as well as recruits.'

They watched as the ride changed reins. A third 'pal' slid to the ground, bringing a welter of expletives from the rough-rider serjeant. The Sixth's methods were thoroughly modern, but a dragoon who would not keep his horse between himself and the ground must be put in no doubt as to his delinquency.

'You missed the best, sir.'

'Indeed?'

'McCarthy. The footiest man on a horse you ever saw. But by God he's determined. As soon as he's proficient we should make him corporal. Collins says he's like lightning with firearms.'

'And Caithlin likes him.'

'She does.'

'I think it settled then,' he said with a smile, but hardly surprised – that affair in France, the only cool head in the company. 'I'd dearly like to know how he lost his rank.'

'Fighting, for sure. Like every other Paddy. What *I'd* like to know is how "BC" lost his name. He's kept his nose clean so far, I grant you.'

As far as the barrack-room was concerned, Private Dodds might as well have been christened 'BC' as branded it.

'Well, it will out sure enough, and probably soon. And you can tell me you warned as much.'

Before Armstrong could protest, Hervey saw the commanding officer approaching, and with him the RSM.

When the colonel had closed with them the officers exchanged salutes, and the serjeant-majors stood to attention as was the Sixth's custom.

'Some way to go, I think,' said Colonel Lankester, with a bemused look.

'I think so too, Colonel,' replied Hervey, managing

not to frown too much. 'We shall need our six months.'

'Mm.'

Hervey looked at Lankester uneasily.

'I shall need to "borrow" your troop, shall we say, somewhat earlier than that.'

'Indeed, Colonel?'

'Nothing too serious, Hervey. I shouldn't worry about it. The Governor-General wants to stage a demonstration, as he puts it. The last of the Pindaree forts was overcome last month and he wants to send a message to all the spies in the city.'

'When, Colonel?'

'We have two weeks.'

Hervey's mouth fell open. 'It can't be done!'

Lankester eyed him warily but was not inclined to take his dissent to task. 'The entire brigade's to turn out – a sort of mock battle. The Governor-General intends it to be a great tamasha, as he puts it. Last one before the rains come. You need have no worry, though. As soon as the brigadier makes his intention known I shall arrange for your troop to be put in a place whence it doesn't have to manoeuvre.'

'Colonel, I fear even that is asking too much. See this ride – and they're by no means the worst. If we had schoolmasters it would not be so bad, but these have no manners whatever.'

Sir Ivo looked again at the ride. There was not a horse on the bit. 'Very well, Hervey,' he said, with a sigh. 'We must think of something that keeps them out of things altogether. Meanwhile, keep at riding school. You may have all the rough-riders, too. And there are more remounts arriving in a day or so. You shall have first choice.'

'I'm obliged, Colonel,' said Hervey. He would have done all in his power to accommodate Sir Ivo, a man of such evident integrity and so wholly lacking in vanity, but he would have been true to no one – not least to Sir Ivo himself – if he had simply said 'yes' to an infeasible task.

But for all his disappointment, Sir Ivo seemed in excellent spirits. He turned to Armstrong. 'Good morning, Serjeant-Major. How is *Mrs* Armstrong? I have not seen her since we disembarked.'

'She is very well, thank you, Colonel.'

'And busy, I hear?'

'She has the wives combining every morning, Colonel.'

'I'm grateful to her. The quarters are better than I dared hope, but the better still for some organization. What say you, Mr Lincoln?'

'I have never seen their like in all my service, Colonel,' declared the RSM. 'I might wish we had come here years ago.'

Only the adjutant knew to what lengths the commanding officer had gone to secure habitable married quarters. Lankester had written to the Court of Directors and then to Mr Canning, President of the Board of Control, and had forced their hand ultimately by pledging a sizeable sum of his own to the provision of separate lines – twice the number normally allowed. And as soon as he had become aware of how many more wives there were beyond even that number, he had sent by the express route a further requisition. The meanest dragoon and his wife had a room of their own in consequence.

'Quite a turnabout, isn't it?' said Armstrong when Lankester had gone.

'It is,' agreed Hervey, but he was disinclined to dwell on it; the memory of Lord Towcester was made all the worse by comparison with such a man as Sir Ivo.

'Well, either way, the RM's going to have a hell of a job getting yon clodhoppers to pass out of riding school this side of the monsoon. I reckon our best bet might be the leading rein for this do of the general's.'

Hervey nodded. 'It may yet come to it. And what a sight we shall then look, eh?'

* * *

The cavalry lines stood on the northern edge of the city, so that dry fodder could be had in plenty from the plain beyond, and so that horse and rider would have easy access to exercise ground. However, in the years since the building of the lines there had been a steady encroachment of squattings, the dwelling places of the little army of syces, bhistis, bearers and sweepers, and all the other 'untouchables' who eased the labour of the cavalrymen or who provided them and their officers with comforts. Their ramshackle huts stood in singular contrast to the whitened stone of the cavalry lines – the verandahed barrack-houses, offices, stores and stables – just as their occupants in their drab homespun stood in contrast to the dragoons in their blue, yellow, silver and gold. In the case of the females, on the other hand, the bright colours of the native women easily eclipsed those of the *gora log*, whose quality preferred white or pastels, and whose others still wore the dark cloth of the tenement or the cottage.

When the lines had been extended in anticipation of the Sixth's posting, many of the squattings had been dismantled and moved half a mile further onto the plain, or had simply been swept away. However, they had still increased in number as the agents began engaging labour for the new regiment; so that almost immediately on leaving the lines – and even, for that matter, the officers' lines, where stood the officers' house and its surrounding bungalows, and the married officers' quarters – the rider was presented with the sights and sounds, the tastes and smells of native India. This morning, the sun just up, the air still fresh, and the cooking fires making yet only a little smoke, Hervey was content. His gelding was getting back to hale condition, summer coat through and shining, muscle regenerate. Gilbert had endured the voyage as well as Jessye had three years before. His mouth was as soft as when the bridoon had been taken off at Tilbury, and his manners had deteriorated not a jot. But that was nothing compared with Private

Johnson's delight, his roan mare. The atrophy of the muscles over her near scapula had been truly alarming, but it had disappeared quite spontaneously – almost overnight, indeed. The veterinary surgeon had predicted that it could, but no one had had any expectation of it, for the ridge on the shoulder blade had been so prominent that it suggested some malignant growth rather than muscle damage.

'What did tha say it were called, sir?'

'Sweeny. That's what the Americans call it – at least, the ones we met in Michigan. Don't you remember that admirable farrier in Detroit who treated the serjeant-major's mare?'

Johnson did. 'Well, I can't wait to get my old girl out for a walk – that's all I'll say. T'vetinary's seeing 'er this afternoon. I reckon 'e'll pass 'er fit.'

'Let's hope so. But it was a very nasty fall.'

Nellie had fallen in a squall off Madagascar and evidently taken her whole weight on her shoulder, for the damage had been massive.

'The veterinarian believes it may be something to do with the nerve in that part, rather than the tissue,' said Hervey.

'Is that why it's come all right?'

'He says that nerves can become snared, and just as suddenly they're released.'

'It'd be a real shame if they didn't. She's t'best trooper I've 'ad.'

Hervey did not doubt it. But this was India. 'What's wrong with the one you're riding?'

Johnson looked surprised. 'What, *this*? I've seen bigger pit ponies.'

'She's going forward nicely.'

'Ay, but . . .'

'Well, what else do you want?'

Johnson looked indignant. 'Well, I'd like summat wi' a bit of reach.'

'That I grant you. But I'll warrant that pony will carry you

213

a deal further in this country than your Irish mare. And I think I'd trade a hand or two for that.'

Johnson was doubtful.

'The first remounts arrive this afternoon,' continued Hervey, brushing a particularly large horsefly from Gilbert's neck. 'I shall look them over with Mr Sledge and choose thirty at once. The sooner those recruits are in the saddle as one body the better.' He looked thoughtful for a moment. 'I ought to stop calling them recruits, I suppose.'

Johnson agreed. 'I wonder 'ow many dragoons 'as spent as long in t'ranks wi'out an 'orse afore!'

Hervey smiled. 'You're right. We must be the footiest dragoons in the line. But their musketry's good, mind – being so long cooped up. You didn't see Harkness bring down that goose at the Cape.'

''E's all right, is 'Arkness, sir. Y'know French 'as taught 'im to read proper and write.'

'Has he indeed? Harkness as well as Mole. Then French has doubly earned his pay.'

'Y'know 'is father's a parson, an' all, sir?'

The short *a* in Johnson's *father* still took Hervey by surprise from time to time. His ear for the peculiarities of Sheffield vowels – indeed, for the whole structure of the speech of those parts – was now finely attuned, but *father* always sounded peculiarly alien. Alien and rather cold, especially compared with the gentle *fayther* of Caithlin Armstrong's Cork – and Private McCarthy's, for that matter. 'Yes, I do know, but he seemed disinclined to speak of his family when first I broached it, so I didn't press him to details.'

'Somewe'er in Wales, 'e said. An' 'e said that folks there used to say them as were on t'parish were as poor as church mice, but not as poor as t'parson.'

Hervey could believe it. His own father's living may have been a poor one, but by the standards of the Welsh dioceses he knew it to be comfortable. 'Is French liked by the others?'

'Oh ay, sir. 'E used to write letters for their sweet'earts, in 'Ounslow. An' 'e's a God-fearing man an' all. Most o' t'troop respects 'im for that. But mind, 'e wouldn't 'ave 'owt to do with Corporal Sandbache when 'e came round.' Johnson lashed out at another of the early horseflies they had attracted.

Hervey smiled at the thought of 'Preacher' Sandbache believing he had a ready-made accomplice in French. Sandbache did little enough harm; that was the general opinion. And from time to time it was acknowledged that he did good. At least, the chaplain had no complaints that a Wesleyan was at work in the ranks, for the chaplain was by any reckoning a good man, and the first to acknowledge that his ministry beyond the church parade was largely ineffective. French was evidently a man to watch, then. Hervey had thought as much from the beginning. But favouring a dragoon who might be a gentleman's son would hardly have been a kindness, especially in the confines of a transport. Better then that he had left him as he had, to earn the trust of his comrades, for once French had won it, Hervey could use his talents keenly.

'What do you think of McCarthy?'

Johnson did not reply at once. It was not that he ever paused to think how best to express something – he spoke entirely as he found – rather that he had no perfect opinion of McCarthy. ''E keeps 'imself to 'imself. T'others've been biding their time wi' 'im, I think. But I'll tell thee this, sir: I can't see as 'e'll ever be 'appy on an 'orse.'

Hervey was all too fearful of this latter. But McCarthy had his talents, for sure. If he could not learn to ride then there were other places he could serve – though it was sabres the troop had need of most. 'The Sisken business was a miserable affair. The first time in the regiment.'

Johnson screwed up his face. ''E pissed 'imself that often everybody wondered if 'e knew where t' 'eads *were*!'

'Johnson!' But Hervey knew it was little use protesting,

even mildly, at the soldier's black humour. It was, in any case, equally the soldier's strength when times were bad. But whatever had driven Private Sisken to hang himself in the ship's heads, it was a poor thing that a dragoon – even one only partially trained – should reach such a state of mind without his fellows or his superiors knowing it. Armstrong, for all his rough tongue, had felt the unstated rebuke as keenly as had Hervey.

But why Sisken had made a crude noose of hemp for himself, when drowning was the easier and surer way, had been the question on everyone's lips. A watery grave was anyway what the man got the following day, the chaplain commending himself to the dragoons by ignoring the statutes against Christian committal of those who had taken their own lives. Indeed, the chaplain preached as perhaps he had never done before, calling upon the assembled company to 'give thanks to Almighty God that he has given us, his unworthy children, the strength to endure where his servant Jeremiah Sisken had insufficient'. So that next day, for the first time, he was received below decks with some regard rather than with mere toleration.

'I should like you to come with me to look at the remounts,' said Hervey, suddenly determined to change the conversation. 'You can ask Mr Seton Canning's groom to stand evening stables for you.'

Johnson saw no cause to object. He trusted Lingard better than any man in the Sixth to stand his duty with the chargers. 'Where will they be?'

'The adjutant says they'll be corralled somewhere out here.' Hervey scanned the plain around him, shading his eyes against the low eastern sun as he turned. To north and west the country was empty but for the odd scrubby tree. The earth was baked and fruitless, for there were no cuts from the Hooghly here by which a ryot could irrigate a little patch for his maize and beans, and no grass that even a goat might subsist on. East of them lay the military lines and the

Chitpore road, which ran north from the Company's city to the 'official' native quarter, with its temples and the prominent houses of grand Bengali merchants. They were white-painted like those of the Company sahibs, and a curious mix of styles – Mahommedan chiefly, the inheritance of the Moghuls, and Grecian, the influence of the Portuguese. 'But I'm dammed if I can see a solitary fence post,' said Hervey, lowering his telescope.

'Which way are they coming?'

Hervey pointed. 'Lucknow. There's a veterinarian who's set up stud farms all over the Company's territory. Apparently Lucknow is his best.'

'Would that be Mr Moorcroft?'

Hervey was impressed. 'Yes. How had you heard of him?'

'One o' t'sutlers used to work for 'im. 'E said that 'e used to keep goin' off into t"ills an' comin' back wi' 'orses. An' ev'ry time they got smaller.'

'What do you mean, "every time"?'

'Ev'ry time, 'e came back wi' smaller 'orses.' Johnson sounded disapproving.

'You don't think he might have been prescient in his breeding policy, then?' said Hervey, trying to suppress a smile at his groom's absolute determination in the matter of size.

Johnson merely shrugged.

By late in the afternoon, the part of the plain where they had stood that very morning was transformed into a sight reminiscent of many a horse fair in England.

'Not exactly as I had imagined,' sighed the commanding officer, casting his eyes left and right dispiritedly. 'I'm not sure that any of them are up to weight.'

Threescore horses stood tethered in running lines, a tail swishing here and there at the odd persistent fly, but otherwise motionless. They were tired from the march, and from the sun which, though low now in the west, had not lost quite

217

all of its formidable strength. The syces had brought them south from Jessor in five days – eighty miles of flat, lush country, at least to begin with, but with two sizeable rivers and a dozen smaller ones to cross. Had the horses been copers' stock, the syces would have rested them another day to let them pick up sufficiently to win the buyer's eye, but these animals were the progeny of the Company's stud department. They were for issue, not for sale.

'They appear tractable, at least, Colonel,' suggested Hervey.

Colonel Lankester nodded, and then smiled. 'But Hugh Rose won't like it much. Especially not when you've had first pick.'

That Captain Hugh Rose had come with his troop to India had been a surprise to many, for it had been assumed he would exchange with some impecunious officer in another regiment and pay the difference (the price of his troop had plummeted as soon as the Sixth had been warned for the posting). But Rose had regained his appetite for the field in Canada, and now wanted to see the east – for a year or so at least, he said. Leaving his bays behind had not been easy, however. Though D with its chestnuts had been unquestionably the prettiest on parade, A Troop had been the more striking, especially when coats were shining with sweat. And there was nothing that Hugh Rose had liked better than to trot them past at a review and hear the admiration of the onlookers, especially if they were female. He had, after all, put no small sum of his own into his troop's horses.

Well, sighed Hervey to himself, the leader of A Troop was not going to enjoy that acclamation with *these* for remounts. 'I think I will leave him the biggest, though, Colonel. From what I observed before, the smaller breeds are the better doers here.'

'And that is what I have heard, too,' said Lankester, sounding hopeful. 'But as the Company expects us to make an impression, I am rather perplexed.'

Hervey did not respond. Big men on big horses might impress the country powers at a durbar, but that might not be enough. Instead he turned his attention to a dozen or more little Marwaris at the end of the line, a mixed bag of colours, none of them standing much above fourteen hands. 'Pit ponies,' Johnson was no doubt thinking. 'I've seen these before, Colonel. They're very tough.'

Colonel Lankester looked at them curiously. 'What extraordinary ears!'

The Marwaris' ears were turned in so much that when they were pricked they almost touched, giving the appearance of horns. 'I don't know why it is so,' replied Hervey. 'There's a lot of Arab in them, but that can hardly be the cause.'

'What is your opinion, Mr Sledge?'

The veterinary surgeon stepped forward, still minded to speak only when spoken to, even with so agreeable a commanding officer as Sir Ivo Lankester. 'I know nothing of their ears, Colonel, but I would not be inclined to regard it as an unsoundness. I would be more troubled by what I am given to understand is their tendency to sickle hocks, and their reputation for uncertain temper.'

Hervey was as impressed as the commanding officer by Sledge's research.

'But sickle hocks you can recognize easily enough, can you not?' Sir Ivo suggested.

'Oh, indeed, Colonel. Anyone may. And if I were buying for myself I should not take such a case: the risk is not worth it. But a fault of conformation is not necessarily an unsoundness.'

Sledge was of the new stamp. Whereas Veterinary-Surgeon Selden, the Sixth's sulphur-tinged veteran of the Peninsula, had turned to the fledgling science from a Guy's Hospital dissecting room, David Sledge, a son of the manse, was a product of the new Veterinary College in Camden Town. Why he had eschewed a lucrative civil practice in

England for the indignities of one in the service was unclear, for his prospects, even under a colonel like Lankester, could not have been greatly appealing. Although he was classed as a cornet for the first ten years of his service, he was on a par with that rank only for the purpose of allotting quarters. And it would be a full twenty years before he could be classed as a captain. For the time being, however, Mr Sledge was an active and diligent veterinarian, and had won an unusual degree of respect among both officers and the ranks alike.

The commanding officer turned to Hervey. 'Am I to take it, then, that you would have these as first preference, subject to Sledge's approval?'

'Yes, Colonel. There seem to be a score or so of them. The rest I should have to search the lines for, but there look to be some promising types.'

The commanding officer now turned full round to Private Johnson. 'And what is your opinion?'

Johnson did not hesitate for a moment. 'Well, Colonel, it won't be so far for t'recruits to fall, that's for certain. But Cap'n 'Ervey says these things is right good doers, so I reckon we should be pleased.'

Johnson's display of both independence and loyalty pleased captain and commanding officer alike. Hervey was especially heartened to hear a private man speak up so, and use 'colonel' to his commanding officer, as had long been the Sixth's custom until the late unhappiness. 'I fear there shall be some rib-bending in this, however,' cautioned Lankester, smiling still. 'You may yet be known as the pony troop, Hervey.'

'Handsome is as handsome does, Colonel.'

'You're right, of course. But you may wait a deal of time before you have a chance to prove them handsome doers.'

Hervey knew it all too well. The review was closer at hand than they could possibly manage.

CHAPTER FOURTEEN
A GREAT TAMASHA

Two weeks later

That fortnight was a time of back-breaking toil for both men and horses. Hervey's troop got the last of their remounts, more Marwaris, only five days before the brigade review. They looked puny even before they stood next to those of the other troops, who could at least form a decent front with their English troopers. But if any dragoons in the other troops had taunted them, E Troop could not have heard, for they were roused a full hour before the rest of the regiment and turned in a full hour later. Yet even by such means – a working day of sixteen hours – the troop was scarcely able to advance in column of threes at more than a walk, and the leading rein, about which Armstrong and others had joked, looked more and more likely to be their deliverer. And the sick list had grown – no malingerers these, for the NCOs would only let them report sick if the farrier had first given his opinion. And only a week ago poor Smith, 'the Boiler' as all and sundry had called him, had fallen to a fever after evening stables and was dead by first parade next day.

'They're so small we could walk next to 'em and at three 'undred yards it'd look as if we were mounted!' Johnson had opined early on.

Hervey had replied that it was not so bad an idea. 'We are dragoons after all.'

The day of the review was on them, however, and finely run it was, for the gathering clouds spoke of the south-west monsoon which would before long engulf this last dry corner of India. On the cusp of what seemed bearable and what was not, the quality and the fashionable of Calcutta were driving out onto the plain north-west of the city to see the review of the 1st Bengal Cavalry Brigade. There could not have been a nabob or a potentate anywhere in the Bengal Presidency who would not be there, as well as many from the adjoining princely states. That, at any rate, was Lord Hastings's intention.

And it seemed that the Governor-General had likewise deported from the city every piece of canvas. For a week and more, bullock carts and elephants had trudged back and forth to the review ground, by a different road so as not to rut the one to be used by the guests, with marquees and rugs and hangings, tables, cushions and chairs, and all manner of little comforts so that the princes and powers might see the wealth to which the Honourable Company had resource. And the Bengal Sappers had constructed a canvas pavilion where the guests might ease themselves, served by fresh running water the like of which no ryot could imagine, the whole bedecked with streamers and bunting so that it might have been the marching pavilion of the Great Moghul himself.

What choice food and wine was to be served, Hervey could only guess; but the whole regiment knew that since midnight the elephants had been porting yakhdans filled from the Fort William ice houses. The dragoons themselves at this minute would have pledged themselves to hefty stoppages of pay for the contents of those hay-boxes, for although their canteens were full, the water in them was warm. They would enjoy the same spectacle of the review as the nabobs, albeit from not so good a vantage point, but without shade or punkahs they could scarcely hope to enjoy it nearly so much.

Orders for the review itself had come at dusk two evenings before, and Sir Ivo had assembled his troop-leaders to discuss how best to expedite them – a sensible course, the captains agreed afterwards, and one which only a commanding officer secure in his own position would have contemplated. The scheme was straightforward enough. Compared with some of the field days they had known at Hounslow it was indeed easy, not to mention the real evolutions many of them had performed for the Duke of Wellington that memorable day five years ago. Save for one thing: the state of training of the remounts. For the first four troops it was not perhaps so great a problem since the dragoons themselves were seasoned, but Hervey faced a compound difficulty of greenhead dragoons and greenhead horses. More than once during the two weeks which had passed since that conversation with Sir Ivo he had found himself wondering why the colonel had not spread the new recruits of both species across the regiment. From a commanding officer's point of view it was better, probably, to be sure of four troops than to be not so sure of five, but Hervey had felt the price of that surety very keenly as he realized that all E Troop might do was stand and watch.

The plan which emerged from the colonel's colloquium was for the first four troops to form two squadrons as the *masse de manoeuvre* on the right of the line; the two other regiments of the brigade were, after all, junior. In close order they would be an impressive sight with their blue coats and pipeclay crossbelts, white shakos and plumes (the brigadier wanted plumes, most emphatically). The trumpeters were good and well practised, and the officers were confident they could carry out the expected evolutions. Hervey's troop, on the other hand, were to remain within sight of the noble spectators, dismounted and in reserve, and would mount only when the 'battle' was won, so that they could retire from the field as the squadrons rallied. There was no distinction in that, Hervey rued, but by the same token there was no danger of his dragoons being overmatched.

And so here, the day of the review, E Troop were mustered, thirty-eight strong, standing easy, sweat glistening on horses and men alike. The NCOs were chafing at being nursemaids when they might have been galloping with their fellows in the other troops, and Hervey was trying hard to conceal his own mixed feelings. The Sixth had worked into the silent hours on their equipment, so that it shone now in the bright sunlight, whether steel or leather. And none had worked harder than E Troop who, though they were to make themselves scarce at the earliest opportunity, knew nevertheless that eyes would be upon them from the moment they led out their horses in the regimental lines.

In troop columns of threes, the Sixth had marched onto the exercise ground behind the Bengal horse, so that when the brigade turned into line they should be on the right, as their seniority required, with the artillery to their right in turn. At any distance it was an imposing sight, speaking of order and discipline, and a disposition for concerted action which must be the envy of the country powers. At the canvas pavilions, the assembled potentates were watching to a commentary by the major of brigade as relays of khitmagars served iced champagne and sherbet.

'The brigadier, having received word that the enemy is approaching, has sent out scouts to range beyond the ridge,' explained the brigade-major through a speaking trumpet, pointing out the direction. 'Mindful that the enemy may deploy his own scouts forward, a line of vedettes will be established to counter them.'

The brigade-major handed his speaking trumpet to the officer who was to continue with the commentary, and rode down to the brigade commander – the signal for the vedettes to deploy and the horse artillery to unlimber. According to the carefully worked scheme there would be a quarter of an hour before the vedettes would signal the enemy's approach, and so the brigadier concluded he had time for one small innovation. He cursed himself for not thinking of it before.

Hervey observed him through his telescope – Major-General Sir Mortimer Massey, a man of whom no one had heard until New Orleans, when he had parleyed successfully with the Americans to take the wounded from the field. He was an impressive figure, tall in the saddle, plumed, scarlet-coated, riding a grey Arab that would have made Bonaparte himself envious.

'Sir Ivo,' said the general, as he trotted up to the Sixth. 'Seeing the ground this morning, I am much taken by the possibilities of that nullah over to your right.'

Sir Ivo looked to where the general was indicating.

'I believe it ought to be possible to get a troop along it unseen to all the nabobs, to come up on the flank of the vedette line.'

Sir Ivo glanced about the field to the points of reference. 'I see it, General. To what advantage, may I ask?'

The general frowned. 'By heavens, you're slow this morning, Lankester! As the enemy come over the ridge and the vedettes pull back, the troop can take them in the flank. It will be the devil of a surprise to the nabobs!'

The proposition was entirely fair, though Sir Ivo wondered why, since this was a day to impress, they had not rehearsed it. Hervey's troop might be in want of riding practice, but the other troops had scarcely had much opportunity for field drill. But he could hardly balk at so elementary a manoeuvre. 'Very well, General. Shall you give me the signal?'

'No, you may judge it for yourself, Sir Ivo. There's no point in waiting for my off when you'll see the vedettes signalling as well as I shall.'

A sensible decision, thought Sir Ivo, if late in the day.

The general reined about and trotted to the centre of the brigade.

'Captain Rose and Mr Assheton-Smith, please.'

The commanding officer's voice was raised no higher than if he were speaking to his charger, but the word was passed at once to A Troop's leader, nearest the guns, and the adjutant in the supernumerary rank.

'Gentlemen, the brigadier has determined a change in the manoeuvres,' said Sir Ivo as they rode up. He explained the intention.

'I'll take a look then if I may, Colonel,' said Rose.

'Yes. But do it covertly.'

Rose saluted and returned to his troop.

'A pity we did not have more time before today,' said Sir Ivo to the adjutant. 'It would have been a fair question of E Troop.'

Bands played for the entertainment of the spectators meanwhile, as the 'enemy', a regiment of native infantry, advanced to the ridge in full view of the pavilions but concealed from the brigade. The design was that when the infantry reached a bullock-cart track which ran obliquely across their front, some five hundred yards short of the ridge, the vedettes would start to signal their approach. The general, a prudent man, had also placed a galloper to observe from a flank so that he could be warned independently. The infantry had rehearsed the manoeuvre twice, but in the early morning; the heat was now unexpectedly slowing their advance, so that the general was becoming anxious. When he saw his galloper approaching, dust rising behind him and exaggerating his speed, he was half convinced that something was amiss.

'The infantry have reached the track, sir,' said the lieutenant, saluting, pleased that he had been able to bring the report his general wished to hear.

But General Massey was disturbed by the news. He turned to his brigade-major. 'Why in heaven's name aren't the vedettes signalling, Neville? Can't they see?'

Brigade-Major Neville could have no more idea than the general. He turned to the galloper. 'You saw with your own eyes they had reached the track?'

'Sir! With my own eyes.'

The general looked about anxiously. He saw Hervey's troop standing dismounted a furlong away. 'Good God, Neville. What's Sir Ivo doing? He's not moved that troop into the nullah yet!'

The brigade-major turned round in the saddle to see for himself. 'If the vedettes haven't reported anything, General, Sir Ivo has no notion he should move them.'

The general, now very agitated, turned back to his galloper. 'Go and tell Hervey's troop to get into that nullah at once!'

'What are they to do there, sir? I did not know of this part of the scheme.'

'Tell him, Neville!' snorted the general.

The brigade-major obliged them both.

The galloper lost no further time. Hervey saw him approaching, the trail of dust indicating more speed than his descent from the ridge. 'Hallo, Shawe,' he said, returning the salute, bemused by the apparent urgency. 'Who are you looking for?'

'*You*, sir! The general says you are to get into the nullah at once. The enemy are approaching the ridge.'

Hervey looked astonished. 'Shawe, I haven't the faintest idea what you mean!' He looked again towards the ridge, then lowered his telescope. 'And the vedettes are stock-still.'

Lieutenant Shawe, his artilleryman's coat more earth-coloured now than blue, was equally perplexed. 'You have no orders at all for the nullah?'

'No! We're to stand here looking alert, that is all.'

Lieutenant Shawe rattled off the brigade commander's intention.

Hervey understood perfectly. 'But those were not Sir Ivo's orders, and I am under his direct command. I think you had better go and see him, and then hare back to the general.'

The galloper saluted, reined about and kicked up even more dust than before as he spurred away.

Hervey turned to his trumpeter. 'Storrs, bring me the officers and sar'nt-major, please.'

It took less than a minute to assemble them. Hervey told them of the exchange, and what they would have to do if it came to it. He had no idea what the nullah was like, how wide it was or how steep its banks. They would have to lead the horses and mount at the last minute, though how much time they would have he couldn't say.

The officers had just retaken post when another cloud of dust signalled the return of the brigadier's galloper. 'Looks like you were right,' said Armstrong.

'I wish I had *not* been,' replied Hervey, handing his reins to Johnson and taking his telescope from the saddle pouch again. 'There's no sign of movement in those vedettes.'

'Captain Hervey, brigade-major's compliments, and would you execute the orders at once.'

With no sign from the vedettes, Hervey could not see the necessity of such urgency. 'Have you spoken with Sir Ivo?'

'Captain Hervey, sir, those are the brigadier's express orders, and they were most imperative.'

'Yes, but have you spoken to Sir Ivo?'

'The general himself has, sir. Really, Hervey, there's no time to lose!'

Hervey had received an order, in front of his troop, and he was not in possession of more information than was the brigadier. 'Very well, Mr Shawe.' Johnson handed him back the reins. 'E Troop, right incline for column of route!'

Dragoons shortened reins to lead, and Hervey took post at the head of the column.

'Forward!'

It took only a few minutes to reach the nullah, and as they began to descend the shallow bank, Hervey glanced at the ridge. The vedettes were circling.

Once the troop were all safely down, Hervey shortened his reins again and called, 'Double march!' for the enemy was supposed to gain the ridge ten minutes after the vedettes began signalling their approach, and he had no idea how difficult the bed of the nullah would get.

E Troop sweated and blew as they struggled over the shingle bed but they made progress, a good hundred yards in the first minute. Hervey thought they must be in line with the squadrons in another two. If they could keep this up they would make the ridge with a couple of minutes in hand.

But in two more, with no warning whatever, Hugh Rose's troop plunged into the nullah in line, checking not the slightest from a fast trot, so that neither A nor E Troop could do anything to evade collision. Men shouted, horses squealed. Many of both fell, for the most part Hervey's. Dragoons cursed each other, some lashed out. NCOs bellowed to regain order. Loose horses raced back down the nullah and knocked over dragoons who had survived the first collision. They would have floored Armstrong had he not already sprung into the saddle. Officers looked stunned. Over to their left the horse-gunners opened blank fire, and in a few seconds smoke was pouring into the nullah to add to the confusion.

'What the deuce are you about, Hervey?' shouted Rose, as he came on him struggling to get his mare up.

'Trying to follow orders!' Hervey almost spat the words. 'What are yours?'

'To get up to the ridge and take them in the flank,' coughed Rose, the smoke engulfing them.

'Mine too. But there's damn little chance of that now. You'd better get on!'

Hervey looked back down the column. He could not recall any greater disorder by daylight. There was nothing for it now but to lick their wounds, real and imagined.

The brigadier was first on the scene, a quarter of an hour

later. By then Hervey had the troop back in column, but two horses, with a broken leg apiece, lay with bullets in their brains. Private Mole sat supported in the saddle, his leg splinted with his sabre, harelip accentuating his sorry state. Private Parkin, one of the 'pals', stood holding a bloody bandage to his right eye. Half a dozen others had burst lips, missing teeth or broken ribs. And two horses were still bleeding severely from severed arteries.

'Hervey, what in the name of God . . .?' The brigadier looked about incredulously.

'Your orders, sir,' said Hervey.

Seton Canning and Cornet Vanneck looked away.

'I *beg* your pardon?'

'We were executing your orders, General, when A Troop plunged on us – with the same orders, it seems.'

General Massey had not the faintest idea what he was talking about. 'What do you mean, "with the same orders"?'

Hervey knew at once what had happened. Perhaps he had the advantage of a quarter of an hour on the brigadier, but he was not sure that that was Massey's handicap. His anger he kept in check, but only just. 'Sir, I surmise you gave Sir Ivo orders to send a troop into the nullah.'

'Of course I did. But not two!'

'But that, indeed, was the effect. You assumed Sir Ivo would order *my* troop to the nullah. Had you sent the hastening order to *him*, General, there would have been no confusion.'

'I don't like your tone one jot, Hervey!' The brigadier sounded more dismayed than angry.

Hervey's anger now matched the brigadier's dismay. 'And, I, with respect, sir, do not like having my troop cut about like this. Had we been in action—'

The brigadier had heard enough. 'Captain Hervey! You exceed yourself, sir! I imagine you lay this blame on me, but I might remind you there is a level of command between the two of us!'

Serjeant-Major Armstrong had closed to Hervey's side soon after the exchange began. He now grasped his captain's arm from behind and squeezed hard.

Hervey made no reply to the brigadier.

'I fancy we shall have all this out on return to the lines,' said General Massey gruffly. 'You had better take your troop back, Captain Hervey.'

Armstrong released his grip, and Hervey saluted.

CHAPTER FIFTEEN
EXTRA DRILL

Next day

'I do not say the brigadier is an *unreasonable* man, Eustace.'
Sir Ivo paused and then sighed. 'But I do believe he might
have had the grace to withdraw on the matter, for the
nonsense was his doing – no one else's.'

Late in the evening, after stables and the colonel's
preliminary inquiry into the affair of the nullah, the brigade-
major had come to the Sixth's headquarters bearing
unwelcome news. While, he said, the brigadier did not hold
Hervey to be responsible for events, he held his manner to
have been insolent, and required his apology in writing at
once. Sir Ivo, having no means by which he might dispute
the brigadier's judgement, had had no option but to instruct
Hervey to comply. Hervey had received this order by
protesting that he did not believe a general officer ought to
take refuge in his position when attempting to discover the
truth of a misadventure. He might have added that neither
did he think it fitting that a general officer should imply that
his – Hervey's – commanding officer bore the responsibility.
But Sir Ivo had persuaded him to write, for, as he explained,
he saw no merit in giving the brigadier a cause which
might in the end eclipse the issue of culpability in the
botched orders. And Hervey had acquiesced because

he saw the logic and held Sir Ivo in absolute respect.

But the letter of apology had not requited the general. 'Does the brigadier say in what measure he considers Hervey's letter to be insufficient?' asked Major Joynson, reading again the fair copy.

'It would seem that his "necessity for establishing the lessons of the affair" and his reference to a "real not imagined enemy" are the offending portions.'

'Yes,' said Joynson, nodding. 'I can see that would go hard with Massey. And he presumably is not best pleased with you for forwarding it in the first place?'

Sir Ivo raised his eyebrows. 'That much was implied, yes.' He sounded philosophical, but everyone knew that his pride was still hurt by the rebukes which had followed the review; the squadrons had manoeuvred well, and even the brigade-major had reported that the fracas at the nullah had remained unseen by the spectators.

'If I may speak, Colonel,' said the RSM.

'Of course, Mr Lincoln.'

'It is causing a deal of resentment in the ranks. Even though they all know Captain Hervey's troop were ordered into the nullah, they know too it was never your intention that they be there. I am afraid, Colonel, very contrary though it is, the view is that E Troop should not have gone into the nullah. And it does not help, of course, that they are largely so raw.'

Sir Ivo sighed. 'It is quite perverse. But thank you, Mr Lincoln. You will, no doubt, be speaking to your mess on the subject?'

'Yes, Colonel. Directly after orderly room.'

'Good. Armstrong behaving well?'

'Exemplary, Colonel. I gather he was a model of restraint in the nullah.'

'Perhaps he can stroll through the lines at evening stables with Serjeant-Major Bowker, and Hervey and Rose the same. A comradely show?'

The RSM returned Sir Ivo's ironic smile. 'Indeed, Colonel.'

Sir Ivo turned to the adjutant. 'Thomas, my compliments to Captain Hervey, and inform him that he'd better pick up his pen again.' He nodded to the RSM. 'And that will be all, too, Mr Lincoln. Your counsel, as always, is appreciated.'

The RSM, matchless in his turnout, even though the heavy air would have made sweat-scrapes busy on them all, saluted and left the office. As he closed the door, Joynson took off his cap and sat down.

'Colonel, I worry about Hervey. He seems his old self a lot of the time, but the anger burns still.'

Sir Ivo nodded. 'It can sometimes be a powerful force for action, Eustace. I saw many an angry man in the Peninsula carry a place with the bayonet or the sabre.'

The major knew that if he himself had had more anger he might have remained with the regiment longer in Spain. He nodded slowly. 'Of course, of course,' he said, as if still measuring the proposition. 'But, I wonder, is it conducive always to good judgement, in hot or in cold blood? Hot blood is probably the lesser to worry about. It's the slow-burning anger, the brooding, the resentment, the loss of reason which sets all the factors in a decision in their proper perspective.'

The Earl of Sussex had warned Sir Ivo that his major would serve him at all times faithfully, and in matters of administrative detail well, but that beyond this he should expect nothing. Yet Sir Ivo had a growing regard for Joynson's general wisdom, not least his modestly perceptive estimates of character in the Sixth's officers. They might all still call him 'Daddy' Joynson, but Sir Ivo had observed that his opinion was sought increasingly by them, and that was ever a sure sign – as, indeed, was the virtual absence of sick headaches. 'A glass of Madeira, Eustace?'

'Thank you, Colonel.'

Sir Ivo took a decanter and glasses from a cupboard. 'You

don't think Hervey has lost anything of his touch, do you? I mean, it just occurs to me that the Hervey of whom I'd heard might have seen that confusion before it happened.'

The major took his glass and considered the proposition. 'In truth, I've thought the same. I know that *I* should never have seen it.'

'Nor I,' said Sir Ivo, with a wry smile. 'Indeed, the notion's probably absurd. But I, too, worry. We must keep a special eye. Who are his friends, though? Eyre Somervile, I suppose.'

'Hervey would count all the officers his friends, but none would own to knowing his thoughts, not even Strickland. And I dare say that Somervile, neither, has ploughed too deep; but he's a shrewd man.'

'A *good* man. I'd have him with me in a fight any day. I'll speak with him – unless you think it better it came from you?'

The major thought about it for a moment. 'I think, let me try first. It might not do for Somervile to think he were being asked to spy on him in some way, which it might well seem if you approached him.'

Sir Ivo smiled. 'Quite so.' He pushed the decanter back across the desk. 'Tell me, Eustace, to change to happier matters, how is Frances? I have not seen her these past two weeks.'

The major smiled too. 'She is more the attention of the garrison officers than ever it seemed in England!'

Sir Ivo nodded. 'It was ever thus, I'm told, Eustace!'

At ten that evening Serjeant Collins, the regimental orderly serjeant-major, entered the wet canteen, as his orders required, to instruct the sutler to close it. It was always a tricky moment, a time when abuse had to be differentiated from good-natured banter in a split-second. Collins never looked forward to the duty, but he was one of the more practised ROSMs in the art of dealing with bibulous dragoons who fancied themselves as wits. His art was tested this night, however, by a barrage of opinion from A Troop men on the question of E Troop's proficiency; it was taken up in turn by groups from B, C and D Troops. Collins stood his ground perhaps a little too long, as if challenging one of them to more than words. He looked about to see where were the E Troop men, to nod to them to beat a retreat before it was too late, but a swaying pug from A Troop was already making his determined way towards the bar.

'I want another fookin' nog, and thou's not gooin' to stop me.' The jabbing finger left no doubt about who was not to do the stopping.

Collins braced himself.

'E Troop?' continued the pug. 'I wouldn't piss on 'em!'

Lance-Corporal McCarthy, sitting in direct line between the pug and his objective, put down his tankard and stood up. 'Time for bed, Brummie.'

The pug looked at him in disbelief. What was a piece of tape compared with *his* brawn? 'Fook off, yo' thick Paddy.'

Corporal McCarthy sighed wearily, clenched both fists, feinted with his left, then drove his right into the pug's nose.

It was the last thing that Serjeant Collins would be able to give any clear account of to the RSM the following morning.

'Major's compliments, sir, and would you attend on him at once.' Scarcely had first parade finished but that Hervey was being summoned to regimental headquarters on account of the wet canteen. He thought it a little unfair that he had not yet had advantage of his serjeant-major's reports in their entirety – Armstrong had been summoned to the RSM's office even before muster – but in any event he did not expect to be given much of an opportunity to speak.

'Sit down, Hervey,' said the major, distinctly tired of the business already. 'You'll have heard of the events of last night, I take it.'

'Yes, sir – in short.'

'In short, eh? I don't suppose any shorter than the brigadier has heard.'

Hervey looked astonished. 'The brigadier? How might he have come to hear?'

'Because the Skinner's quarter-guard had to come and relieve our own while they cleared the canteen.'

Hervey grimaced. 'Is the colonel very dismayed?'

'Not yet. He was at a ball last evening. I don't expect him back until tomorrow.'

'What is there to do?'

'Have you written that letter yet?'

'I was just about to start it.'

'Well, this is what you do, Hervey. You write it as if you had offended against Holy Writ. Is that clear?'

'Perfectly.'

The major took off his spectacles and held them up to the light, before polishing them vigorously with a silk square. 'Your Irishman will be reduced to the ranks, of course. Collins'll be lucky, too, if he scrapes clear.'

'Sir, we're not going to make any great affair of this, are we? E Troop was the butt of every dragoon's joke yesterday. They'd become pretty resentful.'

'Encouraged, no doubt, by their captain!'

'*That* is deuced unfair, sir!'

'Is it, Hervey?'

'I freely admit to my anger, but I thought to have it in good check.'

'Others may not agree. Oh, I have no very great trouble with a fray in the canteen – and neither, I should think, would Sir Ivo. The paymaster's clerks'll be the busier for a few weeks with stoppages, but that's of little moment.' The major took off his spectacles again and began rubbing them once more with the silk. 'Are you not owed any leave you might think of taking, Hervey? Say, a month or so?'

Hervey looked pained, almost affronted. 'If I *were* owed it, sir, I should not dream of taking it now.'

237

The major looked quite shamefaced. 'No, of course not. Silly of me.'

Hervey said nothing.

'You know, the trouble with these little regimental quarrels is that after a while resentment is turned towards the man at the head. Your dragoons'll weary of having to answer on these barbs.'

Hervey was well aware of it, but still made no reply. Then he took up his cap. 'Will that be all, sir?'

'Yes, yes, I think so,' said the major, apparently absently. 'But Hervey, do be a good fellow and write that letter.'

Major Joynson called on Eyre Somervile that afternoon. They had met only twice before, but Somervile was pleased to receive him: the major's note in advance had not been entirely specific, but Somervile had heard already of the affair of the nullah. Over tea, Joynson explained to him the extent of his – and the commanding officer's – concern for their mutual friend. Somervile nodded from time to time, approving the estimation.

'He will not take leave at this time – and very understandably – but he might be inclined to do so if *you* were to invite him,' said Joynson in conclusion.

Somervile thought for a moment. 'I should have said, Major, that once Matthew Hervey had determined where his duty lay, *nothing* would induce him to do otherwise. I am flattered that you think I might have some influence, but if he has determined that leave is contrary to his duty, then I very much fear he will be immovable.'

The major nodded slowly. 'And I fear that he has formed that notion very surely. Might I ask you, however, to do what is in your power to divert him these coming weeks? It will not do to have him in the lines every minute of the day.'

Somervile smiled. 'Of course, Major.'

Joynson made to rise.

'I do have a thought,' added Somervile, appearing to be

turning over an idea. 'Your object is principally to remove our friend from the garrison for a time, not from his troop.'

'The latter, to my mind, would be desirable, but yes, the principal object is to distance him from the garrison – the brigadier especially.'

'Well, an opportunity arises. I am to leave Calcutta next week for Chittagong; I shall be there some months, possibly. I see no reason why I should not apply for a troop of cavalry to accompany me.'

'That would be capital,' said Joynson, much animated by the proposition. 'Indeed, I believe it might be altogether better than his taking leave, for the change of air would serve his troop well, too. Yes, apply, do. I shall speak with Sir Ivo the minute he returns.'

Three days later, Hervey learned of his assignment to Chittagong. The opportunity to bring his troop to a proper efficiency was at once welcome, but he knew also that the talk in stable and canteen – and not least in the officers' mess – would be of 'being sent away'. However, that would be short-lived tattle, he told himself. And when they returned they would be ready to take their place on the left of the line.

'Are you able to tell me why you are sent to Chittagong?' asked Hervey of Eyre Somervile that evening.

'Of course,' said Somervile, holding out his glass to be recharged with a very well-chilled champagne. 'Lord Hastings has asked me to see what can be done with respect to the Burmans and Arakanese who have fled there.'

Hervey thought he detected that Somervile was not altogether enthusiastic. 'Does that please you?'

Somervile shrugged. 'Lord Hastings is of the opinion that *someone* must do it.'

'Lord Hastings considers Eyre to be his most knowledge-able official,' added Emma.

Hervey could believe it. Although Emma would be loyal

to the end, she was no mere distaff. In Madras, Somervile had been wholly absorbed by the language and manners of the native peoples, as fluent in Tamil as he was in Telinga, which Hervey understood had by no means been the rule in the Company for some years. But Madras and Burma were very distant from each other. 'Is this Oxford learning again? For you never said you had been in those parts.'

'Not even Oxford,' replied Somervile, nodding to the khansamah, whose appearance signalled that dinner was ready. 'When I came here to Calcutta no one seemed to know anything of the situation in the east, so wholly absorbed were they by the extirpation of the Pindarees. But the outcome of that campaign was wholly foregone, so I began a study of the eastern question, which seems to me indeed to be very grave.'

'Would you tell me of it?'

Somervile said he would. And long and serpentine would that account be, occupying the five courses of dinner and ending only with the second circulation of the port. Hervey was appalled and thrilled by turns.

When he returned to his quarters – at that time of night but an hour's drive – he was so animated by what Somervile had told him that he set pen to paper at once.

> *Fort William*
> *Calcutta*
> *via The Hnble E. India Co.*
> *Leadenhall Street*
> *London*
> *24 June 1820*

My dear Dan,

The month since I wrote to you has been of very mixed fortunes, which I shall forbear to relate in any detail since they shall like as not seem petty and inconsequential with the passing of time. It is now so excessively hot here that I feel I am melting away, although I think I recall its being hotter in Madras, and the old Company hands say that it is nothing compared with Delhi, and will in any event get hotter as July proceeds, until the Monsoon restores our comfort, at least for a little while each day. Mourning for the late King has now ended. Although we observed it strictly, all our duties of course continued. There is here a good deal of speculation and general gossip as to what shall now obtain, for, besides the question of Queen Caroline's position, it is much rumoured here that King George is in a very bad way with Dropsy, and that we shall soon have King Frederick, who would, of course, be exceedingly popular with the Army as well as the Navy. Do write with the County's opinion, Dan, so far as you can tell it.

My purpose in this letter, however, is to inform you of a further, though temporary, change of station. A few days ago I was instructed by my colonel to accompany Mr Eyre Somervile to the east of the country, abutting the kingdom of Ava, and there to bring my troop to a state of efficiency apart from the distractions of this station – which are too many. You will no doubt recall my telling you of Mr Somervile, and also of his wife, the sister of Philip Lucie, with all of whom I spent such eventful days in Madras. In the three years which have passed since my leaving, it seems the Governor-General, Lord Hastings, has taken the most vigorous and concerted measures to destroy the Pindaree menace, and there is now such peace in the whole land of India as has never before been. This much is certain, that whatever is said at home about the iniquities of the Company's policy here, the consequence for the meanest ryot, as the peasant farmer is called, is a freedom from the ravages of the bandits to which he has been too long a prey. Everyone says that there should be a peace for a decade or more, in the interior at least. But there are still those who would take advantage from their positions beyond the Company's borders or its dominions, and one such is the King of Ava, whose brutish regimen has driven very many thousands of the people of that land to seek the protection of the Company in its territory along the coast east of the mouth of the great Ganges. These people in their turn have sometimes carried out raids into the King's territory, and there has been a deal of resentment on the part of the Avan – or Burman king as some have it – Bagyidaw, a proud as well as cruel man. Lately he has sent letters to the King of Assam and to Lord Hastings demanding that all those who fled from Ava be returned. Lord Hastings is not, of course, minded to comply with such a demand. Mr Somervile is therefore to proceed to Chittagong to see what may be done to stop the raids by the dispossessed Burmans, and to ease generally the discord which obtains there. I have no great wish to be separated from the regiment at this time, but they have their duties in connection with the various treaties which are being concluded with the country powers in the wake of the Pindaree war, and I do not suppose that it will be longer than six months before Mr Somervile's mission is accomplished, as well as mine, and my troop shall then be able to take its place in the line alongside the others for the season of the winter manoeuvres. The journey is all by sea, but it should be accomplished without trouble since Chittagong is not greatly more than two hundred miles, by coastal water, and we shall have the advantage of two steam-driven vessels to tow the transports if winds are unfavourable, which of course they may well be in this season . . .

The more he wrote, the fewer were his misgivings about leaving Calcutta. The country about Chittagong sounded ideal for his purpose, and Somervile's mission would be instructive to observe. He penned a few more paragraphs – soldier's gossip, of which Daniel Coates never tired – and closed by promising to write from his new station.

CHAPTER SIXTEEN

THE EDGE OF THE SWORD

The cavalry lines, Chittagong, October

Serjeant Collins stood properly at ease facing the dozen
dragoons of the first class. He wore forage cap, coat fully
buttoned, overalls and swordbelt. The dragoons were in
watering order – overalls, shirt but no coat, and no hat –
but they too wore swords. It was more than a year since
they had taken the shilling, and yet today was their
first sword exercise. Hervey had tried to arrange for it
aboard ship from England, but it had been a perilous
business soon abandoned in favour of carbine and small-
arms drill.

'Class, atten . . . *shun!*' bawled Local Lance-Corporal
McCarthy.

A dozen pairs of boots closed together.

Corporal McCarthy marched up to Serjeant Collins,
halted, and with only slightly diminished volume
announced, 'There are twelve men on parade awaiting
instruction, Serjeant.'

'Officer on parade, Corporal,' rasped Collins, now himself at attention.

Corporal McCarthy glanced left to the corner of the
square, where he saw his troop-leader and serjeant-major
watching, and a lady too.

'Sor! There are twelve men on parade awaiting instruction, sor!'

Collins nodded. 'Fall in, Corporal.'

McCarthy turned to his right, paused to a silent count of three instead of a salute (the hatless salute had ceased to be the regimental practice), then took his place as flugelman on the right of the dragoons.

Serjeant Collins surveyed the class. 'Right,' he began, as he walked the length of the line. 'You have been chosen as the first class because Captain Hervey has observed that you have made the most progress at riding school.'

Corporal McCarthy would not have recognized the accolade in his own case; Shepherd Stent would not have thought himself worthy of any *but* the first class; Private Rudd would write home proudly to inform his mother; Jobie Wainwright was relieved only that Spreadbury, Parkin and Needham – the Warminster pals – were in the class, too; French, his dark curls as thick as a sheepskin, was the best of riding school, as everyone acknowledged; Harkness, his broad shoulders occupying the space of one and a half of the smaller dragoons, had found sitting to the trot a great trial to begin with but had mastered it in the end, and had lately become a true proficient, especially at the gallop. The remaining four had shown steady application.

'Right,' said Collins again as he retook his place in front of the class. 'Stand at ease; stand easy. Listen attentively. There are only six ways of directing the edge of the sabre. The action of the wrist and shoulder alone directs the blade; and they admit but six movements, from which every cut is derived, wherever may be its particular application to the body.'

Hervey found his thoughts returning to the first time he had heard the words as a young cornet at the Canterbury depot.

'Of the six cuts, four are made in diagonal directions, and two horizontally. The whole are equally applicable against cavalry, and may be directed on either side of the horse, but their application must depend on the openings given by the adversary and be regulated by judgement and experience in the use of the weapon. Any questions?'

There were none.

'Right then, how many ways are there of directing the edge of the blade?' Collins paused for a few seconds. 'Stent?'

'Six, sir,' said the shepherd, coming to attention.

'Correct. Of the six cuts, how many may be directed on either side of the horse?' Another pause. 'Wainwright?'

'The whole, sir,' Jobie replied, feet together.

'Correct. I shall proceed, then. Now, to make a cut with effect, and at the same time without exposing the person, there are two points which principally demand attention. The first is to acquire a facility in giving motion to the arm by means of the wrist and shoulder without bending the elbow. For in bending the elbow the sword arm is exposed, a circumstance of which the opponent will ever be ready to take his advantage.' Collins drew his sword, demonstrated the points which demanded attention, then glanced up and down the line. 'Is that understood?'

'Yes, sir,' came the reply.

'You don't sound so sure. *Is that understood?*'

'Yes, sir!' bellowed the class.

'Very well,' he growled, returning the sword to the position of rest on his shoulder. 'The next object is to attain correctness in applying the edge in the direction of the blade, otherwise it will turn in the hand, and as in that case the flat part must receive the whole force of the blow, it will in all likelihood be shivered to pieces.'

Hervey turned to Armstrong. 'A long time coming, but I think we may soon have it accomplished. We can begin the second class in a week, and the third a week after.'

'Ay, sir. There's nobody better than Collins for this.'

Emma Somervile was still watching intently. 'You say it is

straight from the manual of sword exercises, Captain Hervey, but your serjeant makes it sound as if it very much comes from the heart.'

'That too, madam. Collins once engaged a French colonel in a most ferocious duel, in sight of hundreds on both sides, and overcame him by superior swordsmanship, though the colonel, a count as I recall, must have been very practised in the art from an early age.' He thought it unnecessary to declare that the deciding blow had been a cut to the Frenchman's head which had cleft his skull in two.

'With your leave then, sir?' said Armstrong, stepping back.

'Yes; thank you, Sar'nt-Major. I shall attend at stables.'

Armstrong saluted and strode away.

'Do we watch any more?' asked Emma, sounding eager.

'If you wish,' said Hervey, willing to oblige her. 'But I had rather not watch for too long. It will only distract them.'

'In that case,' said Emma, 'let us take a turn about the civil lines. I like to see the gardens at this time of a day, when there is no one about.'

This was the time when shutters were closed, affording the occupants their privacy before callers for tea, and then the long evening of dinner and cards. It was by no means too hot to be abroad, as the sword class, hatless, demonstrated, but the customs were observed nevertheless.

Chittagong was nothing compared with Calcutta in the extent and magnificence of her buildings. Wood as well as, or in some cases instead of, stone was more in evidence, and her civil as well as military garrison was but a fraction of that of the capital of the Bengal Presidency. But it had a healthier climate, all agreed, and was a pleasant enough place to serve on temporary duty.

'There is a big black-necked stork which sits on my roof sometimes of an afternoon,' said Hervey as they came to his bungalow. 'But evidently not today.'

Emma was intent on the little garden at the front. 'I envy

you the tamarisks. The pink is so *naturally* pretty. My pots are full of things, but they look as though they're the work of a paintbrush.'

Hervey stopped, held up a hand to bid Emma to do likewise, and pointed to the fence post a dozen feet away.

Emma just saw the orange spots before the object of their attention scurried off along the rail and down the further post into the scrub grass. 'Yes, I think it the same as we have in our bathroom. The colours here are so much more vivid than the Madras geckos. I wonder why it might be?'

'Must there be a reason?'

'God surely has a purpose in Creation, Matthew?'

'Yes, I suppose . . .' He had not before imagined it extended to such details.

'There is a most interesting theory about it all. Eyre was speaking of it only last week. There is a naturalist called Lamarck, a Frenchman. Eyre has collected all his work. He suggests that living things adapt to their surroundings and then pass on the changes to successive generations.'

'How do they do that?'

Emma smiled broadly. 'In the usual way, I suppose!'

Hervey looked somewhat abashed. 'In what way does he suggest an animal's surroundings exert an influence?'

'His exemplar is the giraffe, which lengthened its neck over successive generations through its habit of grazing the tops of trees.'

Hervey frowned. 'I had imagined that it grazed the tops of trees because it had a long neck,' he replied, not altogether facetiously.

'We pass on characteristics of our own family do we not?'

Hervey's home thoughts in that instant told him it was so, and painfully. He almost checked in his stride.

Emma did not appear to notice. 'Ask Eyre to show you his books when you come to dine with us tonight. You are able still to come?'

'Yes; yes, indeed,' he replied, a shade absently. 'But I beg

247

you would forgive me if I leave earlier than usual. I have letters which I must finish if they're to go to Calcutta tomorrow. There's a packet for England at the end of the week.'

'Of course,' said Emma, brushing away a persistent dragonfly. 'Now, I must show you the aviary the collector here has built. You will not have seen it, I think?'

When Hervey wrote home that night, there was an unusual degree of contentment in his letters. Chittagong may have been restricted in its society, but that which there was was entirely agreeable to him. He liked the country, with its wooded hills within an easy day's ride, and the climate was very equable. Its people, both country and city, seemed contented, and there was not the clamour of Calcutta – and certainly not the stench. Above all, his troop was making progress. The horses were in better condition than before, and the dragoons' seats were becoming altogether securer. In sum, Hervey was confident that by the beginning of December they would be ready to rejoin the regiment – as the manual had it – 'fully trained'.

In the weeks that followed, Serjeant Collins worked tirelessly to have each class in turn master the six cuts and eight guards against cavalry, and, too, the point, and the cut and guard against infantry. He drove them hard, and they cursed him when they got to their beds. But Collins had many a time had to parry a sword and wield his own with deathly intent, and he had seen what happened when a man lost his nerve or misjudged his distance and bent his elbow. It would be over in an instant, the cut disabling the sword arm like the serpent's strike, and the mortifying edge following. When a man had seen his fellows, or even his antagonists, fall because of their unproficiency, he was not inclined to stint his charges in their instruction.

And when the dragoons were not at stables or skill at arms, they were at troop drill. Every day but Sunday – when they paraded for church – they rode out onto the wide flood plain of the Karnaphuli and manoeuvred to the bugle. So it was that, one morning in early November, Hervey recognized that before him was a handy troop, not a recruit ride.

'Very well, Sar'nt-Major. We'll have one last turn. Trumpeter, sound "front form line".'

Private Storrs breathed a sigh of relief. It was perhaps the easiest of all the calls: nine notes, all the same – Gs. Only the triplets at the end to worry about. He had blown so much in the last two hours, and his lips were cracking. He blew the call perfectly.

Into line the forty and more dragoons trotted, then halted on the marker. Hervey nodded contentedly. He could not have asked better of them. Private Storrs turned his head towards him, expecting to hear that his troop-leader would ride to the front to dismiss the parade.

'Trumpeter, sound "retire".'

A moment's surprise delayed the call a fraction of a second. 'Retire' was tricky. Storrs cracked the last E semi-quaver. Hervey hardly noticed, and certainly didn't show it. The troop turned about as one, and struck off at the walk in a very fair line. But Storrs knew what to expect next. Although the heat of the summer had long gone, and the dust with it, his mouth was still dry. He began slaking it with all the spittle he could summon.

'Trumpeter, sound "front".'

Demi-semi-quavers this time, but no repeats. Storrs just managed it. The troop fronted with only the merest hesitation here and there, and dressed quickly.

Hervey smiled. 'That will do very nicely, Sar'nt-Major.' He rose in the saddle and looked down the line. Yes, it would do very nicely indeed. He could now dismiss them. 'Fall out the officers. Carry on, Sar'nt-Major.'

Armstrong saluted, and Hervey turned his horse away, followed at the regulation one length by Trumpeter Storrs.

Seton Canning trotted up, his face a picture of satisfaction to equal his captain's. 'My God, Hervey, but that was fine! I wouldn't have thought it possible even a month ago.'

'There's a long way to run yet, Harry. We could scarcely call this a field day.' Hervey's smile, however, said that perhaps it might not be too hard a race. 'We have another month, perhaps two. It should be enough if we can keep up this progress.'

They needed a day or two for making and mending, though; for 'interior economy' as it was known in the Sixth. Hervey would give over the rest of the week to the saddler and farriers. It would be good for Seton Canning to have the charge of things, too. There were ever more letters to attend to, and he felt the need of a break from the routine of the troop – from the cantonment, indeed. Perhaps he could persuade Somervile to ride with him along the coast. It was by all accounts an easy country of sand dunes, scrub and salt jheels, a haven for greenshank and tattlers, and for spoon-bills when the tide was high. On the forest's edge there was plenty of game; tigers were not unknown, his bearer had told him. Their guns would not be idle.

Johnson came out of the stables at the sound of hooves on the hard ground. He wore no hat for the sun had lost its strength, but his stable jacket, made up from stone-coloured local cloth, was stained with the signs of his exertions with body brush and curry comb. 'Parade all right, Cap'n 'Ervey?'

There was no one else within earshot now. Hervey could speak his mind. 'Very well, Johnson. Very well indeed. By the time we're relieved I'd pit the troop against the others any day.'

'T'troop's 'appy 'ere, sir. An' it's not as sticky, an' there's not so many sick. Reckon they'd be glad if we stayed a bit longer.'

Johnson's report was not surprising. Detached duty was always preferred. The eyes of the troop serjeant-major were one thing, but those of Mr Lincoln were another. 'We need to do some regimental drill. We can't call ourselves a real troop until we can manoeuvre in squadrons.'

'Thought yer said all that was done for now, sir?'

'Not the business of working as a regiment. What I meant was that the drill book needs rewriting. There's not enough about work other than in close order, and the evolutions just aren't quick enough. Not for well-trained squadrons, that is. It will do *us* very well for a fair while yet, though.'

''E'll need shoein' soon,' said Johnson, content that drill matters would never be his concern again, and nodding to Gilbert's forefeet.

'I'm going to take leave for the next two days. I thought I'd ride along the coast towards Manikpur and take my gun. Do you want to come? You can bring your mongoose.' Hervey vaulted from the saddle and handed over the reins.

Johnson made a snorting noise. 'Useless bloody thing. That ferret I 'ad in 'Orningsham would've put up a better show – an' 'e were next to useless, an' all.'

Hervey took off his cap and frowned. 'I haven't an idea what you're talking of.'

'That mongoose that I paid two rupees for!'

'Yes, that much I understood. What is its problem?'

'It's frightened o' snakes.'

Hervey could hardly blame the animal, improbable though the idea of a mongoose afraid of snakes sounded. 'Nonsense. They *fight* cobras, don't they?'

'Well, that's what we all thought. An' so 'alf a dozen clubbed together an' bought one, an' put 'im in one o' t'stalls, an' when we put t'mongoose in 'e saw t'snake an' shot straight out through an 'ole in t'wall.'

Hervey had to laugh. 'Can't you get your money back for the mongoose?'

'I've tried already but I can't find 'im as sold it me.'

'And what about the snake?'

'Ay, well, we caught 'im and sold 'im to somebody else. An' made a rupee on it.'

'I wonder you couldn't have made more,' suggested Hervey, smiling quizzically now. 'A snake that can see off a mongoose must be something of a curiosity.'

'I didn't think o' that,' replied Johnson, sounding vexed.

'So shall you come? With or without the mongoose?'

Johnson nodded, still frowning at having missed a trick.

'Good. Well, I shall take a bath and then pay a call on the rissalah's officer. And then I shall dine with the Somerviles. I'll send word about tomorrow. Not too early a start.'

The bhistis had drawn his bath before he could take off his boots. After four months they had the routine timed to perfection. A boy kept watch on the exercise ground, and as soon as he saw the serjeant-major salute and take over the parade, he would run back to Hervey's bungalow to alert the bhistis. They would draw off water from the copper boiler, fired before dawn, and fill the big tin bath to a line which allowed the sahib to get his shoulders under water without displacing any over the side. Hervey still looked about and checked before committing himself to the bathroom, as the old India hands warned (and as he had done in Madras), but now with diminished expectation of finding anything; he had concluded that 'the things that creepeth upon the earth' heard him coming and preferred other company.

He took his bath more content than he could recall in a long time. He bade his bearer wait outside as usual, and poured water over his head with a big conch shell half a dozen times. He languished longer than was his custom, enjoying a soak so well earned, and with an afternoon free of duties. He called to his bearer in another five minutes, just as the water was beginning to lose its heat, and the wiry little Bengali brought him towels and then his dressing gown. If deadly danger were always close at hand here, the pleasures were real nonetheless – perhaps even more so because of it.

Once dry, he sat down in the cane armchair from which he always had so pleasant a view of the country beyond the lines, took his glass of fresh-made *nimbu pani*, which would take the skin from his teeth at first sip but revive him even better than brandy, and dismissed the bearer for an hour. He had not written to Daniel Coates since coming here. He could do so now with real pride, having turned three dozen raw recruits, and as many unpromising native remounts, into a troop which was steady and exact on parade. Next week they would begin on scouting and picket duties. And then, from nowhere, came tears. He had no one to share his triumph with but a sheet of paper, and the words would not be addressed to Henrietta. He did nothing to fight back the tears, for they made him feel a little closer to her. It was all he would ever have. The tears just ran – no sobs – and when they were finished he felt the better for them. Something told him they would not come again. He picked up his telescope to watch a kite hunting the plain beyond the civil lines, and he studied it intently for several minutes. It was curious, he mused, how he wished luck to the bird rather than to its prey.

Hervey went early to the Somerviles'. He and they had no definite time of meeting – they dined together several times each week. The evening was cool and the air fresh, a light breeze having blown off the sea for most of the afternoon. There was no one about so he sat outside, facing west, the bungalow being verandahed on all sides. In an hour he could watch the sun fall, into the mouths of the Ganges it seemed, and listen as the night noises replaced the cicadas. A khitmagar brought him champagne, the glass misted. He did not at first sip it, intent as he was on a flock of hoopoes grubbing at the far end of the Somerviles' short-mown lawn. The birds were at ease, their crests down, almost tame. Pretty birds; Henrietta would have liked them. It was a happy thought.

'Hervey!' came Somervile's voice behind him, enough almost to make the hoopoes take flight. 'By heavens, I'm glad to see you. What a perfectly appalling day it's been. I don't know whether I'm more angry with my fellow countrymen or with that damned barbarian over the hill.'

That 'damned barbarian over the hill', as Somervile was wont to call the King of Ava, had been so frequent a topic of their conversation that Hervey supposed the latest complaint to be routine. The other sounded much more interesting. 'What have your fellow countrymen done to offend you?'

'Not *me*. Nothing to offend *me*. They've offended against every decent principle, that's all!'

Hervey raised an eyebrow.

'Two indigo-planters from just this side of Bangamah, two brothers, flogging ryots, putting them in irons, and the same with their wives. And then of all things parading them through the district sitting astride donkeys, looking arse-end, putting them in fear of their lives.'

'Is it pertinent to ask why?'

'Oh, for some indolence or other. But I shan't have it. The magistrate up there says the villagers refused to proceed against them at the trial, they're so terrified of them, but that there's enough evidence notwithstanding. I shall send them to Calcutta to stand trial. And I shall recommend they be expelled.'

Hervey was not surprised by the strength of Somervile's opinion. Many a time in Madras he had railed against the new breed which saw Indians as somehow inferior, un-deserving of either justice, compassion or simple respect. 'What becomes of people here?'

'They think their Christian religion elevates them.' Somervile sighed. 'But we have had this out many times before, you and me.' He pulled a bell rope for the khitmagar (he hated the practice of clapping or shouting). 'Bring the captain and me a bottle of champagne, please, Rama,' he said in confident Bengali. 'I'll sit with you a while, Hervey, and then have my bath. I'll not trouble you with the Burman affair.'

'As you please,' said Hervey, with a wry smile. King Bagyidaw was tiresome in his demands, in every respect.

The khitmagar returned with a wine cooler, poured Somervile his champagne, replenished Hervey's glass and then retired to the end of the verandah. Somervile took a good measure, breathed deep and pushed his legs out straight. 'Last case. Let's hope there's more on next week's packet. How was *your* day?'

'Very satisfactory. I could report the troop ready for review. I thought to take a couple of days' leave, to ride down towards Manikpur. Seton Canning says there's bustard there.'

Somervile emptied his glass, and the khitmagar advanced at once to fill it. 'Half-size bustard, yes – the Bengal florican, to give it its proper name. Black front and head. Dozy birds, not much sport in them, but good to eat.'

'I thought you might like to come too.'

Somervile sighed again. 'I should like that very much. But not until I have a better sense of what Bagyidaw is up to. Emma will go with you. Take the man from the rissalah as well. He's decent enough company.'

'He's bedded down.'

'Well then, take Emma by herself.'

'I'm not sure that would look proper.'

'Proper be damned!'

'Why don't I wait a few more days? Until your Burman business is resolved.'

'If you can. Yes, that would be much the better. I owe Manikpur a visit in any case.'

That decided on, they returned to ornithology and the behaviour of the hoopoes. But at length, and after a third glass of champagne, Somervile changed his tack suddenly. 'You know, Hervey, it isn't right that a man lives as a monk.'

Hervey made to speak, but Somervile raised a hand. 'No,

hear me. I'm talking only of the primary urges, the want for comfort, nothing more permanent. Hervey, we all had our *bibis*. I don't mean something dirty from the Feringhee bazaar here. Some decent girl in the Paterghatta that you can talk to – with a bit of Portuguese in the blood. Send word to my babu. He knows everything, and he's discreet. He'd never breathe a word, not even to me.'

Hervey made to speak a second time, but Somervile turned and beckoned the khitmagar.

'One more glass and then my bath. I say, look at that night heron!'

Night herons were hardly so remarkable. Hervey understood the cipher.

At dinner, the conversation soon turned to King Bagyidaw. Emma had read her husband's evening despatch before joining them. 'The problem is, it seems to me that the king has some cause for exasperation,' she began. 'It is not many years since that we permitted hostile acts from Company territory.'

'Hostile acts by those dispossessed of their own soil in Arakan,' countered Somervile.

'Hostile acts nevertheless, my dear. We cannot escape the consequences if we permit it.'

'That much is true,' he conceded, refastening a persistent button on his straining waistcoat. 'But it was five years ago at least, and since then there has hardly been raiding on a great scale. Nothing, certainly, to threaten the crown. Indeed, we have almost recognized Bagyidaw's suzerainty in Arakan. But he *will* demand that we surrender the Mughs, the Arakan refugees, and *that* Lord Hastings has made clear we could never do.'

'I am surprised it has not come to a fight long since,' said Hervey, glancing at Emma to know her opinion.

She raised her eyebrows as much as to say she agreed. The candles, though many and bright, still could not light her face fully, so thoroughly bronzed was it by the sun – more so than she would have permitted in Calcutta even. Not for the first time Hervey envied Somervile his fortune in the constant company of so intelligent and handsome a woman.

'It almost did,' said Somervile.

Hervey blinked. 'I'm sorry?'

'I said it almost did. Eight years ago, the late Lord Minto, in his last year as governor-general, put a scheme to the Court of Directors in London to make a punitive war on the court of Ava. But that was hardly the best of times, and the government opposed it. I can't but feel that it might have spared us loss of blood in the long run. And certainly a great deal of native blood – of one sort or another.'

'You think it will come to a fight, Eyre?'

Somervile paused for a second or so. 'There is a restlessness about Bagyidaw. He marched into Manipur last year because the rajah didn't pay homage quickly enough, and I still believe he would have gone on into Cachar had we not sent a force there and taken the place under protection.'

'That was Eyre's doing, Matthew,' explained Emma proudly. 'He pressed Lord Hastings to it very forcefully, for the Governor-General was yet preoccupied with the Pindaree campaign.'

'The trouble is,' continued Somervile, 'that such . . . pre-emption, shall we call it, if successful invariably brings questions as to its necessity in the first place. I made some enemies in Calcutta.'

'Why was Cachar important to the Company?'

'You mean besides the moral duty of standing by a neighbour?'

'I stand rebuked. But who is my neighbour, in the Company's terms?'

Somervile smiled. 'You're quite right. We cannot stand against each and every outrage. The truth is that, from Cachar, Bagyidaw would have been well placed to attack through the river plains into the Company's territory. We would have stopped him, of course, but not before he'd had a fair run at Dacca probably.'

'And was it really likely that he would have invaded?'

'You of all men should know that capability often spawns ambition.'

There was no disputing it. Hervey nodded.

'I'm not sure you're answering my question about its coming to a fight, Eyre,' protested Emma. 'Isn't this fish good, by the way?'

'It is, my dear. And I was. What I intended saying was that I believe he will move against Assam first. And if he is successful there, Chittagong will appear so much like a salient in his empire that it will then come to a fight.'

'That is a very ill appreciation, Eyre. I trust there will be a frigate to take us off at once!'

Somervile laid his forks together, and finished his glass of Chablis. 'Truly, my dear, an *excellent* piece of fish. Shall I make a prediction? In two years, unless Assam seeks subsidiary status of the Company, the kingdom will be annexed. And then Bagyidaw will give the Company an ultimatum, which of course we shall decline, and will then attack Chittagong.'

'Where he will be defeated,' said Hervey.

'Oh yes. But not at once. We shall have to move half the army of Bengal across the bay to evict him.'

'What do you advocate, then?'

Somervile smiled thinly. 'The Minto medicine. Unlike many, I do not rate the Burmans so highly when it comes to fighting. They can be brave, yes. But there's more to it than that, as I don't need to tell you. They're so supremely arrogant that a blow at their vitals would stun them. They have a good general in Mahâ Bundula, that I grant you, though not a *great* one as his name suggests in Hindoostani. But Rangoon, their principal port, is vulnerable, and so is Ava, for it's up a very sluggish river, albeit quite a long way up.'

Hervey was impressed, as ever, by the thought which Somervile had so evidently invested in his 'eastern question'. Nothing the lieutenant-governor said was in itself remarkable, perhaps; rather was it his masterly uncoiling of the serpentine factors in the appreciation of native affairs. He immersed himself in language and manners, and then applied the universal impulses of human conduct – both base and noble – and saw what others did not. Of course, such men were not the easiest of associates in the councils of the Honourable East India Company.

'Have you spoken with the military authorities of this?' tried Hervey, uneasily.

Somervile was very temperate in his reply. 'Sir Edward Paget profoundly disagrees with me. He believes we should fortify our borders and take no offensive action.'

Hervey took a deep breath. The commander-in-chief was a fighting general of the Peninsula. 'What is his principal objection?'

'That the country would kill an army without the Burmans needing to fire a shot.'

Hervey shuddered at the thought.

'Shall we have our partridge now, Eyre?' said Emma, thinking the conversation had reached as far as it should.

Hervey looked across at her. Somervile was indeed a fortunate man.

When they had finished the perfumed curds and candied sweets which the cook had laboured over for a good part of the day, Emma rose and said she would retire. 'Good night, Matthew. Let us hope that Eyre will find the time soon so that we may ride to Manikpur.' She stood on her toes and kissed her husband's forehead. 'Not too long, my dear.' And she drew her fingers lightly down his arm, a gesture of intimacy which jerked deep at Hervey's vitals.

They remained at table for perhaps a quarter of an hour after Emma had gone. Somervile declined more port, unusually, and changed subject three or four times, almost distractedly. At length he put down his glass, and stood. 'Hervey, my dear fellow, you must excuse me. I have not the appetite for our usual diversions this evening. Stay, though. Take some more of this port. It's a deuced fine vintage and there's plenty laid down. And there are newspapers from Calcutta there, too,' he said, gesturing towards the drawing room.

'Do not trouble in the slightest, Somervile. It's exceedingly good of you both to extend such frequent hospitality to me. Retire, do. My day's been easy compared with the affairs you must address yourself to.'

'Ay, perhaps. Well then, I'll bid you good night. Until tomorrow evening.' Somervile took his leave, brushing the crumbs from his waistcoat.

Hervey let the khitmagar pour him more port and then went to find the Calcutta papers. He saw half a dozen of the *Journal* on a sideboard, and settled himself into a low, comfortable armchair by an empty fireplace. He sipped appreciatively at his wine as he turned the pages of the most recent, a week old, but he could find nothing to detain him. He reached for another, and found the same. Perhaps there truly was nothing of moment – mere gossip only. But perhaps his attention was not to be had for the persistent image of Somervile going to Emma, his friend's contentment the very reverse of his own agitation. He put down the paper and the glass. It was the *comfort* of the embrace he missed as much as anything. He got up. He could not decently remain there.

Next day he sent a note of thanks to the Somerviles, as he had on every occasion he had dined with them. But this time he also sent a note for the babu, in English, for it was not long and its content was straightforward.

Within the hour, a note came back saying that a boy would meet him at the Suhrawardi gate at three o'clock. Hervey would have preferred the evening, of course, but he would then have had to make his excuses with the Somerviles. He bathed and then dressed, inconspicuously as if intent on a buying visit to the bazaar, and slipped away from his bungalow unobserved except for the chowkidar, who made low namaste but did not speak.

In less than half an hour Hervey reached the Suhrawardi gate and met the boy. It was the sleeping time, and the Paterghatta was uncrowded. He felt awkward, but no one seemed to take any notice as they walked purposefully through the gate and along drowsy streets to a house like any other, distinguished only by a blue door. The boy pushed it open and gestured him on. Hervey gave him a few annas and muttered a thank-you.

Inside seemed dark after the bright sun. An old woman appeared from behind a painted screen, looked at him and then beckoned to a young woman to come from behind it. Even in the dimness Hervey could see she was as promised, a handsome girl, clean and shapely. And he could see what she was not: nothing which recalled Henrietta, the only thing he had really feared.

They sat awhile drinking tea, speaking a little English and even less Bengali. When there was nothing more to say, they rose and she led him up rickety stairs to a small room with white walls, long muslin curtains at the shuttered windows and a bed with clean white linen. Her skin was lighter than the Madrasi girls he had so admired, but her eyes were darker. And they were big. She was perhaps twenty. He said nothing, though his heart hammered, and she likewise made not a sound. With a modesty that only increased his desire, she began taking the slides from her hair.

CHAPTER SEVENTEEN
RUMOURS OF WAR

Next day

Hervey stood at the front of his bungalow taking in the glories of another Bengal daybreak, fuller in promise, perhaps, than any he had known elsewhere. A sun low but already warming, a mist in the distant hills, the civil lines coming slowly to life – there were gentlemen at home in England, he considered, whose crabbed lives would be made immeasurably the better for just one of these mornings.

He felt better than he had expected to. Maybe the guilt would come later. The girl had been tender to him, and for a while he had not been quite so alone. He wondered how long the feeling would last, how long it would be until he had to renew it, and whether guilt would overtake it before then.

'Mornin', Cap'n 'Ervey, sir.'

Hervey returned Johnson's salute and took the reins from him. He sprang easily into the saddle, compensating for Gilbert's habitual sidestep as he did so, and collected him onto the bit. How good it was to be able to ride with a simple snaffle, for relaxed though the regimental regime was in comparison with its predecessor, a bridoon was still the regulation. 'I thought we'd ride over to see Skinner's Horse at exercise. I heard they were tent-pegging this morning.'

Before Johnson could reply, the orderly serjeant hailed

them from across the maidan. 'Captain Hervey, sir!' There was just a note of urgency in it. Corporal Mossop was doubling, but that said nothing: an NCO would not keep an officer waiting on any account.

'Nothing serious, I hope, Corporal Mossop?' said Hervey with a smile, as the orderly serjeant came to a halt before him.

'Not that I'm aware of, sir. Mr Somervile sends his compliments sir, and asks if you would call on him at once.'

Serious or not, it was clearly urgent. 'Very well, Corporal Mossop. Thank you. Come on, Johnson; we'd better see what agitates the lieutenant-governor.'

Somervile did not so much look agitated as troubled. 'Come in, Hervey, come in,' he said, hardly looking up from his desk as he wrote. 'Take a seat, call for some coffee. I'll be finished in a moment.'

Hervey did as he was bid. There was no sign of Emma, just the babu and a bearer. When the coffee came he took his cup and asked Somervile if he wanted any.

'No. Later perhaps,' he replied briskly, waving a sheet of paper about. When the ink was dry he gathered up the other two sheets and put them unfolded into a large envelope, which he sealed with wax and placed in a leather despatch case, locking it with a key attached to his watch chain. 'The hircarrah, Mohan. He should still be in the cantonments,' he said simply, handing the case to the babu. Then he rose, dismissed the bearer and moved to the other side of the table to sit in the armchair next to Hervey.

'I take it that something's amiss?'

Somervile shook his head and raised his eyebrows. 'I can scarcely believe it. Bagyidaw must be insane!'

'He's marched into Cachar?'

Somervile shook his head again. 'No. He's making threats against *here*. He's sent a letter to the Governor-General demanding we send back all the Arakanese who have fled into East Bengal. And, it seems, laying some sort of claim to sovereignty.'

'Sovereignty in Chittagong?'

'Yes. I had a despatch from Calcutta in the early hours by Governor-General's messenger. He's taking back my assessment. I just don't understand why Bagyidaw sees it opportune *now* to make such threats. Assam ought next to be his objective – as I said last night.'

'Do you think he's testing the Company's resolve, then?'

'That is what I've suggested to Calcutta, although we can't proceed on such a supposition alone. I've asked for a brigade at once. We must at least make a show.'

'Yes,' said Hervey, standing up and going to the map on the wall. 'That much would serve both needs. Where should they best go?'

'I was going to ask *your* opinion of that,' replied Somervile, frowning.

Hervey was a little taken aback. 'My purlieus these past months have been the exercise ground. I could only hazard an opinion from the map.'

'My own knowledge is not extensive, Hervey, and your opinion from a map will be better than mine.'

Hervey returned to his chair. 'Do we know anything of Burman dispositions? Or their equipment and how they fight?'

'I don't believe my office does, no. But the Arakanese will. It goes against the intent of my own mission here, but we shall have to enlist their support – at least, their intelligence. I wish their Chin Payan were still alive, for all the trouble he gave us.'

'How long do you suppose it will take for Calcutta to despatch a brigade?'

'I've asked for immediate advice in that respect. I have a fear it will not be as prompt as is necessary. There's no standing force in East Bengal at present, as far as I know; they're all deployed.'

Hervey had thought it might be the case. He knew his own brigade would be in the field still. 'Colonel Piven will be back next week. That's something.'

'He has a very good knowledge of the frontiers; that much is certain. He would have an idea about where to strengthen our patrols, I suppose.' Somervile sighed. 'What I need is two brigades of cavalry and horse artillery. If we surprised the Burmans with a prodigious amount of fire we might well drive them back.'

Hervey nodded. 'That relies on very fine intelligence. We were humbugged at Waterloo – and that was with some of the best officers at work.'

'We had better make a start, then. I'll send word for the leaders of the Arakanese here in the city to come at once; and the more distant ones we shall have to see as they show. Let us meet here again at noon.'

Johnson waved his hand violently across his face. 'Bastard flies! These are worse than them in Madras.'

Hervey agreed. What their provenance was he could not conclude: there was not a living thing in miles on this plain. 'Let's trot again,' he sighed. 'Perhaps they'll give up this time.'

They had come a good way from the lines, but it had been worth it to see the sowars of Colonel Skinner's regiment of siladar cavalry. Their skill with the lance was breathtaking, equalled only by their horsemanship. Both Johnson and Hervey admitted they had never seen the like. But they had been paying the price since with the flies.

This time, however, the flies were evidently more tired than the horses, falling away after the second furlong. Hervey pressed on for a third and then pulled up to a walk. Five minutes later they were still without their tormentors, so he presumed they could walk the remainder of the way in peace. And peaceful the land looked to be at this hour. The hills to the east were still shrouded with the morning's mist

– it was *Hemanto*, Hervey's bearer had told him, the misty season – and the country looked even greener than in the days that followed the August deluges. An unruly flight of Brahminy duck passed high overhead, their funny clanging call seeming to protest against the intrusion.

Johnson was pleased to be able to resume the earlier conversation. 'And so, this 'ere King Baggydrawers reckons we'd just give 'im t'country an' go 'ome?'

'That's about the long and the short of it,' said Hervey, not imagining there was any point insisting on respectful pronunciation. 'And Mr Somervile says that Bagyidaw would not stop until he reached Calcutta.'

''Ow's 'e think 'e'd get across all them rivers?'

'I think he'd go by sea. They have a lot of war barges, apparently.'

''E wants tipping a settler, that's what 'e wants!'

'Just so, Johnson. But how? There's the rub.'

''Fore 'e's art o' 'is pit.'

Mutual comprehension was by now a matter of context rather than knowledge of vocabulary, especially since Johnson, when aroused to indignation, reverted to a particularly impenetrable strain of Sheffield.

'Yes, but how shall you find the pit? You're right, though. Mr Somervile says that the Governor-General, a few years ago, wanted to do just that – march into Burma and teach them a lesson. Not that Bagyidaw was king at that time.'

'Daft name. Mebbe if 'is men knew what it meant they'd pack it all in.'

Hervey smiled. 'I think they would be parted from their heads first. He's a very brutal man, it seems.'

'Sounds as if they'd be pleased if we *did* knock 'im abaht a bit.'

'Perhaps. Anyway, we might get to know a bit more from these Arakanese in an hour or so.' He checked his watch. 'Come on; we'd better not dawdle.'

* * *

All about Eyre Somervile's study were papers and ledgers, boxes and maps. 'Did you have an agreeable ride?' he asked, without looking up.

Hervey felt rather guilty. 'Yes. I watched the native horse at drill. They go very well.'

'Mm,' was the reply.

'What has engaged *you*?'

'The *Bengal Secret and Political Consultations*. And they would have engaged far less of my time had they a proper index. I found what I was looking for by a most circular exercise – in volume ninety-one, no less.'

Hervey had learned to tread gently when Somervile was in his 'scholarly' frame of mind, as he thought of it. 'May I ask what were you searching for?'

'After you had gone this morning, I remembered that Lord Wellesley had sent an officer to Ava to treaty with the then king, Bodawpaya, Bagyidaw's grandfather. A Colonel Symes it was, and it occurred to me that his reports must include some military assessments, and so I have been searching them out.'

'And do they contain that information?'

'In admirable detail. You must read him. The papers are on yonder table.' He gestured without looking up again.

Hervey turned, but at that moment Somervile looked up and took off his spectacles. 'You know, the real danger is these war boats. There are five hundred of them: every town or village near the rivers has to supply a certain number of oarsmen and soldiers – a hundred or so for each boat – and they mount a gun in the bows. These could swarm on Chittagong – and Calcutta for that matter – and there'd be the very devil of a fight.'

Hervey made rapid calculations. The results were indeed ominous. 'Then the answer would be to destroy the boats before they discharged their cargo. But that too might be easier said than done, though I dare say Commodore Peto would know how.'

Somervile raised an eyebrow. 'I have a sense that we shall feel his want very keenly before too long.' He took out his watch. 'Let us go and see who of the Arakanese is come.'

There were a dozen of them, men who hitherto had been regarded as at best troublesome and at worst practitioners of dacoity. Now they all sat in the lieutenant-governor's audience room as if they were waiting for a wedding. 'I have called you here today,' began Somervile, in confident Bengali, 'to ask you for information on the activities of the Burmans.'

There was at once a hubbub, with keen looks of anticipation on the faces of the Arakanese.

Somervile halted it magisterially. 'I must warn you, however, that this does *not* mean we are contemplating any hostilities. It is simply that the Company in Calcutta wishes to know what movements in general are there.'

None of the Arakanese looked convinced, but that suited Somervile. He wanted their help, and it would be the more vigorous for believing that the fight might be taken to their old enemy. He pointed to the map several times as he elaborated on his requirements, unsure as to its usefulness in that company, but the place names he mentioned, especially the rivers, brought eager nods. At length he promised them the Company would meet all reasonable expenses. 'But I must warn you that the Company cannot extend any protection. And I will not condone any offensive action whatever. Indeed, I shall deal with it with infinitely greater severity than hitherto.'

This latter was unwelcome news, but the manifest disappointment was soon replaced by enthusiasm for the covert action to come, and the meeting was ended with Somervile shaking each of the Arakanese by the hand and bidding them *khudā hāfiz*, and expressing his hope that he would see them again soon – *ābār dekā hobe*. When they were gone he asked Hervey for his opinion.

Hervey smiled. He had understood barely a word. 'I'd

wager those men will bring you your intelligence, and severed heads too to prove their word.'

Somervile nodded, and frowned. 'That is my fear. I wanted them keen, but I warned them there was to be no dacoity.'

Hervey nodded as well. 'What shall you do now?'

'There is nothing more *to* do. I've sent word to the town major telling him to put the border patrols on alert – such as there are. He ought just about to manage that. Any more and I should have little confidence.'

Hervey sighed. 'He is certainly past his prime.'

'He's close to his military dotage!'

They both smiled.

'I've heard tell there are seven ages of the military man,' said Hervey.

'I believe we might examine such a theory, but let us do so at table. I think that Emma will be eager to hear of the morning's work.'

When Hervey returned to his quarters in the afternoon he found letters from England, carried from Calcutta by the same packet as the Governor-General's messenger. He settled to read them at once. They were filled with good news and much cheer. His infant daughter was strong and healthy, and showed spirit and intelligence. Elizabeth likewise enjoyed excellent health and uncommon contentment. His father and mother, it seemed, were more active than ever. There were no reports of depredations by the squatters of Warminster Common, nor of violence by the Hindon Luddites, nor of pestilence in the town workhouse, nor any of a dozen things which periodically threatened the repose of the honest citizens of the neighbourhood. There were not even malevolent clerics. And yet these letters brought about so palpable a dejection that even Private Johnson would be moved to remark on it. For there was no Henrietta in their pages, and nor could there ever be, of course. The finality of it was never more apparent to him than by her absence from these modest records of daily life. It tore at his gut like the eagle of Shelley's masterwork. Perhaps more than anything he was dismayed by the suddenness of his descent from sunny spirits to dark discouragement. How much he wished to see that villainous poet again, if only his hand in a letter. He would tell him all, even that of which he was half ashamed. Only *half* ashamed, though, for had he not prayed for a year and more for the strength to endure? What was his true fault, therefore, if he could *not* bear things as he ought? He was as close to slipping away to the Paterghatta now as he was to falling to his knees.

But he would not go to the bibi khana. Neither would he pray. He would not even pick up his pen to reply at once to Horningsham, as had always been his practice. For he had not the right to put his own desires first. It was not a question of Christian morals but of his soldier's duty: he had spent the last hours, with Somervile, considering the possibility of war with the Burmans – there was no other word for it – and he had done nothing since with regard to his own troop. Part-trained though they were, there would be calls on them for such skills as they possessed: guarding, escorting, the occasional undemanding patrol perhaps. And he might accelerate, or in some other way modify, his plans for the completion of their training. This was what his duty required, and he felt wholly ashamed at having to remind himself of it.

CHAPTER EIGHTEEN
CASUS BELLI

Four days later

Hervey drew his sword and brought the pommel to rest on his foreleg. The morning sun at his back warmed him in a most comforting way, as indeed did the sight before him. Serjeant-Major Armstrong rode up from the centre of the ranks opposite, halted and brought his sword upright from the shoulder. 'Good morning, sir! There are nine non-commissioned officers and thirty-eight private men on parade, sir!'

Hervey returned the salute with a nod of his head. 'Thank you, Serjeant-Major. Take post, please.'

It had been the Sixth's custom for many years to invite its serjeant-majors to take post on formal parades, and many had been the time that the troop captains had done the same in the field as a defiant gesture of composure in the face of the enemy. E Troop was not in review order this warm November morning, but campaign dress, for it was their first field day. Since Somervile's alert, Hervey had worked tirelessly in the troop's instruction – picket work on the first day, patrols and escorts the second, and yesterday the crossing of defiles and rivers. Dry work, first in the 'classroom' and then demonstrations, dismounted, using the NCOs to represent parts of the troop or the enemy, and buckets, ropes and

271

all manner of commissary things to portray the features of the terrain. In the afternoons, while the troop was at stables, Hervey had ridden the country to lay out in his mind the course of the field day, the culmination of which was to be a crossing of one of the tributaries of the Hooghly – a stream deep enough to have the horses swim, and yet not so wide as to unnerve the unpractised dragoons. The river was sluggish and the banks were low, making for easy entry and exit. They would be lucky to find so accommodating a crossing site on campaign, that much was certain. He had seen men and horses come to grief in Spain in rivers not much trickier than here. But it was a start.

'Fall in the officers!'

Seton Canning and Vanneck pressed their chargers forward.

Hervey glanced up and down the line. He saw dragoons now, not recruits. Here and there he picked out a face and remembered what it had been when first he had seen it. He saw French that day in the barracks when they were being sluiced down, indignant at Armstrong's suggestion that he had enlisted after losing his name. He saw Harkness at the same parade looking confused when Armstrong said he must answer 'sir', though it must not be addressed to him. There was McCarthy, flugelman, his rank restored by virtue of Hervey's powers as detachment commander, but local rank, limited and unpaid; Hervey recalled McCarthy's awkwardness when first he had sat astride a horse. He saw Shepherd Stent when first he had come to The Bell in Warminster, a silent, brooding, wounded man, and Rudd in that same place, smart, eager, but answerable to his mother in the millinery shop. And there were the Warminster pals themselves, in the squalor of the Common, Wainwright above all, a lad to whom others looked for the lead. A year had made dragoons of them, all but. Another month and—

Off to his right, Hervey saw a mounted orderly approaching. He nodded to his trumpeter to intercept him.

'The troop will return swords. Retu-u-urn swords!'

By the time the drill was complete and they had formed two ranks, Trumpeter Storrs was handing Hervey the orderly's message. Its terse contents startled him: 'Come at once to my quarters. Imperative. ES.'

'Mr Seton Canning, if you please!'

His lieutenant raised a small trail of dust as he trotted up. 'Sir?' The formalities were always observed on parade, even without earshot of the ranks.

'Take the troop out to the exercise ground and put them through skirmishing drill. The lieutenant-governor wants to see me. I'll join you directly.' Hervey turned without waiting for an acknowledgement and put Gilbert into as unhurried a trot as he could manage.

At the Somerviles' he found the lieutenant-governor in his study and still in his dressing gown. As Hervey came in, Somervile's look of anxiety turned to one of near relief. 'I've been up since the early hours again. I almost sent for you a dozen times.'

'I wonder you did not. What has happened?'

'Two reports, that is what; and notice from Calcutta that it will be the best part of two months before the brigade arrives. The Burmans are assembling a force within reach of the headwaters of the Karnaphuli. They'll deliver an ultimatum before the month is out and then march on the city, splitting the country in two.'

Hervey peered at the map lying on Somervile's desk. 'This is very precise intelligence.'

'It is. And I've paid handsomely for it. We have a Burman fugitive from the court of Ava. And the intelligence of the force assembling has been corroborated by the Chakma tribesmen from the hill tracts.'

'What say the Arakanese?'

'I've heard nothing yet. But they wouldn't go into the hill tracts alone.'

'You had better ask the town major to take defensive

273

measures, then. We shall at least know their route.'

'I shall summon him shortly. What do you think his force can do?'

'Two battalions of native infantry and guns? Well sited they might stop five times their number.'

'My agent says there will be twelve thousand, and war barges with guns.'

'Then they can do little but inflict losses and delay on them, but not, I think, for two months.'

'No, nor I. I've sent word this very morning to Calcutta to hasten the brigade. They might at least send them in whatever groups they muster.'

Hervey frowned. 'That could be a scheme for losing them piecemeal. I doubt the commander-in-chief would commit anything less than in battalion strength.'

'That's why I've sent for you, Hervey. You shall have to take charge of the defences of this place. You have experience of these things, and you've seen the way of war here in the east. We both agree the town major's a dear enough man, but not a match for this.'

Hervey narrowed his eyes.

'If rank is the problem I can give you a local colonelcy. That's well within my powers.'

'No, rank is not the problem,' said Hervey, shaking his head. 'A King's officer always takes seniority over one of the Company's. The problem's topography. The country's too flat to make defences. It's only numbers of men – men able to manoeuvre – that could tell.'

Somervile looked dismayed. 'I have to do *something*, Hervey!'

Hervey did not have to think what that something must be. It was, in his view, obvious to the newest cornet. 'You shall have to forestall the attack.'

Somervile looked at him uncertainly.

'We have spoken of it. The Burmans must be defeated before they can fall on us from those boats. Before they embark in them, indeed.'

Somervile's look of astonishment was sufficient.

'Truly, there's no alternative.'

At last the lieutenant-governor found his tongue. 'But how in heaven's name do you propose we do it?'

'I don't know. We did something of the same in Chintal, but that was a madness I thought never to repeat, and five years past. Do you have licence to attack the Burmans, by the way? In their own country, I mean?'

'I have plenipotentiary powers, yes. But as far as the Company goes we should be licensed ultimately by success.'

Hervey frowned. 'My dear Somervile, we must face the possibility that if we undertook such a thing, you are more likely to be arraigned in failure, and I court-martialled.'

Somervile sighed. 'Hervey, I have no wish to prompt you to rashness, to any adventure that might bring such a thing to you.' He scratched his head and called for his bearer. 'No wish at all. Would you therefore make an assessment, a thorough, measured affair? It might reveal some course we have not imagined.'

It was reasonable in one sense, thought Hervey, but the facts were unpromising and time was not on their side. An assessment could only betray how desperate were their straits, and that was too evident already: his own troop was still scarcely better than half-trained – unpractised, at least. 'I shall make a very measured assessment,' he replied, and in a tone intended to reassure Somervile that he would have his best efforts. 'But directed only towards an attack on those boats with all the promptness to be had.'

Somervile, though defied, looked surprisingly relieved.

'I think I should first like to hear all that there is of the Burman force. Are your agents here yet?'

At four o'clock, as the sun's strength was fast diminishing, Hervey left his quarters and went to the stables. His neck was aching from holding his head too long in the same position as he pored over books, manuscripts and maps in order to make his 'measured assessment'. Somervile's Burman agents had not appeared, however, and so all his calculations were based on a supposition that the scant intelligence of the enemy was accurate. This worried him. It was one thing to go bald-headed for a rabble of mutineers, as he had done in Chintal; quite another to undertake an expedition against an organized force which was itself preparing an offensive expedition.

And then there was the problem of the maps. He could hardly expect that they would be as faithful as the Ordnance sheets with which the most part of England was served, nor even the military surveys of Bonaparte's legions which had tramped over the best part of the Continent. However, those with which he was obliged to make his assessment were sketchy in the extreme.

'It's the rivers which give me the greatest trouble,' confided Hervey, as Armstrong listened to the summary of the appreciation. 'There are too many of them and they're too unpredictable.'

Armstrong shifted his weight on the sack of gram, pushed his legs out straight and reached into his pocket for his pipe. 'Rivers are rivers, aren't they?'

To another, the remark might have meant nothing. To Hervey, who had consulted many maps and negotiated many rivers in Armstrong's company, there was no need of elaboration. 'Not here, by all accounts. I've been reading the natural history of the country, and strange it is too. Only thirty years ago the Jamuna shifted its course a full fifty miles.'

Armstrong was not overawed. 'But if these Burmans is coming down a river to attack, then they must know where it leads. And in that case we just hunt the heel line. That's what you'd call it, isn't it?'

Hervey smiled. Armstrong had never followed hounds, but he had always studied his officers' pastimes to advantage. 'We need guides, though. And from what Mr Somervile says, they don't much travel in these parts. I've yet to see these Burman agents who brought him the intelligence. They ought to have some idea of the country between here and there, even if they've not seen the assembly area for themselves.'

'I've always distrusted guides. Ever since that time in Spain.'

A searing experience that had been. Hervey could see it now – Armstrong's ferocious strength unleashed on the Spanish guides who had proved treacherous the night before Corunna. Never again had he had much trust in men who did not wear a uniform. 'Mr Somervile places great faith in the hill tribes, the Chakma especially. They know the forest well, and they're no friends of the Burmans.'

Armstrong made a face as if to say they would have to prove it first. 'And what do your books say about the weather, sir? Thank God it's over the worst, at least.'

Hervey knew that if Bagyidaw had threatened invasion but two months before, there could have been no thought of an anticipatory operation. The humidity at that time induced a torpor which would have prevented any expedition. The monsoon, which battered them daily, made the going so treacherous that no man was permitted to leave camp except in the company of two others. It had been a time when the stoutest hearts had begun to wonder how long they could endure. 'Yes, it's surely over the worst. We must hope the rivers are falling.'

Private Johnson appeared. 'Oh, there thee is, Cap'n 'Ervey. Mr Somervile's man's been lookin' for thee.'

'What does he want?'

Johnson took off his forage cap and wiped his brow with his sleeve. 'Somethin' abaht some blackies that needs to talk to thee.'

'This sounds promising,' said Hervey. 'Where is Mr Somervile's man now?' he asked, turning back to Johnson.

'Waitin' outside. Shall I fetch 'im in?'

'No, no. I'll be along shortly. Would you ask Mr Seton Canning to take evening stables for me? And tell my bearer to expect me late; and to leave some collops or whatever.'

'Ay sir.' Johnson replaced his cap, glanced at the serjeant-major and nodded his respects, then turned to leave the feed store.

'Nearly got his name in the incident book last night, did Johnson,' said Armstrong when he was gone.

'Really?' Hervey thought Johnson long past the orderly serjeant's notice.

Armstrong blew out a great cloud of sweet-smelling smoke from the last of the Tokay-soaked leaf he had bought in Calcutta. 'He put BC on his back. With a left hook, too!'

'Did he indeed? Do we know why?'

'Disputed ownership.'

'Of a woman?'

'None of 'em'd come to blows over that. They'd share 'em quite happily.'

'Well what, then?'

'A razor.'

'Great heavens.'

'Seems there's been a bit of light-fingering of late. Thought was that it must be one of the darkie-wallahs. There are so many of them that come and go.'

'And Dodds was found with Johnson's razor?'

'Seems so. But the circumstances sounded a bit queer. Dodds swore blind it must've been put with his kit by mistake.'

'Is that likely?'

'It's *possible*. Half the troop's shaved in bed of a morning. So rather than make anything formal of it, Johnson tipped 'im a settler.'

Hervey smiled with a certain pride, though the inference of Dodds's recidivism worried him. 'I thought he'd been treading a straight path. You yourself said so.'

'I did, and he had, to start with. He needs chasing, though. That sort just can't stick with it.'

Hervey sighed. But even if he needed chasing, Dodds was still a sabre. He could only hope that he was not a prigster, as the men had it. 'I have a feeling that between them, Corporal McCarthy and that subdivision will keep his hand to the task.'

'They better had,' Armstrong muttered. 'What about dhoolies and syces and the like?'

Hervey shook his head. 'No dhoolies, no syces, no gram-grinders – no *anything* but what we would have had with us in France. Half a dozen cacolets, perhaps. And pray God we shan't need them.'

Armstrong made notes. 'And Boy Porrit?'

Porrit had come with four other boys at the last minute in Chatham, sons of the gun or dockyard foundlings. He and another had been mustered with E Troop, though his 'twin' had died of a fit not long out to sea.

'It's a year since he was enlisted – at sixteen – Sar'nt-Major. The farrier will need him.'

'Sir, he was nowt but a bairn when he 'listed – barely fourteen, I'd reckon.'

'His papers say otherwise, and now's not the time to be counting. He'd want to go, anyway.'

Armstrong kept his peace. Porrit would be another that he would have to keep an eye on, albeit a paternal one; as if there weren't enough already.

'One more thing. Who should be my coverman?'

Armstrong turned the question over in his mind for a moment. 'Stent or Harkness.'

'Not McCarthy?'

'Not with that seat. Not yet. I'd go for Stent. Harkness is stronger with a sword, but Stent's the better jockey. And he's more of a thinking head.'

Hervey stood and brushed the dust from his overalls, put on his cap and made his excuses. 'One way or another we'll have something by morning. I'll say whatever at first parade. Good night.'

Armstrong rose too. 'Ay. And I'll keep my peace, no matter. Though God help us if it ever comes to a fight.' The imprecation was more than the soldier's casual profanity. Armstrong had seen Hervey in his determination many a time before, but there was a distinctly new edge to the steel now – an edge he feared might cut both ways.

CHAPTER NINETEEN
FULLY TRAINED

10 November, next day

'Stand a-a-at . . . ease! Stand easy.'

Hervey's command put the half-hundred on muster parade next morning into an attitude at once relaxed and yet full of anticipation. Muster was normally a prompt affair, little more than a count of heads – the serious business of inspections began later with 'boot and saddle' – so that the order for standing easy presaged an announcement. It might be good news or bad; it was the practice in the Sixth to announce defaulters' punishments at muster; or there might be a court circular 'to be read at the head of all troops' (Hervey had been dreading the despatch which would give the report of their erstwhile colonel-in-chief's trial, for the arraignment of Princess Caroline had been long spoken of with very decided views in the regiment). Or it might be that, as this morning, the officer commanding would have some instruction for them which could not be trusted to the written page of routine orders, being either too oppressive without fuller explanation, or else too portentous to be conveyed from the notice-board. There was a buzz of expectancy now, barely audible but a buzz nevertheless.

'You will have heard talk about the lines these past weeks regarding the warlike antics of King Bagyidaw of Ava,' began Hervey, glancing from right to left along the front rank and into the rear rank as best he could. All eyes were alert and turned to him. 'The lieutenant-governor has therefore concluded that it shall be prudent to reinforce the regular patrols along the borders of the Company's territory, and to obtain reinforcements for the security of Chittagong and the other principal settlements. Accordingly a brigade is being assembled at this moment in Calcutta to augment the garrison, and we have orders to proceed to the border this day.'

Hervey paused to let the announcement take its effect. The earlier buzz returned, even stronger. And it was the sound of approval. Hervey wondered what it might be if he were able to tell them the whole truth. But that would have to wait until they were gone from earshot of any who would retail the intelligence to the Burmans – however impossible the act might seem.

'The remainder of the morning is to be spent in preparation for taking to the field, in accordance with standing instructions. The troop is to muster at two o'clock in campaign order, and in all respects ready to march. That is all for the present. Carry on, please, Serjeant-Major.'

'Sir!' snapped Armstrong, and with a relish that made some of the dragoons shudder. 'E Troop!' he barked.

The two ranks snapped back to the braced 'at ease'.

'Atte-e-en*shun*!'

Armstrong's right hand shot to the peak of his shako as Hervey and his two officers turned away.

'Don't ask of me anything more at this time,' said Hervey when he saw Seton Canning's mouth open. 'There'll be fuller orders when we march. Just keep a close eye on things. They'll need the *jaldi* putting into them, that's for sure, even with the likes of Armstrong and Collins chasing.'

It was strange, thought Hervey, even as he said it, how in a matter only of months they had adopted so much of the Bengal army's cant.

'Do you want me to take boot and saddle?' asked Seton Canning.

'If you please,' said Hervey, without a glance. 'And go to it this morning on the assumption that we'll see action before the week's out.'

His lieutenant seemed surprised. 'Do you really think so, Hervey?'

'Don't be a bloody fool, Harry. I'd not say so if I didn't think it!'

Seton Canning was taken aback. It was the first time Hervey had spoken thus to him. 'Shall you give us orders before we march?'

'No,' said Hervey, keeping up his pace. 'I'm not trusting myself to say a word. You'll learn why soon enough.'

The lieutenant could still feel the edge in his captain's tone, and he decided to withdraw. 'Anything more, sir?'

'No,' replied Hervey briskly, his mind now intent elsewhere. 'I have to see Skinner's Horse about something. Carry on.'

Hervey walked alone to the native horse lines. He had no clear idea how he would secure his intent, for he had no warrant from the lieutenant-governor, and, moreover, the Skinner's commandant had yet to return from his long furlough. To Hervey, the other British officer, the adjutant, was a man of uncertain temperament. He was no gentleman, and therefore inclined to some resentment; but he was diligent, the commandant had said, and he had the respect of the native officers. He had dined with E Troop's officers several times, but none had found him a boon companion, although the hospitality ought at least to make for civility now.

As Hervey approached the Skinner's lines, the daffadar of the quarter-guard began shouting, and soon sowars in yellow kurtas and fur-edged lungis were doubling from the guard-room, snatching lances from the rack on the verandah and

283

falling into line in front of the yellow-painted bound-stones. The daffadar called them to attention, and a dozen pennants fluttered then fell uniformly to the right side of each vertical lance. He marched up to Hervey, halted and saluted. Then he spoke in a high and melodious voice – Hindoostani, clear and measured, as if he were not a native speaker. So near was it to Urdu that Hervey grasped its purport: the daffadar had sent a runner to inform the orderly jemadar, and the daffadar would conduct him to regimental headquarters.

'Is the adjutant at orderly room, daffadar?' asked Hervey, the Urdu simple enough.

'Yes, sahib.'

'Very well.'

The daffadar saluted again and turned to lead the captain-sahib to the headquarters. Hervey looked at each sowar as he walked past the guard. They were big men, full-bearded, from the country west of Bengal. He would wish them with him if it ever came to a fight. He had no doubt they would sooner come with him across the border than stay here, but that he could not risk.

At regimental headquarters, the white dressed stone was brilliant in the morning sun, the guttering, downpipes and fittings painted the same yellow as the kurtas and guard-room bound-stones. The hand of the commandant and the presence of the rissaldar-major were at once evident to the visitor – as indeed was the intention.

The adjutant appeared on the verandah, booted and wearing the kurta rather than the regulation King's pattern short coat. Bareheaded, he pulled his arms to his side and bowed. 'Good morning, Captain Hervey. Unheralded? Is there some alarm?'

The salutation was friendly, even if it suggested a chiding. Hervey touched the peak of his forage cap, and smiled. 'Good morning, Captain Pollock. No, no alarm. I am sorry there was no *nakib*; I have set every last man to work.'

The adjutant smiled. 'You had better tell me of it then.' He turned and called inside to his assistant. 'Woordi-Major-sahib!'

Out came the woordi-major, as martial-looking a man as any, but wearing spectacles. 'Yes, sahib?' he asked in English, bowing also to Hervey – an English bow rather than namaste.

'Please have my bearer come to my bungalow with beer and limewater.'

'Very good, sahib.' He turned to Hervey and bowed again. 'Good morning, Captain Hervey sahib.'

'Good morning, Woordi-Major-sahib,' replied Hervey, with a smile, touching his peak again.

'Very well, Hervey: let us be along. Whatever it be, it be better done with iced beer and limewater.'

Hervey would only too gladly concede that that was true in general and not just this morning. 'I'm afraid you will not like what I have to tell you, and just as little what I have to ask,' he warned as they set off for the officers' lines.

'You had better begin then,' replied the adjutant, sounding more curious than troubled. He laid a hand on Hervey's arm to stay him as a half-rissalah, back from morning exercise, turned into the camp road from the direction of the guard-room, horses and men as sweat-stained as E Troop had been the day before.

Hervey found the sweat reassuring. 'I'm sorry we've not had an opportunity to drill together yet.'

'You're not leaving, are you?'

Hervey had already decided that he could not practise any deception on the Skinner's adjutant, for to do so would be tantamount to practising it on the commandant himself; and that he could never contemplate – not, at least, when he was to ask for men who might have to risk their lives, even if he did not imagine it to be in any degree likely. He therefore told him of the intelligence on which they were to act, and his general design. By the time he was finished, they had reached the adjutant's bungalow. They sat down in deep cane armchairs on the verandah, and in not many minutes the punkah began to swing and the bearer brought them iced beer and salted limewater.

At length, the adjutant – the acting commandant – expressed his opinion. 'I can't see that you will get one league into those forests.'

Hervey was dismayed. 'Are they so much worse than elsewhere?'

The adjutant frowned. 'I have no taste for the jungle, Hervey. I have never seen what was so diverting about collecting tiger skins directly.'

It seemed, thought Hervey, that he himself might be Pollock's superior in affairs of the forest, though his experience in Chintal had been precious little. 'There are good tracks, and we shall have guides.'

'Don't mistake me, Hervey: your scheme is admirable. It's only that there are not the troops to execute it.'

'I don't follow.'

'You yourself have said you have a troop in the making. And such a scheme as this would need a made troop for certain.'

Hervey saw no advantage in debating the point. 'You will not give me a galloper gun?'

'I didn't say that. But I do not see what use they would be to you. However good are the tracks they'll scarcely admit a gun.'

'I had thought to carry them broken down, chapman-fashion.'

The adjutant was silent. He had evidently not considered it.

'At least lend me the guns and have your men instruct mine in how to use them.'

Now the adjutant looked dismayed. 'Hervey, these men would do anything I asked, no matter how perilous – "sahib bolta", "the sahib says" – but I should not hazard to disarm them!'

Hervey fixed him with a steady look: they were at a fork

in the road. 'Then I must ask if you would have them accompany us.'

The adjutant paused long. 'Hervey, taking cavalry into the forest is as desperate a scheme as ever I heard. I might say *foolhardy.*'

Hervey continued to look him in the eye.

'But without guns it would be madness.' He paused again, as if to emphasize the narrow margin of sanity. 'You shall have my best men.'

Hervey nodded in gratitude, the faintest smile upon his lips – a knowing, confiding, grim smile.

'Come,' said Pollock, getting up. 'I'll turn out the daffadar and his guns. And I'll tell you of the forest in those parts – what little of it that I know.'

'Where have you been?' asked Somervile anxiously. 'Your groom said you'd left parade not long after seven.'

'To see the Skinner's commandant,' replied Hervey, matter of fact, pouring limewater for himself from a large glass jug.

Somervile's jaw dropped. 'You haven't told him what you're about?'

Hervey turned with a look like thunder. 'Somervile, you trust me to embark on a foray which some would call harebrained, and then you think I would tattle it about the bazaars!'

Somervile was clearly angered by his own ejaculation, though not entirely disposed to remorse. 'It is a deuced tender time for me too, you know, Hervey.'

That it was, Hervey saw at once: for whereas he risked but his life, Somervile hazarded his reputation. 'I have told Captain Pollock the design, yes, but let us not quarrel over it. I had a tricky mission with Skinner's. I wanted their galloper guns – they have two.'

Somervile looked dismayed again, but stayed his protest. 'Have you got them?'

'Oh yes. They're readying them at this moment.'

'Could you not have had them without letting your intent be known?'

Hervey drained the glass and poured himself more. 'There was nothing in honour I could say to the adjutant but *why* I had need of his guns, and that I confided that he would tell no one.'

Somervile looked at him anxiously for further assurance.

'You need have no fear on that account. I would trust his pledge with my life.'

'You have indeed done so, by all accounts. Pollock is an efficient officer, but . . .'

'You mean he would not have secured a King's commission.'

'Just so. And in these circumstances it is hardly something one may overlook with impunity.'

'I don't gainsay it, Somervile. But Pollock's a soldier to his fingertips.'

Somervile raised his eyebrows. 'And of the "yellow circle"?'

Hervey nodded, with just the degree of mock solemnity that the question had implied. 'Just so, Somervile. The fellowship of the sabre is felt most keenly.'

Somervile frowned indulgently. 'You fellows – you feast on Malory, no doubt, fancying yourselves all Sir Gawains.'

Hervey returned the frown. 'And you *civil* servants of the Crown have ever need of questing knights for your ambitions.'

A khitmagar brought in a tray of coffee. Somervile gestured towards his guest. 'Shall not the guns be a hindrance in the forest? Indeed, shall you be able to traverse the country at all with them?'

Hervey took a cup of blisteringly hot coffee, stronger even than Somervile's normal taste required, then sat down. 'We shall dismantle them at the forest edge and port them on the horses like woolpacks.'

Somervile nodded at this evidence of Hervey's ingenuity, but he still wore an air of concern. 'What then, in general terms, is your intention?'

Hervey sipped at his coffee. 'The intelligence we have is quite precise, although how reliable we cannot tell. The Burmans are assembling just inside the country, on the river where a road appears to lead all the way from Ava and to the middle of nowhere, though perhaps it is the other way round. Either way it seems curious. Has the road some significance, do you know?'

Somervile answered at once. 'I think you need not concern yourself on that account. The road leads *from* there to Ava. The story goes that a great white elephant was found in the forest, and the local zamindar took him as a gift to the king, making the road as he went.'

Hervey was gratified there was no more complicating detail than this. 'The only difficulty is finding the road on our maps. The river divides near the border, and it's by no means apparent which is the place. You say the Arakanese know how to get there, and the Chakma guides know the border well, but I prefer to know where I'm about.'

'It is ... what, fourscore miles?'

'Nearer the hundred, I should say. There's a diversion of some dozen or more in order to avoid one of the settlements. I intend we march twenty this day, and then make camp, and then strike it well before dawn tomorrow so that we shake off any followers. There's a good place for such a halt, your Arakanese say – just beyond a fording place on the Karnaphuli, on the Bandarban road. And thence it's into the hill tracts.'

Somervile looked unsure. 'I doubt you will find a ford so low on the Karnaphuli, even at this time of year.'

Hervey was not greatly perturbed. 'The Arakanese said there might be a little way to swim, but this doesn't trouble me. It's a torpid stream and the horses will know what to do even if half the dragoons don't. It will be good practice. I would have had them doing it in a month or so in any case had we not been stood-to to this. The Arakanese say it's called the Bandarban ford, so the chance of our needing to swim seems very low.'

Somervile nodded. 'So be it. And what are your intentions for the assault?'

'That I can't determine until I've seen for myself the assembly place. I'm trusting to the intelligence that there will be more boats than fighting men. I shall want to secure the site against surprise, and then set to with the breaking-up of the boats. I'm inclined to think we might fire them, except that I can't risk setting alight the forest.'

'No, that would be most hazardous,' Somervile agreed, nodding with some disquiet. 'But what shall you do if there are more men than the intelligence suggests?'

Hervey raised his eyebrows. 'So much depends on their attitude. If they are without much discipline in their security we might yet be able to prevail over them. But if they're alert we shall give them a fright and make good our escape. You would want me to make a demonstration, failing all else?'

'Oh yes, indeed. It risks a *casus belli*, of course, but they are at any rate intent on an attack – of that we are quite sure – and a check such as that might unsteady them a consider-able degree. But I do urge that you have a care. I should not ask you to throw away any man's life in mere speculation, Hervey. I leave to you absolutely how intent you press your attack.'

'Thank you, Somervile. You may be assured I have a proper regard for the dangers, but I'm grateful to have your trust reposed in such a manner.' Hervey made to stand. 'Now, let me show you the difficulties as far as I can discern from this map.'

'Dodds is absent, Hervey,' said Seton Canning as they walked to the stables before the two o'clock mustering.

Hervey stopped dead. 'When? Where?'

'He didn't parade for boot and saddle.'

'I'll have Dodds hanged if we have to set off without him!'

No one could be sure if the threat were more than just exasperation, but the edge was such as to make Seton Canning start. 'The sar'nt-major has sent people out looking for him, but he couldn't spare too many.'

And doubtless Armstrong was not much grieved by the loss, thought Hervey – beyond the affront to discipline. 'I suppose we must own that bad character will out,' he hissed.

Seton Canning said not another word.

At the stables Johnson stood holding the little Marwari which his captain had taken as his second charger. Hervey took the reins and mounted at once. 'Gilbert is seen to?'

'Ay sir. I told yon cripple I'd lame 'im good an' proper if there was as much as a stable mark on 'im when I got back.' Private Hicks's leg was all but mended after his fall a month before, but he had limped about the lines for so long that he could be sure 'St Giles' would remain his nickname for as long as he wore uniform.

Hervey frowned. 'He'd better believe it,' he rasped, leaning forward to pull up a keeper on the bridle. 'And you told him, a pectoral morning and evening? That cold came on so quickly; I don't want it turning to anything worse.'

'I told 'im, sir.'

Hervey nodded grimly. 'Where d'ye think Dodds is hiding, by the way?'

'In t'rear rank if 'e's any sense.'

Hervey looked at him, puzzled.

Then Johnson realized. 'Tha doesn't know 'e's back then?'

'No, I did not. How so?'

'Corporal Mossop found 'im in a cunny-warren in t'town!'

A syce led out Johnson's own horse, together with

Hervey's new second. Hervey frowned at his groom, wanting more from him.

''E were too fuzzed to stand, Mossop said.' A hint of a smirk betrayed Johnson's pleasure at the pun.

Hervey was not inclined to share it. 'Johnson, you do realize he would have been hanged for his absence?'

'Ay sir,' replied his groom, the smile gone. 'And to tell thee t'truth, there'd not be any as'd put in a good word for 'im.'

Hervey fumed, but at himself. It was he who had wanted to enlist Dodds, and since then he had seized on any sign of amends to his 'bad character', and in the face of Armstrong's continuing doubts. For a moment the lash seemed appealing.

He tried to put it from his mind as he rode with Seton Canning to the maidan. He halted at the edge to let his lieutenant go forward to take over the parade from Armstrong, and then he in turn took command. As he rode along the front rank and then the rear, his humour was much restored by his dragoons' appearance. Green his troop might be, but they looked likely enough this day. Just so long as they went to it with a will, and luck went with them, they would manage.

'Dodds is with the bat-horses, sir, in open arrest,' said Armstrong as they cleared the rear right marker. 'For my part I'd have him nowhere near, except that he should stand his chances like the rest of them.'

Hervey could not help wondering, even now, if Dodds had truly intended to absent himself. 'Are we sure he *was* at first parade? Unless he'd heard the warning for the field, he couldn't very well be charged with desertion.'

Armstrong had not considered it. The troop had been reported present or else accounted for. 'I'll get 'is corporal to vouch, sir,' he replied doubtfully.

Hervey checked in front of one of the Warminster pals. 'Are you quite well, Parkin?' he asked, seeing an unusual amount of perspiration about his face and neck.

'Not feeling too good, sir. I expect it'll pass though, sir.'

Hervey glanced at Private Wainwright next to him.

'He were all right until last night, sir, but he didn't want to report sick after what you said at first parade, sir.'

'Report now to the surgeon, Parkin.'

Parkin saluted, a shade awkwardly thought Hervey, as if his arm were constrained, and fell out to his right. 'You'll find him with the bat-horses, lad,' said Armstrong as he passed.

'What did he have to eat last night, Wainwright?' asked Hervey.

'Mutton, sir, same as us.'

'And drink?'

'Just a measure of rum, sir. That's all. He never has more, sir.'

Hervey pressed on down the line, looking into faces more intently now, determined on seeing any sign that Parkin's ailment might not be entirely his own. But all looked none the worse than usual.

They rode round behind the rear rank to where the two galloper guns were, their teams – each of three sowars – sitting like ramrods in the saddle, the kurtas as vivid as sunflowers. Hervey had asked for a daffadar who could understand some English and the adjutant had assured him that he would oblige; but he tried a few words of his Urdu, if as no more than a courtesy.

The daffadar braced in acknowledgement: '*Hazoor!*'

There was a strange noise from beyond the guns, a bleating. Hervey peered between the sowars to see what was the cause.

'Rations, sahib!' said the daffadar, with a grin.

Now he could see it. One of the packhorses carried two live goats strapped either side of the saddle. Hervey nodded to the daffadar, as much in amazement as approval, then reined about, trotted to the front of the troop, and faced. He looked left and right along the ranks. All eyes were still front, and horses' heads were steady. The regiment did not draw swords for inspection in campaign order, so his command was merely 'Sit easy.'

He stood in the saddle to address them. 'E Troop, I am well pleased with your appearance – as serviceable as anything I saw in the Peninsula. It is a good beginning. We march from here presently some twenty miles, in the direction south-east towards Bandarban. After fording the river thereabouts we make camp for the night, and there I shall give a fuller account of our mission. For the moment it is as well that you understand that, as always, your first duty is the care of your mounts. To that end we make no show of pushing off. We shall cover the first half of that distance at the walk, leading the first half-hour.' He turned to his lieutenant and asked him to carry on, then beckoned Johnson over. 'Go and see what the surgeon says about Parkin, will you? I want every man I can have on parade, but we can't carry sick.'

Ten minutes later, with the troop dismounted and drawn up in column of route, two native guides leading, Johnson returned. 'Mr Ledley says 'e thinks it could be just a chill, but 'e can't be sure. Parkin were swearin' blind it were nowt but a sweat, so t'surgeon 'as dosed 'im an' 'e's fallen in again.'

Hervey nodded. Ledley had no worse a reputation than any, so he might as well trust to his optimism. 'Very well. Trumpeter, "walk-march"!'

CHAPTER TWENTY

COLUMN OF ROUTE

Later that day

E Troop had never marched twenty miles before. For the first half-hour they tramped the road from the cantonment to the river, at times in no better order than a train of tinkers. Hervey set too fast a pace to begin with, the dragoons at the rear of the column finding it difficult to get into their stride, with gaps suddenly opening up and then having to be closed rapidly at the trot. And some of the horses would not take to long reins, so that there was a deal of napping, which in turn opened more gaps. After twenty minutes the NCOs were hoarse with their efforts to keep a semblance of soldierly appearance, and more than one dragoon was looking as though he would not stay the distance. But at last the troop settled to a rhythm of sorts, sustained by each man in turn taking up the pace-count; no mean achievement, Hervey and Seton Canning agreed, considering that at least half of them had not been able to count reliably beyond half a dozen when they enlisted. And then they had tightened girths and mounted, and ridden for the next hour at a steady trot, and very creditably together, Hervey thought from his perspective at the column's head. More than one dragoon found the exercise a powerful thirst-maker, but Hervey had given orders that on the march a strict water discipline was to be maintained. At the first halt, after an hour and a half, several men at the rear of the column believed themselves to be so parched as to be close to expiring, and Corporal McCarthy was obliged to seize with some force a canteen from one of them. McCarthy, though he knew nothing more of horses than what every man had learned since enlisting, was nevertheless entirely convinced of the necessity of discipline. His best Cork 'Horses first, you heathens!' stung would-be defaulters with its obvious appeal to duty as well as with the native authority which an Irish NCO possessed.

The river was slow by the standards of those they had known in Spain, and the colour of earth. At the first halt it was set about by tall rain trees, and the grasses at the edge were not so high as in the open stretch from the city – no higher than a man's knee, and in places grazed shorter or uprooted altogether by cattle and game preferring to drink in the rain trees' shade.

'By sections, mouths into the river and then straight out again,' called Armstrong, handing his own horse to his groom and taking his whip in hand as he began to walk along the line, rapping the other hand with it in a manner that signalled there would be no mercy for the 'idle' dragoon. 'Just enough to wash their mouths with. And then a wisp of a hay. One quarter of one hour!'

Hervey slipped the bridle off his little Marwari and put on the head collar. He was pleased to note how little she had sweated, and how light was her breathing. He led her to the river's edge and let her drop her head. She swallowed twice and he pulled her head up again, quite easily – she did not struggle. She was as fit as ever Jessye had been. He turned her away and walked back to where Johnson waited with a handful of hay. Armstrong came up. 'How are the galloper-gunners?' asked Hervey, picking up each of the Marwari's feet to check for stones.

'Not a bead of sweat on any of them, sir! Horses or men.'

Hervey smiled to himself. 'I wonder what they make of us, Sar'nt-Major.'

'I wouldn't rightly know, sir. But let's wait till we've done what we're doing before we ask 'em.'

Hervey smiled again. 'You're quite right. We'll stand judged by our effect, not our appearance. I'll warrant that if they knew how little time we'd had they'd never believe we could have come this far.'

Armstrong looked puzzled. 'Bloody 'ell, sir. We've come nought but ten miles on a warm afternoon. I reckon my Caithlin could manage that!'

Hervey frowned. Armstrong knew well enough that his captain was speaking of more than the day's march, but the latter knew his serjeant-major's proposition was undoubtedly true. An hour and a half into a 'campaign' was a deal too early to be drawing any conclusions, favourable or otherwise.

'Very well then, five minutes more by my watch. At your order, Sar'nt-Major. Then two leagues at a good trot.' And with that he began replacing the bridle.

The next leg they covered at a flying pace. The ground had a spring in it, neither too hard-baked, as in the early part of the year, nor yet soaked by the heavy rains of the middle months. Horses were fit enough, and riders too – at least for a six-mile trot on good, level going. Hervey glanced behind him from time to time and was pleased by what he saw. The jingle of bits and the striking of hoofs fell into a rhythm, which in turn served that regular order which was the mark of seasoned cavalry. So good a rhythm, indeed, that many a head could have nodded a while in perfect safety.

Hervey judged it by his watch. Forty-five minutes at such a pace – two leagues. He held up his hand and ceased rising in the saddle (the Sixth, in common with many another regiment, had for some time given up 'bumping' in the trot), then brought the Marwari to a walk for a full five minutes more, before holding up his hand again for the halt. In a trice he was off and unsaddling his little mare, patting her neck and making much. She was sweating a bit under the saddle blanket and along her shoulders, but scarcely more than a hunter on an English autumn's day. He pulled the stable rubber from the carry-all on the saddle, and set to removing the worst of it. He picked out her feet – nothing troubling her there either. He pulled her funny little ears, turned in like horns, and spoke keenly to her again before taking off the bridle and slipping on the halter. Now was the time to let her take a good drink. He led her to the river's edge and let her drop her head awhile – not too much, though, not enough to bring on the colic. And then again, a little longer, and then once more, until it was safe to hold the lead-rein loose.

He looked down the line of dragoons as they watered by half-sections so as to be under the eye of an NCO. Perhaps not all the NCOs were the best of that breed, but they were adequate, he felt sure. He thought back to those corporals and serjeants who had crossed the Pyrenees all of seven years ago. Was it so long? Would there ever be their like again? How could there be? Surely they would never see a campaign the like of the Peninsula. And without its like, how could such men as they be forged? He knew it to be true of himself, especially. A God-fearing home he had had, and a soldierly tutor of exemplary quality in Daniel Coates, and the best of learning at Shrewsbury, but it had been the winter of Corunna and the summers afterwards on the Spanish plain that had made him no longer a boy.

'Captain Hervey, sir,' came the voice of Serjeant-Major Armstrong upon his reveries, as it had done innumerable times before in less exalted rank. 'Yon Parkin's a sick man. I've a mind to turn him back.'

Hervey frowned at him. 'Shall I take a look?'

'I think you'd better. Surgeon'll take a look when he's put a stitch or two in Rudd's bonny face.'

Hervey raised an inquisitorial eyebrow.

'That nappy little lass of his threw her head up a bit sharp when he'd taken her bridle off.'

Hervey sighed, handed his reins to Johnson and set off back down the column. He came on Parkin sitting with his head in his hands, with Private Wainwright next to him holding both horses. 'What is it, Parkin?'

'It's nothing, sir,' replied Parkin, struggling to rise.

'No, keep where you are,' said Hervey, squatting on his haunches to take a proper look at Parkin's face. It was undoubtedly worse than at muster, beads of sweat trickling almost continuously down his cheeks and neck. But they had since been in a brisk trot, and for the best part of an hour. 'Do you have any pain?'

'No, sir.'

Wainwright evidently considered the reply incomplete. 'He's got the cramps, though, sir. His joints are aching bad.'

The surgeon had by now come up. He too squatted by Parkin's side, and laid the back of his hand on the dragoon's forehead. 'A fever all right. And a sight worse than at muster. Do you have any head pain?'

Parkin hesitated. 'A headache, sir, yes.'

'And his joints are aching, sir,' added Wainwright.

'Is that right, Parkin?'

'I'll be all right, sir. Just need a bit of a rest.'

The surgeon stood up, then Hervey. 'What is it?'

'I don't know, Hervey. It could be any number of things.' His tone was not optimistic.

'What's the worst it might be?'

'He has the symptoms of breakbone fever, though I must say I have never witnessed the condition myself.'

Hervey looked blank.

'Well, it won't kill him, but the aches will become so bad that he'll not be able to stay in the saddle.'

'I don't want to be fell out, sir,' insisted Parkin, albeit limply.

'No, Parkin, I'm sure you don't. It does you credit. But I can't risk it.'

'Let me just go on to the camp tonight, sir. I'll sweat it out then, and likely be better in the morning.'

Hervey glanced at Wainwright.

'I can see to him, sir,' said Wainwright, reluctant but resigned: he knew Parkin would never want to go back to Warminster Common without the same tale of action to tell. And after all, the surgeon *had* said it would not be fatal even if it were the worst.

'Very well then,' said Hervey briskly. 'But I shan't risk taking you beyond the night's camp if there's no amendment.' It was not a difficult decision; after all, he would still have to send another man back with him whether it were now or then.

Armstrong was not convinced of the logic when Hervey told him, however. 'You've been in these parts a sight more than me, sir, but yon Parkin's going to get a whole lot worse before he gets better. It'd be kindness to send him home now, with less of a distance to do.'

Hervey knew that Armstrong was right, in one sense at least, but he was disappointed nevertheless to hear it. How things had changed – Armstrong, the hardest of men, now speaking of *kindness*. How had it come about? Moreover, how far would it go? 'These are green men, Sar'nt-Major. I'm not going to discourage an instinct for the fight.'

They were sufficiently out of earshot for Armstrong to voice his opinion further. 'Aw, come on, sir! Parkin's a babby still. He's no more idea of a fight than a brawl on a Saturday. We can't afford to carry anybody as can't look after themselves. Send him back with one of the syces.'

Hervey was angered. 'That's a judgement I've got to make. This side of the river there's hardly a risk.'

Armstrong looked equally black. 'Of *course* it's a judgement you've got to make, sir! But what good am I supposed to be if I don't give *my* opinion?'

300

Hervey did not reply at once. 'And you'd trust one of the syces?'

'I would while Parkin's still able to do for himself. We can't afford to send one of ours with him.'

Hervey could not make things out; Armstrong, if he were indeed going soft, was as determined as ever. 'Well, I've told him he can stay with us now. If I have to leave him at the river then it will have to be with a syce. I think there'll be a dak bungalow there anyway.'

Private Johnson led up Hervey's Marwari. 'Parkin looks proper poorly to me, Cap'n 'Ervey. Is tha gooin' to send 'im back?'

Armstrong answered. 'Johnson, you'll look a sight poorlier than Parkin if you don't keep that potato-trap of yours shut. And who said to unbutton that coat?'

Johnson knew he was vulnerable on both counts, and did not even glance at Hervey for support. He braced up instead, and turned away.

Armstrong smiled a little. 'You know, when I kept that place at Datchet I was of a mind to take him on if ever, as they say, you'd dispensed with his services.'

Hervey relaxed, and smiled too. 'That might come as a great shock to him.'

'Oh, I'm not so sure, sir. It's water off a duck's back to our Johnson. He knows his worth, that's one thing.'

Hervey shook his head. 'And that's the problem with half the poor beggars who showed for the shilling. They thought so little of themselves.'

Armstrong took out his pipe. There was no time to light it, but he could prick at the bowl in the familiar way. 'It's a queer place this. Most of these 'Indoos as does for us sleeps on the floor, and yet I don't see 'em cringe for all of that. And as for them Skinner's men, you'd think they were maharajahs the way they carry themselves.'

'And what conclusions do you draw from these observations, Sar'nt-Major?'

Armstrong paused. 'Let's just say that when this lot is shot over the first time, we'll have our work cut out.'

Hervey hoped profoundly he was wrong. 'We can thank God at least that by all accounts the Burmans are not famous fighters.'

Armstrong tapped out his pipe on his boot. 'Ay, well we've heard that afore.'

Hervey knew it, but it was time they began resaddling, and he stood up. 'A couple of leagues at most, and then we'll see what their spirit is when I tell them our orders.'

Armstrong rose too. 'Ay. Crossing yon river'll leave 'em in no doubt we've work to do.'

The Karnaphuli river, at the point where they were to pick up the Bandarban road, was not quite as Hervey had imagined. In one respect it was familiar enough: tall rain trees interlocked their canopies so that the sun could not penetrate in any strength, just as in his memory of the Chintal forest. They were indeed at the edge of the great jungled wilderness that stretched as far as Ava itself, and this much his maps told him; but the Arakanese had described the place as a ford – or that, at least, had been the translation through Bengali. If it was a ford, it was a deep one. Hervey sat contemplating the river for some time. Had he come to the wrong place? The native Arakanese guides seemed sure enough, and after all they had merely had to follow the river upstream to where the only road crossed it. This here was undoubtedly a road of some importance, for there on the far bank was a little ferry – whose ferryman would, in any case, be able to confirm it was the place. Then it tumbled to him: a ford it might be, but for whom? The elephants and their mahouts now wading into the middle from the far side were his probable answer. Their day's work done, it was the hour for a cooling soak, and here, it seemed, was the time-honoured place where they came. To a mahout it was indeed a ford.

Some of the troop-horses became unsettled at the sight and smell of the half-dozen elephants, although they were hardly a novelty. Some of the dragoons likewise showed their unease as they saw the river reach half-way up the flanks of the great beasts.

Hervey put on a brave face. 'Well, the current's pretty slow. Now's as good a time as any to try it.' It was probably true. Swimming was the last drill they had to practise, and although they would first have tried it without saddles, they were not nearly so encumbered as they might have been. And the little rope ferry would take the galloper guns and the farrier's packhorses.

'I'll get them to start waterproofing then, sir,' said Armstrong. 'D'you think we can get them elephants to stand sentinel downstream in case we have a few fallers?'

'I think we may. We'll take a rope across, too.'

It took a full half-hour to make waterproof the firelocks and cartridges, binding carbines and pistols with oilskin and wrapping cartridges in waxed paper. When they were ready, Hervey had the troop remount and face the river in line, then he rode to the centre and cast his eyes left and right. 'I have just two things to say, and you will do well to remember them. First, your horse will swim across without any help from you. All you need to do is to let him have his head and sit tall in the saddle. Second, your carbine: you will have no greeting from me if you emerge from the river without it!'

Hervey paused to let the message be understood. Some of the NCOs added their own warnings, though muttered.

'Those elephants will stand in line in case anyone is unseated,' Hervey went on, and then, slowing his delivery to emphasize the point, added, 'which there is no reason to be!' He nodded to Serjeant Collins.

Collins rode out of the ranks, halted and drew his carbine from its bucket and clipped it to his crossbelt in the approved fashion. Then he took the coil of rope, the end of which the serjeant-major had secured to a tree, looped it in the crook of his right arm, took the carbine in the same hand and rode straight for the river's edge.

'See how he holds the carbine up to keep it dry,' called Hervey, glancing left and right again along the line.

All eyes were on Collins. He rode straight into the river as if it were no more than a field of barley, his horse not hesitating a fraction. For half a minute the water came no higher than Collins's toes, then his knees, and then there was no longer a footing, and the horse struck out into the peculiar lunging motion that was its swimming method, head pushed forward flat on the water.

'See how he has let his horse have the rein, and keeps his back straight and carbine hand raised,' continued Hervey.

For another half a minute Collins's horse paddled powerfully until its feet touched bottom again.

'When the horse first gets a footing he'll lurch a bit until he gets his stride. Don't let your weight be thrown forward or you'll unbalance him.'

The water was now back to Collins's knees, and soon to his toes, and then he was riding up the shallow bank and out of the river.

'Serjeant Collins will secure the rope, and that shall be to save the unwary. But I say again, I do not expect any one of you to have recourse to it!' He nodded to Armstrong, who took up post at the entry point.

'Right, you dryfeet! From the left, begin!' barked the serjeant-major.

Armstrong had numbered off the NCOs carefully so that there would be a good spreading of experience. First in went Private French. 'No harder than driving a pair, lad,' said Armstrong encouragingly. 'Probably a lot easier.'

French rode in confidently.

'Keep that carbine up. He'll be up to his neck in no time.'

Next went Corporal Mossop. 'Go on, Eli. Show 'em how it's done.'

Mossop was by no means the best, but Armstrong knew he would be better for a good word.

Then came Mole, the hireling, and Shepherd Stent. Then Corporal Ashbolt and Harkness, and Corporal McCarthy. 'Look careful there, Paddy,' said Armstrong with a smile. 'It's not the River Jordan.'

'No, sor, it isn't. And I was baptized an infant already.' McCarthy had crossed rivers before, many a time, and by no means as warm and sluggish as this, but always on his feet. He looked gingerly ahead, but he had been trained, and he trusted his officers.

A dozen more entered, as regularly as those in front clambered out on the far bank. Johnson took his own mount and Hervey's second across, knotting his reins and holding his carbine high, and with no more trouble than if he had been crossing the parade ground. Parkin and a clutch of Warminster pals came next. Armstrong eyed him fiercely: 'Parkin, you keep that carbine hand up, mind!' That was going to be the least of his worries, Armstrong knew, but this was not the time for second thoughts. He fixed Corporal Tait, following, with a glare. Tait knew what he meant, and nodded. And if there was a better corporal than Tait in the saddle then he wasn't in the Sixth. Then came Wainwright and Rudd, eager to ride up close to Parkin, but Armstrong held them back awhile (it was no use too many in the stream at once).

Parkin was doing well, sitting upright if a little hunched, struggling manfully to keep his carbine up by his shoulders. Corporal Tait was alongside, Wainwright and Rudd a couple of lengths behind. In less than a minute they would be in the shallows. And then the very worst happened, so quick that none saw it coming. The ferry rope, straining to hold the raft with its two galloper guns, snapped with a crack like a rifle. It startled the horses on the near bank and even unsettled the elephants. The raft swung free as if propelled by a paddle, and bore down at once on the swimmers.

There was nothing they could do. Tait was struck first and knocked clean from the saddle, but he managed to grab the side of the raft. Then it hit the packhorse carrying the goats. The horse lost balance, and the current, though weak, began to take the drowning animal towards the elephants, the goats bleating frantically. Then the raft swung round and caught Parkin, still struggling manfully to keep his carbine dry. He disappeared beneath the big teak logs with a shout of 'Jobie!'

Jobie Wainwright did not calculate. He threw himself from the saddle towards the raft, but he fell well short. He had swum many a time in the rivers and ponds about Warminster, but the weight of all he bore was too much, and he too sank like a stone. Corporal Tait threw his crossbelt and carbine onto the raft and slid below after them. Armstrong likewise threw off all his equipment and coat and raced powerfully to the middle of the river, bellowing at Rudd to stay in the saddle. Serjeant Collins plunged in from the far bank astride his gelding, and Shepherd Stent dived headlong after him. Hervey shouted for the remainder to stand fast and then put his own horse into the river. The Skinner's daffadar struggled to hold the galloper guns on the raft as it swung towards the rope which Collins had paid out.

Tait surfaced gasping, struggling desperately to bring up his man. Armstrong reached him first and managed to pull up Wainwright's head. Collins was close enough now to reach out and grab hold of his crossbelt. Tait, exhausted, seized the rope, coughing and trying to catch his breath. 'Parkin, sir! Just under!'

Armstrong dived once more, then Shepherd Stent. After half a minute Armstrong came up for air, then Stent, and then both went under again. It seemed an age. The raft went over the rope, but the mahouts were already moving the elephants towards it. Up came Armstrong and Stent together, gasping worse than Tait, and with a lifeless Parkin. Hervey grabbed his crossbelt and took the weight from them so they could both make for the rope. And in a minute it was all quiet, the river empty but for two of the elephants, the others having edged the raft to the far side.

The surgeon had been the last out. He had never so much as ridden his horse through a dewpond before, but he had put him straight at the far bank as soon as he had seen cause. And now he worked frantically to revive Parkin, even as the crowding knot of men saw there was no life in him. A full five minutes did Ledley pound at Parkin's chest to have him cough up the water. Never would Hervey have believed a surgeon had such faith. But it was to no good. At length he rose, and pronounced him dead.

Two hours it took to dig Private Parkin's grave. The troop carried only a few entrenching tools, and Hervey wanted it deep, so that the scavengers at the jungle's edge should not disturb Parkin's resting place. The pals – Wainwright, Spreadbury and Needham – dug alone for the first hour, until finally they relented and let Rudd, the 'milliner', join them. Needham cried quietly for a lot of the time. He and Parkin had lived cheek by jowl on Warminster Common since they could remember, longer even than had Jobie Wainwright, for he had come with his mother from the parish when he was full five years old. Only once did anyone speak, when Spreadbury, exhausted, sat down and said, 'Danny should have been let off sick.' But Jobie had simply taken up the pick and quietly explained, 'No, Billy. We's all soldiers now.' And the others had accepted it because Jobie had said it. But even Jobie could not rest, for he had told Parkin's mother he would look after him, and he hadn't. What would he say to her? She was as good a mother as any there was on the Common.

When it was done, the pals brought Parkin's body, wrapped in his cloak, and laid it beside the grave, where the rest of the troop was drawn up, hatless.

'I am the resurrection and the life, saith the Lord: he that believeth in me, though he were dead, yet shall he live: and whosoever liveth and believeth in me shall never die.' Hervey spoke the words with sad assurance. Though the rubric of the Prayer Book required that the office was not to be used for any that died unbaptized, he had not been minded to enquire of Parkin's status. He wanted to commend a stout-hearted dragoon to his maker, and to show to the others that the Sixth honoured its dead. 'We brought nothing into this world, and it is certain we can carry nothing out. The Lord gave, and the Lord hath taken away; blessed be the name of the Lord.'

The words settled on the troop like a chill evening mist. All movement ceased.

Then Hervey read Psalm 90, with its promise of a longer span of life than Parkin had enjoyed, and, probably, than many of those gathered could expect; there were few grey hairs in a regiment, and even fewer in a troop. Afterwards came Saint Paul's epistle to the Corinthians, long and bewildering, and the ranks were not now so statue-like. Hervey sensed it, and hammered out its concluding questions: 'O death, where is thy sting? O grave, where is thy victory?' And he raised his voice in authority at its final command: 'Therefore, my beloved brethren, be ye steadfast, unmoveable, always abounding in the work of the Lord, forasmuch as ye know that your labour is not in vain in the Lord.'

Hervey nodded to Armstrong, who in turn nodded to the pals, who took the ends of the knotted reins by which Parkin's body would be lowered into the earth.

'Man that is born of a woman hath but a short time to live, and is full of misery,' began Hervey again, as the pals played out the reins. And then, the body at rest and the reins recovered, Hervey threw a handful of earth into the grave, and the pals did likewise. 'Forasmuch as it hath pleased Almighty God of his great mercy to take unto himself the soul of our dear brother here departed, we therefore commit his body to the ground . . .'

Hervey had always liked the appellation 'brother' applied to a fellow dragoon, irrespective of rank, and hoped that it would strike the same chord beyond just the pals. For it was the strength of the regiment that a dragoon would fight for his friends – would lay down his life, even – and that those friends, those brothers-in-arms, numbered many more than might ordinarily be the case. Indeed, at its principled best, the regiment was a body of friends, whose connection was no more than the sharing of the Roman 'VI' in their headdress.

The rest of the Order for the Burial of the Dead Hervey abbreviated, leading next the Lord's Prayer – and hearing a respectable rendering of it by many of those present – and then pronouncing the Grace. But 'Amen' could not be sufficient to a military occasion, and so he ended with a peremptory 'Parade dismissed.' He turned away and closed his prayer book. It had been the first time he had opened it in many months.

CHAPTER TWENTY-ONE
THE LEAFY LABYRINTH

Later

The noise of the river crossing, and then the solemnity of the burial service, had masked the peace of a rainforest afternoon. From dawn until late morning there was a procession of sound. Some of it, such as the birdsong, was entirely obvious in its origin, but much of it was far from so. Cicadas were easy to tell, like crickets in some vast echo chamber, but what started quite evidently as a chorus of cicadas would then metamorphose in the strangest way, so that it was not clear whether the cicadas had changed their tune or whether another creature had taken it up in imitation and begun its own development. Sometimes, especially at night, the noise seemed as if it were made by machine – hammering and drilling, and rasping like a saw drawn across wire. And all the time there was whistling, whooping, growling, screeching, snarling – terrible other-world noises that could chill the marrow even as the flesh ran with sweat. But not in the afternoon. Then, as in the early hours of the pre-dawn, the forest became progressively silent, as if every creature had flown or slid away. This was the time that Hervey knew, the time he had ventured a little way into the mysterious jungle. It had been silent that afternoon in Chintal, five years ago nearly, when the raj kumari had tempted him. And it had been silent that night when he had crept with the rajah's sowars through the tangled blackness to fall upon the mutineers, so imprudently asleep at their post. Hervey had not heard the rainforest's full-throated chorus. He knew of it only from what men had told him, usually men wide-eyed with the telling.

With little more than an hour to darkness, there were many things for officers, NCOs and dragoons alike to attend to; but Hervey was determined to speak to them about the march ahead, and indeed of the ultimate purpose of that march. He therefore ordered the campfires to be built high so that he could address the troop in full view of them, even if they for the most part would be in the shadows.

It was a joy to watch Armstrong at field duty. This time of the day was his, and he knew precisely how to fill it. His eye missed nothing, nor his ear. His whip swished, jabbed and pointed this way and that, without ever making contact with a man, and certainly never a horse. An NCO considered himself well worthy of his rank if he escaped wholly without censure. Hervey could think himself in Spain once more, when death was an almost daily affair, and as he sat alone beneath a magnolia tree he found it easier than he had expected to lay aside thoughts of Private Parkin, and to apply himself instead to his maps. Such was the worth of a serjeant-major of Armstrong's line and service.

'Five minutes, sir,' said Armstrong.

Hervey looked up. The light was failing and he could no longer make out the detail on his maps, such as it was. 'Very good. All's well?'

'As you'd expect, sir. They're just getting on with things. Surgeon's got his work cut out trying to stop 'em pulling them leeches straight off, though.'

Hervey nodded. 'A very noble effort of his with Parkin.'

Armstrong sighed. 'It was scabby luck: Parkin of all people to be in its way.'

And that was the only way to look at it, Hervey

considered. But he knew he had yet to bring the occurrence to a close in the minds of many of the troop, the greenheads especially.

When they were assembled, standing easy with carbines piled, Hervey began at once on the task of putting the spirit back in them. He knew how a Frenchman, or perhaps an Italian, would go about it, with soul-stirring rhetoric and appeals to patriotic sentiment. But the English soldier, in his experience, responded best to something simpler. 'Private Parkin died today because he was too good a man to go sick when his companions were embarked on something hazardous. I have to tell you now that many of you – all of you, perhaps – will be put to the same test as Parkin in the days ahead.'

The silence was now absolute.

'We shall strike camp tomorrow morning, two hours before dawn, and shall be taken by the native guides north to the Burman border through thick forest, a march of perhaps two or three days. We shall rendezvous with tribesmen from the hills who know that border well, and we shall cross it and enter Burman territory, and we shall seek out the force which is at this very moment assembling with the intention of bearing down upon the place we have just left.'

He paused to judge the effect. The silence held as acutely as before.

'Having discovered their location, we shall attack them with the greatest ferocity and destroy their capacity to do this vile thing.'

The promise of action was too much – just as he had hoped – and there was a murmur of approval. He must now encourage it.

'Do not ask me what is the plan of action, for until we know where is the enemy and what his dispositions, such plans are futile. Only remember this: surprise is our shield and our spear, but without our horses we can have no advantage once surprise is lost. We shall struggle therefore to take them through the forest in the expectation that their appearance alone will shock the enemy.' He had toyed with the idea of reference to Hannibal, but the allusion would have been absurdly high-flown, and much worse understood. 'And we should be grateful they are good little tats, all of them.'

He saw the nodding of heads. Now was the time to promise and to challenge. 'Very well, you new men are to become soldiers full and good. See to it that you do not dishonour Private Parkin! Parade is dismissed.' He delivered this last as fact rather than an order, which allowed the challenge to carry over into the conversation that at once arose. And he would stand aloof from it, but ready to respond if approached. It was not yet the time to go among them.

Armstrong knew it from old, and busied himself with the roster of sentries. Seton Canning sensed it and sought out the quartermaster to discuss some matter of provisions. Even Johnson found other things to be about. Eventually some NCO would come and share his enthusiasm for what Hervey had promised, but for the moment he would watch the little knots of men alone. And he could think of what he might be able to say to the Skinner's men who had stood loyally but uncomprehendingly throughout.

It was cold that night. Even near a fire, and wrapped in his cloak, Hervey felt the earth giving up its warmth to the sky and taking with it his own, for they were bivouacked in a clearing. He had turned in at once after rounds at last light, the night noises just beginning – the men would have to bear them for themselves – and he had slept fitfully. He had not risen at all, leaving to his lieutenant instead the job of picket-officer, for he knew it was no advantage his having a man like Seton Canning if he didn't use him. When he did wake, the silence surprised him, with only here and there a whicker from the horse lines or a grunt from a sleeping dragoon.

Nothing sounded the passing of the early hours in the forest. In Spain there had always been something – the cockcrow, a tocsin, or a watchman's call. He imagined that he had not slept this far from habitation in three years. He could look at his hunter if he wished, by the light of the dying fire, or the luminescent one which Daniel Coates had given him, but he had seen no point, instead lying still, keeping what warmth remained to himself.

An hour later, as Hervey dozed, Johnson shook him gently by the shoulder. 'Tea, Cap'n 'Ervey. An' a good mashin' it is an' all.'

Tea at this time and in these circumstances had always had but one important quality as far as Hervey was concerned – that it was hot. Whether or not it was strong or sweet, or had milk, was of no moment compared with this requirement. And it had been Johnson's singular ability in this direction which for some years now had marked him out in Hervey's mind as a special sort of man. Since coming to him in Spain, Johnson had never failed to bring him tea at reveille. Even on the morning of Waterloo, when the rain had poured all night, Johnson had brought 'a good mashing' before stand-to, so welcome a drink that Hervey truly believed he would choose to give up all other before he would give up tea.

'It's four o'clock, sir,' added Johnson without having to be asked.

Hervey would record in his journal, later that day, that the dawn stand-to went passably well, except that the troop made too much noise. And he would be pleased with the day's march, too. The going was easy, and they met with no setback in the forty miles they covered, most of it by midday. The camp that evening therefore had an altogether different air from that of the one before. The NCOs were agreeably surprised by the way the march had gone, and were now giving their orders with not quite so much of a snarl. Armstrong, especially, had been pleased to be able to march

314

and ride for long periods without having to open his mouth. The private men, for the most part, were very tired, for to those unaccustomed to such a distance in one day, the bodily and moral exertion was prodigious. But a tired soldier was almost invariably a contented soldier, a maxim Hervey had learned from Joseph Edmonds when first he had joined, and which he had confirmed for himself in no time at all. And so it would be a propitious time for him to go about the troop in their bivouac as fires were beginning the work of making their supper – just to show himself, just to be there to let the private men share their contentment with him. It would make it so much the easier when he needed to go among them when things looked perilous.

Hervey walked the horse lines by himself, in the main content with what he saw. But the mosquitoes were back, and the men were occupied in rubbing a foul-smelling liquid about their horses' faces and ears – and, indeed, their own – which the commissary in Chittagong had dispensed. Hervey had brought some citronella from Calcutta, which seemed to work just as well as the camphor or whatever was the other, but had the advantage of a pleasant scent, if the disadvantage of a hefty price.

At the end of the line he came across Private Mole sitting on the ground, who, when he saw Hervey approaching, began struggling to pull up his overalls to stand. He looked more doleful than usual, even taking account of his lip.

'Are you quite well, Mole?'

'He's got a leech on his pennis, sor!' said Corporal McCarthy, taking an ember from the fire, blowing it red-hot and handing it to Mole.

Hervey kept the shiver to himself. The surgeon had warned them all about the jungle leech's habits and preferences, but this seemed uncommonly early proof of it. 'Sit yourself down, then, Mole. Would it not be better to call Mr Ledley, Corporal McCarthy?'

'Ah, there's no need, sor. That ember'll do it. I've done it meself many a time afore, though I must say never with the crown jewels.'

Hervey watched as Mole braced himself and applied the ember to the engorged worm. It curled up at once and in another second let go its grip, falling wriggling to the floor, where Mole's angry boot finished the job.

'Just as Mr Ledley told us, sor,' said McCarthy, with a look of satisfaction. 'An ember's the thing. That or salt. I've seen 'em pulled off in a panic and the wound become very pussy afterwards.'

Mole looked unhappy still. Hervey thought it best to leave him to recover his humour as well as his modesty. He turned and walked back along the line contemplating his good fortune in having McCarthy. It was clear the man was possessed of something in his field habits which commanded the dragoons to imitate him. He had recognized McCarthy's fighting spirit in an instant when first they had been hurled together in France, but he had for long months retained a suspicion that an NCO who had once lost his stripes might ever be doing so again. McCarthy was probably no more impulsive a pugilist than Armstrong, and probably no more enamoured of a drop or two than he, but Armstrong had never been reduced to the ranks; that was the difference. Was it, perhaps, that discipline was in some way administered differently in the infantry? He wished he had been able to enquire of the 104th what had been the circumstances. But there was no denying now that McCarthy was an exemplary corporal. Hervey didn't even have to trust to his own judgement in that; Armstrong was certain of it.

It was not the same with Corporal Mossop, though. Mossop did not do anything wrong; he did it, indeed, to the best of his ability. And there lay the problem. Mossop tried, but nothing came easily or naturally. Mossop was awkward, even in conversation. He would have thrown himself into the flames for his captain, but Hervey would dodge the other side of a horse so as not to have to pass the time of day with him. And that, he knew full well, could not but convey itself to the man, and so he would make himself go through the motions of bantering, if only to display his confidence in him in front of the dragoons. But Mossop would never be a serjeant; that was certain. With McCarthy, on the other hand, there could be no such certainty.

When Hervey looked at Collins, though, he wondered how any other corporal might aspire to serjeant. How might they measure themselves against him – his celerity in action, his composure in routine? It was Collins's misfortune, however, to be a serjeant at this time, for the wait would be long for the fourth piece of tape. He needed the toast to 'a short war and a bloody one', but India looked unlikely to oblige him, even with forays such as this. It was a sorry thing to wish for dead men's boots, thought Hervey, but he hoped very dearly that Collins would not be spent before his time came for a troop of his own.

However, it was the little knot of Warminster pals that intrigued him most. They were three now, the original pals, but Rudd was messing with them this evening. His mother would have been appalled at the notion of her son's associating with the roughs of Warminster Common – and in ordinary the son too would never have had occasion to speak with them – but the bond of a shared home place when so far distant from it was ever strong. Even Shepherd Stent, although an Imber man by birth, felt some kin with Rudd and Wainwright and Spreadbury and Needham. Indeed, he had been more welcome in the high street, at the sheep markets with his father, than ever the roughs of the Common had been. Hervey stood watching them for some time, unnoticed. Stent was the older by ten years, perhaps, and by experience and temper should have been the chosen man in their case. But he seemed always to want nothing of it, to want that nothing extra be required of him other than honest duty as a private soldier. Hervey still had his doubts about him as coverman. As for Rudd, he was a shiny dragoon – no

317

doubt about it – but as yet there seemed no edge to him that would make him fit for command. It was Wainwright, not yet twenty, who held the pals' esteem. Indeed, the more Hervey saw of him, and the more he thought about it, the more he was convinced that Wainwright had singular promise. What was beyond doubt was that yesterday both Jobie Wainwright and Shepherd Stent had shown instinctive and selfless courage. England bred her heroes rough, mused Hervey; but breed them she did.

They were late striking off next morning. Hervey had been expecting a rendezvous with the Chakma guides the evening before, but there had been no sign of them. By eight o'clock, the troop having breakfasted and done an hour's making and mending, there was still no sign of them. Hervey spoke with Seton Canning and Armstrong. 'I don't like just sitting and waiting. The track we're following is clear enough, and the Chittagong guides say they're certain it leads to the border. The Chakma will have no difficulty finding us if they're as good as they say. I intend pressing on and making up lost time.'

Armstrong made as if to turn, but Seton Canning looked mildly troubled. 'Why might the Chakma not be here, Hervey? You're not inclined to see any mischief?'

Hervey grimaced to himself. 'No, I'm not inclined to, not yet. There are any number of reasons why they mightn't have shown – the haste with which we mounted things, to begin with.'

'These folk work to a different clock from us, Mr Seton Canning, sir,' added Armstrong. 'It were just the same in Spain. There you'd wait days for some bandit to leave off what he was doing.'

'And in any case, I don't see any alternative.'

Hervey's voice had an edge to it again. Seton Canning made no reply.

* * *

Just after midday, with close on four hours of marching behind them, the troop halted for the second rest. The going had become harder than the day before, the ground now climbing towards the tribal tracts, but the way was wide enough still to permit two horses to go abreast. This was important for it allowed the NCOs to patrol the column, although, as yesterday, they found remarkably little dereliction or inactivity to reprove.

The troop had taken longer than prescribed at the first halt since they had ridden for longer, the way being too steep to pull up for some miles; and it had been the same with the second halt, for Hervey had wanted to draw closer to the river. By his calculations they were now within three hours of the border. The Chittagong guides seemed sure of it too, although they conceded that their knowledge of these parts was sparse. There was still no sign of the Chakma, however, and Hervey knew that soon the guides would be wholly beyond their reach. Not that they had shown the least hesitation so far. Quite the opposite, indeed: one of them, an Arakani boatman whom Somervile had said knew the rivers well, seemed positively fired with the notion of the coming blow at his people's oppressor. He told Hervey, in broken Urdu, that he knew the country well enough to take them to the boats, and Hervey could but admire the man's determination to be at them; and, he reasoned, he was not himself entirely without resource in navigation. The way they had come had been the way of the Karnaphuli, and that was the essential detail, even if for much of the time the river had been out of sight.

Hervey leaned back against a tree, where Johnson had placed a blanket for him to sit, and peered again at his map. That morning he had checked constantly by his travelling compass, and he was as confident as any might be of their position and course. He decided to press on as soon as the rest was up. But he judged it time to make packhorses of the troopers pulling the galloper guns, for if the way deteriorated much more, wheels would be an encumbrance. Also, he did not want to be disassembling guns in a place not of his own choosing. He sent word for the daffadar to make ready as soon as he could.

In a quarter of an hour he got up and walked to the back of the column. There he was surprised to find wheels and trunnions, barrels and trails already stripped down and distributed between the two gun-horses and the four spares. He hoped they would be as quick, if not quicker, reassembling them when the time came: a ball and a bag of grape would be a powerful blow to the enemy, not for its material effect so much as for the shock of cannon fire in so wholly unexpected a place.

The afternoon was the hardest. For the most part the dragoons had to lead, not only to spare the horses but because the way was ever more overgrown. Saj trees crowded the way, their grey bark like crocodile skin and bhorla creepers coiling like snakes about their trunks. Soon the horses were being led single-file. So heavy were the vines and creepers that here and there a branch, and sometimes a whole tree, had collapsed across the way, and the farriers' axes would be called up. And while the axes swung, the dragoons stood, the respite welcome. They had shed their coats at the second halt, on command, but the sweat ran freely still. Some swore there was less air to breathe, others feared that trees might fall behind them like coffin lids. Some thought secretly of flight; but what chance might they have in this green prison, and with NCOs like Armstrong and Collins – ay, and McCarthy – after them? Only a very few of them could take pleasure in what the jungle offered their eyes: orchids, little dabs of colour in the gloom, or the strange shapes of the dhak trees, dark crooked skeletons which in two or three months' time would burst into flower, orange and red, the 'flame of the forest'. Jobie Wainwright could. Jobie saw pleasing things in the most wretched of places. It was why the Common had not made a felon of him as it had many another. For the rest, there were not half a dozen who might share Jobie's pleasure in the forest. They might be sons of the crowding streets of a great city, but cities weren't forests: they were not haunted by all manner of beasts that might kill in an instant, whose strike was sudden and unseen. And at night, even in the drearest, foggiest rookery, there were not ghostly creatures that slid or shuffled as here about the forest floor, that darted between the trees, or crept about their branches.

Hervey could see their unease all too well as he walked back along the column when they were halted to clear a third tree. But at the rear was Armstrong, looking for all the world as if he were merely at stables, at Hounslow even. Armstrong was neither fearful of nor partial to the forest. He was entirely unmoved by it: the forest was there, and he was in it; that was that. 'This is chatty country all right,' he opined as Hervey pushed past the last dragoon. 'And getting chattier by the looks of it.'

Hervey took off his shako, wiped his brow with his sleeve, and raised his eyebrows. 'The guides say it will get no worse – well, not *much* worse.'

'Do they know what they're about?'

'Well, they're putting on a good show if they don't. They say we should reach the river again before six' (it was now a little after three), 'and that's the border, and then we can ride its length for about a mile and that will place us to advantage above where the boats are.'

'Where do you want to make camp for the night then?'

'Just short of the river. We can water and then retire a furlong or so to bivouac.'

'You'll be wanting to push out scouts, then.'

'I think I'd better. Is all well with you?'

'Ay, sir. Them packers have been struggling a bit of late, but they're sticking with it.'

'The gun-horses or the quartermaster's?'

'Both. But them Skinner's men are good.'

Hervey nodded. A cheering report was ever welcome. The struggle past the column was worth it for that alone. He replaced his shako and made to turn. 'Well, the river will be a fine thing again. The canteens are getting empty.'

It was fortunate that the third saj had lain where it had, for within half an hour the scouts signalled alarm. Corporal Ashbolt, first scout, hurried back to report, finding Hervey now at the front of the column, just behind the point-men.

'T'river's ahead, sir, three hundred yards. But there are voices.'

'What sort of voices?' asked Hervey, his unease at once apparent to the guides beside him.

'Difficult to tell, sir,' replied Ashbolt. 'High-pitched, like women, but they might not be. Corporal McCarthy reckons there are three different ones at least.'

Hervey was even more dismayed. Women meant a village. The guides had said they would encounter no settlement. He decided he would tell them nothing for the moment. 'Mr Seton Canning and the serjeant-major, please,' he said to his trumpeter. 'And Serjeant Collins.'

It took a full five minutes to assemble them.

'The scouts have come on the river and heard voices which might be female,' said Hervey, as matter-of-fact as he could. 'I want to take a look for myself, with you, Serjeant Collins.'

Collins nodded.

'Mr Seton Canning to have the troop stand to, if you please.'

His lieutenant nodded likewise.

'How are the packhorses, Serjeant-Major?'

'They're managing all right, sir.'

'Good. Well, let's make a start. Storrs will come as relay. And, Sar'nt-Major, I want a close eye on the guides.'

'Ay, sir. Mine it'll be an' all.'

Hervey took his carbine from the saddle bucket. A sudden thought of the repeater falling from Henrietta's hands made him hesitate, the first thought of her in days. He recovered himself quickly by shaking his head at Private Johnson. Johnson didn't need to ask aloud if he could come. He always wanted to, and the answer was always 'no'. Stent did not even look; his duty it was to go with him.

They had gone not more than a few dozen yards when a noisy flock of lorikeets took off from a tree to their left, a whistling whirl of red and blue and bright green. Hervey swung round, carbine raised, to face whatever would be the manifestation of the enemy. Just as suddenly, all was still-ness again. They waited a while, Hervey now more aware than ever of just how vulnerable was the troop. The jungle offered cover from view, but at a price. Once discovered, the troop would be an unwieldy body, overwhelmed in an instant. They had practised a little in the time they had had between the warning order and leaving Chittagong, but it had not been much more than picketing front and rear. If they were assailed from a flank there was little they could do – nothing, indeed, but draw sabres and fight.

Hervey signalled the others to follow. They trod slowly and carefully, eyes searching left and right into the thicken-ing undergrowth. It took a full ten minutes to come up to Corporal McCarthy. He looked relieved to see them. It could not have been more than half an hour since Ashbolt had left him, but the forest had a way of stretching time.

'Well?' said Hervey, voice lowered, gesturing for him not to stand up as he approached.

'Voices went about five minutes ago, sor,' replied McCarthy, rising to a crouch. 'They didn't stop sudden, though. Just trailed off.'

An intelligent observation, thought Hervey. 'Have you been forward to look again?'

'No, sor. I was going to give it a few minutes more in case they were coming back.'

Hervey nodded, approving.

'But another thing, sor,' he added, sounding puzzled. 'The river doesn't run as you'd expect it to.'

Hervey narrowed his eyes.

'Well, sor, I expected it would run from our right to our left. But it runs the other way.'

Hervey was astonished. He looked at his watch: there was but two hours' light left. 'We'd better take another look.'

They rose and began to advance, half-crouching.

After fifty yards they heard voices, angry ones. Hervey looked at McCarthy and Ashbolt. They nodded. 'Same ones, sir,' whispered Ashbolt.

Hervey dropped to one knee and motioned the others to do the same. He listened intently, not knowing for what, only for some clue to inform his next move. Then the voices sounded closer. He strained every nerve to hear. There was no doubt: the voices were coming towards them. He waved his hand at the others to get into cover on the left, then he himself backed a couple of yards into the undergrowth, all that was needed to conceal them.

He had less than a minute to calculate. He had no idea if the voices were hostile. He could let them pass and rely on the point-men, but they might have no warning. He dared not draw his sword for fear of being heard; how many times in the past had he lamented the steel scabbard? He could not risk a shot.

Suddenly there were men in coloured shirts on the track in front of him, and a woman with a rope around her neck. In that instant he judged them to be false. He leapt forward with his carbine at the port. The others followed, drawing swords as best they could. The woman screamed and dropped to her knees. One of the men drew a knife, but Collins gave him the point under the breastbone and the man fell, squealing like stuck pig. Another lunged at the woman, his eyes wild. Corporal Ashbolt cut the knife from his hand with a deft flex of the wrist, then drove the point into his side. The man fell without a sound, eyes even wilder, legs and arms thrashing. The third took off back down the track. Collins and Hervey gave chase, but he was too fleet.

'Shoot!' bellowed Hervey.

Collins dropped to a knee, took aim with his carbine and fired. The shot felled the man and at once set the forest alive with noise.

'Christ!' hissed Hervey. But what choice had he?

They ran to the body and Collins began searching. 'I reckon this is probably ill-gotten, sir,' he said, holding out a bag of gold coin.

'You'd better put him in the undergrowth, Sar'nt Collins,' said Hervey, shaking his head. 'I'll go and see how the others are.'

The other two men were dead, and their bodies too had yielded up gold. The girl was now silent, though she looked fearful. Her features were not those of the men, which were the same as any about the bazaars in Chittagong. Hers was a face of some refinement, the nose smaller than the Chittagong women and her eyes turned up a little. Her salwar kameez, a deep blue silk, was quite unsuited to the forest. Hervey tried his Urdu, but to no avail.

Seton Canning and Armstrong arrived breathless, with the guides in tow. 'Was that your shot, Hervey?'

Hervey nodded. 'It will have put every man on his guard for miles. What can the guides tell us about these two, I wonder?' He gestured at the bloody bodies.

The guides did not need long. '*Dacoiti, badhja.*'

Seton Canning looked at Hervey for enlightenment.

'Bandits and gypsies.' Hervey thought it some relief, at least, to know they had not despatched innocent men.

'And the girl?' added Seton Canning. She was, indeed, not long out of her teens, if at all.

Hervey asked the guides, but they couldn't speak to her either. He cursed to himself. 'You'd better get the surgeon up.'

'Pretty little thing,' said Armstrong approvingly. 'I'll get the daffadar to try talking. Just stepped out of a pallerquin by the looks of her. I wonder how.'

'That's not the half of it, Sar'nt-Major.' Hervey told them about the river. 'I'm going to take a good look. We'd better expect the worst, too. Keep the troop stood to till I return.'

'What about burying these, sir?' asked Armstrong.

'Shallow graves only,' was the reply, almost casually.

Hervey groaned as he saw for himself the worst. The river looked the same as before, but it flowed the wrong way. He took out his compass and laid it on the ground. A carbine Daniel Coates had given him had once been his saving; Coates's compass might yet prove as valuable. The needle settled in a direction he had not expected, indicating north much further to the left. The track had evidently been veering, and so gradually he hadn't noticed. He cursed for not having checked in more than an hour.

'What do you reckon, sir?' asked Serjeant Collins.

'We've come more to the east than we ought. That's all I know. Those guides . . . I'm just not sure.'

'All we've done is follow the same track, sir.'

It was true. The guides had led them nowhere but along the same well-trodden track. 'I wonder then what the Chakma would have done. I suppose they would have led us off the track; there was no undergrowth to speak of for a lot of the way.'

Collins looked at him for the next move.

It was at such a moment that the privilege of command could almost be measured by weight. Hervey was thinking for all he was worth. 'I'm trying to picture the country without the trees, Sar'nt Collins. But it's strange for all that. This river can't join the Karnaphuli: there isn't any junction between where we crossed and Chittagong.' He picked up a stick and started to draw in the earth. 'It must mean there's high ground between here and where we should be. Do you see?'

'Ay, sir.'

'So if we follow the needle due north, and the ground rises, we should recover ourselves.'

'There's no chance your compass is false, sir?'

The thought had occurred to Hervey too. 'Well, I can't picture the ground any other way. The river can't be the Karnaphuli; we can't have crossed it without noticing.'

'We bivouac here, then, sir?'

'I think we'd better.'

A strict rule of silence was the order of the bivouac that evening. Hervey posted sentries well forward, towards the river, and he allowed cooking fires only in pits. The tethering lines were cramped, the track being so narrow, but the horses were quiet enough. Indeed, it seemed to Hervey that they had taken to the forest extraordinarily well, unmoved by its strange noises, and content to chew its green shoots whenever there was a halt. His admiration for the Marwaris grew daily, not least for what fine doers they were, seeming happy with a few handfuls of gram of a morning and evening – rations on which an English trooper would soon have lost condition. In the case of the dragoons, their appetites were not in the least diminished. Hervey had gone to some trouble to find good salt beef before they left, and it boiled up well in the surprisingly sweet river water of which they had had ample since leaving Chittagong. Only the Skinner's sowars were less than content, for no amount of salt mutton could altogether replace the live goats. Even so, the instinct for fresh rations remained strong with the dragoons, for Hervey watched with admiration as one of the Warminster pals plucked a coucal which had fallen to the slingshot as it clambered too sluggishly in the branches above.

After he had looked at every horse with the farrier, Hervey called together Seton Canning, Vanneck and Armstrong and told them his intentions for the morning. He began with his assessment of how they had come too far to the east, and what action they must take to remedy it. He confessed freely that the absence of the Chakma guides now worried him, for whereas the Chittagong guides had previously given him confidence that they could proceed without them, he was no longer so sure – not least because he wondered if he could trust them. But, he declared resolutely, the Avan war barges, astride a river such as the Karnaphuli, could not be concealed from those determined to find them, even in jungle like this. Seton Canning asked what should be done about the woman – little more than a girl, indeed – to which Hervey confessed also that he neither knew what to do with her, beyond entrusting her to the surgeon, nor what her presence signified. The daffadar had been able to have but few words with her, concluding that she was as respectable as her rich silks suggested. Beyond the general intelligence that her people were Avan, there was little more he could discover.

Hervey saw no necessity to deviate from his course, however, especially since Collins had scouted some way along the river and found no sign of habitation. But he wanted the dragoons to know what difficulties lay ahead, and he said he would be obliged if they, his officers, would be as candid with the men as he had been with them. In Spain once, he told them, after a day in which everything that might go wrong had, Joseph Edmonds, then captain, had spoken frankly with his troop. The men, cast down by the events, had been visibly stiffened by their captain's confidences, and their spirits restored on hearing what was his plan for the morning. As a consequence, added Hervey, he himself had come to trust more than many in the innate good sense of the private dragoon, even when his instincts sometimes told him otherwise.

As ever, theory was not wholly justified by practice. At stand-to in the morning, Armstrong was beside himself with anger as he reported to the troop lieutenant.

Hervey, standing close by, could scarcely believe what he heard. '*Absent*, Sar'nt-Major?'

'Ay, sir, absent – gone.'

Hervey felt a wrench at his gut. 'When? How?'

'He's been gone since before midnight, that's all I can tell. Mossop couldn't find him for the sentry change then, but he supposed he was bedded down somewhere else. It was as black as pitch last night.'

'*Damned fool* Mossop!'

Armstrong did not at heart disagree. 'There's not much we could have done about it, even so.'

'There's no fear he's lost himself in the thick of all this?'

'I couldn't say for certain, sir, but the orders were that no one was to leave the lines, even to ease himself. If it were anybody but Dodds I might be inclined to give it a thought.'

There was no rebuke in Armstrong's voice, but Hervey presumed there was one in his mind. 'The bad character is out at last, Sar'nt-Major?'

'I fear so, sir.'

Hervey fell silent for a moment. 'I shall see him hanged.' He almost spat the words.

He pronounced sentence so very determinedly, indeed, that Seton Canning shivered.

Armstrong stood, silent, awaiting orders.

'Very well, Mr Seton Canning, Sar'nt-Major: stand down. Rounds in five minutes if you please.'

A morning round should not have been necessary after the inspection the night before, but Hervey wanted to look each man in the eye. In truth, he doubted them less than he doubted his own judgement, and that indeed was the reason for the rounds – to restore his own pride, and his authority perhaps, for it was well known that it had been he who had championed the reform of a known bad character, against all the usages of the service and the instincts of his NCOs. He need not have troubled, though. There was not a man who appeared in the slightest degree dismayed by Dodds's desertion. Dodds's flight earned the contempt of the bold, and showed to the most timid that they possessed more courage than did another, whereas before they might have thought that none could be possessed of less – a discovery to fortify their own resolve, indeed.

Hervey was much brightened by the round. He wished he could get the whole troop back into the saddle now, to parade in threes and have them in a brisk trot to put the swing into them again, rather than another morning's plodding as yesterday. But that would have to wait. If his calculations were right it would be a day before they broke cover. *Then* they could go at it with a swing all right! He felt his hand twitch to be at the sabre. But for now, he could not even give an animating word of command to advance, let alone sound the trumpet. Only a hand signal, a wave to have the troop set off in single file. And it could not be a wave that set them off as one, as on parade; rather it had to be the French way, each man in turn, so displeasing to an English eye. If Hervey disliked the jungle as much as did his men, it was for different reasons.

In an hour, to his immense relief, the ground began to rise as he had calculated, and with that change in inclination he felt a general rise in spirits. The pace was slower, the sweating – men and horses – even more prodigious, but with each step came the satisfaction of nearing the quarry. If any dragoon were anxious of what was to come, his fear was dulled by the anticipation of at last being able to swing his sabre to a purpose, and to discharge his carbine at more than a roundel. That, and the standing he knew it would bring when they returned to Calcutta.

A fearful cry broke the toiling silence. Hervey swung round. 'Who in God's name is that?' he cursed, reaching for his sword as if he would inflict his own punishment. The column faltered for an instant then struggled on, with anxious glances over shoulders.

A short while later, garbled word reached Hervey that Private French had been attacked by something and could not move. He halted the column and pushed his way back roughly, past two dozen dragoons and more, until he came to the unfortunate French lying motionless, his face swollen beyond recognition, his arms across his chest and his fingers puffed up like cucumbers. 'What in God's name—?'

'Snake, sir. It must have been,' suggested Corporal Mossop, the NCO nearest.

'Beggin' yer pardon, sir,' piped Private Rudd, the rank behind. 'It were bees.'

'*Bees?*' Hervey knelt to feel for French's pulse – he could see the rise and fall of his chest well enough.

'Ay sir. I'm sure of it. They just seemed to be rushing at him.'

'That's not bees,' said Mossop, certain of the symptoms plain to see. 'Bees don't do that.'

Hervey shook his head. 'I wouldn't be too sure. English bees perhaps not. But here . . .'

French remained silent and immobile.

Hervey searched for the obvious clues. 'Well, there's no sign of any bite. And I can't see how a snake could have bit through those overalls.'

Armstrong and the surgeon arrived.

'Ah, Ledley: bees or a snakebite? I can find no sign.'

The surgeon made a tutting sound as he saw his patient. 'How's his pulse?'

'It seemed weak, but I couldn't tell for sure.'

The surgeon took up French's wrist, not troubling with a watch. 'I'm not surprised. His hand's so swollen it's hard to find the pulse at all. Who saw the snake?'

'I didn't actually *see* it, sir,' replied Mossop, his confidence only slightly diminished.

'Then don't speculate,' said Ledley brusquely. 'Worse than useless.'

Corporal Mossop looked crestfallen.

'Who saw the bees then?'

'I did, sir.'

Ledley turned to see his patient of a few days ago. 'Those stitches can come out tomorrow, by the look of them. You saw these bees?'

'I didn't exactly *see* the bees, sir, just French flaying his hands about his head as if he were being *attacked* by 'em.'

'Mm,' said Ledley thoughtfully. 'Not definitive, but good enough in the circumstances.'

'Bee stings, then?' asked Hervey, anxious for confirmation so that they could decide their course.

'Near enough.' By now the surgeon had had a close look at French's face – plumped and red like a gourd on a scarecrow. 'Not bees, though,' said Ledley, shaking his head. 'Hornets, jungle hornets. Brutish little devils by all accounts and the evidence before us.'

Even Armstrong looked appalled at the transformation of the dragoon's features by so small an agent and in so rapid a manner. Only the thick black curls gave away its owner. 'Will he live, sir?'

'I don't know,' said the surgeon briskly. 'If he lives the next quarter of an hour then he ought to be safe.' He reached into his saddlebag. 'Water, if you please.'

Private Rudd unslung his canteen and handed it to the surgeon. Ledley poured a cupful into an enamelled bowl and added five drops of clear liquid from a glass phial. He lifted French's head with one hand and put the bowl to his lips. 'Drink this, my lad. All of it.'

French, who had hitherto shown no sign of sentience, began at once to sip.

'What is it?' asked Hervey.

'Digitalis. To stimulate the heart. That's his greatest need at present.'

Hervey took Armstrong to one side. 'I'll leave one man with him – Rudd – and a surgeon's orderly, but even them we can scarcely spare.'

Armstrong nodded. 'But Rudd's too good a man when we're short already. The orderly ought to be able to mind him on his own. Why not make the woman stay an' all?'

If Dodds had not stolen away in the night like some— Hervey bit his lip and nodded. 'You're right. Just the orderly and the woman. And Boy Porrit. You'd better see to it, then. I'll get the troop moving.'

At the next halt, French's misfortune was retailed through the ranks from the back of the column to the front, and by the time it reached the point-men hornets were no longer the culprit but giant batlike creatures which tore at the flesh and sucked blood more voraciously than a dozen bull leeches. Hervey had to walk the length of the column again to allay the consternation. With some difficulty he managed also to inform the Skinner's sowars of the affair, but they knew full well what had been the cause, and revealed that they had left powdered cow dung with the orderly, to be made into a paste and applied to the swollen parts. Hervey, whose respect for native medicine had been settled during his previous sojourn in India, hoped the orderly would not scruple to use it.

At three o'clock, at the scouts' bidding, they halted. Hervey went forward to see what had prompted them.

'The cover's changing, sir,' said Serjeant Collins. 'It's getting thicker. It must mean we're coming to the edge.'

Hervey smiled thankfully to himself. There were but half a dozen men in the troop who would have drawn such an inference. He checked his map and his calculations. It was certainly possible. 'And it's been flat going for a full two hours,' he said, pleased to be able to corroborate Collins's observation.

'I think I'd like to scout forward a little more, sir. Can the troop hold a while?'

'I think I'll gamble on a bivouac, Sar'nt Collins,' said Hervey, sensing they might make contact with the Burmans sooner rather than later. But how he wished the Chakma were with him, for it was now that their intimate knowledge would be of most use. To stumble on outposts, or make camp too close, would be the devil of a thing after all they had been through. He turned to his trumpeter. 'Storrs, my compliments to Mr Seton Canning, and we'll bivouac where they stand now. I shall go forward with Serjeant Collins to spy things out. Have the point-men sent up to join Corporal Ashbolt here as picket, and have the daffadar reassemble the guns.'

'Very good, sir,' said Storrs, closing his notebook.

Hervey laid down his carbine and pistol. 'And yours too,' he said to Collins and Stent. 'If we come upon an outpost we shall have to carry it with steel. One shot and it might be the death of us all.'

334

CHAPTER TWENTY-TWO
IMMEDIATE ACTION

Later

'It's a fine-balanced thing, Sar'nt-Major, but I think it best to attack at first light. The camp had the look of receiving troops at any minute, but they're not likely to be marching in during the night, so there's nothing to lose in that respect.' Hervey sipped gratefully at the hot sweet tea which Johnson had waiting for him. He took out his watch again: they had been gone for the best part of two hours, and there were but two more until darkness.

Armstrong relit his pipe, sat back on the fallen tree which served as the troop orderly room, and put his heel on a tiny scorpion emerging from under a dead leaf. 'About half a mile, you say, sir? We could just about do it before dark. At least we'd have the night to burn the boats.'

Hervey was conscious of going against every cavalry precept. 'We couldn't be sure they'd not march in once we began the fight, though. No matter how afeard they were of moving about the jungle by night, if they heard the sound of a fight they'd surely make for it? You would!'

'Ay, and it's as well never to suppose the enemy's any less canny.'

'Just so. In daylight we surely have a better chance of holding them off, if only to make good our escape.'

'Ay, you're right, sir. How many do you reckon there are there now?'

'Three hundred, perhaps four. Most of those are bargees, but there are lines laid out for a thousand more, and I reckon the boats will carry twice that number.'

Armstrong did not so much look dismayed at the numbers as incredulous. 'And they would assemble that many men in the forest and paddle 'em all that way to Chittagong? What a business when they could be on the place from the sea with not a fraction of the trouble.'

Hervey had rehearsed the same doubts with Somervile. 'They couldn't do it unnoticed, though, and if there were one frigate in sight then they'd be blown from out of the water. No, Sar'nt-Major, I think this is a deuced clever plan, and I think we have come on it not a day too soon.'

Armstrong took his pipe from his mouth and looked at the bowl in despair. He hoped the troop's powder was drier than his tobacco. 'Just so I'm sure, which side of the river do we come out of the forest on?'

Hervey smiled to himself: Armstrong the world-weary NCO, resigned to whatever his officer had embroiled him in! 'The Avan side, Sar'nt-Major – just as we'd always intended.'

'No more wet feet, then?'

'I can't promise that, but there is a bridge.'

Armstrong was not inclined to dispute it further. 'And so how shall we go at them?'

Hervey had yet to finish writing his orders. 'The whole assembly area is open grass and planting, nothing that I could see above four feet high, and firm going. It's not rice planting or the like.' He cleared the ground of leaves in front of where they sat, and took up a stick to make a sketch in the earth, drawing two lines like the letter X. 'Here's the river,' he began, pointing to the line which ran right to left. 'It's not much more than a chain across, two dozen yards at most, and no deeper than an elephant's ears.'

Armstrong raised an eyebrow. 'Are there many of them?'

'I'm coming to that. But no, half a dozen. And I should say the water's no less sluggish than where we crossed.' He now pointed to the other line in the earth. '*This*, I surmise, is the white elephant's road. It's certainly running in the right direction. *There* is north,' he added, bisecting the right quadrant's angle. 'We are *here*.' He pointed to where the line representing the river would project, explaining that it turned south-west not far below the assembly area. 'And *here*,' he pointed to where the lines intersected, 'there's a bridge of sorts. I couldn't get a good look, but all I saw on it were men on their feet, so I've no idea if it will take the weight of a horse, let alone a bullock cart – or a galloper gun.'

Armstrong nodded silently.

Hervey then made marks either side of the line representing the river, below the intersection. 'This is where the barges are, pulled up on the banks either side, and most of them on logs so they can be launched the more easily. The elephants seem to be used for hauling them out of the water, but their work looked done for the most part.'

'A pity they're on both sides,' said Armstrong.

'Just so. We can't avoid a crossing. Now, the Burman fighting men are all in tented lines *here*,' added Hervey, pointing to the northern quadrant. 'So they're all on our side of the river. *They* must be our immediate objective, for if they get under arms there'll be the very devil of a fight.'

'We should attack in darkness, then,' said Armstrong without hesitation.

'You're right. But how might we ever keep the troop in hand? We both have the memory of that beach at Brighton.'

Indeed they did. Yet Armstrong would still have reckoned it the only course . . . except for one thing. 'We have the guns, of course, this time.'

'Exactly so,' said Hervey, with a faint smile. 'A whiff of grape: I don't see why it shouldn't work for *us*. And I shall want you to have command of those guns. I shall want you to have them play wherever there's need of them without my even having to think of it.'

Armstrong had not a moment's doubt.

'All the Burmans who surrender are to be driven across the bridge and held there by Corporal Ashbolt, like Horatius.'

'Who?'

'It doesn't matter. Cornet Vanneck will take half a dozen men to picket the road where it debouches from the forest, and the rest of us will set about destroying the barges. Also the bridge, and then we'll withdraw the way we came.'

'Sounds easy enough.'

Hervey smiled wryly. 'It *is* easy. Until the first shot.'

Armstrong raised his eyebrows. 'Ay, always: first shot and bets are off. How much kindling did you see, by the way?'

They had brought four gallons of lamp oil with them, enough for a pint to each barge, but each would need packing with combustibles to guarantee a good blaze. 'There's a fair amount of tentage, and a good stack of hay,' replied Hervey confidently. 'And the oars.' He had already decided to fire the barges off the water rather than risk having them recovered if they sank only partially burned.

Private Johnson came up and, ever wary of Armstrong, saluted. 'Leave to speak, sir. There's some snap ready when tha's a mind.'

'Thank you, Johnson,' said Hervey, throwing aside the stick and wiping his hands on his overalls. 'Five minutes more.'

Armstrong resumed his questions, taking out his notebook. 'What time do you want reveille then?'

'Four o'clock. That will give us two hours of darkness to get close. We should move off sharp at five.'

'And—'

There was a terrible squealing from the middle of the tethering line, made worse by the surrounding silence.

Hervey sprang up. 'Christ! They'll hear that a mile off,' he rasped, reaching for his carbine.

Armstrong was already on his feet. They hurried to the noise.

'Broken like a dry stick,' said Corporal Ashbolt, crouching by the trooper's foreleg.

'Yours?'

'No, sir. Stent's.'

The horse, one of the Marwaris, stood silent now, sweating heavily, her cannon bone hanging limply. The kicker had already been slipped from the tether line and taken away.

'That other were being proper riggish,' cursed Stent, just come up. 'I should have kept mine apart.'

Hervey thought it pointless to agree or otherwise. 'Where's the farrier?'

'Here, sir,' came the reply from an equally sweating Farrier Brennan. 'I was at the back, tightenin' them Skinner's shoes.'

'This one to despatch, then, I'm afraid,' said Hervey, shaking his head.

'Not with the pistol though, sir?'

'Good God, no! Silent work, if you please, Brennan.'

A dragoon was sent to fetch the farrier's axe. Meanwhile, they unslipped the horses either side of the doomed trooper to make space, not an easy job at the best of times. Hervey did not know whether Brennan had despatched an animal in this way before, but he did not think it the time to ask. Instead, without a word, but with a great deal of care, they pulled the little mare onto her side. She kept her head up, though, and Stent put his knee on her withers to discourage her from trying to rise. 'Bring her a couple of pecks of oats please, Corporal,' he said, stroking the mare's neck.

The axe was brought a minute or two later. By then, Farrier Brennan had cut away the mane just behind the poll to expose the occipital depression, where the axe's spear-point could most easily penetrate and sever the cervical cord. Shepherd Stent gave his mare a handful of oats, and pulled one of her ears fondly.

'Hold 'er 'ead steady,' said Brennan, raising the axe.

Stent crouched with his knees either side of her muzzle as she ground the oats in her mouth. Brennan swung the axe down – powerful, confident. The mare squealed then grunted, lashing out with her legs, though the shepherd held on. Brennan put his foot to her neck to get enough purchase to pull out the axe. There was remarkably little blood.

'Again?' said Hervey, anxious.

The mare's eyes were wide and her legs were still kicking.

'No, sir,' replied Brennan.

Stent would not let her go. 'Mick?'

'No,' said Brennan simply.

And in a few seconds more she was motionless.

Stent closed the mare's eyes and got up. 'Thanks, Mick.'

Hervey saw the look, too – the first sign of emotion he had detected in the shepherd.

'I've butchered a good many sheep, Mick, but I couldn't have done that.'

Brennan looked satisfied rather than pleased with his skill. 'I've not had to do that since Corunna. But you didn't flinch when I swung the axe, mind, Shep.'

'Well done, Farrier,' said Hervey. 'We could not have afforded the noise otherwise. Right, Private Stent, take one of the led horses.'

'And look sharp, bonny lad,' added Armstrong, with just enough of a bark to put an end to the condoling. 'I've stood-to the front section, sir,' he added.

Hervey nodded. 'We'll just have to wait, then. Perhaps one more beast calling in the jungle won't raise the alarm. But a gun at the point would be prudent. I think I'll go forward to the pickets to see how strong it carried to them.'

'I'll do that, sir,' said Armstrong. 'You have something to eat and then give them orders out.'

'Yes, Geordie, you're right. Thank you.'

After stand-down, when it was dark, Hervey went round the troop and spoke to every man, the sowars too. Not of things of any moment, just a few words – whatever seemed appropriate, if only whether they knew the password. Sometimes it was a thought about home, sometimes about India. It did not matter, just as long as he spoke to each man and thereby assured them of his own peace of mind about the morning; as Seton Canning put it to Cornet Vanneck, 'a little touch of Hervey in the night'. Every man knew that their captain had found the Burmans without the aid of the Chakma guides, and most of them knew in their hearts that they themselves would have given up long before. They liked their captain's determination; it made it so much the harder to do anything but follow him.

When he was done, Hervey found his way to the place where his groom had laid his blanket, and sat down tired yet content.

'I've kept thi snap warm, Cap'n 'Ervey, sir, but it'll be nowt like it were.'

'Johnson, I could eat . . .' He almost said 'a horse', but it was not the thing. 'I could eat that wretched bird I saw Spreadbury plucking last night!'

Johnson sensed rather than saw Hervey's frown. 'They didn't eat it in the end. They chucked it away.'

'It tasted so bad?'

'They found a length o' snake in its gizzard.'

Hervey could have retched. 'I've just discovered I'm not hungry.'

'Tha'll be all right, sir. It's 'taties and beef. But it's a bit of a squash. I'll make a fresh mashin' o' tea.'

That was what Hervey would prize above all, now. More so even than the whisky in his spare canteen.

He slept well. Checking the picket he left to Seton Canning and the serjeant-major. That was their job. His now was to rest, to find the sleep that had eluded him these past three days.

Just before four o'clock Johnson's hand shook his shoulder, as it had more times than had Henrietta's. But as Hervey took the enamelled cup – he could see the steam rising even in the darkness – he thought of her. And it was the first time since Chittagong that the thought had been more than momentary. What made him hold it now he did not know, but he puzzled over her absence from his mind for so many days. And he did not know whether to be discouraged or the very opposite.

'I'll be glad to be gone from *this* place right enough,' grumbled Johnson. 'I were bitten alive by mesquitoes last night.'

Now that Johnson mentioned it, Hervey too found himself scratching at bites about his hands and face. 'Because we're nearer the river, I imagine.'

'Bastard things, they is. I wonder 'ow French's gooin' on wi' them bee stings?'

'Say your prayers that we see him later today,' replied Hervey in a supplicatory tone.

At five o'clock the troop stepped off, Hervey with the point-men, and no scouts (he knew what lay ahead). The men had put rotting leaves from the forest floor in the backs of their shakos, the curious phosphorescence, as on the hands of his watch, a useful beacon in the pitch dark of the jungle pre-dawn. Stand-to and breaking camp had been a model. How quickly these men had mastered the game, he mused. Would older dogs have been so quick to learn new tricks? Perhaps. After all, the NCOs had done the teaching as well as the jungle. And this morning they had all eaten hot – a rare achievement indeed in a bivouac.

By six they were close enough to the forest's edge to see fires burning in the Burman camp. Hervey felt the thrill that at last their progress was over. From now on it was battle, and the fortunes of battle, and the price of battle. He did not doubt the outcome, for he did not think of it. 'Pass the word: ball cartridge, load. Guns make ready.'

He heard the ramming-home of charges in carbines behind him, but no louder than it need have been, and he peered towards the east for the signs of lightening in the sky. The dawn came quickly on them in these parts, and five minutes made a difference. He wanted a sign before they broke cover. He took out his watch. How practical a contribution to killing the King's enemies had Daniel Coates's presents been! The old soldier would revel in its telling when he received Hervey's letter after this was all over. It was so accurate a watch, too. It told him there were but ten minutes to the first rays of the sun, and thereafter he knew he would have six more before there was sufficient light to see a white horse at a furlong. 'Pass the word: mount!'

He heard the jingle of bits, the creaking of leather, the whickering of horses keen for the off. The thrill of it never palled.

'Draw swords!'

The chilling chafing of steel on steel – it sent a shiver down his spine as if he had touched rubbed amber.

'Troop will advance!'

Out they came, at the walk so as to make no more noise than they need. He could feel their eagerness somehow, though, and wanted as much as they to lower his sword and gallop at once on the Burman lines.

He waved the sabre to left and right above his head. Those immediately behind him would see it and repeat it, and begin the movement into line, just as he had told them last night.

The first wisps of sunlight broke the line of the forest canopy to their right, almost to the minute of his calculation – auguries of success, dared he hope? The nearest campfires were only fifty more yards. Would this spell the end of their stealth?

On they walked. The fires were dying, untended. There

was no one afoot, just a huddle of sleeping figures by the first of them. Collins and two others jumped from the saddle and made sure they would never rise again – swift, silent execution. Hervey was proud of them.

The line had scarcely slowed, but Collins and the other sabrists were back in the saddle and in their places before another twenty yards. The next would be easy – no sentries, no alarm. They might go through the Burman lines and sabre every one of them in their sleep. Except that no luck ever held so long. Hervey knew he must stick with his plan, even if it meant surrendering some of the surprise that was his for the reaping.

The light was now enough to make out the whole of the camp, the white tents standing like snowcaps. 'See your opportunity, Sar'nt-Major?' Hervey's voice was hushed, but his exhilaration evident.

Armstrong beckoned his guns. 'All in lines – like regulars on Chobham Common. A shame we're loaded with grape!'

Nevertheless they could wring havoc in minutes. And the Skinner's sowars knew it, wheeling full about and unhitching the guns with the fervour of hounds on to a fox.

There were no orders. Portfires went to touch-holes just as soon as the gunners dropped their hands to signal 'On!' The guns belched flame and a thousand pieces of iron at the first tents not a dozen yards away, their reports becoming as one roar in that forest arena, all the louder for the enforced silence of the past days.

The nearest tents, and the ones just beyond, blew down like corn stooks in a sudden squall. Then came the screaming, a terrible, devilish noise that unnerved many a dragoon as he sat contemplating the gallopers' work. For Hervey it meant nothing more than his prevailing over the enemy; it was what he wanted to hear. The sowars almost bayed as they reloaded, urged on by Armstrong waving his sword and shrieking every kind of profanity. Hervey urged them just as fervently, but below his breath.

The right-hand gun beat the left by barely a second. Another two angry explosions, louder than before with increased charges for the double shot, sent four two-pound balls bowling down the tent lines, doing untold slaughter within. Out from those still standing tumbled half-naked Burmans, dazed, not even able to take up their muskets from the arm-piles. With the sun rising above the forest, it was time to test the age-old business of cavalry. 'And we shall shock them!' said Hervey aloud.

'Bible again, Cap'n 'Ervey?' came the voice at his left.

'No, Johnson. Only Shakespeare. Trumpeter, sound "Charge"!'

He would never have done it against formed troops – not put untried dragoons into a charge from the halt. But he didn't need weight, only the noise of hoofs and the sight of sabres lowered. The Burmans ran this way and that, like rabbits scattering before greyhounds. One or two ran into swords, but for the most part the dragoons had not the skill to despatch their prey. It did not matter. The Burmans were broken.

'Go to it, Harry,' called Hervey to Seton Canning, then looked about for his trumpeter. 'Storrs!' he bellowed.

'Sir!' called Storrs, struggling to remount the other side of a tent.

'What in God's name—?'

'Didn't see the guy-rope, sir.'

Corporal Ashbolt and Johnson closed to help him.

'Look sharp, Storrs! I hope that bugle of yours is whole. Sound "Rally"!'

Storrs, back in the saddle, blew it well – octave intervals, by no means easy when winded. 'Good man,' cheered Hervey. 'Mr Vanneck!'

The cornet was close by. There was blood on his sabre. 'Well done, Myles. Take your picket off. Drive well up the road to begin with. I'll send the guns up when I can.'

'Very good, sir.' He turned and started gathering his half-dozen.

Hervey rode back to the guns, which the sowars had already hitched up. '*Shabash, sipahi! Shabash!*'

Armstrong looked impressed.

'*Very* good shooting indeed!'

The quartermaster had not been idle during the skirmish. Hervey saw him and his men already piling oil and kindling into the barges. The sooner they could get the canvas in, the better. Hervey told Seton Canning to have the Burmans begin the work for them.

The surgeon had difficulty bringing his horse to a halt. He had work to do and was keen to be about it. 'Have a care, Ledley!' called Hervey, and then turned to Johnson. 'Go and help the surgeon dismount,' he said despairingly.

Ledley made straight for the stricken tents. From the shrieks and groans he knew that his skill was sorely needed, though he feared he would not be able to do much but staunching and binding. He was the only man in the troop who wished the Burman battalions would come soon, for they would be the only hope for their fallen comrades. Hervey watched as the surgeon set about the carnage with his assistants, coolly assessing the scale and priorities of his task.

After days of moving at a snail's pace through the forest, the sudden liberation made everything seem as if in double time. And the exhilaration of the assault, and the utter rout, gave each man an ardour that the duke himself would have been proud to see. But Hervey knew this might change at any moment with the arrival of the Burman battalions. He looked at his watch: it was half an hour since they had crept out of the forest, and not much less since the first gun had fired. If the Burmans were encamped anywhere within five miles he could expect some of them here within an hour, for the noise of the galloper guns had surely carried that distance, even through the forest. He surmised the Burmans would not have made camp closer than that, for would they not have pressed on the extra hour or so to where canvas awaited them? If they had cavalry, they would be so much the quicker, but Somervile had not spoken of it. Why, indeed, would they have cavalry if they could not embark them?

Hervey took his compass from the carrying case on the saddle. The needle swung to where he expected, but he wanted to make sure beyond the influence of the iron and steel about him. Out of the saddle he climbed, unfastened his swordbelt and handed it and the reins to Johnson, then walked ten paces before he was satisfied that the compass reading was a true one.

'Is it all right, Cap'n 'Ervey, sir?' enquired Johnson, confident equally in his officer and in officers' apparatuses.

'Yes, it's all right, Johnson. Yon other road into the forest goes just as it should. I'd be powerfully tempted to take it homewards were it not for French and the others.'

Johnson handed him back his swordbelt and reins. 'I'll 'ave a prog around, if tha doesn't mind. I'll peg this'n, an' let 'im 'ave a bit o' grass.'

Hervey had no objection; his second charger had its head down already. He climbed back into the saddle. 'Search those bigger tents first – maps, letters, anything. I'll take a look myself when I've had the guns moved.'

The quartermaster and Armstrong had got all but five of the barges on their bank ablaze. Another quarter of an hour and all would be done this side. Some of the Burmans were already taking canvas across the bridge, their double time prompted more by the sabres of Seton Canning's men than natural ardour. Hervey wondered if their spirit would return once the troop were gone, if they would try to follow and harry them. That was another reason to have them all on the far side of the river – and the bridge burned – when the time came.

He glanced over to where the surgeon was working. He would not go to him, though. He would not trouble himself with the sight of dead and dying men when there might be more yet to add to the butcher's bill. He had never been qualmish of such things – well, rarely – but he had never been indifferent to what the ball and the cutting edge did to a man's flesh.

'Guns ready, sahib!' reported the daffadar, his yellow kurta begrimed with black powder smoke.

'Very good, daffadar; follow me if you please.' Hervey reined right towards the white elephant road, but before he led them away he would speak with his lieutenant. 'Mr Seton Canning!'

The lieutenant spurred at once from the bridge.

'See to it sharp, Harry. Every minute makes me keen for the off.'

'Of course, Hervey,' he replied. 'Half the trouble's that bridge. It creaks and sways in a crazy fashion with only half a dozen on it.'

Hervey nodded. 'Well, at least it won't take much chopping at when the time comes. I'll leave Storrs with you. He can sound recall when you're ready.'

Seton Canning saluted as Hervey dug his spurs into the Marwari's flanks.

Johnson lifted the pot from the fire and poured boiling water into an enamel cup. Hervey meanwhile studied the papers and map in the leather-bound portfolio.

'What's tha think, sir?'

Hervey furrowed his brow. 'I can't make out a word. I don't know if the guides could. But the map's suggestive, I'd say. It seems to have Chittagong and the river, at least.'

Johnson lifted the muslin bag from the cup and laid it to one side. He poured in sugar and arrack, and stirred the liquid with a twig.

Hervey took it without looking up. 'And there seems to be a list of some sorts.'

'What's tha think o' t'flag?'

Hervey sipped his tea and smiled. 'I shall send it to Mr

348

Somervile just as soon as we have fired the last barge. It and these papers.'

'Pity there were nowt else.'

'Shiny things, you mean? I suspect they thought they'd be garnering plenty enough of that in Chittagong.'

'Is tha gooin' to 'ave a look for thisen?'

Hervey looked to where he had posted the galloper guns by the debouch from the forest, three hundred yards off, and then to the other side of the river. He saw Armstrong torching the first of the barges there. 'No, I think I'll stay here. It can't be many more minutes before—'

A sudden fusillade in the forest beyond the guns made him spring up. Johnson rushed to unpeg the horses. Hervey leapt into the saddle and galloped towards the guns without once looking back, Stent, his coverman, and Johnson hard behind him. Vanneck's picket was half a mile up the white elephant road: Hervey reckoned there would be scarcely a minute before the contact-man galloped out. He reined the Marwari to an abrupt halt by the guns. 'No firing, mind, daffadar. First out shall be Vanneck-sahib's men.'

'*Acha, sahib!*'

Hervey turned back to the river and took his telescope from its saddle case. He could just make out, through the smoke, Ashbolt corralling the Burmans on the far side, just as he'd ordered, lest the firing embolden them. But the smoke was too thick to see how many barges still awaited the torch. Seton Canning was assembling the remainder of the troop, perhaps two dozen men, no more, on Hervey's side of the river. He saw them extend into line, at the halt, and draw swords. 'Well done, Harry,' he said to himself. 'They'll be the keener for coming up sabres drawn.'

A minute later they were with him. 'Walk-march!' called Seton Canning.

They bumped from the trot.

'Ha-a-alt!' Up went his hand.

Trumpeter Storrs took his place next to Hervey.

Serjeant Collins rode at once to the middle. 'Your leave, sir?'

Seton Canning nodded.

'Now listen, you men! Listen hard!' began Collins, in a voice that set every nerve on edge. 'That we did this morning was about as hard as bobbing for apples – dhobi-wallahs fast asleep and pissing themselves. This lot'll mean business. You'd better remember everything you was taught. You keep them arms straight no matter what – a man on 'is feet can cut as bad as one astride. *Arms straight!*' he bellowed, thrusting out his sabre. 'Infantry, give point front!' He leaned forward and lowered his sword to reach beyond his horse's head. 'And *follow through!*' Up swung the sabre behind him, his arm straight as a die.

There was another fusillade. It sounded much closer. Some of the dragoons now looked apprehensive.

Collins was undaunted. 'If those Burmans come out astride then don't be in too much of a hurry to cut at them. If we go with the point, remember your flank! Sword pressed against the shako to keep it steady! And mind your horses' heads!'

Not a minute later Corporal Mossop galloped out of the forest as if the hounds of hell were at his heels. He had to snatch hard at the curb to pull up his little mare. Her flanks were in a worse lather than Hervey had seen in months. '*Sir*,' he gasped, saluting once he could afford to free his right hand. 'Mr Vanneck's compliments, and there's a column of Burmans coming along the road, and at the double like light infantry, sir. We can't tell the numbers, for we can't see beyond the front ranks, sir. We fired on 'em, but they didn't check, even to pick up them that was hit. We fired on them another twice, I think, sir.'

'I heard so. What do they carry?'

'Muskets of some sort, sir. They fired on us, but no one was hit.'

Hervey turned to Johnson. 'Gallop to the serjeant-major,

and tell me how many of the barges have still to be set alight.'

'Ay, sir,' said Johnson calmly, not even forgetting to salute. He reined about and sped off.

'Daffadar, shot loaded?'

'Yes, sahib!' His voice betrayed no emotion but resolve.

Hervey wished he were standing now by Mercer's troop, as he had at Waterloo. Now was the time for six-pounders and shell, rather than half that of solid shot. He toyed with the idea of putting them where the road debouched from the forest, like a cork in a bottle, and firing grape. It would be much the more destructive. But he knew the gunners would not be able to reload quickly enough – two discharges at most before being overrun. If he could hold the Burmans at arm's length with shot for a while (they could not know at once how many guns there were), then the quartermaster and Armstrong might just complete their work.

Another fusillade, and not more than a hundred yards off. Hervey braced himself. 'Do not fire, daffadar. It will be Vanneck-sahib first.'

'*Acha, sahib.*'

Hervey looked back to the river. He could see Johnson galloping towards him, but the smoke was so great he could see nothing beyond. How much longer could it take to fire those boats?

'Daffadar, we shall hold our ground until the barges are all alight and then withdraw to the forest whence we came.'

'*Acha, sahib.*' Hervey had explained the orders well enough before.

Johnson pulled up beside him just as the picket, five strong – not a man lost – galloped out of the forest, Cornet Vanneck at the rear. 'Another five to fire yet, sir,' Johnson reported. 'Not enough oil to prime with, though. They're using powder. Serjeant-major says they'll need another half an hour.'

Hervey grimaced.

'Have we not burned enough, sir? They could scarcely invade Chittagong with half a dozen boats,' asked Seton Canning.

'Those boats have got to burn out, Harry. And the others. There's no saying what they could do with them if they put out the flames.'

'But is that likely?'

'It's a *possibility*,' Hervey snarled. '*That* is the point!'

Cornet Vanneck pulled up hard in front of him, his charger throwing its head about wildly. He saluted while struggling with the reins.

'In good time, Mr Vanneck,' said Hervey calmly, returning the salute.

'There are so many of them, sir. No sooner did we do our execution but those behind took their place. And they came on the while in double time.'

'Very well. We shall see if hot iron and cold steel shall check their ardour.'

Hervey's manner was so composed as to make his cornet look at him askance, as indeed was partly his intention.

'Take post, please.'

Cornet Vanneck reined away, and with a sheepish look, for the little line of dragoons appeared so calm compared with his own agitation.

Not many minutes more, and they saw their adversary for the first time. But only for a moment. 'Fire!' bellowed Hervey, startling his own horse.

The galloper guns thundered, enveloping them all in black smoke, thicker than the grapeshot's, for the two-pound ball needed more powder to see it the distance. Hervey trotted forward a little way to see the effect. The Burmans had checked. Another volley might see them withdraw – if only he could have it *now*.

The sowars worked methodically: swab to damp the barrel and make safe, powder charge rammed home, ball tamped with the other end of the swab; then the struggle to realign the pieces, and the gunner re-laying, then the prick of priming powder and slow match.

Both guns fired as one again.

More smoke billowed over them. Once more Hervey trotted forward to see the effect. There were even more Burmans now, but so many dead or dying, and the confusion looked the greater. He drew his sabre and pointed. '*Charge!*'

Out of the smoke galloped thirty dragoons, swords lowered. The Burmans had no time to deploy. They knew it and they turned for the forest. But Hervey's men were on them before they could clear the line of their own dead.

It was easy. No need to guard, protect or parry. First the point and then the cut, and simple – Cut One, nearside, Cut Two, offside. Every sabre was bloodied, many of them several times over.

Ragged shots from the forest edge checked their ardour, and Hervey rallied them to a flank, thankful he could see no horse riderless.

As soon as Hervey's men cleared their line, the guns fired again. It would surely make the Burmans fall back, he thought.

But no. Out they poured again, still in an ill-ordered fashion, for the debouch was too narrow to permit otherwise. Hervey formed his men into line as best he could, then charged again from the flank. With only fifty yards a bigger horse might have done greater damage, but the little country-breds were into their stride quickly, and sheer momentum broke up the Burman ranks with scarcely need for the sabre this time.

But the pressure did not slacken. Out of the forest poured more and more of the enemy. No matter that they were ill-ordered, force of numbers must soon tell.

Hervey turned to rally the line. He saw Private Spreadbury's horse tumble fifty yards off, Spreadbury himself thrown clean from the saddle and dropping his reins. A dozen Burmans rushed him. Jobie Wainwright saw, and spurred at them at once. In seconds he was among them, turning in the saddle for each cut, just as Collins had taught him, swinging his sabre for all he was worth – Cut One near-side to the rear, Two offside to the rear, Three offside to the front, Four nearside to the front. Each time he felled one of the pal's attackers, and each time he recovered the sabre from side to side above his shako in the manner prescribed. Collins, reordering the line, watched in admiration. But bayonets jabbed at Jobie and his mare – too many of them, so that soon he could only protect and parry. Corporal McCarthy, galloping back to the rally, saw the fight and turned. Hervey looked over at Collins and gave him the nod.

McCarthy got there first, leapt from the saddle and ran at the Burmans, grasping his sabre by handle and blade as if it were a musket and bayonet. Collins was there a second or so later and made three cuts so fast that it scarce seemed possible. Those untouched began to run.

'Paddy, you dumb, cursed Irish bastard! What the hell d'you think you're doing?' yelled Collins.

'It's just a bit easier to me still, serjeant,' replied McCarthy equably, picking up his trooper's reins and making for Private Spreadbury.

'Christ alive, Paddy. Never again!'

'No, Serjeant. Will ye help me up with Private Spreadbury please, Jobie?'

Meanwhile Hervey had rallied the rest of the troop, taking them back at the trot to where the sowars were calmly serving the guns, and forming line to the rear.

'Ready, daffadar?'

'*Ji, sahib!*'

How long they could keep this up he had no idea. If the Burmans came out each time the same way they ought to be good for another dozen goes. But they would surely not keep hurling themselves on guns and steel so willingly?

The field went silent now. It ought to have been welcome, the sign that they had done their work well, but not knowing what would follow was unsettling. Hervey considered dismounting and having them make ready with the carbines, but the range was too great to guarantee the effect. He looked back at the river. There was smoke and fire the length of it, but he could still see boats unburned. He looked at his little command. 'Well done, E Troop!' he called. 'Smart work. We may yet have more of it!'

Not many minutes later, E Troop saw the work to be had. Out from the forest burst as one a dozen horsemen. The guns fired, the shot arched and plunged beautifully into the defile, but by the time it fell there was no target. Seconds later more horsemen began pouring out. The Burmans had the measure of the time to reload. The collective inrush of breath behind him left Hervey in no doubt of what chance the troop believed it had.

'Jesus!' muttered Collins to himself.

Hervey counted quickly – fifty of them. Had they stopped coming? The guns fired again. No more appeared. 'Daffadar, grape, load!'

'*Ji, sahib*,' came the reply, as cool as ever.

The Burman horse took their time. They were so regular that Hervey reckoned it would take the same number, at least, to prevail over them.

'Now *remember*,' began Collins, trotting forward, his voice as matter-of-fact as the daffadar's. '*Guard*;' he thrust his arm straight and front, sabre across his chest parallel with the ground. '*Left Protect*;' he flexed his wrist upright and to his left, the sabre perpendicular. '*Right Protect*;' he swung it back across his chest and out to his side. '*St George*;' and up went the sabre to protect his head. 'Those are the ones you'll want. Then make your cuts!'

Hervey knew the guns were useless, for the Burmans would not ride at them. He could stay close and be safe, therefore – indeed, if he didn't the Burmans would ride the guns down from a flank – but that would leave the field open for them to take the bridge. There was only one thing he could do. 'Daffadar, guns to the bridge! Troop advance!'

E Troop marched forward a dozen paces to mask the guns, then halted. Hervey could only pray the Burmans were not as quick as an English cornet was expected to be.

It took the sowars less than a minute to hitch up the guns, but it seemed more. As they made to gallop back, Hervey knew he had at least saved them. A minute more and he could retire too.

But the Burman horse began to advance, at the trot. Hervey looked back at the galloper guns: it was still too close. 'Troop will advance, walk-march!'

He did not want them to cover too much ground: every yard they advanced was another painful one to withdraw. He had to judge the speed of collision, though. A fair gallop was what they'd need.

'Trot!'

Some of the horses broke into three-time instead. Collins's curses took their riders' minds off the enemy for the moment.

Hervey raised his sword above his head. 'Gallop!'

Every sabre went up.

'Arms straight, curse you!' bellowed Collins. 'Close up! Close up!'

'*Charge!*'

The ragged line of sabres dropped to the guard. An instant later they crashed into the Burman horse, flesh on flesh, steel on steel, steel on flesh. Hervey parried an artless cut from a tulwar and sliced its sword arm with a Cut Two as he swept past. He looked behind as he reined about, and saw two dragoons unhorsed by the violence of the collision. He saw Mole brought to a halt and bend his elbow in the instinct to protect his face. The tulwar sliced his forearm, Mole dropped his sabre, then the tulwar sliced his neck. He fell sideways from the saddle, his face contorted with terror. Hervey, raging, made straight for his executioner and took him between the shoulder blades with the point. He cut left and right at Burmans who had not yet turned. He saw Collins duelling and McCarthy hacking artlessly but bloodily. He saw Seton Canning in a desperate fight with two Burmans at once, and then Lingard and Vanneck coming to his aid. He saw Armstrong. Then the Burmans were wheeling and trying to fight back the way they had come.

'Rally! Rally!' he shouted.

Storrs, breathless and his own sword red, just kept sounding the G and the C. Somehow the troop, battered and very bloody, formed line and fronted, Armstrong and Collins chivvying them straight and cursing those who had not sloped swords properly. One or two of them could barely stay upright; Corporal Mossop's sword arm hung limp like a rag doll's, Needham had lost an ear. But every horse was on its feet, one way or another.

'I brought up all we could spare when I saw what was happening, sir,' called Armstrong as he closed to Hervey's side. 'But only the half-dozen of us. Gutless bastards, them Burmans!'

Hervey looked at him askance.

'Did you not see, sir? Half of 'em sat still on their arses back there when the others came on.'

Hervey took out his telescope. 'There's a very pretty flag there. That was their trouble. They wouldn't leave whoever was bottom of it.'

'Well, thank Christ for flags. Another dozen and we'd have lost it!'

Hervey looked at Mole's lifeless body thirty yards or so in front of them. 'Troop will advance!'

'Jesus, Jobie, not again!' gasped Needham.

'I reckon we've got to, Sammy.'

'Ha-a-alt!'

They stopped just short of where Private Mole lay.

'If you please, Corporal McCarthy,' said Hervey simply.

'Thank you, sor,' replied McCarthy, as if it were a favour

to him. 'Give me a hand, boys,' he said, nodding to Harkness and Rudd.

Hervey watched as they lifted their fellow dragoon across McCarthy's saddle. 'Troop will retire, at the trot!'

They about-faced three times in the first furlong to the river. Each time Hervey expected to see the Burmans pressing them, but each time he saw the distance between them only lengthening. Were they really gutless, or merely artless? The third time he decided it was probably the latter, for now he saw them extending, and a far longer line than his. The Burman horse could not outrun him now – not take his flanks – but if he judged it badly they might give him another mauling. He tried to calculate if it was worth standing long enough to give them a round from the carbines to check their zeal. He would lose men to theirs if he did, and it would do little to slow their advance. He could now see Corporal Ashbolt at the bridge with half a dozen men, dismounted, the led horses trotting along the river's edge behind the line of burning barges. Ashbolt could hardly have had the best view of the field, but he had judged at once that their withdrawal could no longer be by the way they had come. Hervey was relieved. He had feared he might have his force divided.

Two more fronts and they were close on the bridge, but Hervey saw to his dismay that the second gun was still not across. The sowars struggled desperately to remove the pin that held fast the barrel to the trail. Seton Canning looked hard at him. 'What do we do, Hervey?'

Hervey was only certain of what he would *not* do. 'I could never abandon a gun, Harry.'

He saw Corporal Ashbolt mount and gallop towards him.

'That bridge won't take any more horses, sir,' called Ashbolt from a dozen yards. 'The decking's broken away and the supports are gone. The farrier's breaking the pin on that gun now and we'll have it across in a minute. The other can fire grape. I'd like to put my Burmans in the river if it's all right with you, sir.'

Hervey looked back to where Ashbolt's prisoners sat – more than a hundred of them, for the moment, quiet.

'You would only be able to drive them in with the point, and there are too many for that. Are they bound?'

'Yes, sir.'

'Then cover them with the other gun. And give no quarter if any try to break free!'

Ashbolt raced back to the bridge to drive the sweating sowars and dragoons across before setting to with the charges he had made – enough, he hoped, to destroy the centre of the span at least.

In two more minutes Hervey saw the Burman flanks turning to pen him up against the river, and behind the centre of the line a column of infantry coming on at the double. He glanced over his shoulder again. The second gun had made the far bank: it was time for them to do the same. But how would he then check the Burmans, for they could surely swim the Karnaphuli as well as the troop could?

He glanced back again. Ashbolt had a dozen men along the bank, carbines ready, and the second gun would be in action soon. He wondered if one more sabre charge might demoralize the Burmans. It was not unknown in India. Indeed, it had been the sole tactic of many a campaign. He looked at the Burman line and then at his own. 'Troop will retire!' he called, as calmly as he might. He thanked God they had swum the Karnaphuli once before. At least he was asking nothing new of them now.

In they plunged, needing no urging. Ashbolt's men began their covering fire, and then the gun thundered. Hervey heard the whistle of grape above his head, just like the night at Brighton, except that there it was so dark he had no idea how many or how close the enemy was. His mare jumped from the bank and struck out confidently. The current was stronger than the first time, but nothing to worry about. She swam freely, seeming to enjoy it. Not long now to the far bank, another ten yards at most. She gained a footing, lost it, then stumbled, almost throwing him. He looked right and left to see how the others were faring – well enough. Some were even ahead of him. He let her get her footing again – one more try and then he'd slip from the saddle. But she got all four feet firm and up the bank she struggled, until Hervey jumped off near the top to let her clamber up the overhang the easier. He turned about. Johnson was just behind him, almost out too, but his mare couldn't get the measure of the overhang and Johnson was a fraction too slow in leaving the saddle. The mare fell on her side, pinning him under the water. She couldn't shift, for all her flaying. And now shots were ringing out from the Burman bank, ragged at first, but close. Hervey scrambled back down the bank. The mare squealed as a musket ball struck her quarters, but still she lay thrashing. Shepherd Stent followed him down, and Storrs, and then Corporal McCarthy, last across the bridge with Private Mole's body. The firing increased, though fortunately not its accuracy. Hervey would himself have put a bullet in the downed mare's head had he not thought the dead weight would impede them greater. But somehow, slipping and sliding, with ball flying about them and the frantic mare's legs liable at any second to propel them into the river, they pulled Johnson free and dragged him up the bank. And there he lay, like Parkin before him, reliant on the skill of the surgeon.

The firing slackened and then stopped altogether. Hervey couldn't for the life of him think why, for the Burmans now had every advantage. Perhaps they were gutless as well as artless after all. Then came the cheering behind him, loud and hearty.

'*Himmat-I-Mardan!*'

And the gun sowars, faint by comparison, but fullthroated: '*Madad-I-Khuda!*'

'*Himmat-I-Mardan!*'
'*Madad-I-Khuda!*'

Hervey stood up. The sight astonished him. The Skinner's men debouched from the forest as if trotting to exercise. He lost count at fifty – there must be half that number again. Lance pennants fluttered, then out came the carbines as the sowars slung their lances over the shoulder. The line of yellow stretched the length of the bank. It was a sight he would never forget, like the solid walls of red at Waterloo. And all the time the cheering: '*Himmat-I-Mardan! Madad-I-Khuda!*'

CHAPTER TWENTY-THREE

NEMESIS

Chittagong, two days later

Eyre Somervile stood by his desk in the lieutenant-governor's new residency on the hill north and west of the Sadarghat. It was a fine building of white stone in the classical manner, the interior of which, though unfinished, spoke of the permanence of the Honourable East India Company's investment in the country. Somervile wore a dark blue coat and a cream stock, and around his neck the order of Knight Companion of the Bath, a military honour of which he was at the same time both proud and abashed, for the circumstances of the honouring had been peculiar in the extreme. Nevertheless, for his coming encounter, to wear it this morning suited his purpose very well indeed.

As the clocks began striking eleven, his secretary entered and announced, 'His Excellency Wundauk Maha Thilwa, envoy of the Viceroy of Arakan.'

Somervile turned to face the envoy and bowed. The Viceroy of Arakan was King Bagyidaw's vassal; there was no doubting the reason for the envoy's calling.

Wundauk Maha Thilwa bowed by return. He was an arresting figure, if shorter than Somervile, clean-shaven and with searching eyes. He wore a long green robe fastened about the waist with a wide cummerbund, and carried an ornately carved ivory staff. He came alone, having no need of an interpreter.

'To what do we owe this honour, Your Excellency?' asked Somervile gravely.

Wundauk Maha Thilwa lifted his head so that his eyes could look down at his interlocutor rather than up. 'I bring you an ultimatum from His Highness the Viceroy,' he began, making a small bow at the mention of the rank. 'For many months, now, the domains of His Majesty the King,' he made another, deeper bow, 'have been violated by fugitive subjects of His Majesty here in Chittagong. On numerous occasions His Highness the Viceroy has asked for the expulsion of the fugitives, for their return to face justice, but this has been refused.' He paused for an effect of greater portent. 'I am therefore commanded to inform your excellency that unless by the going down of the sun today I on His Highness's behalf receive word that the fugitives will be delivered up to His Majesty's justice, an immediate attack shall be made upon Chittagong and the territory annexed.'

Somervile did not flinch. Indeed, he would play the envoy for further intelligence. He made himself speak with an air of cool detachment. 'Laying aside, for the moment, the propriety – some would say impudence, *infamy* even – of such a threat, how might you be able to execute it? There is a squadron of frigates in the bay, a brigade will arrive within the fortnight from Calcutta, and on the border with Arakan is a force of cavalry.'

Wundauk Maha Thilwa looked at him contemptuously. How could this high representative of the British be so dull-witted as to think that these were the only ways by which the superior troops of Ava could come? And how careless of his own secrets was this mere man of government!

Somervile was satisfied. Now was the time. 'Your Excellency, I beg you would accept my compliments for your faultless command of English.'

Wundauk Maha Thilwa inclined his head, condescendingly.

'The Avan court is superior in every respect to those of the outer world.'

'Indeed. You would not say then – you will be familiar with the phrase – that you had burned your boats in coming here?'

Wundauk Maha Thilwa smiled like a jackal: how unfortunately apt was this . . . *functionary*'s choice of words. 'No, Excellency,' he replied, shaking his head pityingly. 'We have by no means burned our boats!'

Somervile pulled open the drawer of his desk and took out a bundle of silk. He flung it down so that its royal emblem was at once apparent. 'No, Your Excellency, but *we* have!'

At one o'clock, Eyre Somervile rode back to his bungalow in the civil lines and told Emma what had transpired with the Burman envoy.

'I do wish you had let me observe, secretly,' she said, pouring him a glass of claret. 'Not so much to see the envoy but *you*!'

'Oh, I was nothing, I assure you. I've played wilier fish on the Nagari! Anyway, the honour is all Hervey's.'

Emma sighed. 'I shall only be able to rest when we see him. What else did the serjeant say?'

'Nothing more than you heard yourself at breakfast. Except that there was a man of his who had deserted before the action, and that he would not be surprised if Hervey didn't want to hunt him down himself!'

'Where is Serjeant Collins now? I should very much like to hear more of their time in the jungle.'

Somervile smiled. 'Sleeping, I shouldn't wonder. The poor devil had ridden day and night – *two* days and nights!'

'Well, I shall send word for him to come here to bathe and take his ease the minute he wakes.'

'I beg you would. But I also believe the native horse are due high honours. Captain Pollock emerges from this a considerably stouter man than I'd imagined.'

'Oh . . . yes,' said Emma, a little uncertainly. 'I didn't rightly understand the circumstances of their being at the river.'

'It was deuced resourceful,' pronounced Somervile, holding out his glass for Emma to refill. 'All their orders said was for them to patrol the forest edge – nothing about the border. But Pollock, it seems, heard tell of the Chakma guides who'd arrived at the rendezvous with Hervey's troop two days late. Well, not *late*; they'd got there as soon as they could. They just hadn't received word in time. So Pollock took it upon himself to go with them after Hervey, but he'd taken a more roundabout route, so they met only at the river. How in God's name Pollock could make himself understood with the Chakma I cannot imagine.' His glass was empty again.

Emma shook her head. 'I think we're bidden to luncheon.'

Somervile put his glass down. 'I'd better summon a hircarrah and send off a despatch to Calcutta this afternoon. They can have a fuller one when Hervey returns. With any luck we'll see him by tomorrow evening.'

Hervey angrily brushed away a barbed attap frond which hooked into the sleeve of his tunic. The jungle was becoming thicker. Did these Chakma guides really know where they were going? Yet for all the trouble he was having, they were making faster progress now than they had on the wide tracks at the start of the expedition. It was just one of those imponderables: six men and horses with tribal guides made quicker headway than forty on uncertain bearings, even on better going.

He wondered again about Johnson. Not a rib unbroken, said the surgeon. How could a man be half drowned and have every rib broken and the surgeon say he would live? He wished he had allowed some dhoolies to be brought. They had fashioned a decent makeshift one, but Johnson's ride back to Chittagong could not be comfortable. But Ledley had said that he wouldn't feel a thing – or *know* a thing – by the time he'd had the laudanum. It was just the worst time to leave him, that was the trouble. He had to recover French, though. But poor French might be dead. Would the surgeon's orderly and Boy Porrit make their own way back, in that case? Then there was the girl . . .

Thank God – thank *all* their gods – that Pollock and his men had come when they had. He didn't want to think what would have happened had they had to limp back, fighting all the way. A rearguard of Skinner's Horse – he could scarcely have hoped! And not a shot after the first hour. The Burmans had undoubtedly given in. Seton Canning would have the troop back in Chittagong tomorrow night, and if these Chakma really knew their business he would not be long behind them. And then what a tamasha they'd have – a celebration with Skinner's the like of which the Sixth hadn't seen since they'd got to Paris!

Another attap frond struck him in the face. He broke it off and gave it to his mare behind him; she would eat anything. And then suddenly there were no more attap fronds, just a track, the hoofmarks plain to see, as the Chakma turned left.

'Captain Hervey, sir!'

Private French, now more recognizable than when Hervey had last seen him, and certainly more mobile, came towards them with a look both relieved and anxious.

'Don't sound so surprised, French. I'm not in the habit of forgetting people,' said Hervey drily.

'Do those buttons, up, young French!' came Corporal Ashbolt's voice from behind. 'And where's your carbine?'

'Porrit has it, sir.'

'*Porrit?*' said Ashbolt, disbelieving.

'He's guarding Dodds, sir.'

Hervey pushed past him roughly and almost doubled to where Boy Porrit, Otway the surgeon's assistant and Dodds sat. Porrit and Otway scrambled to their feet, but

Dodds remained seated, his back against a tree, eyes closed. His thigh was bandaged and bloodstained. Hervey turned back to French. 'Well?'

'Sir, Dodds came yesterday morning. He said he'd got lost going for water. We told him which way you'd gone but he said he'd better wait with us. Then yesterday evening he tried to take the food you'd left us and wanted the girl to go with him. Then it came to a bit of a fight, sir, and Dodds threatened his pistol and grabbed the girl, and that's when the boy fired, sir.'

Hervey glanced at Porrit, who lowered his eyes. 'You did well, boy,' he said grimly. He would not quibble about his aim at this time.

'And where is the girl?'

'She . . . she went for some privacy a few minutes ago, sir,' said French, with admirable decorum.

Hervey raised an eyebrow, glanced at Dodds and then the surgeon's orderly.

'He's been unconscious an hour and more, sir,' said Otway. 'He bled a lot.'

Corporal Ashbolt took a closer look. 'You'd better check 'im again, Ottie. I reckon 'e's gone.'

The surgeon's orderly felt in vain for Dodds's pulse, then opened an eyelid. 'Ay, 'e's dead.'

Hervey cursed. 'Then he's cheated the gallows just as he's cheated in everything before!'

CHAPTER TWENTY-FOUR
UNDER AUTHORITY

The maidan, Chittagong, a week later

'E Troop, carry . . . swords!'

Up from the slope went the points of forty sabres in white-gloved hands. Horses threw their heads about as if to add their own salute. Gilbert's throat plume danced as Hervey shouted the command.

'Skinner's Horse, atte-e-en*shun*!' echoed Captain Pollock.

Four hundred heads atop yellow kurtas braced up, lance pennants caught the breeze, and the sun glinted on the gleaming barrels of the galloper guns.

An uneven parade, but an apt one, thought Hervey as he rode up to the dais and dropped his sword in salute.

Eyre Somervile was dressed the same as when he had faced the Avan envoy. In his hand were a few notes, in Hindoostani and English. He would alternate between the two, and leave both King's and native horse in no doubt of the great service they had rendered, and the esteem in which the Presidency in Calcutta held their actions. 'Gentlemen, I stand before you humbly in the face of courage and resource beyond what it is common to behold.'

'That's nice,' said Johnson, painfully, from a chair at the edge of the maidan, his chest swaddled in bandages. 'I was sure it'd end up a lagging matter.'

Hicks frowned. 'I just wish *I'd* been there. There'll be no talking to anybody now. Bloody leg!'

'It were no place for a cripple, *I* can tell thee!'

Somervile's Hindoostani found its mark just as surely among the ranks of yellow, where heads nodded approvingly. He sang the praises of King's troops and Company's fulsomely, though he warned that the King of Ava was a predatory and corrupt man, and that the day might be sooner than they thought when an altogether bigger expedition would have to be mounted to put an end to his designs on the lawful territory of the Honourable Company.

'See, Hicksy, tha'll soon 'ave a chance to get thi' own back!' said Johnson, almost smiling.

Somervile said that he had recommended to the Council of the Presidency that some pecuniary reward be given (there were murmurs of approval everywhere), and that he was pleased even now to be able to announce that the Company's gold and silver medals would be awarded respectively to Captain Hervey and Captain Pollock.

The approval of both yellow ranks and blue was at once apparent. 'Bloody right, an' all!' said Johnson, nodding his head too vigorously for his own good. 'I bet there isn't another officer as could have done better than Cap'n 'Ervey – not even as good as!'

'I am pleased, meanwhile, to grant three days' furlough,' added Somervile. 'At the end of which I shall deem it a privilege to hold a tamasha to honour both gallant regiments. God save the King!'

The response was hearty, if dominated by the sowars' *hazoors*.

And then, as at the river: '*Himmat-I-Mardan!*'
'*Madad-I-Khuda!*'
'*Himmat-I-Mardan!*'
'*Madad-I-Khuda!*'

Later, at lunch with the Somerviles, Hervey expressed himself grateful for the words on parade. 'It was, after all, the reason we came here, was it not? To restore our self-regard.'

'You think the words were not too cautious then?'

Hervey smiled. 'No, indeed. You have a very noble way with them.'

'You think I was too *florid*?'

'Not in the slightest. I envy you your eloquence. The men appreciated it, of that I'm sure.'

Somervile nodded, content, and beckoned the khitmagar to bring champagne. 'I have a mind, too, you know, that that girl you rescued – all Sir Gawain-like – will turn out a handsome investment once returned to her father.'

Emma picked up her glass. 'I must say for my part I thought her very handsome even without her father. What say you, Matthew?'

Hervey smiled back at her. 'Yes, very handsome. The men call her the china doll.'

Somervile looked puzzled. 'Though she is Shan?'

Emma smiled again. Punctiliousness in these affairs was one of the things she so admired in her husband.

Hervey raised his hands. 'We are far from home.'

'You should speak with her, Hervey,' said Somervile, dabbing at his forehead with his napkin. 'She is the most engaging of company.'

Hervey frowned. 'With you to interpret for us?'

Somervile looked puzzled. 'I'm surprised you didn't try Portuguese with her.'

Hervey felt deflated, almost foolish. He remembered how well just a very little of the language had served him in the Peninsula. He smiled. 'Missionaries again, I suppose?'

'And *merchants*, Hervey. No, I tell you, we have made a most grateful and gratifying connection there.'

'You are being most abstemious, Matthew,' said Emma, feeling a little sorry for him. 'Can we not tempt you to more champagne?'

'No thank you, ma'am. I intend riding out this afternoon.'

He drained his coffee cup and accepted more, then returned to Somervile's speculation. 'You believe, I imagine, that she and her father might be a grateful source of intelligence on events in Ava?'

'No doubt of it. I've seen it before many a time.'

Hervey took another sip of his coffee. 'Tell me, Somervile, you were very frank on parade in your views on the prospects with Bagyidaw. What is your true estimation?'

Somervile sat back in his chair and sipped at his champagne. 'Two years, three perhaps. The problem is Assam. Until Calcutta decides what its connection is to be with the king there, the whole of the Presidency will be hostage to Ava. And as soon as we're drawn into a fight with Ava, every little nabob in Hindoostan will think he can make mischief. Believe me, Hervey, before your regiment sees the English coast again, you'll be deep in the thick of fighting on one side of Bengal or the other, perhaps even both. And it will be no mere troop affair!'

Hervey raised his eyebrows. 'It can feel devilish hot even in the middle of a troop affair!'

'Yes, yes, Hervey, I know,' said Somervile, waving his hand. 'Don't let's confuse matters!'

Hervey smiled. 'Perhaps just a *very* little champagne before I ride?'

Hervey took off Gilbert's saddle and handed it to Private Hicks. Then he unfastened the headstall and slipped the reins over the gelding's ears, taking off the bridle and putting on the halter in one movement. 'I'll rub him down, Hicks. Bring his flysheet if you will. And Hicks . . .'

'Sir?'

'You made a good job of looking after him. Thank you.'

'Thank *you*, sir.'

In the adjacent stall Emma Somervile attempted the same with her mount but met with a firm refusal. 'No, ma'am. She can be a mite rancorous.' Lingard's words carried conviction, and though Emma would count herself a proficient, sidesaddle and astride, she readily deferred this evening.

'She can indeed,' Hervey affirmed, going hard at Gilbert's saddle mark with the curry comb. 'But she's been as handy as Jessye, almost, these last weeks.'

'High praise indeed,' smiled Emma.

'But you thought her worthy of it, did you not?'

'Of course. I said so before. I don't think *my* mare would jump ditches so freely.'

Hervey stood aside to let Hicks put on the flysheet. 'Thank you for riding with me. It would have been a dull affair otherwise.'

'It was good for me too. I haven't been able to tempt Eyre to ride out in weeks.'

Hervey nodded to Hicks to say he was finished, then turned to Emma again. 'Come, or we shall be late for the lieutenant-governor. Dinner as well as luncheon – I am excessively honoured.'

She smiled again. 'And he is excessively proud of you. I read his despatch to Calcutta.'

'But to him is due the real honour. To decide to act was the truly courageous thing. Any soldier should have been able to do what I did.'

Emma's smile half-turned to frown. 'Matthew Hervey, can you *possibly* believe your conduct was commonplace?'

He would not answer at first. They walked a little way. 'Parkin's death goes heavier for not being the Burmans' doing, you know.'

She took his arm.

'Drowning's so casual a thing, and played out before your eyes in spite of every exertion. And, likely as not, he was unfit to be at duty.'

Emma gripped his arm a little tighter. 'I'm sorry. I didn't mean to imply—'

'No, of course not,' said Hervey, touching her hand in

return. 'I'm being recalcitrant, as my sister would say. The truth is, it could so easily have been three to the river.'

Emma nodded. 'Private Johnson was in cordial spirits this morning. I came across him watching the parade. He kept calling me "miss".'

That was what Johnson always called Henrietta, thought Hervey, but he wouldn't mention it today. 'The surgeon says he'll be at light duties within the month. But he swallowed so much of that foul river that I should have thought it weeks before he was purged.'

Emma nodded again. 'He said it was nothing. At least, that is what I think he said.'

Hervey smiled. 'Oh indeed, indeed. Johnson would be the first to tell you it's nothing compared with what he suffered in the workhouse. There's bound to be a river in Sheffield at least twice as noxious as the Karnaphuli!'

'You are very fortunate to have such men as he and your serjeants, so devoted.'

Hervey knew it, though devotion would not have been his word. 'That is why I'm anxious to return to Calcutta. A troop doesn't fare well on its own for too long, although they're mightily pleased with themselves at present – and with very just cause.'

'And your regiment will be equally anxious to welcome you there, too. That was a very handsome letter from your colonel.'

'Yes,' agreed Hervey, a little bashfully.

They walked on a few paces in silence. It was Emma who broke it, and with a change in her tone to something less assured. 'You are content to be in these parts, then, Matthew? I mean in the Company's domain?'

Hervey sighed to himself. Was it possible to give a complete answer to such a question? '*You* are the Sunday-school teacher, Emma – or were, in Madras. You should know there cannot be perfect contentment here on earth!'

'But I know we must strive for it: we cannot be content until the kingdom of God is come on earth.' She hesitated again. 'And shall you find here, do you think, the . . . complete society for contentment?'

Hervey smiled, a little indulgently. 'My dear Emma, I am a soldier. The past ten years have set their seal on things. I have ever found the centurion's a sure voice, though.'

'"For I also am a man set under authority, having under me soldiers."'

'Yes. And each element derives from the other. You told me how it cheered you so much when Serjeant Collins reported that I had gone back to search for those dragoons. But I could not imagine it any other way. Don't mistake me. I have no excess of sentiment in this. Had he lived, I would have had that dragoon who deserted brought to the regiment and hanged. And just as surely, I will never be a slave to authority.'

So powerful a testament required a respectful silence, at least for a while. But when they reached the point where the path divided, one way to his quarters, the other to hers, Emma put her hand on his arm again. 'Matthew, you will ever have loving friends in Eyre and me, and we shall resume our intimacy at Calcutta soon. You will be fêted for your feats of arms – and rightly so. But do have a care, for not everything in India can fit so exacting a pattern as yours.'

He smiled again. How well did she understand him.

A trumpet sounded in the lines beyond, at once commanding his attention.

Emma looked dismayed. 'A trumpet, and at once you forget where you are. How do you know it sounds for *you* and not the native horse?'

Hervey smiled the more. 'Madam, every dragoon recognizes his regimental call!'

THE END

The adventures of Matthew Hervey continue in
THE SABRE'S EDGE
– now available from Bantam Press.

HISTORICAL AFTERNOTE

The Burmese were not to be deterred. In 1822 they reduced the kingdom of Assam and the principality of Muneepore. The following year they demanded the surrender of the island of Shaporooree in the estuary of the Teek Naaf, which formed the boundary between Chittagong and Arakan (incidentally, the Karnaphuli, known more usually at this time as the Chittagong river, follows a very different course today). The new Governor-General, Lord Amherst, sent troops to dislodge them, but also a letter to the King of Ava which convinced the Burmese court that the British had no stomach for a fight. The Burmese general and national hero, Mahâ Bundoola, was despatched with a large army to Arakan with orders to drive the British from the whole of Bengal. Lord Amherst found himself with no alternative but to declare war on the king in February 1824.

The commander-in-chief, Lieutenant-General Sir Edward Paget, had profound misgivings about offensive operations, for in Burma, he said, 'we should find nothing but jungle, pestilence and famine.' He therefore favoured a maritime and riverine strategy, and accordingly a combined naval and military expedition was assembled in the Andaman Islands under command of another Peninsular veteran,

Major-General Archibald Campbell. To the inexpressible surprise of the Burmese, the flotilla arrived off the great port of Rangoon on 12 May. Thereafter, the expeditionary force, ill-prepared in so many ways, was to discover the truth of the commander-in-chief's foreboding . . .

Skinner's Horse, the regiment of irregular cavalry founded by James Skinner, the son of a Scotch officer in the Honourable East India Company and a Rajput woman of rank, is today second only to the President's Bodyguard in seniority in the army of India. Skinner's Horse wear the yellow kurta still, the colour chosen by Colonel Skinner from Rajput legend. A Rajput prince, riding out to fight, would vow that if he could not win he would die. His men, accepting the commitment, put saffron on their faces and a yellow cloak over their armour. These were called the clothes of the dead, and the warriors were known as the 'Yellow Men', who would not return from battle unless victorious – they were 'sworn to die'.

In 2003 Skinner's Horse, at one time better known to the world, perhaps, as the 1st Bengal Lancers, celebrate the bicentenary of their founding. It is certain that the words given them by James Skinner will ring out on parade that day:

> *Himmat-I-Mardan! Madad-I-Khuda! –*
> *The Bravery of Man!*
> *By the Help of God!*

Brigadier Allan Mallinson is a serving cavalry officer. He originally trained for the Anglican priesthood, but joined the army in 1969 and served with the infantry in Malaya, Cyprus and Northern Ireland. He commanded the 13th/18th Royal Hussars in Cyprus and Norway, and has since worked in the Ministry of Defence and for the Foreign Office. The author of *Light Dragoons*, a history of British cavalry, and a regular reviewer for *The Times* and the *Spectator*, he is currently the British Military Attaché in Rome.

A Call to Arms is the fourth book in Allan Mallinson's series featuring Matthew Hervey. The first three novels, *A Close Run Thing*, *The Nizam's Daughters* and *A Regimental Affair*, are also available in Bantam paperback, while the fifth novel in the series, *The Sabre's Edge*, is published in Bantam Press hardback.

A CLOSE RUN THING
by Allan Mallinson

'An astonishingly impressive début . . . convincingly drawn, perfectly paced and expertly written . . . a joy to read'
Antony Beevor

As the war against Bonaparte rages to its bloody end upon the field of Waterloo, a young officer goes about his duty in the ranks of Wellington's army. He is Cornet Matthew Hervey of the 6th Light Dragoons – a soldier, gentleman and man of honour who suddenly finds himself allotted a hero's role . . .

'Now at last a highly literate, deeply read cavalry officer of high rank shows one the nature of horse-borne warfare in those times: and Colonel Mallinson's *A Close Run Thing* is very much to be welcomed'
Patrick O'Brian

'Allan Mallinson has a splendid feeling for period and for soldiers. His tale of Waterloo will delight all those who share his enthusiasm'
Max Hastings

'Effortless and impressive . . . it is a pleasure to read a book based on so much genuine knowledge, no doubt painstakingly acquired, but lightly worn'
Spectator

'O'Brian's equal in accurate knowledge of the equipment, methods, weapons and conditions of service of the fighting men of whom he writes . . . An imaginative feat of high order, owing as much to thorough scholarship as it does to compassion and sensibility . . . Brilliantly conveyed'
Country Life

A Bantam Paperback

0 553 50713 3

THE NIZAM'S DAUGHTERS
by Allan Mallinson

'A marvellous read, paced like a well-balanced symphony . . . full of surprises and excitement'
The Times

Fresh from the field of Waterloo, Matthew Hervey, newly appointed *aide-de-camp* to the Duke of Wellington, is dispatched on a mission of the utmost secrecy. Leaving behind his fiancée, Lady Henrietta Lindsay, he must journey across tempestuous seas to India, an alien, exotic and beguiling land that will test his mettle to the very limit. For the princely state of Chintal is threatened both by intrigue from within and military might from without, and Hervey, sabre in hand, finds he is once more destined for the field of battle . . .

'Mallinson writes with style, verve and the lucidity one would expect from a talented officer . . . His breadth of knowledge is deeply impressive even if it is modestly entwined in the fabric of this epic narrative. Kick on, Captain Hervey, we cannot wait for more'
Country Life

'An exciting, fast moving story, full of bloody hacking with sabre and tulwar'
Evening Standard

'An epic adventure . . . with a texture as rich as cut velvet, and a storyline as detailed as a Bruges tapestry. Patrick O'Brian may no longer be with us, but Mallinson has obviously taken up the historical baton'
Birmingham Post

A Bantam Paperback

0 553 50714 1

A REGIMENTAL AFFAIR
by Allan Mallinson

'Confirms his undoubted talents and marks him as the heir to Patrick O'Brian and C. S. Forester'
Observer

THE SPLENDID SEQUEL TO *A CLOSE RUN THING* AND *THE NIZAM'S DAUGHTERS* . . .

The year is 1817, and Captain Matthew Hervey has returned from India to an England in economic and political turmoil – close, perhaps, to revolution. The onerous task of policing falls increasingly to the army, especially the cavalry.

And there's unrest too within the 6th Light Dragoons. Their new commanding officer – a wealthy, arrogant and cruel man – takes an immediate dislike to Hervey who must somehow earn promotion while retaining his integrity and the loyalty of his men. The trauma of a regimental flogging is swiftly followed by action against the Luddites and it comes as something of a relief when the 6th are dispatched to Canada. But there, in the aftermath of war with the United States, tension along the border is still high and although Hervey doesn't know it yet, he and his commanding officer are on a collision course, and the consequences for them both will be devastating . . .

'Assured and capable . . . a fine read'
The Times

'Enthrallingly informative . . . beautifully told . . . in Hervey, Mallinson has a character worthy of comparison with Forester's young Hornblower'
Punch

'A riveting tale . . . Matthew Hervey has now joined Bernard Cornwell's Sharpe and Patrick O'Brian's Jack Aubrey'
Birmingham Post

A Bantam Paperback

0 553 50715 X

THE SABRE'S EDGE
by Allan Mallinson

The year is 1824; the 6th Light Dragoons are still stationed in India, and the talk in the officers' mess is of war.

The Burmese are increasingly challenging the Company's dominion, and skirmishes are becoming common on India's borders. Meanwhile, across the country in Rajputana, a princely succession has been usurped. The rightful claimant to the raj, Balwant Singh, has been forced from the throne by the war-monger Durjan Sal. A conflagration looks set to flare, taking the surrounding provinces with it. With the threat of war on two fronts, British troops must intervene.

The trial ahead will test Hervey and his newly blooded troop to their very limits, for Durjan Sal has taken refuge in the infamous fortress of Bhurtpore. The fortress stands within a five-mile perimeter, a deep ditch runs around it which can be flooded at a moment's notice, and thirty-five turreted bastions rise from its thick and lofty walls. And as the Tower of Victory, built two decades before with the skulls of Lord Lake's defeated men, bears witness, it has withstood all attacks.

But no fortress is impregnable, given the will, the wit and the means. Of one thing Hervey can be sure: the siege of Bhurtpore will be hot and dangerous work. Once again, the fortunes of Matthew Hervey and his courageous troop will be decided by the sabre's edge.

NOW AVAILABLE FROM BANTAM PRESS

0 593 04728 1

BY FORCE OF ARMS
by James Nelson

'Nelson writes with the eagerness of a young man sailing his first command'
Patrick O'Brian

As the War of Independence begins in earnest, American merchant seamen prepare to strike the first blows. None strikes more deftly than Isaac Biddlecomb, captain of the *Judea*, whose smuggling activities are making a mockery of His Majesty's Royal Navy. Pursued by the HMS *Rose*, he sacrifices the ship he loved to the depths, together with the fortune he stood to gain, rather than surrender.

On the run from the enraged forces of King George, Isaac disguises himself as a merchant seaman. He is reunited with Ezra Rumstick, a comrade and fierce rebel, as the revolution gathers momentum. On a brig bound for Jamaica, and now serving as a lowly mate, fate tests Isaac's mettle as he is captured by the enemy and faces a life of servitude under the deranged captain and sadistic crew of the HMS *Icarus* . . .

The first in his enthralling REVOLUTION AT SEA series.

'First rate action writing'
Publishers Weekly

0 552 14960 8

THE BLIGHTED CLIFFS
by Edwin Thomas

Set in the early 19th century, when Britain was fighting hard to rule the waves: a wonderfully entertaining, swashbuckling adventure series, and a dashing hero, for whom life – and love – does not always turn out the way he intends it to.

January 1806: Martin Jerrold comes to Dover in order to restore the reputation he ruined at Trafalgar, in which trapped below deck for the duration of the battle, he finally emerged – in deepest disgrace, but alive. Before he has been in Dover a day, however, he finds himself standing over a corpse at the foot of the cliffs. This might not matter, except that the body is too far from the cliffs to have fallen accidentally or even suicidally, and Jerrold is suspected of murder. His captain seems to despise him; and the magistrate, Sir Lawrence Cunningham, wants to hang him, but no one can be found to identify the body, let alone press charges. When word reaches Jerrold's long suffering uncle at the Admiralty, the choice is stark: he must either clear his name or be cut off without a guinea.

Somewhere in Dover's twisted streets, someone knows something, but can Jerrold find them? Nothing is as it seems, especially in Dover where smuggling is a way of life, everyone has well stocked wine cellars, and the local banker has a lucrative connection with the French. And all the time, Jerrold is under suspicion, finding sympathy only from the unlikely direction of Sir Lawrence's wife Anne, and in the rather less respectable arms of Isobel, the girl who seems – without any great effort on Jerrold's part – to be becoming his mistress. Distrusted by his superiors, set upon by curiously well informed smugglers, attacked by the French at sea, Jerrold has two weeks to save his skin – or perish in the attempt.

0 593 05064 9

COMING SOON FROM BANTAM PRESS

A SELECTED LIST OF FINE WRITING
AVAILABLE FROM TRANSWORLD